THE LAST COIN

Books by James P. Blaylock

THE DIGGING LEVIATHAN
HOMUNCULUS
LAND OF DREAMS
THE LAST COIN

THE LAST COIN

JAMES P. BLAYLOCK

ACE BOOKS, NEW YORK

THE LAST COIN

An Ace Book
Published by The Berkley Publishing Group
200 Madison Avenue, New York, New York 10016

Book design by Jill Dinneen

First Edition: November 1988

Library of Congress Cataloging-in-Publication Data

Blaylock, James P., 1950–
    The last coin.

    I. Title.
PS3552.L3966L34   1988   813'.54   88-14665
ISBN 0-441-11381-8

Printed in the United States of America

10 9 8 7 6 5 4 3 2 1

"—Nay, if you come to that, Sir, have not the wisest of men in all ages, not excepting Solomon himself,—have they not had their Hobby-Horses;—their running horses, their coins and their cockle-shells, their drums and their trumpets, their fiddles, their pallets, their maggots and their butterflies?—and so long as a man rides his Hobby-Horse peaceably and quietly along the King's highway, and neither compels you or me to get up behind him,—pray, Sir, what have either you or I to do with it?"

Laurence Sterne
Tristram Shandy

BOOK I

The Second Joke

"There is no duty we so much underrate as the duty of being happy . . . A happy man or woman is a better thing to find than a five-pound note."

Robert Louis Stevenson
"An Apology for Idlers"

Prologue

HE SAT IN the back seat of a sherrut, a whirling dervish taxi, slamming down the road out of the Jerusalem Highlands toward the Ben-Gurion Airport in Tel Aviv. The driver was a lunatic, and Pennyman bounced and rocked on the back seat of the old Mercedes-Benz as it wheeled around curves and plunged over dips. In his pocket was a leather bag of silver coins, uncomfortably hot. The day was declining behind them, and the buildings of old Jerusalem were sun-washed and pale. Ahead, the highrises of Tel Aviv threw shadows out over the flat Mediterranean landscape. Pennyman could barely recognize it. It had been years.

He'd been through the airport once before, when it was the Lod Airport. Before that, uncounted years earlier, he'd sailed from Haifa to Cyprus on a fishing boat, carrying another of the coins—only the third he'd ever possessed. The crew had sensed that he was fleeing from something, and when a storm had blown up in the night and nearly capsized them, the ship's cook, a

Jordanian with wide, holy eyes, had called him a Jonah, and Pennyman had come close to being pitched into the sea. They had taken the coin from him when it had begun to crackle with St. Elmo's fire in the static-charged air. They'd flung *it* over the side instead, and then watched silently when a vast shadow rose from the dark sea and swallowed up the glowing coin as it tumbled into the depths.

The years had shuffled his memory, dealing away bits and pieces of it. Time diminished a man; there was no denying it—even a man who possessed certain methods. Now the coins in his pocket made him feel almost young again, although it was a feeling that was tainted and corrupted, like the youthful flush of a well-nourished vampire.

He looked back out the window. There appeared to be no sign of pursuit. In well under an hour he'd be in the airport, and then on a Pan American jet to Paris and New York. He would angle across to Vancouver on the way to Los Angeles in order to pay a visit to his old coin-collecting friend, Pfennig. Pfennig might have heard about the murder of Aureus by then, of course, and might have fled. He might as easily have decided to sell. Perhaps Pfennig was the sort who would come cheap, or at least who could be convinced that it was better to come cheap than dead. The world was filled with fools, it seemed, who thought they'd been called upon to be Caretakers. He himself had been called upon to be something; but it was he, and no one else, who would determine what that something was.

He'd left the old man named Aureus dead in Jerusalem, and with any luck the man's corpse would lie in his locked shop for days before it was found. The shades were pulled and a sign hung in the window. He was gone, it said—on holiday. No one on earth expected the store to reopen for another week. The blind beggars in the man's employ would know that something was wrong. They sensed something, no doubt about it, behind their strangely Asiatic, sightless eyes. But they were almost certainly mad. One had followed Pennyman for half a block, and then had cocked his head, as if listening, when Pennyman had climbed into the taxi and driven off. Pennyman had made the mistake of rattling his bag full of stolen silver out the window at the man, just as a lark. At the sound of it, coins had flown out of the beggar's cup like popcorn out of hot oil, and the man had thrown open his mouth and howled so high and shrill that his howling was silent, and the rising lamentation of baying dogs had followed the taxi out of the city to the highway. None of the beggars would have keys to the shop, though. Old Aureus wouldn't have trusted them with a bag of shekels much less with the coins. His corpse would have ample time to ripen.

Pennyman patted his coat pocket. His papers, as the saying went, were in order. It was too bad he had to fly out of Tel Aviv. Security at Ben-Gurion was tight and mean, and there was nothing of the bazaar atmosphere of Athens or Beirut airport. That would keep the beggars out, though, which was just as well. Tackling the metal detector would be interesting. He'd send the coins around it with the papers of requisition from the British Museum. Carrying out old Hebrew coins would have been tricky, but these thirty silver coins—of which Pennyman possessed twenty-five—had their origins farther east, much farther east, and so weren't of local historical significance. He wouldn't be accused of trying to smuggle out relics from the Holy Land.

The coins were old when the Cities of the Plain had burned, and they had been scattered in the years since, to be collected, all of them together, only once in the last thousands of years. The man who had held all of them briefly in his grasp had cast the coins into the dirt and hanged himself in remorse for the ruination his greed had fashioned.

But he hadn't been allowed to die. The thirty silver coins, all together, had assured his immortality, and he had wandered the earth since, for over two thousand years, seeking to redeem himself by assuring that the coins were kept forever scattered. Old Aureus, trusted as a secret Caretaker, had sought to betray him, and had sought out more and more of the coins, hoarding them. Aureus had failed, though, in the end. Jules Pennyman didn't intend to fail.

Some few of the coins had been used by temple priests twenty centuries ago to buy the potter's field where wandering strangers would be buried—the first one of whom was interred with two of the coins pressing his eyelids shut. And so it was thought by the priest who had buried the man that even if twenty-eight of the coins were gathered again in a distant time, at least these two would be lost forever. But in the end he betrayed his own secret, for his own meddling with the coins had tainted him.

When the grave in the potter's field was robbed, though, the coins were gone, and it was said that the weight of the coins had driven them through the dead man's head and that they'd burnt through the winding sheet and into the earth beneath it and that one day, ages hence, they would complete their travel through the earth and appear on the other side of the world to set into spinning motion the prophecy of revelation.

The twenty-eight unburied coins had been carried off singly, and now and then two or three together. Most had been squandered, sometimes sold as curiosities. In the right hands, though, they were something more than curiosities. Benjamin Aureus, finally, had buried fourteen of them in the sand beneath the floor of his shop, and it was said that early on autumn mornings, an hour or two before sunrise, the air over the shop seemed to be agitated by flitting spirits, like an illustration of the opening of Pandora's box.

Jules Pennyman had long suspected that Aureus possessed some of the coins, but he hadn't half-expected what he'd found. Powerful as Aureus was, he couldn't have hoped to keep the coins silent. The coins had a way of finding Caretakers, and of searching out weaknesses in them. In the absence of weaknesses, the coins would create some. Aureus at first had been nothing more than a Caretaker himself, a disciple of the Wandering Jew whose penance for the sin of betrayal was the two-thousand-year task of keeping the coins apart. But Aureus had fallen to greed and to the corruption that came inevitably from the process of accumulating the coins. And now he was dead.

Jules Pennyman wasn't anyone's disciple. He was a stone in the desert—linked to nothing at all, a self-contained, self-satisfied entity. And unlike Aureus, he was alive, and he possessed nearly, but not quite, twice the number of coins. His power would be incalculable. Unlike Judas Iscariot, he wasn't a man given over to remorse . . .

At the thought of Judas Iscariot he pulled a flask full of Pepto-Bismol out of his coat and drank off half the contents. He had more in his luggage.

The taxi banged over a pothole as the driver felt around on the floor, coming up with a bottle of sweet Carmel wine. Pennyman leaned forward to complain, but the man shrugged and tilted it back, then spat the wine through the open window, cursing and throwing the bag and then the bottle out after it, muttering about vinegar. He turned and glared at Pennyman, as if the wine's turning was his fault. And in a way it was.

Just then it began to rain, great muddy drops that fouled the windshield. Pennyman peered up out the rear window at a nearly cloudless sky. Overhead, as if following them, was a single black cloud, and out over the desert a thousand little wind devils seemed to be whirling up, dancing in a riot of dust and dry twigs. They raced along beside the car for a way, the twigs and debris swirling into vaguely human shapes, like spirits again, peering in at the window. A dead bird plummeted from the sky, thumping onto the hood of the taxi, and then another followed, slamming against the windshield. The rain of birds lasted half a minute, and then the sky cleared abruptly and the wind devils died away. Pennyman waited. He had expected something, but he hadn't known what.

There was a lead box waiting at the airport, in his suitcase in a locker. He ought to have brought it along. The leather bag wasn't enough to *contain* the coins. Even the weather, suddenly, was sensitive to them, as if it knew that they'd fallen into—what?—not evil hands. Evil wasn't the word for it. Evil was a word used by the ignorant to explain powers and forces they feared. Jules Pennyman feared nothing at all, short of being stopped when he was so close to winning through.

The rearview mirror spontaneously cracked to bits just then, showering the front seat with tiny fragments. The driver glanced sideways at Pennyman. He had a look of frightened incomprehension on his face now. The taxi swerved toward the shoulder, then back again, and then started to slow down. Pennyman had seen that look before. He pulled out his wallet, withdrew a wad of shekels, and waved it at the man. The taxi drove on. In ten minutes they'd be in Tel Aviv.

It was true that Pennyman didn't yet have all of the coins. There were still two in the earth, and the one that had been thrown into the sea. Pfennig, it seemed certain, possessed another one—or rather the coin possessed him. And then there was the coin in California. That one was veiled by mystery. He would have them all, though, in the very end; for the more he possessed, the more certain he became of the whereabouts of the rest, as if the coins sought each other out.

"Skirt the city," Pennyman said, not wanting to get caught in the downtown press of people. The road had flattened, and the air was sticky and warm. The muddy rain had given out, but the sky over the Mediterranean was black with approaching clouds.

Something was happening to the weather. The pressure was dropping and the atmosphere seemed to be bending and warping —tensing like a coiled spring. When the taxi lurched to a halt amid honking traffic and Pennyman stepped out onto the curb, the ground shook, just a little, just enough to make the hurrying masses of people put down their luggage and stop, waiting.

Pennyman paid the taxi driver and strode toward the airport doors—casually, nodding at an old woman with a dog, and pausing for one precious moment to hold back the milling crowd so that she could drag her bags and her dog in through the door. He didn't want to seem to be in a hurry to get to the locker, to be a man possessed, although in truth there wasn't a man in the world at that moment more thoroughly possessed than he was.

He peered up at what he could see of the sky and grimaced as lightning arced across it. An immediate blast of thunder rattled the windows, followed by a wash of wind-driven rain. The air suddenly was full of the smell of ozone and sulphur, and the ground shook again, as if it were waking up.

ONE

"I was told that he was, in his heart, a good fellow,
and an enemy to no one but himself."
                              Robert Louis Stevenson
                              Prince Otto

ANDREW VANBERGEN USED a pruning ladder to get to the attic
window—the sort with flared legs and a single pole for support.
The pole clacked against the copper rain gutter and then hung
uselessly, the top rung of the ladder seesawing back and forth
across it. He looked over his shoulder at the silent midnight
street and wiggled the ladder, worried that it might slide down
along the gutter and pitch him into the branches of the camphor tree that grew along the side of the house. But there was
nothing he could do about it now; it was the only ladder he
had.

He could hear Aunt Naomi snoring through the open window.
The whole street could hear it. That's what would give him
away—not any noise he'd make, not the scraping of the ladder
against the gutter, but the sudden stopping of the snoring if she
woke up and saw him there outside the window, peering in.

Neighbors would lurch awake in their beds, wondering. Had they heard something? It would be like in an earthquake, when you're not aware of the rumbling and the groaning and creaking until it stops.

An hour ago he had lain in bed beside his sleeping wife in their second-story bedroom, listening to Aunt Naomi snoring through the floor. It drove him nearly crazy, the snoring and the mewling of her cats. He couldn't sleep because of it. He had pitched and tossed and plumped up his pillow, watching the slow luminous hands on the clock edge toward morning. He swore that if he saw the coming of twelve o'clock, he'd act. Midnight had come and gone.

He had lain there knowing that the old woman would sleep the night through, like a baby. She'd awaken in the morning, about five, proud of herself for rising early but complaining about it anyway. She couldn't sleep: her poor nerves, her "sciatica," her sinuses, her this, her that. She'd demand tea with milk in it. Her bed would be covered with cats, and the air in the room would reek of mentholated vapor rub and litter boxes and old clothes. Taken altogether it would smell like—what? Words couldn't express it. They *wouldn't* express it; they'd mutiny first and become babble.

It was the hottest April he could remember. Even at nearly one in the morning it was seventy-seven degrees and not a whisper of wind. The ocean sighed through the pier pilings half a block away, just over the rooftops. Now and then the light of headlamps would swing around the curve from Sunset Beach, and a car full of sleepy night owls would go gunning up the Pacific Coast Highway toward Belmont Shore and Long Beach. They were too far off to see him though, hidden as the house was down the little dead-end street that it shared with half a dozen other houses. Lights shone in one; the others were dark.

Andrew climbed the ladder slowly, his faced blacked out with ash from the disused fireplace. He wore a black shirt and slacks and black burlap shoes with crepe soles. A long fiberglass pole with a loop on the end lay tilted against the ladder. On the shingled gable in front of him was an empty flour sack and a bit of rope with a loop already tied in one end. Lying there awake in bed an hour earlier, hot and tired and unable to sleep through the mewling and the snoring, he'd committed himself to the idea of tackling the cat problem that very night. Sleeplessness was maddening. There was nothing else on earth like it when it came to sheer, teeth-grinding irritation.

The idea now was to snatch up a cat, hoist it into the flour sack, and tie the sack off with a slipknot, then go in after another cat. One of them stared at him through the open attic window. It seemed to find his sudden appearance boring and tiresome. He smiled at it and touched two fingers to his forehead, as if tipping his hat. Civility in all things, he muttered, peering in at the window, past the cat. Thank God there wasn't a window screen to remove.

He listened—to the snoring, to the sounds of distant, muted traffic, to the faint music coming from a tavern somewhere down the Pacific Coast Highway, probably the Glide 'er Inn. It drifted past him on the warm night, reminding him of the world, stealing away his nerve, his resolve. The moon was just rising over the rooftops. He'd have to hurry.

"Nice kitty," he whispered, making smacking noises at the cat. They liked that, or seemed to. He'd decided that he wouldn't throw the cats into the salt marsh after all. A half hour ago, when he was crazy with being kept awake, it had seemed like the only prudent course. Now that he was up and about, though, and had put things in perspective, he realized that he had nothing against cats, not really, as long as they lived somewhere else. He couldn't bear even to take them to the pound. He knew that. Cruelty wasn't in him.

He hadn't, in fact, entirely worked out what he *would* do with them. Give them away in front of the supermarket, perhaps. He could claim that they'd belonged to a celebrity—the grandmother of a movie star, maybe; that would fetch it. People would clamor for them. Or else he could give them to the neighborhood children and offer them a dollar-fifty reward for every cat they took away and didn't come back with, and another dollar apiece if the kids hadn't ratted on him by the end of the month. That would be dangerous, though; children were a mysterious, unpredictable race—almost as bad as cats. Pulling a smelt out of his shirt pocket, he dangled it in front of the open flour sack. The cat inside the window wrinkled up its nose.

He smiled at it and nodded, winking good-naturedly. "Good kitty-pup. Here's a fishy."

The cat turned away and licked itself. He edged up a rung on the ladder and laid the fish on a shingle, but the cat didn't care about it; it might as well have been an old shoe. Andrew's shadow bent away across the shingles, long and angular in the moonlight, looking almost like a caricature of Don Quixote. He turned his head to catch his profile, liking that better, and thinking that as he got older he looked just a little bit more like Basil Rathbone every year, if only he could stay thin enough. He squinted just a little, as if something had been revealed to him, something that was hidden to the rest of mortal men. But the shadow, of course, didn't reveal the knowing squint, and his nose needed more hook to it, and the cat on the sill sat as ever, seeming to know far more than he did about hidden things.

He reached for the pole, jumping it up through his right hand until he could tilt it in through the open window. The pole wasn't any good for close work. The cat in the window would have to wait. He peered into the darkened room, waiting for his eyes to adjust, listening to the snoring. It was frightful. There was nothing else like it on earth: snorts and groans and noises that reminded him of an octopus.

He had been tempted at first, when he was seething, to poke the pole against her ear and shout into the other end. But such a thing would finish her. She'd been ill for ten years—or so she'd let on—and an invalid for most of them. A voice shouting into her ear at midnight through a fifteen-foot pole would simply kill her. The autopsy would reveal that she'd turned into a human pudding. They'd jail him for it. His shouting would awaken the house. They'd haul him down from the ladder and gape into his ash-smeared face. Why had he shouted at Aunt Naomi through a tube? She owned cats? She'd been snoring, had she? And he'd—what?—got himself up in jewel-thief clothes and crept up a pruning ladder to the attic window, hoping to undo her by shouting down a fiberglass tube?

Moonlight slanted past him through the tree branches, suddenly illuminating the room. There was another cat, curled up on the bed. He would never get the noose over its head. There was another, atop the bureau. It stood there staring into the moonlight, its eyes glowing red. The room was full of cats. It stank like a kennel, the room did, the floorboards gritty with spilled kitty litter. An acre of ocean winds blowing through two-dozen open windows wouldn't scour out the reek. He grimaced and played out line, waving the loop across the top of the bed toward the dresser. The cat stood there defiantly, staring him down. He felt almost ashamed. He'd have to be quick—jerk it off the dresser without slamming the pole down onto the bed and awakening Aunt Naomi, if that were possible. A *little* noise wouldn't hurt; her snoring would mask it.

He had practiced in the backyard when the family was gone. His friend Beams Pickett had helped him, playing the part of a surprised cat. Then they'd pieced up a false cat out of a pillow, a jar, and a gunnysack and snatched it off tree limbs and out of bushes and off fences until Andrew had it refined down to one swift thrust and yank. The trick now was to balance the pole atop the windowsill in order to take up some of the weight. Another arm would help, of course, if only to hold open the sack. He'd asked Pickett to come along, but Pickett wouldn't. He was an "idea man" he had said, not a man of action.

Andrew let the pole rest on the sill for a moment, watching the strangely unmoving cat out of one eye, the cat inside the window out of the other eye. He picked up the flour sack, shoving the hem of the open end into his mouth and letting it dangle there against the shingles. He was ready. Aunt Naomi snorted and rolled over. He froze, his heart pounding, a chill running through him despite the heat. Moments passed. He worked the pole forward, wondering at the foolish cat that stood there as still as ever. It was a sitting duck. He giggled, suppressing laughter. What would Darwin say? It served the beast right to be snatched away like this. Natural selection is what it was. He'd get the cats, then pluck up the corners of Aunt Naomi's bed sheet and tie them off, too. It would be a simple thing to lock her into the trunk of the Metropolitan and fling her, still trussed up in the sheet, into the marsh in Gum Grove Park.

It was easy to believe, when you looked at the wash of stars in the heavens, that something was happening in the night sky and in the darkened city stretched along the coast. The whole random shape of things—the people roundabout, their seemingly petty business, the day-to-day machinations of governments and empires—all of it spun slowly, like the stars, into patterns invisible to the man on the street, but, especially late at night, clear as bottle glass to him. Or at least they all would become so. Clearing the house of cats would be the first step toward clearing his mind of murk, toward ordering the mess that his life seemed sometimes to be spiraling into. He and Pickett had set up Pickett's telescope in the unplastered attic cubbyhole adjacent to Aunt Naomi's bedroom, but the smell of the cats had pretty much kept them out of it—a pity, really. There was something—a cosmic order, maybe—in the starry heavens that relaxed him, that made things all right after all. He couldn't get enough of them and stayed up late sometimes just to get a midnight glimpse of the sky after the lights of the city had dimmed.

All this talk of unusual weather and earthquakes on the news over the past weeks was unsettling, although it seemed to be evidence of something; it seemed to bear out his suspicions that something was afoot. The business of the Jordan River flowing backward out of the Dead Sea was the corker. It sounded overmuch like an Old Testament miracle, although as far as the newspapers knew, there hadn't been any Moses orchestrating the phenomenon. It would no doubt have excited less comment if it weren't for the dying birds and the rain of mud. The newspapers in their euphemistic way spoke of solar disturbances and tidal deviations, but that was pretty obvious hogwash. Andrew wondered whether anyone knew for sure, whether there were some few chosen people out there who understood, who nodded at such occurrences and winked at each other.

The city of Seal Beach was full of oddballs these days, too: men from secret societies, palm readers, psychics of indeterminate powers. There had been a convention of mystics in South Long

Beach just last week. Even Beams Pickett had taken up with one, a woman who didn't at all have the appearance of a spiritualist, but who had announced that Andrew's house was full of "emanations." He hated that kind of talk.

He shook his head. He'd been daydreaming, so to speak. His mind had wandered, and that wasn't good. That was his problem all along. Rose, his wife, had told him so on more than one occasion. He grinned in at the cat on the dresser, trying to mesmerize it. "Keep still," he whispered, slowly dangling the noose in over its head. He held his breath, stopped dead for a slice of a moment, then jerked on the line and yanked back on the pole at the same instant. The line went taut and pulled the cat off the dresser. The pole whumped down across the sill, overbalanced, and whammed onto the bed just as the weirdly heavy cat hit the floorboards with a crash that made it sound as if the thing had smashed into fragments. The cat inside the window howled into his ear and leaped out onto the roof. The half-dozen cats left inside ran mad, leaping and yowling and hissing. He jerked at his pole, but the noose was caught on something—the edge of the bed, probably.

A light blinked on, and there was Aunt Naomi, her hair papered into tight little curls, her face twisted into something resembling a fish. She clutched the bedclothes to her chest and screamed, then snatched up the lamp beside her bed and pitched it toward the window. The room winked into darkness, and the flying lamp banged against the wall a foot from his head.

The pole wrenched loose just then with a suddenness that propelled him backward. He dropped it and grappled for the rain gutter as the ladder slid sideways toward the camphor tree in a rush that tore his hands loose. He smashed in among the branches, hollering, hooking his left leg around the drainpipe and ripping it away, crashing up against a limb and holding on, his legs dangling fourteen feet above the ground. Hauling himself onto the limb, trembling, he listened to doors slamming and people shouting below. Aunt Naomi shrieked. Cats scoured across the rooftops, alerting the neighborhood. Dogs howled.

His pole and ladder lay on the ground. His flour sack had

entangled itself in the foliage. He could climb back up onto the roof if he had to, scramble over to the other side, shinny down a drainpipe into the backyard. They'd know by now that he wasn't in bed, of course, but he'd claim to have gone out after the marauder. He'd claim to have chased him off, to have hit him, perhaps, with a rock. The prowler wouldn't come fooling around *there* any more, not after that. Aunt Naomi couldn't have known who it was that had menaced her. The moment of light wouldn't have given her eyes enough time to adjust. She wouldn't cut him out of her will. She would thank him for the part he'd played. She'd . . .

A light shone up into the tree. People gathered on the lawn below: his wife, Mrs. Gummidge, Pennyman. All of them were there. And the neighbor, too—old what's his name, Ken-or-Ed, as his wife called him. My God he was fat without a shirt on—out half-naked, minding everybody's business but his own. He was almost a cephalopod in the silver moonlight. His bald head shone with sweat.

There was a silence below. Then, hesitantly, Rose's voice: "Is that you, Andrew? Why are you in the tree, dear?"

"There's been some sort of funny business. I'm surprised you didn't hear it. I couldn't sleep, because of the heat, so I came downstairs and out onto the porch . . ."

"You did what?" His wife shouted up to him, cupping a hand to her ear. "Come down. We can't hear you. Why have you got the ladder out?"

"I don't!" he shouted. "A prowler . . ." but then Aunt Naomi's head thrust out through the open window, her eyes screwed down to the size of dimes. She gasped and pointed at him, signaling to those below on the lawn.

"I'll go to her," said Mrs. Gummidge, starting into the house.

Andrew had always hated that phrase—"go to her." It drove him nearly crazy, and now particularly. Mrs. Gummidge had a stock of such phrases. She was always "reaching out" and "taking ill" and "lending a hand" and "proving useful." He watched the top of her head disappear under the porch gable. At least she paid her rent on time—thanks to Aunt Naomi's money. But Aunt Naomi held the money over her head, too, just like she did with the rest of them, and Andrew knew that Mrs. Gummidge loathed the idea of it; it ate her up. She was sly, though, and didn't let on. The wife couldn't see it. Rose was convinced that Mrs. Gummidge was a saint—bringing cups of tea up to the attic at all hours, playing Scrabble in the afternoon as long as Aunt Naomi let her win.

"Of course she lets her win," Andrew had said. "She feels sorry for the woman."

Rose hadn't thought so. She said it was generosity on Aunt Naomi's part that explained it—natural charity. But it wasn't. Andrew was certain it was something loathsome. It would almost be worth it to have Aunt Naomi gone, and her money with her. They'd get by somehow. If they could just hold on a couple of weeks, until tourists began to flock through, until he could get the cafe into shape and open up for dinners. They'd see their way clear then.

He shivered. It had gotten suddenly colder. An onshore wind had blown up, ruffling the leaves on the tree, cutting through his cotton shirt. At forty-two he wasn't the hand at climbing trees that he'd been at ten. There was no way he was going onto the roof of the house. He was trapped there. He'd stick it, though, at least until Pennyman left—Pennyman and Ken-or-Ed. The man's head was a disgrace. He looked like a bearded pumpkin.

There he was, down on the grass, peering at the looped end of the rope attached to the pole. Tied into it was the head and shoulders of the plaster statue of a cat, its red glass eyes glowing in the moonlight. Andrew Vanbergen had risked his life and reputation to snatch a painted plaster cat off a dresser at one in the morning. He shrugged. Such was fate. The gods got a laugh out of it anyway. Pickett would see the humor in it. So would Uncle Arthur. Ken-or-Ed pitched the cat head into the bushes and leaned the pole against a branch of the camphor tree, shaking his head again as if the whole business were beyond him, as if it beat all.

Murmuring voices wafted up toward Andrew from the lawn. "Are you coming down, dear?" his wife asked suddenly, shading her eyes and peering up into the branches.

He waited for a moment, then said, "No, not for a bit. I'm

going to wait. This man might return. He could be lurking in the neighborhood right now. Wait! What's that! Off toward the highway!''

Ken-or-Ed loped away, looking around wildly, alert for prowlers. Pennyman watched as if unconvinced, then muttered something and strode off into the house. When he found nothing at all to confront, Ken-or-Ed slouched back up the street and onto the lawn. He explained loudly to Andrew's wife just what it was a prowler was likely to have done under the circumstances. He had done some police work when he was younger, he said, and it paid off in situations like this. Andrew rolled his eyes and listened from up in the tree, shivering again in the breeze off the ocean. He could just see the top of his wife's head.

"I'm certain it does," Rose said diplomatically, and then she excused herself and said "Don't be long" to Andrew, up into the branches of the tree. "And don't tackle him alone! Just shout. There's enough of us here to help you, so forget any stupid heroics." Andrew loved her for that. She saw through him as if he were a sheet of glass. He knew that. She hadn't swallowed any of it, but here she was letting him off.

She deserved better than him. He made up his mind to turn over a leaf. He'd start tomorrow. Maybe he'd paint the garage. It needed it, certainly. Thinking about it depressed him. He'd do something, though. He watched as Rose followed along in Pennyman's wake, shutting the front door after her. Finding himself alone on the lawn, Ken-or-Ed went home, squinting back up toward the tree as if he only half-believed there was anyone in it. Aunt Naomi's window slammed shut just then, and Andrew sat by himself in the filtered moonlight, sheltered by the canopy of leaves, listening to the lonely chirping of night birds and the quiet splash of seawaves.

Andrew's family had come from Iowa, all of them Dutch with remarkable last names. There'd been dozens of them: aunts and uncles and cousins and far-flung this and thats who had never been entirely explained.

Rose's family was the same way, but Dutch with Scottish mixed in. They'd grown up in Alton, he and Rose, and had married out of love. There'd been farms and corn and shiftings west, to Colorado and California. The family had scattered. Like old home movies, elements of it had been grand, but you had to have been there. There were bits and pieces of it, though—largely uninteresting even to those who *had* been there—that *meant* something. Andrew was pretty sure of it. Beams Pickett would be positive. They kept swimming into focus through the murky waters of passing time, refusing to be submerged and swept away into the gray sea of lost memories. That's the way things went: the crumbling of empires, the front-page news, the blather yodeling out of the television; all of that was nothing, a blind, a red herring.

It was the *trifles* that signified: the cut of a man's beard, the too-convenient discovery of forgotten money in a disused wallet, the overheard conversation between two fishermen early in the fog-shrouded morning as one of them hauls out of the ocean a crab trap with an ink-stained note in it. There was a secret order to things.

In Iowa, in 1910, almost forty years before she was born, Rose's family had lived on a farm. There were a dozen of them in all, including the vast grandmother, who was so wide that her voluminous skirts wedged tight in doorways. There were aunts and uncles, too—Rose's Aunt Naomi, for one. Uncle Arthur lived nearby. He wasn't exactly an uncle, but was an old and trusted friend, and now he lived some two miles down Seal Beach Boulevard at the Leisure World retirement community.

Family legend told how, one autumn morning, back on the farm, there had been a furious clatter on the back porch. It was as if a portable earthquake were rattling the windows. It was hot and muggy outside, and somehow the banging and shaking didn't surprise anyone, not even the children. Jars toppled off the pantry shelf and broke; the porch railing groaned; the house shuddered as if some fearful Providence waited impatiently outside, tapping its foot and frowning, checking its pocket watch.

The grandmother, clutching a fireplace poker, cast the door open. A half-score of children peered past her skirts.

There on the stoop had stood a pig, broad as a buggy, with a silver spoon in its mouth. It waited, watching the family gaping there, until the grandmother, very calmly and solemnly, took the spoon from between its teeth. The pig turned and ran away on idiotic legs, lumbering around the side of the chicken coop, out of their lives. The thin spoon was dented on the edge from the pig's teeth, and there was an almost rubbed-off profile on the concave surface of it. If you held it in moonlight, and tilted it just so, it seemed to be the bearded face of a pharaoh, perhaps, or an Old Testament king with a stiffened beard and an unlikely hat. There was a moon on the other side, or maybe a curled up fish, or both, one inside the other; it was too dim and rubbed to tell.

It created a stir in Alton for a week. Conversations sprang up around it, as if one of the grandmother's ten children had been born with the same article between *its* teeth. By week's end, though, the business of the spoon dwindled until nobody, in the family or out of it, cared any more. But Rose's grandmother polished and kept it, and it fell out, years later, that the spoon was given to Naomi, who met her husband because of it—or so the story went—and that the husband had considered it some sort of talisman. The spoon disappeared when he died—or was murdered, as some thought. Rose had heard that years later his young widow had had his corpse exhumed and cut open, and the spoon was found in his stomach and recovered.

Even more years later—almost seventy-five years after the arrival of the pig at the family farm in Iowa—Andrew and his wife had moved from Eagle Rock to Seal Beach, and bought, at least partly with Aunt Naomi's money, a thirteen-room craftsman bungalow with the idea of renovating it and opening up an inn and a restaurant. They would rent out rooms, by the day, week, or month. They'd take in boarders and feed them breakfast. There would be a cafe with a price-fixed menu and a bar, open on weekends. Aunt Naomi would live upstairs.

Her spoon came west with her and sat now in a mahogany china hutch, along with a collection of old Delft pottery and the last cracked pieces of a porcelain chocolate set.

There was something about the spoon. Andrew couldn't define

it. It was vaguely loathsome, like an enormous snail, maybe, or the wrong sort of toad, with an almost visible trail behind it leading through a dusty old Iowa graveyard and into antiquity. Maybe it was the idea of the thing's having been cut out of the stomach of a dead man. It all signified, somehow.

It meant something, but what it meant he wasn't sure. Rose was indifferent to it. It was just another bit of family history—probably lies. She hadn't yet been born, after all, when the fabled pig had arrived on the back porch. It sounded suspiciously like one of Uncle Arthur's tales, Andrew had to admit. It sounded *just* like one of Uncle Arthur's tales—which made it all the more curious.

They'd moved into the bungalow and rolled up their sleeves, uncrating boxes for weeks. They painted. They crept around in the cool cellar replacing galvanized pipes. They ran electrical conduit to replace the old single line and insulator wiring that rats had chewed into rubble. Andrew converted one of the rooms into a library, with a couch and easy chairs and footstools and a painting of a clipper ship on the wall. He hauled out his aquaria with an eye toward setting up half a dozen.

Rose objected to Andrew's aquaria. There wouldn't be time for them. There never had been. They had been a mess half the time—a brown muddle of half-eaten waterweeds and declining fish. Andrew insisted, though. He would set up *one*, he said, to house a Surinam toad. It was the only aquatic creature he wanted anymore, and she could hardly object to his caring for it. A Surinam toad reminded him of Aunt Naomi, poor thing. Outside her aquarium-like room she'd dry up and wither. Without the family gathered round to conceal her, Aunt Naomi was a sort of unlikely horror, and couldn't be expected to survive without their charity. His wife scowled at the comparison, but she understood Aunt Naomi's plight well enough. Unlike Andrew, though, she rarely said anything ill about anyone, especially about Aunt Naomi, whose money they were almost completely dependent on.

Andrew shook his head sadly over the plight of the toad, which, in fact, he'd already bought from the aquarium shop that used to belong to poor old Moneywort, before he'd been murdered. The toad lived at that moment on the back porch, in a five-gallon bucket lidded with a copy of *Life* magazine. Andrew wouldn't treat the creature shabbily. He *was* his brother's keeper, after a fashion. His soul wouldn't be worth a drilled-out penny if he abandoned the toad now. In the end he had set up the aquarium on the service porch just behind the kitchen and beside their bedroom.

He and Rose slept in a downstairs room during the first two months they lived in the bungalow. One night late, a week after the setting up of the aquarium, there'd been a fearful clatter on the porch—a scuffling and sloshing and a banging of aquarium lids, and then the odd, Lovecraftian sound of something slurping across the floor of the kitchen. Rose had awakened in a sweat. It was a burglar; she was certain of it. The noise was unnatural—the noise of a fiend. Andrew had picked up a shoe, but he was thinking of the pig, making its racket seventy-five years ago on the back porch of an Iowa farm. He dropped the shoe, certain that he wouldn't need it. In his nightshirt he peeked out through the half-open door. There was the escaped toad, scurrying across the linoleum floor toward the front of the house, toward the living room, chirping as it ran. He confronted it on the threshold of the kitchen, scooping it up and dropping it back into its aquarium, then weighting the lid with a brick before going back to bed.

It wasn't until dawn that it occurred to him that the toad must have had a destination. In the living room, against the far wall, sat the china cabinet in which lay the pig spoon. It seemed unlikely at first, then possible, then wildly likely that the toad had been bound for that china cabinet, that it, too, was caught up in the adventure of the spoon. Andrew lay for an hour thinking about it, and then, without waking his wife, he tiptoed out onto the service porch, scooped the toad out of the tank, and set it onto the floor. It sat there, pretending to be dead.

Of course it *would* with him looking on and all. He'd missed his chance—bungled it. It might have been very different: the toad, thinking itself undiscovered, making away across the floor toward the hutch, wrestling it open somehow, plucking out the spoon, going out the mail slot with the spoon gripped in one of its webbed paws. Andrew might have followed it—to the sea, to a den beneath the old pier, into the back door of one of the derelict carnival rides at the Pike. It would have demonstrated, at the very least, a symphony of mysterious activity. At best—and not at all farfetched—it hinted at the sort of veiled, underlying order that bespoke the very existence of God.

But the toad had sat mute. After long minutes had passed, Andrew plucked it up and returned it once again to its aquarium, where it sank innocently to the bottom and pretended to sleep. He hadn't proved anything, but he was left with the uncanny suspicion that one foggy morning there would come a rattle at the door handle and a scuffling on the front porch. He would rise, wondering, and throw open the door. On the porch, giving him the glad eye, would be the pig, come round for the spoon. The toad would appear, yawning and stretching, and the two of them, the toad and the pig, would take the spoon and go.

Andrew sat at the kitchen table, surrounded by open boxes of breakfast cereal. He scowled into his coffee. It had gone stale. He would mail-order another two pounds that very morning. Coffee shouldn't sit in the refrigerator for more than two weeks. *One* week was plenty. The precious aromas were lost, somehow. He'd read about it. He'd compiled a notebook full of coffee literature and was toying with the idea of ordering a brass roasting oven from Diedrich. Rose wasn't keen on it.

She held her coffee mug in her hand, satisfied, not understanding his passion for brewing perfect coffee. She didn't see that it *had* to be done just so, or it was barely worth doing at all—they might as well boil up jimsonweed. A cup of coffee was a cup of coffee to her. Well, that was overstating it. She lacked some sort of vital instinct for it, though. "What I don't get," she said, peering at him over the top of the mug, "is why you smeared ashes all over your face."

"I tell you I really *was* after 'possums," he said, putting down the coffee and gesturing. "Do you know what 'possums would do to the wiring in the roof if they got up there and built a nest? We might as well burn the place to the ground ourselves. They're nocturnal. You know that. I went out after them, that's all. Traps don't work. They're too smart for traps.''

"Did you *try* traps?'' She looked at him skeptically. He rolled his eyes, as if to suggest that he didn't see the necessity of *trying* anything, when a man could round up a ladder and noose and just lasso the creatures. "One got in through the window, you say? In among the cats?''

"That's right.'' He nodded broadly. That was it exactly. In among the cats. He'd seen it leap in, and knew there was going to be trouble. Anyone who understood 'possums could have seen it. It wouldn't do for the beast to awaken Aunt Naomi. *She'd* think it was an enormous rat that had gotten in. So he had gone after it with the noose affair he and Pickett had put together. The beast had run across the dresser, and he'd looped the noose over the head of the statue by mistake. If Aunt Naomi's bedroom hadn't been so full of trash, he'd have gotten the 'possum instead of the statue. But as it was, the thing went back out through the window—made a rush at him and nearly toppled him onto the ground. Rose had heard the racket, hadn't she? Fat lot of thanks he'd gotten for the effort, too.

"What was all that rigamarole about a prowler on the roof, and then him running down toward the boulevard?''

He blinked at her, stared into his empty coffee cup, and then blinked at her again. "Health Department,'' he said. "With neighbors looking on, I had to pretend it was something other than 'possums. They'd report us, and the Health Department would close us down in a shot. I don't half-trust Ken-or-Ed. Did you *see* him parading around out there? And then there's Pennyman. Do you think he'd stick it here for another moment if he thought there were 'possums around? He'd be packed and gone, and there goes two hundred a month, like clockwork. It's the psychology of a 'possum that you've got to understand. A common criminal leaves when he knows you're onto him. A 'possum doesn't care. He moves in wholesale, meaning to stay, and Pennyman moves out. There goes the two hundred, like I said, in a shot. And then the cry goes round that there's 'possums positively haunting the place, and we don't get a nickel's worth of customers this summer. There's your inn for you . . . 'Possums could have the place; they've nearly got it already.'' He shook his head darkly, as if he was surprised that he had to explain such a thing.

"Have another cup of coffee?" his wife asked, looking at him sideways and picking up the Chemex beaker. "What's wrong with the electric drip pot?"

He shook his head at the proffered coffee. "Temperature's not right. Too hot. Over 180 degrees the water releases all the bitter oils. Wrecks your stomach. And it shouldn't sit and stew on the hot coil, either. All that does is make the coffee taste like turpentine."

"Wash your face a bit," she said. "There's still ashes all over it. And later on this morning you might look in on poor Aunt Naomi. Explain things to her. I wouldn't half-wonder at her packing up and leaving."

"You wouldn't half-wonder at her making *me* pack for her, and then drive her down to the train station in order for her to sit around for three hours before relenting and coming home again."

"Just look in on her. Mrs. Gummidge is with her now, but *she* shouldn't have to do all the smoothing over. Not when it was you chasing . . .''

"'Possums. I was chasing 'possums.'' He turned away and walked toward the door. "I'm going out to the restaurant and inventory supplies. Have you seen my copy of *Grossman's Guide*? I can't make another move without it."

"There's work that needs to be done worse than that."

"Later. I promise I'll do it this afternoon. Draw me up a list. Either the restaurant will open or it won't. I don't think you're as keen on it opening as I am."

"I think we need a chef, and I don't think we can afford one."

"That's just it. *I'm* the chef. Pickett has volunteered as *maître d'* until we get onto our feet. But unless I get things squared away out there, we don't have a chance. I'll need more money, by the way. I'm over budget now."

"Talk to Aunt Naomi."

"Maybe *you* should, what with this 'possum business and all."

He bent across and kissed her on the cheek, trying to look cheerful and matter-of-fact and swearing to himself that he *would* set in to paint the garage that afternoon. For certain he would, just as soon as he finished the business of shaping up the bar. Talk to Aunt Naomi—the idea of it appalled him.

"Square it with her this afternoon," Rose said. "She doesn't bite. Explain yourself a little bit, and she'll see reason. And don't carry on about 'possums, for heaven's sake. She thinks you're insane. You know that, don't you? Remember when you told her about how many baby 'possums could sit in a teaspoon, and then tried to say that that's how 'possum mothers carried their babies around? In a spoon? Don't talk that way, not in front of Aunt Naomi. You can talk nuts like that all afternoon with Pickett, but for goodness sake, leave it alone in front of people who don't understand it."

He nodded, as if he thought Rose had given him good advice. But she gave him a look, seeing through him again, so he winked at her and went out, trying to seem jolly. She was right, of course. He'd have to confront the old woman after lunch. He'd bring her chocolates and flowers and explain about the mythical 'possum— not terrify her with it, of course, or say anything nuts. He'd just tell her about how it was big as a dog and had threatened her cats and about how the beasts burrow under bedsheets and build nests. If he spread himself a little bit, there'd be no telling what he might convince her of.

Jules Pennyman crouched outside the kitchen door, dabbing at his shoes with a rag. The shoes were already polished—they were new, in fact—and so didn't, maybe, need much dabbing. But he dabbed at them anyway, with the same methodical squint and tilt of the head with which he regarded himself in the mirror each morning when he trimmed his mustache and beard. His feet hurt, actually, as if his shoes were two sizes too small. There was damn-all he could do about it though, except hide the pain and wait for it to get worse.

He wore a Vandyke beard, razor-cut to a point that could have impaled a potato. His silver hair was brushed back cleanly—the sort of hair that wouldn't allow itself to become tousled unless the situation absolutely called for it. He might have been a barber, talcumed and rose-oiled and with a mustache that curled at the ends. What he was, though, no one was certain. He was "retired" and had been in the import-export business. He wore white suits. He collected silver coins. He was a product, he said, of the "old school." He had appeared at the doorstep some weeks back, having returned from travel in the east, and looking for a place, he said, where he could "watch the sea." And he had the habit of paying his rent on time—even early. This last virtue alone was enough to recommend him, at least to Rose.

He was well read, too. Andrew had liked that at first, and had made a show of consulting him when it came to setting up the library. They had two dozen old stackable bookcases, which, along with the furniture, the clipper ship, a pole lamp and an old Chinese rug made for a tolerably comfortable room. Andrew picked through his own books, finding copies to fill the shelves. The idea of transient tourists thumbing through anything good, though—perhaps slipping volumes down their pants and into their purses—made him cautious. He took Pickett's advice and plied Aunt Naomi with chocolate truffles and latex cat toys, and the following day he and Pickett made a serious trip to Bertram Smith's Acres of Books and, spending Aunt Naomi's money, brought out enough crates to half-bury the old pickup truck.

But the shelves still weren't quite filled up. Rose suggested knickknacks, but Andrew stood firm against them. Pennyman, in a show of kindness, lent them two hundred or so volumes from his own considerable library. His books looked right—old dark spines, dusty, comfortable—but most of them had to do with faintly unsavory subjects or were written in foreign languages, mostly German. Andrew secretly doubted that Pennyman knew the languages. He was just being ostentatious. "Pennyman is a phony," Andrew had said to Pickett, showing him an old German volume inked up with what appeared to be alchemical symbols. Pickett shook his head and studied the drawings, then asked to borrow the book. There were other books—on Masonic history, on the Illuminati, on gypsies and Mormons and suppressed Protestant ritual.

Andrew saw a clear link between Pennyman's obsessive self-barbering and his interest in secret knowledge. There was something slimy about it. Rose didn't see it at all. She didn't say so, but he feared that after she would talk with Pennyman she would size Andrew up—study his old shirts, his burlap shoes torn out in the toe, his hair rumpled west in the morning and east in the afternoon. Andrew couldn't stand Mr. Pennyman. He couldn't, in fact, call him *Mr*. Pennyman. The name was idiotic.

Pennyman adjusted his collar, dusted off his hands, and stepped into the kitchen. He bowed just a little to Rose—something which had struck her from the first as being "European" and gallant. "Trouble with opossums, then? I didn't mean to listen, but I couldn't help hearing just a bit of your conversation."

Rose hesitated a moment, smiled weakly, and admitted that there was, apparently, trouble with 'possums. Nothing that should concern Mr. Pennyman, though. Andrew had taken steps. It was poor Aunt Naomi that they were worried about. A 'possum in her room could be the last straw. She had such delicate health.

Pennyman nodded his head. "I might stop in and see her this morning, in fact. She was understandably upset last night. She quite likely still doesn't fathom all the clamor." He paused and picked up Andrew's empty coffee cup, peering at the trout painted on the front of it. He set it down, frowning. "I'm not sure, now that I think of it, that *I* entirely understand all the ruckus. Andrew, though, has it all sorted out, I'm certain. He's a stout lad, Rosannah, a stout lad. You won't find another like him." He nodded at her pleasantly. "May I call you Rose, do you think? I feel as if we've gotten rather closer in the last month. All this formality wears me out. I'm a simple man, really, with simple ways. That's why I admire your husband. He's so—what? Simple, I suppose." He gestured at the tabletop, at the half-dozen boxes of breakfast cereal: Captain Crunch, Kix, Grapenuts, Wheat Chex.

"Rose will be just fine. That's what everyone calls me." She blushed faintly and stood up to pour Pennyman a cup of coffee. He watched her, smiling. He seemed to admire the way she moved—sure, quick, never a wasted gesture. She worked almost like a machine—washing the stove front and wiping down cabinet doors even as she poured coffee. He nodded for no reason at all, except to communicate his admiration.

"Aah," he said, sipping the coffee. "Wonderful." He sloshed it around inside his mouth, making noise, as if he were tasting wine. "Quite a lot of fancy coffee-brewing apparatus, eh? What is that affair there with the tube and valve?"

"It's a milk steamer. He's got three of them, actually. Lord knows why."

Pennyman grinned and shook his head slowly. "Rather like a child with toys, I suppose." He held up a hand as if he anticipated a response. "I don't mean anything by it. I appreciate that sort of thing, in fact. I'm a fan of—what is it?—eccentricity, I suppose. It's . . . charming in its way. That creamer there—the elongated toad with the open mouth, sitting on the stump; that's it, the one wearing trousers and a cocked hat. I bet that's something Andrew brought home. Am I right? I knew it. This place has his mark on it. Positively."

He grinned again and nodded widely while he looked around, as if he were appreciating the labored artwork of a six-year-old. "He has so much *fun* when he's at it. I envy that. I've always been a little too serious, I think. Too . . . well, grown up." And he said this last bit in a theatrically deep voice, as if to indicate that he saw very clearly through his own shortcomings, and that his seeing through them made them all right after all. He drank his coffee and regarded Rose with the eye of an artist.

"You're French," he said, squinting.

"On my mother's side. Originally, anyway. They were—what do you callums?—Huguenots. Always sounds like Hottentots to me. They were filtered through Holland for a few years, though, before transplanting to Iowa."

"You can see it in your cheekbones. Very finely chiseled. My own ancestors were French. We've a certain amount in common, it seems."

Rose smiled at him and pushed a wisp of dark hair out of her eyes, tucking it back in under the scarf that she wore tied across the top of her head. "I've got to get these dishes washed, I'm afraid."

"Of course," he said. "Of course. *Devil* of a lot to this business of opening up an inn, isn't there? I shouldn't wonder that you were ready half the time to throw it all over. Looks like six months work to me, and here you are struggling to be ready for the public in June. Andrew will fetch it all together, though. He's quite a character, quite a character. I don't mean to muscle in, but if this were *my* inn, I'd throw another coat of paint on the west wall outside. The sun and the ocean will alligator that paint off quick."

"Andrew mentioned something of that sort. It's on his list."

"His list! Of course; he's a man of lists. I should have guessed it. Pity you can't get a real workman in to do it, though. I have faith in this little venture of yours, Rose. I've loaned my books to Andrew; I could loan you the price of a housepainter." He held up a hand again to cut off any objections. "I wouldn't suggest it except that we Huguenots have to rally round. Don't give me a yes or no. Just remember that the offer stands. I like this place. The ocean air suits me. I shouldn't wonder that I'll spend a few years here, God granting me the time. I rather feel as if I have a right to offer."

"Thank you, Mr. Pennyman. Andrew has it on his list, though, as I said, and he's promised to get at the list this afternoon."

"*Jules,* Rose. No more Mr. Pennyman. No backsliding now."

"Jules, then."

Pennyman touched his forehead and smiled. Then, as if suddenly remembering something, he asked, "Tell me, does Naomi collect coins? She has the look of a person who might—a sort of—what is it?" Rose shrugged and shook her head. "Not at all then? Perhaps when she was a girl, or a young woman? You haven't heard her talk about such a thing—a particularly valuable coin, perhaps?" Rose said she hadn't, wondering at Pennyman's curiosity. Under the right circumstances, she might rather like him for it. He seemed to make such an effort to *talk* to people. The world needed more of that, when it was genuine. She wondered whether with him it *was* genuine, or whether he was simply playacting. She watched him stride out, brisk and humming, his shoulders square. In a moment the front door slammed and he walked away down the sidewalk toward Ocean Boulevard, just as he did every morning, tapping along with a stick topped with an ivory sea serpent that curled back around onto itself.

TWO

"—Mr. Shandy, my father, Sir, would see nothing
in the light in which others placed it;—he placed
things in his own light;—he would weigh nothing
in common scales."

Laurence Sterne
Tristram Shandy

ANDREW STOOD IN what had become the bar. He very carefully poured cold coffee into a cup. Beams Pickett watched him. "So I fill it once," said Andrew, "like this." He finished, set the coffee down, and picked up the cup. "And I drink half of it, like this." He drank half of it, then set the cup down. "Now I fill it up again, and, once again, drink it." He poured the coffee down his throat, finishing it off entirely, then set the cup down once more, with a flourish, like a stage magician. "So this cup has been entirely full of coffee twice. Is that right?"

Pickett squinted at him for a moment before nodding.

"And now it's empty, right?"

"That's right. Empty."

"And yet," said Andrew, smiling, "though the cup has been full two whole times, I only drank a cup and a half of coffee, and the cup is *empty*." He turned it upside down to illustrate. A single dark drop plunked down onto the countertop.

"I think I see," said Pickett, calculating. He touched the first two fingers of his left hand with the index finger of his right, as if working the problem through thoroughly. "My advice to you is to drop it entirely. There's no profit in it at all. I swear it. Einstein was in ahead of you anyway."

"Einstein? He worked with cups of coffee, too?"

"No, cups of tea I think it was. And it didn't have anything to do with drinking the tea, either, like yours does. His had something to do with rivers—oxbows, I think. He figured them out."

"Did he? Einstein? From reading tea leaves?"

Pickett shrugged. "That's what I've read."

Andrew rather liked that. Science was a satisfactory business all the way around. One of Rose's cousins had spent years whirling frog brains in a centrifuge, with the vague hope, apparently, of working the experiments into something telling. The papers he'd written were full of the most amazing illustrations. One man whirls frog brains, the other measures coffee in a cup, and one day—what? A man walks on the moon. Another steps into a black hole and disappears. Who could say what might come of it all, for good or ill? That was the wonder of it. "It's rather like infinity at first, isn't it, this vanishing coffee business? Like the notion of endless space. When I was a boy I always imagined that there was a chain-link fence out there somewhere, like on the edge of a schoolyard, where things just ended."

"Couldn't you see through it? Chain-link, after all . . ."

"I can't remember. Coffee?" He held the rest of the cold coffee out toward Pickett and slid a clean cup down toward him. Pickett shook his head. "I love mathematical mysteries," said Andrew, "especially when you bring them down to earth, to where they apply to cups of coffee and that sort of thing. Not an unprofitable consideration for a restaurant man."

Pickett nodded, but looked puzzled. "You know, I don't think it *was* filled twice; I think . . ."

"Of course," said Andrew. "Of course. I figured that out

myself—last night. It's a matter of language, isn't it? What do we
mean when we use the word 'filled'? Do we refer to the empty cup
having been filled up twice, or do we mean that it's merely been
topped off? It's rather like the word 'window.' Look that one up in
your *Webster's New International*. No one on earth can tell you
whether 'window' refers to the solid business that keeps the wind
from blowing in or to the hole in the wall, the hiatus itself. You can
close the window and you can climb through it and you can wash it
and you can break it. Imagine being able to climb through
something solid enough to break.

"It's an astonishing business, language, and I'll tell you that it
seemed a lot more astonishing last night after a couple of glasses of
scotch. I thought at first that I'd fallen onto the secret of the
bottomless cup of coffee, except that it seemed to work against
me. I could see straightaway that I couldn't profit from it. Just the
opposite. I pour two cups and the customer only gets a cup and a
half out of them. I lose a half a cup for every two I pour. Imagine
the loss over the years. What is it? Say two hundred cups a day,
two days a week, and half a cup each disappearing due to
mathematics—that's fifty cups a day gone, multiplied by . . .
Will we close this place down on holidays?"

"And Mondays, maybe. Everything closes down on Mondays."

"Yes," said Andrew. "We weren't going to be open on
Mondays anyway. Now I've lost count. Fifty times what?"
Andrew shook his head and shrugged. "Anyway, I wanted to show
it to you. I've written up a brief explanation and mailed it off to the
'Mr. Wizard' program, just as a sort of joke. Kids love this sort of
thing. Don't tell Rose, though. She'd think I was wasting time."

"I won't. Don't worry about that." Pickett sat on his stool and
stared out toward the street, as Andrew sipped at the cold coffee
and studied his copy of *Grossman's Guide*. "How are people going
to find you here, tucked away like this off the highway?"

Andrew looked up from his work. He was drawing up a list of
bar implements—three lists, actually: the necessary, the desir-
able, and the questionable. He'd rulered the page into three
columns and headed each with an N, D, or Q. Neatness was

impossible in broad matters, so he made up for it in small ways when he could. The first list covered an entire column and spilled over onto the back of the page; the Q list had only one item on it—flex straws, which it seemed to him were children's items. He didn't intend to cater to children, not from the bar anyway. "Reputation," he said.

"You need to do some footwork. Xeroxed flyers aren't enough. The best menu in the world isn't enough."

"I rather thought we might slip something into the *Herald*, with you on the staff part time and all." Andrew picked up a comical napkin and studied the grinning, pipe-smoking dog on the front of it. "Do you know anyone in advertising?"

Pickett nodded. "There's Pringle, but he's a wash-out. He hates me for the gag letter I printed with his name on it. He'd boasted about being one of the founders of the Pringle Society, but that turned out to be a lie. They wouldn't even let him in. Anyway, I ribbed him about it and now we can't stand each other. He'd ruin any ad we ran. I could trust Mary Clark, though. She's sharp. Has an eye for design. Speaks French, too."

"A pity no one else in Seal Beach does. We'd better run it in English, I think."

"Of course, of course," Pickett said, gesturing. "But it should have a Continental air to it. This isn't going to be a hamburger joint. I'll draw something up. Leave it to me. Have you worked out a menu yet?"

"No. I'm still experimenting. Never having worked in the restaurant business is a handicap. I can see that. But I can turn it to advantage, I think. The customer is bound to find something here to surprise him. The Weetabix, for example. Show me another restaurant that serves them. They don't. All they've got are those variety pack cereals—the same everywhere. That's the truth of it. A man in the business sees nothing but the business; he's hidebound, blown by the winds of the obvious. A man from outside, though, he'll take his chance on the peculiar, because he doesn't know it's peculiar. Success out of naivete. That's my motto. Speaking of the Weetabix, when are you driving up to Vancouver?"

"Day after tomorrow. Are you *sure* they're contraband? I can't fathom the idea of contraband breakfast cereal. Can't you just order them from some local distributor?"

"Not a chance of it. And as I was saying, there's not a restaurant in the continental United States that serves them, not that I've heard of. All the best restaurants in England and Canada wouldn't open up without a supply. Used to be you could get something called Ruskets. These Ruskets weren't identical to Weetabix, of course, but they were close—flat little biscuits of wheat flakes. Some people broke them up before pouring on the milk and sugar; other people dropped them into the bowl whole, then cut them apart with a spoon. I had a friend who crushed them with his hands first. What's the use of that, I asked him. Might as well eat anything—Wheaties, bran flakes; it wouldn't make a lick of difference. That's the point here, the strategy. Give the customer something out of the ordinary. Make it wholesome, but don't make it like the competition makes it or you're good as dead."

"But all the way to Canada in the pickup truck?"

"Don't use the truck. They'd probably just confiscate the crates of Weetabix at the border—spot them in a second. They'd wonder what in the world a man is doing smuggling Weetabix in an old pickup truck when he's supposed to be in Vancouver at a convention for writers of columns for the lovelorn. The truck doesn't run worth a damn anyway. Fill the trunk of your car. That'll be enough. We'll make another run somehow in a few months." He paused for a moment and thought. "I'll pay for gas."

Pickett nodded, as if he trusted Andrew's weird native genius for this type of thing, for seeing things roundaboutly and inside out and upside down. It was too easy to doubt him, and if there was anything that Beams Pickett distrusted, it was anything that was too easy. Simplicity almost always wore a clever disguise. If he was caught with the Weetabix at the border, he could claim ignorance. "Contraband? Breakfast cereal?" What would they do to him, shoot him?

"When does the first lovelorn column appear, anyway?" Andrew asked.

"Friday after next. I'm still putting it together. It'll run daily in the *Herald*, but if it's good enough, I don't see why I can't syndicate it sooner or later. Georgia's helping me with it."

"Lots of letters? How does anyone know to write?"

"I'm making them up, actually, addresses and all. Georgia's answering them. She's too bluff, though. Too unkind for my tastes. Her advice to everyone is to dry up. I submitted a letter by a woman in Southgate whose husband had lost interest. 'Lose weight, get a face lift, and tell him to go to hell,' that was Georgia's response. *My* advice was to buy diaphanous nighties and packets of bath herbs. That's going to be my standard response, I think."

"Bath herbs?"

Pickett nodded. "You can order them through women's magazines—little bags of dried apples and rose hips and lavender. You mix them into the tub water along with bath oils and then climb in, winking at your mate, you know, provocatively. Turns them into sexual dynamos, apparently."

"And all this stuff floats on the bathwater? God help us. Isn't there an easier method?"

"It's the rage," said Pickett. "The word from the public is that they want whatever's the rage. That's one reason I'm going up to Vancouver. The convention up there is the cutting edge of the lovelorn business."

"That's where we part company," said Andrew. "The science of breakfast cereals runs counter to that, and I mean to prove it. To hell with the rage. To hell with the cutting edge. If it were my column I'd advise celibacy. Either that, or go wild in the other direction. Advise them to heap the bed with suggestive fruit—peaches, bananas, split figs, that sort of thing. Call it the Freudian approach, just to give it legitimacy. And use *Dr*. Pickett as a byline." Andrew studied his list again, then went after it with his eraser. "I've got ice picks, ice tongs, ice scoops, ice shavers, ice buckets, ice molds, and ice dyes. What have I left out?"

Pickett shook his head. "What kinds of molds?"

"Mermaids, toads, comical hats, and high-heeled shoes. I'm purposely staying away from gag items. No eyeballs, bugs, or naked women."

"Wise," said Pickett, nodding. "No trash." He looked over the list. "What's a muddler?"

"I don't know, entirely. I looked it up but there was nothing in the dictionary after muddleheaded. It has something to do with stirring things up, I think."

"Couldn't just use a spoon, then?"

"Go down to the Potholder if you want spoons. Here we use muddlers. At least I think we do. I've got to call down to Walt's to find out what they are."

Pickett stepped across to the street window and rubbed off a little circle of glass wax so that he could peer out better. "I've been having a look at Pennyman's books. At several of them."

Andrew nodded. "Anything telling?"

"I think he bears watching."

"In what way? Has an eye for the silver, does he? Waiting to rob us blind and go out through the window?"

"Hardly. I don't think he needs to rob anyone. I've got a hunch that your Uncle Arthur would know something about him—though he'd never let on. It's more than just his name."

"Names, names, names. Remember what you said about old Moneywort. If anyone was less likely than Moneywort to be involved in that sort of thing, I can't think who it might be. Poor devil, crippled by some wasting disease. What was wrong with him, anyway?"

Pickett frowned. "I'm not sure, exactly. Age, maybe. A bone disease. He couldn't get up from his chair there in the end."

"And then cut to bits in his shop by a dope-addled thief! My God that was grisly." Andrew shuddered, remembering the account in the newspaper. "I'll say this, though, if Moneywort was up to some sort of peculiar shenanigans, that wouldn't be the way he'd die. You know that. It would be something exotic. Something out of Fu Manchu."

"That's exactly what it *wouldn't* be. Not necessarily. That's where you've got to get 'round them. Sometimes it's the slightest clues that give them away, rather than anything broad. You won't see them driving up and down in limousines. Have you gotten a glimpse of Pennyman's walking stick?''

"Of course I have."

Pickett squinted at him, nodding slowly. "Remember Moneywort's hat—the one that was all over fishing lures?"

"Vaguely."

"Well *I* remember it. There were things hanging from that hat that no sane man would try to entice a fish with. Most of them were smokescreens, if you follow me. But there was one that signified—a sea serpent, curling around on itself and swallowing its own tail. What did he hope to catch with that? A blind cave fish? That wasn't any lure, and you can quote me on it. And the devil who sliced him up wasn't some down-and-out dope addict looking for a twenty. Do you know that the murderer died before coming to trial?''

Andrew looked up at Pickett, widening his eyes. "Did he?"

"For a fact. Poisoned. Fed the liver of a blowfish, scrambled up in his eggs. Pitched over nose-first into his plate. I got it out of the police report.''

"Just like—what was his name? The man with the eyeglasses. Or with the name that sounded like eyeglasses—impossible name. Must have been a fake. Remember? Sea captain. Died in Long Beach back in '65. *You* told me about it. Didn't they find blowfish poison in his whisky glass?''

Pickett shrugged, but it was the shrug of a man who saw things very clearly. "That was one of the explanations that turned up later. Hastings made an issue of it, but the man was dead and buried, and ninety-odd years old to boot. Nobody cared what killed him. He could have been carried away by a pterodactyl and it wouldn't have interrupted anyone's lunch. There goes Pennyman,'' Pickett said, watching through the window again. "Where in the devil does he go every morning? Why haven't we followed him?''

Andrew shook his head. "Haven't time. Rose is all over me with her list. It's long enough to paper the hallway with. She doesn't understand the fine points of setting up a bar—of setting up the whole damned restaurant, for heaven's sake. She has doubts about my chefing. She doesn't say so straight out, but I can sense it. I'll be damned if I'll back down now. There's got to be something around this place that I can do right. Rose got the upstairs coming along, though. I'll give her that.''

''Well,'' said Pickett, sitting back down, ''for my money, your fellow with the walking stick there amounts to more than we can guess. I bet *he* could tell you a little bit about poisoning a man with the guts of a fish, except that you couldn't get anyplace close to the subject in a conversation with him. You'd suddenly find some damned half-eaten thing in your sandwich and him grinning at you across the table. That's the last thing you'd see this side of heaven.''

''Look at this.'' Pickett reached into his pants pocket and pulled out a newspaper clipping—a photograph. He glanced around the room before opening it up. In the clipping was a picture of a man on a hospital bed—apparently dead. Three other men stood by the bedside: a doctor; a trim, no-nonsense looking man in a suit; and a man who looked for all the world like Jules Pennyman. It was a fuzzy shot, though, and the third man, really, could have been anyone.

''Who is it?'' asked Andrew.

''Pennyman,'' said Pickett, plonking out the answer without hesitation.

''Does it say so?''

''No, it doesn't say so. It refers to an 'unidentified third party.' But look closer.''

Andrew squinted at the picture. The Pennyman figure held something in his open palm—two coins, it seemed, as if he were handing them over or had just had them handed to him or as if he were getting ready to do something else with them, like lay them on the dead man's eyes. ''Good God,'' Andrew said, mystified. ''Is he going to put coins on the corpse's eyes? I didn't think they did that anymore.''

''That depends upon who 'they' are, doesn't it?''

Andrew looked at him. ''They?'' he asked.

"The ubiquitous 'they,' " said Pickett. "Who do *you* suppose we mean by using the term?"

Andrew shook his head again. "I don't know. It's just idiom, I guess. Just a convenience. Like 'it,' you know. Like '*It* won't rain this afternoon.' Nothing more to it than that. If you try to put a face on it you go mad, don't you? That's schizophrenia."

"Not if it's *true* it isn't. Not if it actually *has* a face. And in this case I'm afraid it has. Any number of them, known in fact as 'Caretakers.' "

"Pardon me," said Andrew, smiling. "Who are? I lost you, I'm afraid."

"*They* are. That's what I'm trying to tell you. This reference to 'they' isn't idiom, not in any local sense. It comes down out of antiquity, and it has specific application—deadly specific." Pickett let his voice fall, casting another glance at the door to the kitchen. "You've read of legends of the Wandering Jews?"

"Was there more than one of them? I thought it was singular."

"There might have been a heap of them, over the years. Throughout Europe. The peasantry used to leave crossed harrows in fallow fields for them to sleep under. It was a magical totem of some sort, meant to protect them. Animals brought them food. There was a central character, though, a magician, an immortal. The rest of them were disciples, who extended their lives by secret means. I'm piecing it together bit by bit, and it involves fish and coins and who knows what sorts of talismans and symbols. What I'm telling you is that this is not fable. This is the real McCoy, and like it or not, I think we've been pitched into the middle of it."

"So you're telling me that there's—what?—a whole company of 'them'? What do they want with you?"

Pickett shrugged. "I don't know enough about it, mind you. And any ignorance here is deadly dangerous. But it could be that they control everything. All of it. You, me, the gatepost, the spin of the planet for all I know."

Andrew snapped his fingers. He had it suddenly. He'd read about it in a novel. "Like in Balzac! What was it?—*The Thirteen*. Was that 'them'?"

Pickett looked tired. He shook his head. "What Balzac knew about it you could put in your hat. Some few of them might have been assembled in Paris, of course. Or anywhere at all. Here, even."

"*Here*, at the inn?"

"That's what I mean. One of them's here already, not at the inn *necessarily*. Here in Seal Beach."

"So Pennyman, you're telling me . . ."

"I'm not *telling* you anything. Some of it I know; some of it's speculation. Go easy with the man, though, or you'll find yourself looking at the wrong end of a blowfish."

Andrew wondered which end was the *right* end of a blowfish. He poked idly at the newspaper clipping, still lying in front of him. "Who's the dead man, then?"

"Jack Ruby," said Pickett.

Andrew suddenly seemed to go cold. He looked again at the picture. It *could*, certainly, be Pennyman. But coins on a dead man's eyes . . . The idea was too morbid. And it didn't amount to anything either. What did it mean? "Why coins on his eyes?" Andrew asked, folding the clipping in half and handing it back to Pickett. Somehow, he'd seen enough of it. It hinted at things he really didn't want to learn more about.

"*I* didn't say anything about coins on his eyes; you did. I don't believe it's that at all. It's payment, is what I think. Somebody's dead, and somebody else has killed him. The coins are payment for services rendered. Payment for a long series of betrayals."

"Comes cheap, doesn't he?" said Andrew, referring to Pennyman, or whoever it was.

"We haven't seen the coins, have we?"

"Why did They do it?"

"I don't think They did. I think *one* of Them did, working at cross purposes to the others. There's something in those coins . . ."

Andrew tried to study *Grossman's Guide* again; all of a sudden *Grossman's* talk about appropriate gins and bitters had begun to sound wholesome and comfortable. When it got around to particulars, this talk about conspiracies gave him the willies.

Something was pending. He'd felt it last night when he was in the tree. He wasn't sure he was ready for it. Pickett and his mysteries! The truth of it was that if you didn't go looking for them you'd never see them. Let well enough alone; that was what Rose would advise. And it would be good advice, too. "Why do you suppose he recommends stainless steel fruit knives?"

"Who? Pennyman?"

"No, Grossman. What's wrong with a carbon steel knife? It holds an edge better."

"Turns the fruit dark. Stainless steel doesn't. It's chemistry is what it is. I can't explain it better than that. A *glass* knife is what I'd advise. That's what they use somewhere."

"*They?*" asked Andrew, picturing Pennyman stepping out of the fog with a glass knife in one hand and a frightful looking fish in the other.

"No, not *Them*. I forget where. Hotel in Singapore, I think."

Andrew nodded, relieved. "How about one of those Ginzu knives? I saw them on television. Apparently you can beat them with hammers if you want to."

Pickett gave him a puzzled look. "Why do you want to do that?"

"I don't have any idea," said Andrew, shaking his head. "Just on general principles, I should think. I'll stick to *Grossman* here, though. Distrust anything modern, that's my motto. Stainless steel fruit knives it is—three of them."

His list looked pretty healthy, all in all, but it would cost him a fortune to buy the whole lot of it. He couldn't bear the idea of a half-equipped bar, though. He was an all-or-nothing man at heart. "The Balzac book," he said to Pickett, "have you read it?"

"Years ago."

"What was the old man's name? Ferragus. That was it. Remember? 'A whole drama lay in the droop of the withered eyelids.' Fancy such a thing as 'withered eyelids.' I love the notion of all that sort of thing—of the Thirteen, the *Devorants*."

"You'll love it a lot less when they come in through the door."

"So you think this is Them, then?"

"No," said Pickett. "This is not the same crowd. That was the wrong Them. This isn't the Thirteen nor ever has been. This isn't a fiction. Mr. Pennyman is who it is, and I'm telling you that you'd better be careful of him."

"But is there thirteen of Them, of our Them?"

"How on earth do *I* know? There might be ten; there might be a dozen."

"A baker's dozen, for my money. That's what we'll call the inn."

"What, The Baker's Dozen?"

"Sounds foody enough, doesn't it? And with all this Thirteen business, it seems to fit. It'll be our joke."

"Sounds cheap to me. Like a chain restaurant, a coffee shop."

"Then we'll call it The Thirteen. Just like that. And it'll work, too. That's our address, isn't it? Number 13 Edith Circle. Destiny shoves its oar in again. That's just the sort of thing that appeals to me—the mysterious double meaning. To the common man it's merely an address; to the man who squints into the fog, though, it signifies. You like that notion, too. Admit it. The number is full of portent."

Pickett shrugged. "It has a ring," he said. "But . . ."

"But nothing," said Andrew. "It has an inevitability, is what it has." He looked up at Pickett suddenly and then stepped across to peer through the half-open door that led down the hallway to the kitchen. Apparently satisfied, he said in a whisper, "Speaking of poisons and conspiracies, what's the name of your man at Rodent Control? The guy you interviewed for the newspaper?"

"Biff Chateau."

"That's the one. Fancy my having forgotten a name like that. What's he got in the way of poisons?"

"Mostly anticoagulants."

"Work quick, do they? Feed a 'possum a dose of one of them and—what?—he's dead in an hour?"

Pickett shook his head. "I don't think so. Most of them are cumulative. Rat nibbles a little bit on Monday, snacks on it on Tuesday, still feels in top form on Thursday. A week later, though, he's under the weather. Then, as I understand it, all his blood turns to vapor or something and just leaks out through every available pore. Grisly sort of thing, but effective.''

''Do they ever murder a dog by mistake?''

''In fact, yes. It's rare, though. A dog has to eat a heap of the stuff. They could kill an elephant with it, I suppose, if they took the time to do it right.''

Andrew nodded and stroked his chin. ''Can this man Chateau get me a dead 'possum?''

''More than one, I should think. They're always turning up dead in someone's backyard and being taken for enormous rats. They probably have a half dozen in the dumpster right now.''

''I only need one,'' said Andrew. He stepped across to the window and looked out, as if he were suddenly in a hurry. The street was in shadow, since the sun was behind the house, but the rooftops blazed with sunlight, and Pacific Coast Highway, a block away, was thronged with barefoot beach-goers, taking advantage of the hot spring weather. Andrew peered back down the hallway, listening.

A vacuum cleaner rumbled somewhere on the second floor. Rose was working away. God bless her, thought Andrew, as he and Pickett slipped out through the back door and headed toward Andrew's Metropolitan, parked at the curb. Knowing that Rose was at work wrestling the bungalow into submission was like knowing there was coffee brewing in the morning. It gave a man hope. It made things solid.

There were days when it seemed to him that the walls and the floor and the chairs he sat on were becoming transparent, were about to wink out of existence like snuffed candle flames, leaving only a smoky shadow lingering in the air. But then there was Rose, looming into view with a dust rag or a hammer or a pair of hedge clippers, and the chairs and walls and floors precipitated out of the air again and smiled at him. He'd be a jellyfish without her, a ghost. He knew that and reminded himself of it daily.

So what if she was short-sighted when it came to beer scrapers or imported breakfast cereals or just the right bottle of gin or scotch? She had *him,* didn't she? He had a genius for those sorts of things. She didn't have to bother with them.

The Metropolitan grumbled away toward the highway, blowing

out a plume of dark exhaust. If he was lucky, Rose wouldn't have heard them go, and he could slip back in later, undetected. Pickett would want to stop at Leisure World and look in on old Uncle Arthur, but there wouldn't be any time for that. This was business. He'd have to settle the score with Aunt Naomi that afternoon, or there'd be trouble.

Good old Aunt Naomi. In the light of day—when she wasn't snoring, when her cats were out stalking across the rooftops—it was easy to take the long view. The idea of Rose pulling things together made it even easier. Sometimes. In truth, sometimes it just made it easier to feel guilty. He sighed, unable to keep it all straight. Well, *he'd* look to the delicate work. It was the best he could do. No one could ask more of him than that. What had his father said on the subject? If it was easy, his father had been fond of saying, they would have gotten somebody else to do it. Or something like that. It seemed to apply here, in some nebulous way that didn't bear scrupulous study. He realized suddenly that Pickett was talking—asking him something.

"What? Sorry."

"I said, what do you want with poison?"

Andrew stayed up late that night reading in the library. Mrs. Gummidge and Aunt Naomi played Scrabble upstairs until nearly eleven; then they went to bed. Rose had been asleep for hours. Pennyman had turned in at ten. By midnight the house was quiet and dark; only the pole lamp in the library burned. Andrew felt like a conspirator, but in fact he wasn't conspiring with anyone. This was *his* plot, from end to end. He hadn't even discussed it with Pickett, although his friend had agreed to come round early in the morning, pretending to be on his way to the pier to fish. At six A.M., Andrew thought, smiling, the tale would be told.

He waited for the stroke of midnight, just for the romance of it. Then, feeling as if his chest were empty, he tiptoed up the attic stairs carrying the dead 'possum in a bag. It was starting to ripen, having been found yesterday in Garden Grove, already dead and torn up by something—cats, probably. That would be a stroke of luck if he played his cards right. It was dark on the stairs, but he couldn't use even a flashlight. Being discovered now would mean . . . He couldn't say. They'd take him away. Men in lab coats would ask him deceptive questions. They'd whirl his brain in a centrifuge and come to conclusions.

He let himself into the little, gabled cubbyhole, so that he could climb out the window onto the roof. The ladder had been a wash-out the night before; he wouldn't chance it again. He could see the shadow of Pickett's telescope in front of the casement. Slowly, carefully, he hauled it aside, eased open the window, and stepped out. Thank goodness there wasn't much of a slope. He pulled the bag out after him, left it lying on the roof, and edged down the asphalt shingles toward where the pole lay tilted against the house, hidden by the foliage of the camphor tree. There it was.

He pulled it up through the leaves, scraping it over a limb, and then set it on the roof with the noose in front of him. The moon wouldn't be up for an hour yet; last night he had learned that much, anyway. The 'possum cooperated admirably. Dead 'possums tell no tales, he thought, grinning. He tightened the noose around its neck, and, towing the pole behind him, crept toward Aunt Naomi's window.

It was closed. Of course it would be. She wouldn't want any more marauders. Last night had been enough to put the fear into her. Andrew slipped a hand into his back pocket and pulled out a long-bladed spatula, then shoved it through the gap between the two halves of the ill-fitting casement windows. It was the work of an instant to flip up the latch. In the hot, still night there wouldn't even be a breeze to disturb the sleeping Aunt Naomi.

If there was trouble, if she awoke again, he could just let the 'possum lie and drop the pole back down into the tree. He'd go across the roof and climb down onto the carport, and from there onto the top of his pickup truck. The library window was wide open, and there was a pile of bricks outside it. He'd be reading in his chair inside of two minutes, and all they'd find on the roof would be a dead 'possum. He had thought it through that afternoon—studied it from the street. It was as if Providence had come round to set it up: the bricks, the 'possum, the pole already lying beneath the tree; all of it had been handed to him with a ribbon tied around it. But if his luck held, he wouldn't need to use the escape route. It would be a neater job all the way around if he could plant the 'possum in Aunt Naomi's bedroom and let her find it in the morning.

Nothing stirred inside. Aunt Naomi snored grotesquely; the cats slept through it. He slid the pole in through the window, barely breathing. Dropping the 'possum onto her bed would lead to spectacular results, except that she'd probably wake up on the instant and shriek. Near the door—that would be good enough—as if the beast were trying to escape, but hadn't made it. He positioned the pole just so, paused to breathe, then played out the line. Immediately it went slack; the 'possum whumped to the floor, and Andrew hauled the pole out into the night.

He pulled the casement shut and slid along on his rear end toward the tree, dropping the pole down through the leaves so that it rested on the same branch that it had been tilting against all day. Crouching, listening, he counted to sixty. The snoring continued, uninterrupted. She hadn't even stirred.

He crept back to the casement, pulled out his spatula again, and pushed the latch back into place, neat as you please. In a moment he was back in at the window, shifting Pickett's telescope, shoving the 'possum bag in behind the foil-backed insulation stapled into the unplastered studs. He tiptoed back down the narrow stairs, washed his hands in the kitchen sink, and opened a beer to celebrate. It was 12:13 by the clock, and he'd already accomplished a night's work.

Far too full of anxious energy and anticipation to sleep, he lay down on the couch with the idea of reading a book, and in a half hour got up to pour himself another glass of beer. He read some more, half-heartedly, his mind wandering away from the book, until he found himself studying in his mind the complexities of coffee mugs. That led him on to silverware and to copper pots and pans and enormous colanders suitable for draining twenty pounds of fetuccini. He dreamed about extravagant chefs' hats, about his wearing one, standing in front of an impossibly grand espresso machine that was a sort of orchestrated tangle of tubes and valves, reaching away to the ceiling.

A pounding on the front door awakened him. There was a simultaneous screaming, coming from somewhere—from overhead, from the attic. Andrew stumbled out into the living room, rubbing his face. He felt like a rumpled, dehydrated hobo. Wrapped in her bathrobe, Rose pushed past him, bound for the front door. She threw it open. There was Pickett, holding a fishing pole and tackle box and wearing a hat. He started to speak, to play out the role he and Andrew had written for him the previous afternoon, but Rose dashed away toward the stairs, shouting at Andrew to follow along.

Upstairs, Mrs. Gummidge stood with her hand across her mouth, outside the open door of Aunt Naomi's room. Somehow the 'possum had deteriorated sadly in the early morning hours. In the closeness of the room, it outstank the cats, which had, apparently, been at the corpse just a little bit—investigating it, but finally giving up and leaving it alone. It was perfect. Andrew bit his lip and winked at Pickett.

Aunt Naomi sat in bed, her hair curled as it had been the night before. She breathed like a tea kettle. "How," she demanded in a hollow, lamenting voice, "did that creature get into my room?"

Andrew cleared Mrs. Gummidge out of the way. "Bring me the scoop shovel," he said, taking command. "Out of the garage. The broad, aluminum scoop."

"I'll get it," said Pickett, hurrying away down the stairs.

Andrew examined the dead 'possum. "Cats have done for it." He nodded at Aunt Naomi, who stared at him as if he were talking like an ape. "The cats," he said, louder. "They've worried the beast to death. Look at him, he's all over scratches. Like the Chinese—the death of a thousand cuts. Very nasty business." He shook his head. Pickett came stomping up the stairs, carrying the short-handled shovel. "What do you think of this?" asked Andrew stoutly.

Pickett stared at him, then said, "Looks like—what?—the cats got him, I guess." He bent over to have a closer look, then screwed up his face and backed away. "He's rather had it, hasn't he?"

Andrew nodded. "Does he look like the fellow we saw on the back fence two days ago? Same size, I'd say."

Pickett nodded. "I'm certain it is." He looked up at Rose, who seemed to be staring at him particularly hard. "Couldn't *swear* to it, of course, not absolutely. Wouldn't want to sign an affidavit. If he were in a police line-up, you know . . ." He let the subject drop and pretended to examine the creature again, shaking his head at the very idea of it.

Rose sat down on the bed beside Aunt Naomi and patted the coverlet over the old woman's leg. "Can't you get it out of here?" she asked Andrew, nodding toward the door.

"At once. Back away there, Mrs. Gummidge. One dead 'possum coming down the stairs. Call Rodent Control, will you? There's a man there named Biff Chateau who has done some work for me in the past. This is right in his line. Thank God for the cats, eh? This place would be hell on earth without them. There wouldn't be a room in the house safe from monsters like this. He stinks to high heaven, doesn't he?"

There were more footfalls on the stairs, and Mr. Pennyman hove into view. Imposter, thought Andrew. He's taken the time to massage his scalp before coming up. There might have been any kind of trouble at all up here—thieves, cavemen, Martians—*he* wouldn't have been worth a curse. It occurred to Andrew that he could trip right then, and pitch the spoiled 'possum into Pennyman's face. No one would claim it wasn't a flat-out accident. But he wouldn't. This was art, this 'possum business. It demanded subtlety. There wasn't any room for farce.

"Excuse me, Mr. Pennyman," Andrew said, shoving past the man on the landing. "There's been a 'possum fooling about in Naomi's bedroom. Half-terrorized her before the cats got to it. God bless the cats, like I was saying. Lord love a cat. Nothing like them." He angled away down the stairs, holding the scoop shovel out in front of him, Pickett following. "A cat by any other name . . ." he said over his shoulder. "Sacred in Borneo, I understand." He continued to chatter long after Pennyman could no longer hear him. If he stopped, he'd pitch over laughing. He'd convulse. They'd have to call in a doctor to sedate him. The whole successful business would be spoiled like an old fish.

There was Mrs. Gummidge, looming out of the kitchen. She'd gotten nothing but a recording over the phone at Rodent Control. Of course she would have. He'd known it when he'd sent her off, but *she* hadn't thought of it. What Mrs. Gummidge didn't think of would fill a book. It wasn't even six in the morning yet. She'd left a message, and Chateau would discover it later. He'd send a man out in a van later in the day, full of stories about renegade 'possums, about the land being overrun with them.

Andrew was vindicated. That was the long and the short of it. He held the truth on a scoop shovel. They'd been suspicious of his 'possum, had they? Now here one was, giving them all the glad eye. Or the glazed eye. Andrew very nearly laughed out loud. He had taken up the reins and steered the morning out of chaos, right under the nose of Pennyman. He would look in on Aunt Naomi later that morning, after she'd had a chance to compose herself, to haul the god-awful curl papers out of her hair. He would ask her for a small sum, for the restaurant. Five hundred dollars would . . . Well, it wouldn't go far. A thousand, though, would buy him the bar implements on his list, with money left over to buy single malt whiskies. His importer listed forty-two, at an average of thirteen dollars a bottle. That was five hundred and what, altogether? Something. He wasn't any good at sums.

He paused to smile at Mrs. Gummidge on his way out the door, thanking her for making the useless phone call. She grinned back at him and nodded. Pickett stood silently, holding his hat. His mustache desperately needed trimming.

"I'll just go to Naomi," said Mrs. Gummidge. "I'll bring round her tea."

Andrew winked at her. "You do that, Mrs. Gummidge. I'd suggest chamomile, for its soothing properties. Avoid anything containing caffeine. I'd fetch it up myself, but this fellow here ought to be dumped into a trash can and lidded, before the whole house moves out on account of him. Then I'm going fishing. You've met Mr. Pickett, I believe.''

Mrs. Gummidge nodded, still smiling, her teeth set.

''Yes, of course you have,'' said Andrew. ''Any number of times. Goodbye, then. If Rodent Control calls back, tell them the beast is in a trash can behind the garage. Normally it's the animal shelter that handles this sort of thing, but I particularly wanted Rodent Control to be in on it. They're equipped to test for plague fleas.''

Mrs. Gummidge blinked. Andrew nodded to her and went out through the door, dumping the 'possum in an empty trash can and shoving the lid on, then leaning the shovel against the clapboard wall of the garage. Pickett followed along into the cool darkness inside, waiting in the doorway until Andrew turned on the lights. ''She's the grinningest woman I've ever seen,'' Pickett said, putting his hat back on. ''I'd guess she was a waxwork statue if I didn't know any better. Or an automaton. You can't trust a face like that. Impossible to read.''

Andrew nodded, messing with a little bag full of white granules on the workbench. On the side of it, in black felt pen, was scrawled something impossible—a chemical name. ''She has a vocabulary of about thirty stock phrases, most of them involving tea and Scrabble and changing poor Naomi's bed linen. All of it sounds programmed. For my money she's got some dark motive beneath it all.''

Pickett watched him untie and then tie the plastic bag. He looked uncomfortable. ''Which one is that again? Chloro-what?''

''Chlorophacinone,'' Andrew said. ''No, I haven't mixed it up yet. You use wet cornmeal—press it into cakes.'' He put the bag down on the bench, as if he suddenly found it distasteful. ''I'd thought of setting the cakes around as if I were poisoning 'possums. Rose would have to take the whole business more seriously then.''

''I dare say she would,'' Pickett said. ''What if you *do* poison something—a 'possum, say? What if by accident you poison a *cat*, for God's sake? You'd never get out of the soup.''

Andrew stared at the powder in the bag. ''I'd hate myself if I poisoned anything at all. It was just going to be a blind, a ruse. Only because the cat-stealing trick went bad. I'm certain Rose saw through it. So I've got to press on, somehow, and make her doubt herself. Make her see that I'm serious about this 'possum business.''

"*Are* you serious about this 'possum business? My advice is to let it drop. Cut bait and get out. It's a shame there *isn't* a 'possum around the neighborhood. That would settle things.''

Andrew sighed. "There is, actually. I think there's one living under the house. That's where I got the idea in the first place.''

"Well there you are! Point him out to Rose. There's your evidence, right where you want him.''

"I can't let on that there's *really* one living under the house. She'd want him out of there.''

Pickett stared hard at Andrew, as if trying to make sense of nonsense. "So you're telling me that despite the poison and the dead 'possum in Naomi's room and your fears about having been caught up on the roof in the middle of the night, what you really want to do is *protect* the 'possum living under the house?''

Andrew shrugged and then nodded weakly. "They're such great-looking little guys, with that nose and all.''

"I can't do anything for you then,'' said Pickett. "You've made a mess of your priorities.''

"I can't stand talk about 'priorities.' They tire me out.'' Andrew picked up the sack full of poison. It seemed suddenly to contain a coiled snake or a nest of spiders. "I ought to pitch it into the trash, right now, while I'm thinking straight. Don't tell Chateau, though, will you? I don't want him to know that I tossed it out after begging five pounds of it off him to assassinate non-existent rats.''

Pickett shook his head. "Toss it out. That's what I'd do. I'm afraid of poisons, especially with Pennyman around. There's no telling what you'll find in your beer.''

Andrew nodded. "Done,'' he said, and he stepped out into the daylight, dropping the bag into another trash can and hauling the can across the backyard, away from the garage so that Rodent Control wouldn't find it while looking for the 'possum.

"I left my pole and tackle box in the living room," said Pickett, remembering suddenly.

"Go after them then. I'll get my stuff together. I'd better not go back in—not just now." Somehow the idea of coming face-to-face with Rose filled him with terror. He'd wait until the dust settled.

Just as Pickett turned to go, the house door slammed shut, and there was Mrs. Gummidge, carrying a dripping coffee filter full of steaming grounds. She grinned at them. "Can't put these down the disposal," she said. "They'll clog the septic tank."

"We haven't got a septic tank," Andrew said, grinning back. "Nothing but sewers for us."

She stepped across and lifted the lid from the trash can that Andrew had just moved. She set the lid down and looked in suspiciously, then dropped the grounds in. "No 'possums in that one," she said cheerfully, bending over to pick up the lid. She banged it back down onto the trash can and hurried away toward the house, muttering about "poor Naomi" and "given such a fright," her voice trailing away into nothing.

The door slammed again, and Pickett stood watching the empty porch, lost in thought. His eyes had that vacant, dangerous look that meant he was "onto something," that he was beginning to see things clearly at last. He was lost in plots, assembling and disassembling them, thinking of blowfish and assassins and lights in the sky, thinking of Moneywort and Pennyman, thinking of Uncle Arthur steering across foggy midnight oilfields in his red, electronic car, bumping over ruts, watching, perhaps, for the telltale glow of a suddenly uncovered lantern that would reveal to him in the instant of illumination the secret tiltings of world banks, the moment-to-moment machinations of governments. He turned around stiffly and set out after his fishing pole.

THREE

"See the rings pursue each other;
All below grows black as night . . ."
Robert Louis Stevenson
"Looking Glass River"

WHATEVER WAS HAPPENING had the feeling of nightfall about it, the feeling that twenty centuries of battles and betrayals, of civilizations and the shifting of continents, were crashing to a stony close. Something was coming full circle—slouching in on a wind out of the east. It was hot and thin—a desert wind with the smell of sagebrush and riverbeds on it, yanking off roof shingles in the night and scattering sycamore leaves and blowing spindrift off the back of the cold north swell as it hammered through pier pilings and surged up onto an almost deserted spring beach.

The wind tore fruitlessly at the newspaper in the hands of Jules Pennyman, who sat at a redwood table in the shade of the old pier and drank black coffee from a Styrofoam cup. He knew as he sat there, idly sipping his coffee and watching the sea across the top of his newspaper, that something had loosened in the world; something had awakened, and was plodding toward him, or with him, across the aimless miles. He smiled and stroked his beard, then flicked a bit of thread from the knee of his white trousers. He could hear the deep, hoarse breathing of it on the wind, like an out-of-tune, bedlam orchestra. There was just the suggestion of the first trumpet behind it all, and there would follow in the days to come a rain of hail and fire and blood, maybe literally. He rather hoped so.

Pennyman's coffee was terrible—probably brewed early that morning and then burnt up on a hot plate. Andrew Vanbergen made a good cup of coffee. You had to give him that much. It didn't matter much to Pennyman anymore, though; coffee was coffee. He drank it because he had to fill his stomach; that much was still required of him. He would have liked to see the world rid of its curious little habits. If it were up to him—and it soon might be—he'd have the beaches swept clean of sand and its seashells ground into powder and mixed into cement. He'd pave everything, is what he'd do. The pattern of mussels and barnacles and starfish on the pier pilings offended him, almost as much as the sunlight did. The shouted laughter of an unseen fisherman up on the pier rasped across the back of his brain like the serrated edge of a scaling knife.

He'd gotten back just four weeks past from his trip to the Middle East. His coins were tucked away, waiting against the day that he'd possess them all. There was still only one of the remaining five that puzzled him, and he suspected that somehow, somewhere in antiquity, something had been done to it to render it unrecognizable. He'd find it, though. Someone knew what it was and where it was, and it was only a matter of time before, one by one, he'd wring the information out of them.

He wasn't the only one who sensed that something was in the wind. There'd been a rash of odd stories in the newspaper over the past months—and not in the tabloids, either, but in big-city papers. A goat had climbed into a truck owned by a shadowy delivery service and had knocked the handbrake loose and steered the truck down a hill and into a tree, jumping out the open window a moment before the truck had caught fire and burned, along with its contents. Two pigs a month back had terrorized a doughnut shop, making away across a parking lot with half a dozen glazed doughnuts and rooting through a drive-in dairy until the startled clerk had given them milk to drink. When they were rounded up at last they seemed to be playing a complicated game on the asphalt of the parking lot, snuffling the doughnuts up and down with their noses. And then there were reports in Huntington Beach of a hippopotamus that had appeared through the mist of a foggy morning and then disappeared just as thoroughly and quickly. Thirty whales had beached themselves in Mexico.

It had all been very funny to the journalists, but it wasn't funny to Pennyman; it reminded him a little too much of the demoniacs and the Gadarene swine. It was as if an unseen hand were stirring nature out of her long lethargy, as if there were counterplots and divine conspiracies that he didn't entirely see or understand. There was nothing he liked less than something he didn't understand.

Someone would rise up to take the places of Moneywort and Aureus. And when Pennyman had his way with Pfennig, there would be a person in the world unwittingly ready to take his place, too, if any of the coins found him. The trick was recognizing them when they appeared; and they *would* appear— one of them possessing the untraceable coin. It had been thousands of years that they'd worked as one, all the Caretakers, and all the time there was someone's shadow cast across their enterprises. There were surreptitious visits, disappearing coins, coins reappearing in the possession of apes or in the pouches of opossums after being lost for decades—all of it a sort of shadow symphony, orchestrated by—whom?

Pennyman knew the secret identity of the man who conducted the orchestra; he knew who the overseer *really* was. And he knew that the man sought to ransom himself by keeping the coins apart. It was a two-thousand-years-old good deed. The man's *assumed* identity was a mystery to him, though. One couldn't simply look up "Iscariot, Judas" in the Seal Beach phone directory and come up with an address. It might be the mayor, or a television repairman, or, even more likely, the hobo that slept right now against the wall of the concrete rest room beneath the pier. He might call himself anything at all. There were certain tests that betrayed the identity of one of the Caretakers, but their master wasn't susceptible to tests, not unless you caught him out—in the moonlight. Well, he would show his hand soon enough, whoever he was. Pennyman would force it. He'd been forcing it for close onto two hundred years now—hoarding and hiding the coins, giving up one here to gain two there, committing any sort of atrocity, buying and selling kings and presidents and piling up the silver coins one on top of another. And now the pot was almost full. Almost.

Things were falling into disorder—a condition that suited Pennyman just fine. He sometimes, more often lately, preferred white noise to music on the radio. He sought out the hoarse, chaotic cry of nighttime terror and closed his ears to the insipid laughter of human beings pretending to be jolly. He found his flask in his coat pocket and drained off the rest of the chalky, pink antacid in it. The skin of his scalp felt as if it were crawling, and for a moment it seemed as if he were breathing dust. He could almost feel his pulse creeping along like a tired, rusted engine. With a shaking hand he fumbled after a glass vial in the pocket of his trousers. He squinted at the little dribble of elixir in the bottom of it, and he shook his head, as if dissatisfied. Then, grimacing, he drank it off, capped it and put it away.

He poured the rest of his coffee onto the ground and nodded his head at a man who approached along the sand. He felt the elixir from the vial seeping along his arteries, bracing him. The man coming toward him was a bore, all full of drivel about flying saucers. He'd insisted Pennyman come to a literary society thereabouts, and he wouldn't take no for an answer. It was always possible, of course, that the man knew more than he let on—that he was a Caretaker, that he had the coin. Maybe it was in his pocket right now. Maybe he possessed it and didn't know what it was. Was he the one? Pennyman gestured toward a chair and half stood up, as if in greeting. He rummaged in his pocket for a silver quarter, and winked as the man sat down, a wide, stupid grin on his face. "Take a look at this," said Pennyman, flipping the coin end over end. The coin seemed to vanish, and then, as if by a miracle, Pennyman, looking vastly surprised, hauled it out of the man's ear.

Halfway down the pier, affixed to an old, rusted swivel that used to be painted a jaunty red and white, stood a telescope that you could aim out to sea on a clear day in order to catch a glimpse of Catalina Island. Or you could point it north, toward Los Angeles Harbor or south toward the oilfields of Huntington Beach. A tall old man with brush-cut hair dropped a dime into the slot and cranked it around toward the beach, slowly turning the focus. Parked beside the telescope was a red car, a little electric car like a golf cart, that was about twenty percent interior space and eighty percent fins, as if it were an old Cadillac shrunk down by an urban witch doctor. It was driven by a twelve-volt battery that plugged into a wall socket for a recharge, and you could drive it on the pier if you were old enough or if your legs were no good.

Arthur Eastman squinted through the lens. He could read nothing in the face of the man he watched, except that the man was waiting for something, or someone. There was desperation in the wind, the slow creak of a century turning fitfully to a close, the quiet whisper of the shuffling of the last pages of a book. Uncle Arthur didn't like it a bit. The next week would tell. He swung the telescope around and scanned the sea. There was nothing.

The telescope shut off, and Arthur stepped down off the little plinth that the thing stood on. He might as well stroll down the pier and see what people were catching. The air would do him good. He caught sight, just then, of Naomi's nephew, Andrew Vanbergen, fishing by the bait house along with young Pickett, both of them laughing out loud. Apparently they hadn't seen him yet. It was best, perhaps, to leave them alone. Pickett would ask too many questions. The pot was boiling, and there were too many cooks as it was. He didn't need Pickett to come staggering toward the broth with a saltshaker. He was a good man—both of them were—and their time would come. But right now wasn't their time. He would let them fish.

Climbing into his car, he noticed that Jules Pennyman had struck up a conversation with one of Andrew's idiot friends. Pennyman was desperate—but then desperate men were as often as not dangerous men. He was plying the man with coin tricks. Uncle Arthur sat and thought for a minute, then looked out once again at the open sea before motoring silently away up the pier and down onto Main Street.

The doctor visited Aunt Naomi that afternoon. "She's had a fright," he said under his breath when Andrew poked his head into the room. The doctor stepped out onto the landing and half-shut the door behind him. Andrew shook his head sadly, hiding a bag full of chocolates behind his back. The doctor paused to take his glasses off, then wiped them slowly and carefully with a shred of tissue before putting them back on, squinting, taking them off again, and wiping some more, turning the activity into a sort of drama. Andrew stared at him, controlling himself.

"Bed rest; that's what I'd advise. And a certain amount of quiet, too." The doctor was a fraud. Andrew could see that in an instant. There was a look in the man's eyes that advertised it, that seemed to say: "I know nothing at all about anything, and so I look very grave instead." He was perfect for Aunt Naomi, who wanted a doctor that knew nothing. A decent doctor would merely tell her to get out of bed, to quit whining, to pitch out the cats and air the room for a week.

The doctor had almost no chin, as if he were inbred or had evolved in a single generation from the fishes. And his hair had fallen out in two symmetrical clumps, so that he was bald as a vulture above his forehead and on the very crown of his head, and combed the little strip of wispy hair in between so that half of it fell forward and half of it backward, making him look as if he were wearing a rare sort of foreign hat.

He made housecalls, though, for an exorbitant sum that Aunt Naomi gladly paid. Andrew was happy enough about that, for it would be he, if anyone, who would otherwise have to cart her across town to the doctor's office. Doctor Garibaldi, he called himself. He wore a black suit and tie in the sweltering heat. "She needs exercise, you know," he said, peering sideways at Andrew as if he were revealing a secret that he ought not to reveal.

Andrew nodded. "Bed rest and exercise," he said. "How about chocolate?"

The doctor shook his head violently. "I wouldn't. Too rich for her."

"Liquor?"

"No more than a glass of dry white wine with a meal."

"What exactly is wrong with her," asked Andrew, "besides her being an invalid?"

"Well," said the doctor, "it's a complicated business for a layman. The veins and arteries, you understand, are like little subways, let's say, for the blood to—what is it?—traverse, perhaps." He gestured with both hands, driving one through the other like a car through a tunnel. "Do you follow me?" he asked. Andrew smiled and nodded. "When we're young, they have a certain elasticity to them, not unlike rubber tubing."

Andrew widened his eyes, as if struck by the extent of the doctor's knowledge of anatomy. "I begin to see," he said. "Elasticity?"

"Yes indeed. The pressures, you know. The heart is like a pump . . ."

"There's biblical precedent for all of this, I believe—all of this elasticity. In Exodus, if I'm not mistaken."

The doctor looked at him sharply and shook his head, as if he didn't quite follow.

"Moses," said Andrew, "was out in the scrub—how did that go? He was looking for something. I don't remember what it was; the fatted calf, I think. We can look it up if we have to. It says, if I recall the substance of the text, that he tied his ass to a tree and walked half a mile."

The doctor stared at him. Andrew smiled. It wasn't worth laughing out loud over, maybe, but it was worth more than six seconds of staring. Nothing came of it, though, except more staring. He thinks I'm insane, Andrew thought. That sort of thing happened to him a lot. It was like the baby 'possums in the teaspoon business. The world wasn't built with a sense of humor. It took itself too seriously. He'd once laughingly informed a gas station mechanic that there was something wrong with the "Johnson rods" in the Metropolitan. The man had wiped his greasy hands on his pants and given him a look that matched exactly the look that the doctor was giving him now. "Ain't no such thing," the man had said, and shook his head over it, as if of all the living idiots he'd seen in his life, none had amounted to half as much as Andrew amounted to.

The doctor opened his bag, looked inside quickly, and stepped toward the stairs. "And no coffee, either. Especially no coffee. The acid could ruin her stomach lining. And the caffeine!—well, leave it at this: She simply shouldn't get worked up. At all. It's the worst thing. I've prescribed Valium. It's tranquility that she needs, poor soul. I gather there was some sort of disturbance this morning—an animal or something in her room."

"That's right," said Andrew, feeling ashamed of himself now. "A 'possum, actually. Cats tore it to shreds in the night. I've read that they're on the march, in their way—migrating south. There's talk of a coming ice age, according to *Scientific American*. Do you read it?"

"Yes . . . That is, when I can. I'm a busy man, what with house calls and all. Are you talking about cats?" He wiped his glasses again, peered at Andrew, and backed away down the stairs. "I'll come round again in a week. Keep these creatures out of her room, cats or no cats."

Andrew followed him down, thinking that if he himself were a bald man he'd have something tattooed on the crown of his head—on the very top, so that almost no one could see it unless he bent over. He thought briefly of writing something on Dr. Garibaldi's head with a felt-tipped pen, but it would quite likely be impossible unless the doctor were asleep or dead. And if he were dead there wouldn't be much point to it, beyond exciting a certain amount of wonder and suspicion among coroners and immediate family. Something completely unfathomable would be best. If you were going to do a job, he thought, watching Dr. Garibaldi step out into the living room from the stairs, then you do a job. You'd have to write something on a man's head that had no sane explanation. Nonsense syllables might do the trick. And if they rhymed, then it would be all the better, since it would seem as if they signified something. He could imagine Beams Pickett innocently noticing such a thing written onto the top of the doctor's head. His eyes would expand like pond ripples until he fell face-first into the bushes.

The doctor went out through the front door and onto the porch. Andrew shook his hand, which, it occurred to him, felt rather like a mushroom, as if pressing it too hard would release a little cloud of spores. He dropped it abruptly. "About animals in the room, Doctor Garibaldi—the cats, that is. All the hair and noise and cat boxes and half-eaten food. That can't be healthful. It would be hard for me to see them go, of course, but perhaps they should. We're fond of them, my wife and I, but we could sacrifice ourselves just a bit if it would improve Naomi's health."

The doctor grimaced. "If it were a matter of asthma or allergies I'd concur," he said. "But this is general debility, so to speak. The cats are a boost to her lagging spirits." He paused, then winked broadly at Andrew. He bent forward and whispered, "She'll outlive us both if she's kept away from rich foods, liquor, and tobacco." And then he turned and hurried away like a fat little animal, a marmot or a raccoon, toward his car.

Andrew stepped into the house, and popped back up the stairs whistling, still carrying his chocolates. He tapped twice on the door before shoving it open a crack and looking in. There sat Aunt Naomi, propped against pillows. She looked tired—but who wouldn't, lying around all day in a room full of cats? In fact, when he looked more closely, it wasn't so much tired as put-upon that she looked—by circumstance, by doctors, by 'possums, by the world in general.

Aunt Naomi was inscrutable; that was her problem, or one of them anyway. Either that or she was merely empty-headed. In truth, Andrew hadn't ever been able to figure her out—not entirely. He had always had mixed thoughts about inscrutable people, about eastern mystics or people claiming to be geniuses or certain sorts of knowing, pipe-smoking men whom he'd meet in bookstores or aquarium shops. Their knowledge could never be clearly defined, and although when he was younger he had assumed that he simply hadn't the brains to fathom that knowledge, when he'd gotten older he began to develop suspicions.

Aunt Naomi's suffering was the same sort of thing. It was this, it was that, it was the other: twinges, pains, general listlessness. Iron capsules accomplished nothing. Orthopedic pillows brought on headaches. An army of doctors had come and gone over the long course of her life, and those that had gone the quickest had been the ones to suggest that her maladies were "psychosomatic." Uncle Arthur had recommended something called a "Bed Massage," which he had peddled, in his day, door to door. It was an electronic contrivance that hummed and rippled the stuffing in the mattress. Somehow it had gone haywire, though, after Andrew had hooked it up, and had, through some kink in the laws of physics, caused the leg on the nightstand to collapse and then couldn't be turned off until, hearing an ominous hammering on the floorboards and Aunt Naomi shouting, Andrew had dashed up the stairs and jerked the plug out of the wall socket.

Andrew preferred maladies that were more sharply defined. If he were a doctor he wouldn't have lasted ten minutes with Aunt Naomi. One time when discussing the death of Naomi's husband after only two years of marriage, Andrew had said to Rose, "Who wouldn't have died?" thinking to be funny. It hadn't been funny, though, and Rose had given him a look.

There were secrets in Aunt Naomi's past, skeletons in the closet. The circumstances of her husband's death was one of them. Mrs. Gummidge was familiar with them. The women had been fast friends in school, if such a thing were possible. There had been a falling out. The two had been in love with the same man—Miles Lepton, but it had been Aunt Naomi who had married him. He'd been fascinated with the story of the pig spoon and had actually come to possess it, or so Rose had heard. Mrs. Gummidge—who hadn't, of course, been Mrs. Gummidge at the time—had felt jilted and swore to do them ill, but Lepton had died, and old wounds slowly began to heal. But it was years afterward that the reconciliation between the two women occurred.

Mrs. Gummidge had come west, down on her luck, and Aunt Naomi had condescended, charitably, to take her in. That gave Andrew a pain. It was *his* house, after all. It had been *him* who had taken Mrs. Gummidge in, and yet Aunt Naomi had become a sort of saint because of it.

He regarded Aunt Naomi with a smile. "How are you feeling?" he asked, sitting softly on the end of the bed. She opened one eye and looked at him as if he were some creature in a zoo and had wandered inadvertently into the wrong cage. "Piece of chocolate?"

"I can't tolerate chocolate," she said, sighing. "You can't imagine what it does to me."

"Really?" Andrew shook his head, trying to imagine it, but failing. "I've brought truffles. All natural. I'd be wary of preservatives. I read an article about chemical preservatives in chocolates—a list of poisons half a mile long."

Naomi lay silent for a moment, then opened her eyes and looked at the bag of chocolates. A warm afternoon breeze billowed the window curtains. "Could you adjust an old lady's pillows?" she asked suddenly.

"Of course, of course." Andrew stood up and, as Aunt Naomi bent forward, he plumped up the half-dozen pillows, arranging them into a little box canyon. She leaned back and immediately pitched forward again, as if he'd hidden a cactus among them.

"My back," she cried, screwing up her face. "Mound them, Andrew. I can't stand that sort of thing."

"Of course!" he said, not knowing, exactly, what it was her back couldn't stand. There was no satisfying her, no dealing with her unfathomable maladies. "Here now. There it is. Slide back just about an inch. How's that now?"

She settled into the pillows, as if into a too-hot bath, hunching her shoulders and souring her face. Then she shook her head, tolerably dissatisfied. She didn't invite him to rearrange them again, though. She'd given up on him, the look on her face seemed to say. "What do you mean, natural?"

"Cream," he said, "and cocoa and butter. That's it, except for flavoring. And not chemical flavoring, either—walnut extract, liqueurs, berries. All very healthful. Dr. Garibaldi particularly recommended them.''

She gave him a look. Andrew smiled, thinking that by the time Dr. Garibaldi left the house next week he *would* have recommended them. Aunt Naomi would see to it. She plucked out a cocoa-covered piece and nibbled it. Then, without a word, she nodded toward the nightstand as if commanding him to set the bag down, to leave it.

''I've rather brought these as a peace offering,'' Andrew said, shrugging just a little. ''The incident with the 'possum—I blame myself for that. If it hadn't been for your cats . . .''

She said nothing. She might have been dead, except that she was still chewing on the chocolate.

''I've set traps all around the house—a sort of Maginot Line. I think I can guarantee that there won't be any more of the creatures in at the window.'' There was a silence, during which Aunt Naomi finished chewing, then sucked the chocolate from her fingers. Andrew smiled down at her. ''Would you like a telephone in your room?'' he asked.

Her eyes shot open. ''What on earth for?'' She looked at him as if he'd uttered an obscenity. ''A telephone would drive me mad, ringing all day long. That's what you want, isn't it? I've seen through you from the start, and I told Rose so when she introduced you. A telephone.''

''I meant your own phone, of course. Not an extension. Your own number. You could ring up your friends, the drugstore. You could call downstairs. We could put a phone in Mrs. Gummidge's room. It would be better than a bell on a rope.''

''I have no friends.''

''Well,'' said Andrew, stopping the compulsion to merely shrug and nod. ''There's Mrs. Gummidge.''

''Mrs. Gummidge,'' said Aunt Naomi flatly—as if that was all she had to say on the subject of Mrs. Gummidge. She squinted into space, looking, perhaps, at some little piece of distant history, when she and Mrs. Gummidge had been young together.

''What *do* you want, then?'' asked Andrew patiently. ''A television?''

She waved the suggestion aside.

"New glasses?"

She pretended to sleep.

"A subscription to a book-of-the-month club?"

Nothing would satisfy her but that Andrew would leave her alone and send Mrs. Gummidge up. He would, said Andrew. Straightaway. It was rest she needed. He paused, trying to think up some way to ask her for the thousand dollars for the restaurant. A lie would do, and nothing less. He could hear a flock of wild parrots, out ravaging the neighborhood carob trees, probably. They'd been hanging around lately, about thirty of them, big Amazon parrots, up from Mexico. "I do have one little surprise besides the chocolate," he said, smiling.

She waited, breathing deeply, fanning herself with a little Japanese fold-out fan from the nightstand.

"I've found a chef for the restaurant. I think you'll approve. I had you in mind, in fact, when I talked to the man. He studied in Paris, under Girot. He ran a pastry kitchen in Pasadena. In fact, he made these truffles. That's partly why I brought them up, to give you an inkling of the sort of man we'll have in the kitchen."

She opened one eye, almost imperceptibly, like a toad regarding an unsuspecting fly. She had, somewhere along the line, developed a reputation as a gourmet, although Andrew was fairly sure that she couldn't tell milk-fed veal from dairy cow. He'd found that she liked a drink well enough, but again, maybe just out of perversity, he'd concluded that it didn't much matter how you defined "drink." Mrs. Gummidge, he was fairly sure, had the same tastes, and kept Aunt Naomi well enough satisfied. Rose would have been too temperate. Dr. Garibaldi's advice would have struck home with Rose.

The news of the hiring of the French chef seemed to revive Aunt Naomi just a little. She nodded at Andrew in almost a "good man" sort of way. "And you say you've actually hired this man? When?"

"Yesterday," Andrew lied. There was no such man, although there might be someday soon. It was only half a lie. "He's given notice, but he has to stick it out for two more weeks at the pastry shop. The honor of the French, you know. Then he'll be here. I'm hustling to get the restaurant in order. They're installing the equipment that you helped buy, in fact. But it's still an expensive thing—hiring chefs, buying this and that, stocking the shelves. These foreign chefs want fresh materials. It's not just a matter of hauling a truckload of canned goods back from the market. I've got three different suppliers on the hook—two of them importers. Pickett is drawing up a menu. We'd be grateful to you—Aunt—if you'd give it a look-over when we've got it roughed out.''

"I should be glad to," she said. "It wouldn't be excessive to say that I've had some experience along those lines."

"I'm certain you have." Andrew sighed. "I'm afraid the menu won't be—what?—as *nice,* maybe, as you're accustomed to." He cleared his throat. "As I said, the expenses of a hired chef and all . . .''

She squinted at him. "How much do you want?"

"No, no. That isn't it at all. Dr. Garibaldi tells me that you've got a delicate constitution. That's all. Under the circumstances a foreign chef isn't a luxury, is it? That's what I said to Rose."

"How much do you want?"

Andrew shook his head, half-sadly, and, hating himself, patted her on the shoulder. "Well," he said, "not to put too fine a point on it, there's wages for the man in advance for a month and the price of copper mixing bowls and pots and pans. He won't have anything less. And he insists on an espresso maker. You won't argue with that, I'd bet. Would you like a cup now, in fact?"

"Have you already bought it? The espresso maker? I thought you were asking for money for it. Now it's suddenly in use."

"No, no, no." Andrew laughed and slapped his knee theatrically. "I've got a small one—one cup at a time. And a milk steamer. For the restaurant we would need something sizeable. I was just thinking that a big cup might go right along with another of these chocolates. Since you press me, though, let's call it . . . two thousand. At month's end I should have a good bit of it back. Rose says we're almost ready for boarders—by the end of the week, she thinks. I've drawn up a placard, and there's a man coming round to hang it out front, facing the boulevard.'' All the talk about getting the money back was perfunctory. Aunt Naomi had never asked for it back, which made Andrew feel guilty, and so he was doubly scrupulous about offering to give it back, even if that were impossible.

Aunt Naomi nodded tiredly and mechanically, and gestured Andrew out of the room.

"I'll just brew up that coffee," he said, and went away whistling, down the two flights of stairs to the kitchen. He loved meddling with coffee machinery—grinders, steamers, even thermometers if he were doing the job right. He poured beans into the hand grinder on the wall, cranked the setting to super fine, and smashed out nearly a half-cup of powdered coffee, which he heaped into the coffee trap in the stove-top espresso maker. In minutes, thick, black liquid, dark as sewer sludge but smelling wonderful, was bubbling up out of the depths of the pot, and his milk steamer hissed through the pressure-release hole. He steamed a third of a mug of milk, topped it off with coffee, and then, before dumping in two teaspoons of sugar, he poured the leftover coffee across the copper bottom of a pan in the sink, tilting it this way and that to cover the entire pan bottom. In twenty minutes the copper would shine like a new penny.

Aunt Naomi handed him a check when he set the mug down next to the chocolates. He could tell that she'd been shoving the truffles down while he'd been out. The checkbook had vanished. She kept it hidden. With it she kept a little spiral binder listing all the money she'd doled out over the months. She had let him catch a glimpse of that more than once, to remind him, possibly, that he wasn't getting away with anything.

He steeled himself, then bent over and kissed her on the cheek. In two minutes he was out the door, striding up the alley toward the bank. Two thousand—it was double what he'd hoped for. He might have asked for three. But if he had, and she'd laughed in his face, then the whole business of the chocolates and the French chef would have come to nothing. And besides, if she'd written a bigger check, the bank might easily have kept it for a week to clear it. They weren't entirely satisfied with the quality of Andrew's banking. They weren't anxious to speculate in questionable new businesses. Bankers were men of little imagination; that was the truth of it. The further truth was that the two thousand would go some distance toward paying the bills. They seemed to pile up so quickly these days. It wouldn't be long, quite likely, before certain of their creditors would get nasty. But then their desperation might be enough to make Aunt Naomi advance them a bit more. Her will was drawn, after all. It would all belong to Rose when Naomi died. Surely it didn't matter to the old woman whether she gave it to them now or waited until the end.

So the two thousand would have to do for the moment. If he were lucky, Rose would never hear about it until, on some future, grim day, Naomi would haul out her binder and show Rose what sort of spendthrift husband she was married to. By that time though, Rose couldn't possibly remember what had happened to any single piece of that money. True, she'd be flabbergasted at the size of the debt they'd run up. But such was life. It would be spilled milk by then. There would be no inn without it, and certainly there'd be no restaurant—no real restaurant, anyway. Speculation was in his blood. There wasn't a winner in the world that didn't bet, and timidity wouldn't buy copper pots. He'd have to work on the French chef business, though. Faking up a beard and mustache for Pickett wouldn't answer. He'd heard of a chef's school in Bellflower, and it would be the work of a moment to ring them up and inquire about the availability of graduates. He could hire one for a week to satisfy Naomi and Rose, then toss him out and do the cooking himself.

It was early evening when Andrew drove along the Coast Highway, listening to an odd rattle in the engine of the Metropolitan. He was entirely ignorant of mechanics, happily so. He didn't have time in his life to meddle with it. There were better things to do, any number of them. In fact, he'd been doing some of them that very afternoon. He'd paid a visit to Polsky and Sons liquor importers and distributors on Beach Boulevard in Westminster, and come away with two cases of scotch, four dozen pint glasses, and most of the items on the list he'd made up out of *Grossman*.

The trunk and back seat were full of stuff, and he still had the bulk of Aunt Naomi's money in his wallet. He whistled tunelessly and looked out the window.

The warm weather seemed to be passing. The sky was gray out over the Pacific, and the wind had fallen off. Twilight cast long shadows across the weedy marshland ruins of boatyards and clapboard bungalows. He drove past heaps of rusted anchors and piles of painted buoys and what looked like an old concrete bridge, collapsed now and sunk into the shallows of the Bolsa Chica Salt Marsh. The Seal Beach Naval Weapons Station loomed off to the right, a broad expanse of what looked like pastureland and farmland, with here and there in the dim distances a weapons bunker sitting toad-like and ominous between grassy hillocks. There were broad wooden doors in the ends of some of the hillocks, with grass and canteloupe vines growing right in around the jambs. What lay under the grass and vines was a mystery.

He slowed the car, bumping off onto the shoulder. A knot of people stood around in front of the roadside stand that sold strawberries and corn and tomatoes in the spring and summer, and pumpkins in the fall, all of it grown on government property, which wore the fruits and vegetables as a clever disguise. Hinged sheets of plywood had been dropped across the front of the stand to close it up for the night, so the people—a couple of families with children from the look of it—weren't buying anything. They were clearly up to something else. Another carload pulled in directly behind Andrew, and what seemed to be a half-dozen children piled out and went shouting away past his car, a large woman in a wraparound garment climbing ponderously out after them and yelling them into submission.

Andrew followed just for the adventure of it—something that Beams Pickett would approve of. There was a sign posted, advertising, of all things, a treasure hunt. It referred to a companion ad in the *Seal Beach Herald*, Pickett's newspaper. The newspaper advertisement no doubt explained the carloads of curious people. Treasures were to be buried, the sign said, no end of them, and the public could come dig for them, on the night of Sunday the 24th, by moonlight. Penlights were allowed, nothing bigger than that, though, and the public could keep what it found. There was a diamond ring, it said, in a hermetically sealed glass box, and a glass paperweight in a wooden box, and tickets for two dinners at Sam's Seafood, which weren't, Andrew assumed, in any sort of box at all. There were five hundred children's toys, and a real treasure chest full of quartz crystals and fluorite and bags of rhinestones and glass beads. No maps would be provided. The public would furnish their own spades.

Andrew recalled such a thing from the past. What was it?—almost thirty-five years ago. It had been a fairly common practice in central Orange County, when vast tracts of houses were routing out orange groves and bean fields, and driving up the price of land so that small farmers couldn't afford to keep it. For a time it had been the fashion for farmers to let the populace spade up their acreage for them. They'd bury rolls of pennies and such, and let suburban hordes do a week's worth of work in a night. It had always seemed an unlikely practice to Andrew, although he approved of the notion because of the mystery and romance associated with digging for spurious treasures in a weedy pasture by moonlight. It appealed to his sense of—what? He couldn't quite define it.

He drove away mulling it over. It made a certain amount of sense two score years ago, when hundreds of farmers owned little tracts of land up and down the roads leading south toward the beaches—just a couple of acres or so—and sold roadside produce to wring out a living. But that was all gone years since, and now what farmland was left was owned by vast real estate companies that, in some indefinable way, let out bits of land for farming in order to gain some sort of nebulous tax profits. Nobody "spaded up" the land anymore.

Still, that didn't mean that there was some sort of secret motive in this moonlight-spading business, did it? He'd have to watch that sort of jumping-to-conclusions. It was too easy to raise people's eyebrows. He suspected, somewhere inside him, that Rose "put up with him" sometimes. In the best possible way, she was conventional. There wasn't any more to it than that. She was conventional; he wasn't. His antics made her tired. He knew that, and he wished it weren't so. But they seemed to inhabit different worlds sometimes, different universes. Hers was neatly mapped out. The streets that seemed to run north and south *did* run north and south, seven days a week, and if a farmer planted pumpkins it was simply because Halloween was drawing near and he could sell them at a profit. Andrew's world was cut with streets that angled and twisted. Fogs rolled through at inopportune moments, seeming to hide the shifting landscape. Slouching farmers planted pumpkins so that the crawling vines would cover hillocks beneath which lay unguessed weapons, cleverly hidden from the eyes of satellites sweeping past overhead, themselves veiled by distance.

And although he was certain that he understood her world easily enough, saw through it clearly, he was equally certain that she had little notion of his. She understood him to be simply frivolous, cockeyed for no apparent reason at all. His enthusiasms were a mystery to her, a closed book. At worst he was stark, staring mad, which didn't, he thought as he drove along, particularly bother him. What was far worse was that she thought him childish, with his coffee makers and his books and his paperweights, his preoccupation with beer glasses and breakfast cereal and his odd car, which, she'd once said when she was angry, no grown man had any business driving. But he was deadly serious about it all. Those sorts of things were the threads which knitted up his world. Pulled out one by one and examined, maybe they were foolish and frivolous things, but if you pulled them all out and pitched them into the dumpster, then what was left? Nothing that was worth bothering with. A lot of airy trash fit for the junkman. That was the truth of it, and Rose didn't quite understand it. She pretended to when he tried to explain it, but in her eyes and in her voice there was something that made him feel as if he were six years old, showing his mother his favorite toy. It made him mad just to think about it.

He drove along feeling half-sorry for himself, neglecting to turn his headlights on. He couldn't tell Rose about Pickett's Caretaker nonsense. It would be evidence of something. Lord knows what would have happened if she were to discover that he'd shamelessly talked two thousand dollars out of Aunt Naomi that afternoon, when what he was supposed to be doing was generally smoothing things over. Now he'd promised a French chef and spent a quarter of the money on exotic liquor, and Beams Pickett was on his way to Vancouver to load up the trunk of his Chevrolet with cartons of Weetabix, charging gas to the company credit card, which Rose had insisted he not use unless it were an absolute emergency. He hadn't *wanted* to give Pickett the credit card, but his wallet had been empty. Now it was full, only a few hours later. That's how life went. It was unpredictable. Just when you thought that the way was clear, that the script was written, wham! there was some new confusion, flying in at the window, overturning chairs.

A horn blared and a car swerved out of the lane in front of him. He'd drifted across the line, into oncoming traffic. He jerked the car back into his own lane, his heart hammering. Rose paid attention when she drove. He didn't, it was true. He couldn't argue with her when she pointed it out. The only human being on earth, she said, who drove worse than he was Uncle Arthur, who was ninety-two.

And she had her doubts about his seeing so much of Beams Pickett. Pickett had developed the reputation of believing in plots and threats, and Rose understood, although she never said it, that Andrew had been contaminated. Pickett believed in the theory that what was obvious was probably lies; the truth lay hidden, and you got at it by ignoring what passed as common sense.

Andrew's mind wandered again as he drove along. He thought about their eventful morning, about the 'possum trick and Pickett's suspicions about Mrs. Gummidge. What was true about Pickett was that he was skeptical of skeptics. He had almost hit one that very morning in a cafe near the pier, after the two of them had dumped the 'possum and went fishing. They had had some luck with bonita, keeping at it until after nine in the morning. Then they'd left the fish in a gunnysack in the back of the Metropolitan and gone in for breakfast at the Potholder. A man named Johnson sat at the counter, sopping up egg yolks with a slab of white toast. They knew him from the bookstore, where they'd attended meetings of a literary society for a time.

Johnson saw through everything. There was nothing that would surprise him. He had "no regrets," he had insisted at the literary society in a hearty, chest-slapping tone, and he'd drained his beer glass at a gulp and smacked his lips. There at the counter at the Potholder he had sat poking at egg yolks and shoving down half a slice of bread without bothering to chew it more than twice. Pickett couldn't stand him, and Andrew could see, as soon as they had walked in through the door, that Pickett was going to go for him straightaway, although what Andrew wanted to do was to nod and sit at the opposite end of the cafe, so as to avoid starting Johnson up. Pickett, braced by four hours of sea air, had wanted to start him up very badly.

Johnson had been reading—old issues of science fiction magazines. He'd come upon an essay that made a hash of Pickett's flying saucer enthusiasm—knocked the pins out from under it, Johnson had said, grinning. He'd nodded at Andrew and motioned down the length of the empty counter. Andrew didn't like sitting at counters. He felt too conspicuous there. But Pickett sat down at once and fingered the menu, grinning at Johnson, who droned along about unidentified flying objects.

"The telling thing," Johnson had said, wiping his face with a napkin, "is that when these things appear, they're always described in the fashion of the day. Do you get me?"

"No," said Pickett.

"I mean to say that a hundred years ago they were a common enough business, weren't they? But they looked like hay wagons, then, with wings and propellers and paddle wheels. I was reading an account of a man in Sioux City, Iowa, who claimed to have seen an airship—this was in 1896, mind you—that was shaped like an Indian canoe with an inflated gasbag above it. It dropped a grappling hook, he said, that caught in the slack of his trousers and dragged him across a cow field." Johnson grinned and laughed to himself, humping up and down with the force of it. He looked sharply at the remaining egg on his plate, as if seeing it for the first time, and then hacked it to bits with the corner of a piece of toast. "A *cow* field!"

"I'm still not certain," said Pickett, "what you mean to say. It's an amusing story, but . . ."

"Isn't it?" said Johnson, interrupting. "Concentrate, now. It's not difficult to grasp. Really it isn't."

Pickett sat stony-faced.

"You see," said Johnson, waving his toast, "that's how it went in 1896. In 1925 it was the same business, only no canoes by then, no airbags, no propellers. They were those inflated-looking rockets that you see in the pulps. After that it was saucers, and now there's cylindrical ships made of polished metal that go very, very fast. What next? That's the point. It's all fakery, imagination, humbugging. If it weren't, there'd be some consistency to it. That was the crux of this essay, anyway."

"Who wrote it?" asked Pickett, sitting very still and stirring his coffee.

"Asimov. He's hard to argue with. Rock solid logic, from my point of view. Shreds the whole UFO business at a single swipe. What do you think?" He leaned past Pickett to put the question to Andrew.

"Absolutely," said Andrew. "It's a dead issue I should think."

Pickett gaped at Andrew, then turned back to Johnson, heating up. Andrew could see it. Pickett was about to burst. It always happened that way with Johnson. That was why they'd given up the literary society. Pickett would be fired up to have a go at him, and then the conversation would drive him mad, and Johnson would go off grinning, having won.

"Of *course* they keep showing up in different craft," Pickett said. Their breakfasts arrived and Andrew started to eat, but Pickett ignored his. "That's the beauty of it. They don't *want* to give themselves away, for God's sake. It's a matter of disguise, is what it is. I wouldn't be half-surprised if the aliens who dragged your man across the cow pasture are the same crowd who appeared in the flying egg six years ago over San Francisco. Why not? If they've got the technology to sail in from the stars, then certainly they've got the technology to design any sorts of ships they please. Look at Detroit, for heaven's sake. They can build a truck on Monday and a convertible on Tuesday, just like that. And what's more . . ."

But Pickett hadn't gotten a chance to finish, for Johnson was

suddenly ignoring him, talking to the waitress and paying his bill.
He laid a quarter on the counter by way of a tip and then scratched
the end of his nose. "Do you know what it was in the airship?" he
asked, grinning at Pickett and Andrew.

Pickett blinked at him. "What? What airship?"

"In Iowa—the cow field ship. Pigs. That's what the man said.
It was pigs. And they stole his money—a rare coin. That's what
he said. I swear it. He was robbed by pigs. Of course, the whole
story went to bits, didn't it? It's simple enough. You don't need
Sherlock Holmes to piece together the truth. The way I figure it
he'd had a run-in with pigs. They were probably out on the road
and knocked him into a ditch. That explains how his trousers came
to be ruined. And he'd lost money of some sort, probably a silver
piece or something, which he shouldn't have had anyway because
his wife needed it for groceries. He was on his way to spend it on a
bottle, probably. Well, he couldn't just up and admit it, could he?
I mean *pigs,* after all. He'd look like a fool. So he made up the
story, lock, stock, and barrel: alien pigs, hooks, draggings across
cow fields, rare coins. He's a hero, isn't he, and not a fool at all,
no longer a poor sod manhandled by pigs." Johnson stopped and
squinted at them, nodding his head knowingly. "He lost a
pocketful of change in ditch water, that's what I think, and soiled
his pants. So he explained it away with the wildest lie he could
invent, knowing that the public would go for it. They always
do—the wilder the better. But mark me, gentlemen, you can bet
that his wife didn't much believe him. Am I right? Yes I am. Right
as rain. There isn't a wife alive that isn't ten times as shrewd as the
public. What do you think, Andrew?"

Andrew gawked at him, not at all knowing what to make of all
this talk about pigs and rare coins. But there was no fathoming
Johnson. There was nothing to fathom. Johnson wasn't deep
enough. You could see the bottom just by looking into his eyes. "I
think," said Andrew, "that if you laid the public out end to end
they wouldn't reach from here to Glendale."

"You're a scholar!" shouted Johnson, standing up. "You, too,
son," he said to Pickett, and he grabbed Pickett's hand and shook
it before Pickett had a chance to snatch it away. "Got to go," he

said. "I've got to see a man about a horse. Do you know what I mean? Spaceships—very interesting business all the way around. We'll take this up again."

Pickett started to speak, to get in the last word, to finish what he'd started. "Anyway, as I was saying, convertibles on Tuesday . . ."

"Yes," Johnson said, setting out. "That's right. Convertibles. Maybe the aliens will be driving convertibles next. Pigs in sunglasses." And with that he giggled and strolled away, letting the glass door slam shut behind him and waving back over his shoulder.

Pickett had left his cold eggs on the counter, Johnson having ruined his appetite. They paid and left, forgetting entirely about the car and the fish and walking the two blocks back to the inn. Andrew tried to bring the subject around to the successful 'possum episode, but his enthusiasm was lost on Pickett, who insisted that he was going to have Johnson killed, that he'd ridicule him in the *Herald,* that before he was done he'd do half a dozen things to ruin the man, to make his life a living hell. That very afternoon, while driving north, he'd compose lovelorn letters in order to publish them in the *Herald* under Johnson's name. "What did you make of the pencil line down the center of his face?" Pickett asked suddenly. "Evidence of insanity, I'd call it."

Andrew shrugged. "Just more of his nonsense. It was best not to ask. He *wanted* you to ask, obviously. He'd probably have had some idiotic explanation prepared, some gag line and we'd be the butt of the joke."

Pickett nodded. "He must have forgotten it, though, if he'd put it there on purpose. Did you see him smear it up with the napkin?"

"He was too fired up about his cow pasture story. You shouldn't work him up so. It doesn't do you any good."

"I'll sell him to the apes," said Pickett, climbing into his Chevrolet. "See you." He started the car up with a roar and drove away toward the Coast Highway, carrying Andrew's credit card, bound for Vancouver. He'd be gone nearly a week.

It had been the middle of the afternoon when Andrew discovered that he'd left the Metropolitan parked at the pier. He'd jogged back down and opened the trunk. There lay the fish, stiff as papier-mâché ornaments. He had emptied the gunnysack into the dirt of the alley behind Señor Corky's restaurant, and was immediately surrounded by half a dozen cats. He waved goodbye, driving away south to visit Polsky and Sons and feeling generous.

Now here he was, parking the car at the curb, home at last after a hellishly long day. He hadn't gotten around to painting the garage, as he'd intended to, but there'd be time enough tomorrow to tackle it. Haste was never any good. The street was dark, and Aunt Naomi's window was shut against night creatures. Andrew locked up the car. It wouldn't do to start hauling stuff in. He'd wait until Rose went out or went to bed. He'd tell her he'd been to Bellflower to interview student chefs, which wasn't entirely a lie. He'd called the chefs' school, after all, and had gotten the name of a likely graduate, a young Frenchman who had grown up in Long Beach but still had a trace of an accent.

Fog blew in billows now, in between the houses and over rooftops. It would be a good night for some cat sabotage, but he'd probably worked the 'possum angle hard enough already. In fact, he'd been pressing his luck all day long. Maybe he'd go to bed early. That would make Rose happy. It would be evidence that there were traces of sanity left in him. He stepped up onto the front porch, humming, tolerably satisfied with things. Then he jumped in spite of himself to see Pennyman sitting in a rattan chair, smoking his pipe. He looked far too polished and stiff, like a waxwork dummy or a preserved corpse, and it seemed to Andrew as if he had the smell of fish about him, as if he'd been swilling cod liver oil. Pennyman pulled his pipe out of his mouth and pointed at an empty chair. "Sit down," he said.

FOUR

"Similarly, a stone with little discs upon it is good to bring in such coins; and if a man found a large stone with a number of small ones under it, like a sow among her litter, he was sure that to offer a coin upon it would bring him the one pig."

Sir James G. Frazer
The Golden Bough

ANDREW STARED AT the figure of Pennyman smoking on the darkened porch. Suddenly he was filled with Pickett's fears, with visions of blowfish and secret societies. The glowing ash in the bowl of Pennyman's pipe burned like a hovering eye in the evening gloom. Andrew opened the door and reached into the house, flipping on the porch light. "I'm home!" he shouted, not wanting to seem to be any later than he was.

Rose answered from somewhere within. "Oh," she said.

Andrew turned and shrugged at Pennyman. "Sitting in the dark, are you?"

"Yes, indeed," came the reply. "I find it strangely relaxing, darkness. It's like the womb. Or the tomb. Funny business, language. Full of that sort of coincidence. Makes you wonder, doesn't it?"

"Of course it does." Andrew sat down across from him,

where he could see Rose through the window, angling back and forth across the kitchen. It was a comforting sight, but it made him feel vaguely guilty, and he wondered suddenly where he'd put his painting paraphernalia. He'd have a go at the garage in the morning, before the day heated up. It wouldn't take him long.

The day's newspaper lay in a heap beside Pennyman's chair. A crumpled piece lay in the shadows, half atop the pile, as if Pennyman had read something in it that he didn't at all like, and had wadded it up in a rage. There was an odd quality to it that caught Andrew's eye. He bent forward to have a better look and discovered that it wasn't a crumple at all, but was an inflated origami fish, with spiny little fins, folded up out of the comic section of the *Herald*. The sight of it was unnerving, although Andrew couldn't entirely say why.

Fog wisped across the lawn, obscuring the curb trees. A soft ocean wind blew, scraping tree limbs across the eaves of the porch, sighing through the bushes and unclipped grass, swirling the fog. The pale mists were a perfect accompaniment, somehow, to Pennyman's white suit and reeking pipe. He cast Andrew a mysterious sideways glance and said, "I've spent some time in the Orient." Then he nodded at the origami fish by way of explanation. "Delicate things, aren't they? Like flower petals. The fog will half-dissolve it in the night—like the fleeting years, like life itself." He sighed and waved his hand tiredly, gesturing, perhaps, at life.

Andrew nodded. He couldn't stand Pennyman. The man acted as if he were on a stage. "I never did get the knack of folding up paper," Andrew said. "Couldn't even fold a paper hat." Pennyman stared at him, as if he expected something more, something philosophic, as if the reference to paper hats couldn't, alone, have been the point of Andrew's utterance. Andrew's hand shook on his knee. He grinned widely. "My sister could, though. She could fold up . . . well, anything."

With a flourish of his wrist, Pennyman opened up his hand. A quarter lay in his open palm. He widened his eyes at Andrew, as if to say, "Watch this," and he tumbled the coin over onto the back of his hand with one smooth movement of his thumb, flip-flopping it back and forth across his knuckles. Then he rolled it around into his palm again, caught it between his thumb and forefinger, and snapped his fingers so that the coin vanished up the sleeve of his coat.

Andrew was at a loss. It was a neat trick, to be sure, but he couldn't at all guess what Pennyman meant by it. He grinned, though, and produced a coin of his own, a nickel, which he balanced on end on the tip of his finger. It seemed to him that their encounter on the front porch was shaping up into a sort of contest, a test of cleverness or harmony or reason—as if they were competing students in some rare breed of martial arts school, learning to tread on rice paper without making any noise or balance on one leg like a swamp bird.

Pennyman nodded at the upended nickel, then smiled in appreciation when Andrew drew back his forearm, allowing the nickel to roll down his tilted finger onto the edge of his palm and then down his arm and off his elbow into the air, where he snatched it up. He bowed just a little. All in all it beat Pennyman's knuckle-rolling. And the open-sleeve trick was amateurish. Anyone could do that.

Pennyman said nothing. He flourished his quarter again, and, looking very grave, seemed to shove it into his ear. Then with a look of sudden surprise he hauled it out of his mouth, rattled it in his cupped hands, opened them, and seemed mystified to find no quarter at all.

That was cheap, thought Andrew, wondering what other coin tricks he remembered. Somewhere, in a shoebox tied with twine, he had a nickel with a nail welded to it. You'd pound the nail into the floor, then laugh and point at people who tried to pick it up. He made a mental note to remember it and play it on Pennyman later, when he suspected nothing. It would do him no good at the moment, though. He was at a loss for another trick. He could wedge quarters into his eyes, or dimes into his nose and ears, but the effect would be lost on Pennyman. It would be lost on anyone, for that matter—which was something in itself. There was always some profit merely in confounding people. Pennyman would at least wonder what Andrew meant by it. There was a certain indignity involved in shoving dimes into one's nostrils, though.

His hesitation made Pennyman tired, it seemed, and he couldn't wait any longer for Andrew to fire a shot. He produced a penny from his shirt pocket, held it up in front of Andrew's face, canted his head at it, and dropped it neatly into the bowl of his pipe, nearly covering the glowing coal. Andrew waited, wondering what in the world the man had in mind. Pennyman winked, and just as he did the penny caught fire—flared up just for an instant, then died, then seemed to be consumed into the tobacco. The penny had disappeared. Pennyman removed his pipe and bowed, acknowledging himself the winner.

Andrew, being gallant, shook his hand regretfully, secretly seething at being taken in by the burning penny trick. Obviously it was a cheap gag bought for fifty cents in a joke shop—a penny pressed out of dry, copper-colored tobacco. That's why he'd had it in his coat pocket instead of his pants pocket—so that it wouldn't be crushed. Pennyman probably had a whole handful of such pennies that he hauled out and burned in his pipe to impress strangers and influence competitors in the world of import and export. He'd probably bought them in the Orient when he'd tired of learning to fold paper.

"You're a good sport," said Pennyman, slapping his knee and settling back into the chair. "You're—what?—playful. I like that in a man. You don't find it often. Everyone's so damned *serious*." And he growled this last word out in order to make fun of it, then tamped his pipe and relit it, blowing an enormous billow of smoke toward the porch roof. "You've traveled, haven't you?"

"Well," said Andrew, fuming, "not extensively. To the midwest. Or rather *from* the midwest. I spent some time in Canada, too. Rose and I manage to get away to San Francisco sometimes. We love San Francisco."

Pennyman nodded, "I have contacts in Chinatown. I've spent some time there myself. You haven't been off the continent, though?"

"Not besides Canada . . ." Andrew began. Then he stopped, catching himself in a stupidity and inwardly blanching. "No. I'd like to, of course, but, with the inn and all . . .''

"How true." Pennyman sighed. "You have a European air about you, actually. That's why I asked. It's the casual cut of your trousers, perhaps. Reminds one of the Provinces—vineyards, cobbled streets, bent old men in backyard gardens. Or, no, this is it—of the Mediterranean. Greek fishermen." He paused and shook his head sadly, as if remembering. Then, in an inflated tone, he said, " 'I grow old . . . I grow old . . . I shall wear the bottoms of my trousers rolled.' " He squinted at Andrew silently, assessing him. Andrew considered poking him in the eye. Pennyman sat back with the air of a successful man, a man who has expressed himself tolerably well. "And your hair—that tousled look. Do you do that on purpose? I mean, is it contrived? It's so . . . so . . . well, *you*. Do you follow me?"

"Not entirely. No. I just don't comb it, that's all. Waste of time, combing hair." He meant this last bit to sting, but even as he said it it sounded like a petty insult. Whatever game they were playing on the porch, Andrew was losing, and he knew it.

"I mean to say that few men would have, well, the *guts* that it takes to wear their hair like that. That's all. I admire the hell out of that. Blast the world! What does it know?" He shook his head again and stared at the floorboards of the porch, and his look seemed to say that he'd found out this truth too late in life, that his manicured nails and sculpted beard were nothing but vanity, nothing but a childish fear of letting himself go.

Andrew saw through the whole despicable charade. There was nothing in Pennyman's chatter, though, that would justify Andrew's hitting him—bonking him on the conk. Or even of outright insulting him. Pennyman suddenly cheered up, as if he'd just then remembered where he'd left a twenty-dollar bill that he'd thought he'd lost, or as if he'd forgotten his name and it had just come to him in a flash. He produced a quarter again. "One more," he said, waving it in the air. "Wait. Let's be sporting about this. I'll bet you a dollar that you can't pull this one off, and as a handicap, I'll let you watch the trick first. If you want to have a go at it, then we'll both ante up a dollar. If you think you can't hack it, we're quits. What do you say?"

"Go," said Andrew, who, with fourteen hundred of Aunt Naomi's dollars in his wallet, could afford to lose one. And he was clever enough at coin tricks. He'd take Pennyman's money and walk away singing.

Pinning the quarter flatwise between both forefingers, Pennyman pressed the edge of it dead center on his forehead, right at his hairline, and then, with his fingers acting like axles, he rolled the quarter down over his nose, across his lips and down his chin. That was it—a manual dexterity trick. Pennyman half stood up and dropped the quarter into his trouser pocket.

"You're on," said Andrew, fishing out a dollar.

Pennyman pulled a bill out of his shirt pocket, waved it, then thrust it back in, as if to imply that he was certain it would stay there, and that in a moment Andrew's would keep it company. "Have one of mine," he said, producing yet another quarter from his coat pocket and handing it to Andrew, who pinned it at once between his fingers, jammed it against his forehead, and rolled it down his face slowly. Just like that, right off the end of his chin. He could have driven it down into the collar of his shirt if he'd wanted to, and he gave Pennyman a look that seemed to say so. Pennyman frowned and shrugged, then handed across his dollar. "It's not many people can do that," he said. "You've got a steady hand, sir; a steady hand."

"Look," said Andrew suddenly, staring at Pennyman's quarter, which he still held, "it's silver. Don't lose it."

"Is it?" asked Pennyman, acting astonished. "Well I'll be damned . . ." He held it out so that the dim porch light glinted off the curve of George Washington's head. "Would you look at that? How much is it worth, do you suppose, a dollar?"

"I'd suppose," said Andrew, shrugging. "Something like that."

Pennyman widened his eyes in mock astonishment. "Imagine," he said. "A whole dollar." He put the coin away, sat back, and smiled, as if the smile were meant to suggest that it was Andrew's turn to dream up the next bit of front porch sport.

Andrew caught sight of the newspaper just then. Partly visible beneath the origami fish was the ad about the treasure hunt. He picked it up and read it, swearing that he wouldn't say another word to Pennyman until Pennyman said something to him—something civil. He could find nothing in the ad that explained the real purpose of the hunt. It was some sort of promotional gimmick, apparently. A charity of some sort, based locally, had leased the farmland for a night. Ah, there it was—the fine print. It would cost five dollars for adults, three for children. How many cars, full of people, would drive up, spades thrusting out of tied-down trunks, only to discover that they had to *pay* to dig for treasure, that they could dump all the five dollars and the three dollars in a box and have their own treasure without dirtying their hands? But it would be too late for them. They'd have to pay, or their children, intent upon digging gold in the moonlight, would wail the tops off their parents' cars.

It seemed the money was going to a good cause, though, although what that cause was the ad in no way made clear. It had slightly liberal political overtones—world hunger, world peace, world sanity—all too nebulous to define clearly.

"What do you make of that?" asked Pennyman suddenly, startling Andrew into dropping the paper.

"What? I mean, I don't know. Looks like fun, I suppose, digging treasures and all. Just the sort of thing I'd have liked as a child."

"I knew it when I saw it. I said to myself, *here's* something that Andrew Vanbergen would appreciate. It would appeal to . . ." He stopped and smiled. "I bet you read Stevenson, don't you?"

Andrew nodded, wondering what would follow.

"I knew it. *Treasure Island*. I read it when I was thirteen. I was attracted to his essays, too, as a boy. Nothing brilliant in them. I can see that now. But they shined when I was a lad. All that adventurous optimism and moody reflection. Playing at soldiers with wooden swords—that's what his writing always reminded me of. Yes indeed. All style though. Not much substance. Great for children. To hell with substance, in fact. Let's ban it. Let's all read boys' books again and go off pirating, eh?" He nodded his head vigorously, then broke into a snatch of piratical talk, saying "aargh," afterward, which, if Rose hadn't shouted just then from the kitchen, might have cost Pennyman his life. Seething and grinning past his teeth, Andrew nodded at him and walked away into the house muttering, leaving him there.

He obligingly flipped off the front porch light so that Pennyman could do all the wombing and tombing he wanted. The man had figured out, somehow, that Andrew was keen on going to the treasure hunt. How he'd figured it was impossible to say, but he'd purposefully been making sport of him, that was sure. All that talk of adventure and tousled hair. The idiot. Nothing brilliant! No matter that most of it happened to be true and that Pennyman was full of lies and falseness. That's why Pennyman despised it. That's why he despised Andrew, for that matter. The truth always appeared despicable to the eyes of someone inherently false. Well to hell with him! The man wouldn't frighten him away from the treasure hunt. Andrew would be there and would take Pickett along. He'd talk Rose into going, by God. They'd bring a midnight lunch, a bottle of wine. Cheese. Smoked oysters. Sardines. Baskets of strawberries.

"What?" asked Rose. "Run this plate up to Aunt Naomi, will you? Mrs. Gummidge has gone out."

"Yes. Nothing. I was just talking out loud."

"Sounded like you said something about oysters. Remember when we had that picnic on the bluffs in Mendocino and ate smoked oysters and chocolate?"

"Yes," said Andrew, smiling. "You liked that. You were happy then."

"I'm happy now," she said, then stopped, looking at him as if puzzled. "What's that on your face?"

"What? On my face?"

"Look in the mirror."

He peered into the mirror over the kitchen sink. There, running down his forehead and nose and chin, dividing his face evenly in half, was a line of graphite or charcoal dust or something. In an instant it was clear to him—the quarter trick. Pennyman had hoaxed him, had played him for a fool. Pennyman had rubbed the serrated edge of the quarter across a pencil lead, perhaps, then tricked Andrew into rolling it down his face. Andrew would kill the man, he'd . . . Suddenly he remembered Johnson, smearing through an identical line with a torn napkin at the Potholder. He slumped, wondering what it meant, nearly putting his hand into Aunt Naomi's chicken.

"What on earth is wrong?" asked Rose, pulling out a chair.

Andrew waved her away. "It's nothing," he said. "I was shaken to see it, that's all. I've apparently interviewed a man at the chefs' school in Bellflower while all the time I've looked like a fool. Heaven knows what they made of it."

"*I* don't know quite what to make of it, actually."

"It's nothing. An experiment, that's all. I was reading psychology. Certain sorts of madmen have faces which are utterly symmetrical. Sane people don't. There's subtle differences—one eye squints, maybe, or one cheek angles toward the chin just a hair steeper than the other. But madmen . . . cut their face in half—or rather a photograph, say—and flop the halves over and . . . Well. It's fascinating, really."

Rose nodded while he talked, as if she were sympathetic to the notion of cutting photographs of madmen's faces in half, or whatever it was that Andrew was suggesting be done, and as if she saw very clearly why Andrew, after having come to understand the peculiar facial characteristics of lunatics, had drawn a line down the middle of his own face and gone out on the town. "Naomi's food is getting cold," she said, patting him on the arm.

Andrew started to wipe his face clean with the dish towel, but Rose snatched it away and handed him a paper towel, tucking the dish towel through the handle on the refrigerator door. "I just took it out of the drawer," she said. "I wish you'd get into the habit of using paper towels instead. It just makes more work using tea towels all the time."

"I will," said Andrew. "I lost my head." He rubbed away with the paper towel, smearing the line. To hell with it; he had to take a shower anyway. He felt as if he'd been wearing the same clothes for a week. *Damn* Pennyman. Andrew would work the nailed-nickel trick on him tomorrow—in public. He'd laugh out loud and point; then he'd twist Pennyman's nose for him and send him packing. They'd do without his stinking two hundred dollars. He gave up and dropped the wadded paper towel onto the countertop, then went back out into the living room, carrying the plate for Aunt Naomi. Inconspicuously, he peered out onto the porch. Pennyman was gone.

The door to Aunt Naomi's bedroom was ajar, although the room was dim. Assuming she was awake, Andrew pushed the door farther open with his shoulder and stuck his head in. "Dinner," he said cheerfully. The bed was empty. Naomi sat in a chair, staring through the little gable window that looked out toward the ocean. There was the muffled boom of waves breaking, punctuated by the footfalls of someone walking on the sidewalk below, but nothing could be seen through the open window except hovering gray mist. A cat rubbed against Andrew's leg, pretending to be friendly.

"Chicken a la Rose," said Andrew, setting the tray down. "And rice, too, and—something. Looks like eggplant, maybe, in little squares." He smiled at the back of Aunt Naomi's head, wondering if the woman was alive or had died in her chair. He caught himself inadvertently petting the cat, so he gave it a hard look and stood up. "See anything out there?"

"Too much fog," said Aunt Naomi, not turning around. "I love to watch the ocean. I wish there were a widow's walk on the roof. I'd spend all my time out of doors, watching."

"For what?" Andrew asked. "Your ship coming in?"

"It went down years ago, I'm afraid. But there's no telling what might be out there waiting. Have you read this business in the newspaper about the whale trying to swim up the Sacramento River? What do they call him—some foolish name. If they understood it they'd laugh out of the other side of their mouth. I wonder where they think he's going."

"I don't know," said Andrew, trying to think of something funny to say—some ridiculous destination for the off-course whale. If it *was* off course. Aunt Naomi didn't seem to think so. He wasn't much in a joking mood, though. Somehow the presence of the old lady, staring out into the fog and talking about things lurking in the sea, took the edge off his sense of humor. It occurred to him that in a moment she'd turn around to confront him, her face a grinning skull, like something out of a late-night horror movie.

She swiveled round suddenly, regarding him strangely, then gasped and half stood up, as if *he* were the grinning skull. He reached down and flipped on the bedside lamp, but the sight of his illuminated face made her recoil even more, and for a moment he was certain that she was going to topple backward out the window.

"Who's done that to you?" she asked.

Andrew was at a loss. He touched his cheek and shrugged. "Pardon me?" he said. He'd humor her. That's what he'd do. It was instantly clear to him. She'd gone round the bend. She was seeing things. She looked straight at him and saw—what?—her long-dead husband, perhaps, or Saint Augustine, or her old grammar school principal. He couldn't deal with this sort of thing at all. He shouldn't have to. She was Rose's aunt, after all. He'd get Rose up here. *She'd* know what to do. She was a marvel in this sort of situation. She'd say it was the 'possum business, though, that had driven Aunt Naomi crazy. If it was ever discovered that he . . .

"The line on your face," she said. "Who did that to you?"

The line, thought Andrew. Of course. She hadn't run mad. "No one *did* it to me," he said. "I was reading a book about schizophrenics. Strangely frightening business, really, about symmetrical faces, and . . ."

"*Books*. You weren't reading books. Someone did that to you and you don't have the foggiest notion why. You're like a child. Tell me. Who was it? It's smeared, isn't it? It must be smeared."

Andrew was seething again. Who was she to call him a child? She was driven half-wild by his having a line drawn down his nose, and she was calling *him* a child. But she'd given him two thousand dollars just that morning, hadn't she? He thought hard about the money in his wallet, about the trunk full of liquor, about the chances of wrestling another thousand or so out of her in a few days, after he'd introduced her to the French chef from Long Beach. It was best not to take offense. Old people as often as not didn't mean any offense to be taken. And she was right, wasn't she? "Mr. Pennyman," he said. "Yes, it's smeared. I'm just going in now to wash it off."

"Pennyman!"

"That's right. A little gag of his. A quarter rubbed in pencil dust. Very funny. Kid's trick, actually. We were horsing around on the porch."

"Yes. A silver quarter."

Andrew stared at her, washed by an entirely new wave of emotion; nearly drowned in it. "How did you know that?"

She waved the question away. "I knew it. Stay away from him. Everything he says to you is significant. There's no such thing as a casual conversation with a man like Pennyman. I know who he is now. Take my word, and steer clear of him. And here," she said, dipping her napkin into the water glass beside her bed, "see if you can wipe that off."

Andrew grinned and took the napkin. Humor her, he thought. Don't say anything. He rubbed at the line, then looked at the smudged napkin. Peering into the mirror over the dresser, he wiped some more until the mark was gone. He handed the napkin to Aunt Naomi, thanked her, and turned to leave.

"Wait," she said, peering at him closely. "Do me a grand favor, will you?"

"Anything," he said.

"Fetch that old silver spoon from the china cupboard. The one Rose calls the pig spoon."

Puzzled, Andrew hopped away down the stairs and was back in a moment carrying the spoon.

"I want to give this to you," Naomi said.

"To Rose?" asked Andrew.

"No, to you. Despite our differences, I'm pretty sure you're a man of honor. Listen closely. This spoon is yours now. It's been mine for a long time, but I'm quit of it now. It belongs to you. Do you want it?"

Andrew blinked at her. In truth, he didn't much want the spoon. It had a curious history and was a moderately interesting relic, but it couldn't be *worth* anything. It was simply a dust collector. He tilted it into the light and stared at the delicate scoring on the concave surface. It seemed to be pulled down into the handle, so that the markings were proportionate at the top of the spoon and then stretched away below. It was thin enough so that he could have bent it in half between his thumb and forefinger. The silver of it was warm, almost hot, but that came from his holding it in his hand, he supposed. It *was* an interesting piece. He'd always been fascinated by it. It felt almost like some sort of magic wand in his hand. Suddenly he didn't want to give it up. He wanted to keep it. And almost as suddenly he felt vastly tired. Of course he did. He'd been up half the night and then awakened at dawn. His back was stiff, too. A hot shower *would* be nice. It would pick him right up. "I'd love to have it," he said. "I'll just put it back into the hutch."

"God bless you," said Aunt Naomi, smiling one of her very rare smiles. It was genuine, too. Andrew felt a sudden liking for her, and he wondered at the tinge of sadness that flavored her smile. That came from age, he guessed. There was always some sadness flavoring your smiles when you stood in the shadow of the gravestone. It was regret, is what it was, for the passing of time. She had fond memories of that spoon. It was all she had left of her husband—aside from his money, of course. It was the last link to the Iowa farm. She lowered her voice suddenly and said, "But I wouldn't put it back into the hutch if I were you. I'd find a safer place. It's really far more valuable than you suppose—very old, actually. In a sense, it will make its value known to you. You'll see. Put it somewhere safe for now."

Andrew smiled back at her. She'd gone mystical on him, obviously. "I'll keep it safe as a lamb," he said. And then, hearing Rose calling from downstairs, he tipped a non-existent hat to Aunt Naomi and stepped out onto the landing, tucking the spoon into his pocket, muddled with mysteries. Halfway down, it occurred to him that Naomi might easily have overheard his conversation with Pennyman, down on the porch. Both of them had exclaimed over the silver quarter. Of course she had. She wasn't filled with arcane knowledge after all; she just wanted to *seem* so.

Rose stood in the living room holding the telephone. It was a long distance call—from Vancouver. Puzzled, Andrew took the phone, half-expecting, impossibly, to hear Pickett's voice on the other end.

But it wasn't Pickett. It was a man who claimed to be named August Pfennig—a dealer in coins and books and curiosities, calling from his shop on the waterfront. He asked whether Andrew was of the Iowa Vanbergens and whether he wasn't related by marriage to the Iowa Zwollenveters, and when Andrew said that he was, Pfennig sighed, as if happy at last. The man's name was vaguely familiar to Andrew, as if he'd run across it in a magazine article, perhaps, and remembered it because of its curious sound. He thought hard while the man rambled on, but he couldn't fit the name with a face.

Pfennig's voice was slow and careful, as if he were half-old and half-calculating. There was a false joviality to it, too, that Andrew recognized at once to be the empty, pretended interest of a salesman. He couldn't stand salesmen, especially salesmen who muttered about mutual friends, since that was always a lie right on the face of it. It was interesting, though, that one had called all the way from Canada. At least it wouldn't be insurance that the man was peddling. Maybe it was light bulbs. Andrew had got a rash of calls about light bulbs—a charity of some sort selling them for fifteen dollars a bulb, guaranteed to outlast everything, still to be glowing after you were dead and living with the worms.

The man wasn't selling light bulbs. He was buying—not selling anything at all. He dealt in estate jewelry and libraries. Andrew had been a hard man to "track down." Since the death of his brother-in-law, said Pfennig, he'd rather lost track of what went on in Southern California, and he said this in such a way that it sounded as if Andrew ought to know who this brother-in-law was.

"Well," said Pfennig, carrying on, "I do like to renew old acquaintances. Things seem to go to bits these days, don't they? The years sail past so."

Andrew admitted that they did, thinking that somehow the conversation was at an end, that Pfennig, whoever he was, had called all the way from Vancouver to chat. Perhaps he was one of

Rose's old school friends, a casual acquaintance from Orange City. He covered the mouthpiece and whispered the name to Rose, who stood waiting, curious. Rose shrugged and shook her head. Andrew shrugged back. The man's voice trailed off into nothing.

"Pardon me?" asked Andrew politely. "I'm afraid I missed that last part. Bad connection."

There was heavy breathing on the other end, like someone hyperventilating. "I'm not well," the man said suddenly. "I'm . . . ill. Bedridden. If you could speak up . . ."

Irritated, Andrew spoke directly into the mouthpiece, talking roundly, "I said, 'What?' "

There was more breathing, and for a moment Andrew thought the conversation had gone entirely to bits, but then the man Pfennig continued. "I was led to believe," he said, "that you were a collector, and I hoped that we could trade this for that, in the spirit of collecting, of course. I'm not in this for the money."

Andrew nodded. Here it was. He wasn't in it for the money, wasn't he? He was in it for sport. He was calling from Vancouver for the jolly spirit of collecting. Pfennig droned on, asking about family Bibles, hymnals, Dutch translations, perhaps, of old prayer books. He worked his way into cookbooks and volumes of medical arcana and books describing home remedies. Andrew didn't have any of them. He had a falling-apart copy of *The Whitehouse Cookbook,* but Pfennig wasn't interested in it. "Not in my line," he said, and then went on to arts and crafts pottery and hammered copper.

"I've got a Roseville vase," said Andrew helpfully. "Fuchsia pattern—green and pink. Fairly rare, actually. But I don't want to sell it."

"Too bad," said Pfennig, clucking his tongue. "My brother-in-law led me to believe you might put me in the way of some rare coins. What do you have along those lines?"

Andrew paused, thinking. He had the remnants of an old childhood penny collection and a half-dozen oval dimes flattened on a railroad track, but beyond that . . . "Are you sure it's me?" he asked. "Maybe . . . My wife's *cousin* collects coins. He's always regretting that he can't put his hands on a curly quarter. Too expensive by half. It would cost him the value of the rest of his collection.''

"This is an *old* coin, that I'm talking about," said Pfennig, and he went on to describe the thing—the hawk-nosed face on the one side, a curious rune on the other. A silver coin, but not as worn as you'd guess, given the thing's great age. They didn't have much silver of this quality any more, not very much at all.

"I'm really very sorry," said Andrew. "Someone's mistaken. I'm just not much of a coin man, actually. I'm afraid that I don't go in much for the kind of collecting . . ."

"You're telling me you don't own this coin, then?"

"That's correct, Mr . . ."

"Have you owned it? Sold it, maybe?"

"No, really I . . ."

"Think about it. I'm prepared to offer a substantial sum. More than the man you're dealing with now. On no account let him have it. I'll be in touch."

"I don't have any coin!" Andrew began. "What *man*?" But Pfennig hung up. In a moment there was a dial tone.

"Who was it?" asked Rose.

Andrew shrugged. "I don't know. Man from Vancouver buying and selling things."

"You shouldn't let them waste your time like that. Tell them very firmly that you won't talk to them and then hang up. You're too polite for your own good, letting people like that waste your time away."

"What do you mean 'people like that'? What kind of person was he? He was an old acquaintance of some sort. How did I know? 'People like that'! I go in for politeness. That's my way. Cheap as dirt, politeness."

Rose shook her head and disappeared into the kitchen, not seeming to want to argue about how cheap politeness was. Andrew took a step toward the kitchen, thinking to press the issue. What, he would ask, did Rose have against politeness? And how on earth, not having listened in to the conversation, did she know that . . . But thinking about the conversation with Pfennig muddled things up. What *was* it all about? A wrong number, likely. Or rather a case of mistaken identity. Surely no one would have recommended Andrew as a collector of rare coins.

"Food's getting cold," Rose said from the kitchen. She looked tired, Andrew thought as he stabbed away at his chicken. This business of opening an inn was wearing her out. She'd run an ad in the *Herald* already, and she was working doubly hard just in case it paid off early. It was premature, certainly, but she was right when she said that it might take time to draw customers. "Anything come from the ad?" Andrew asked, deciding to let the politeness issue drop.

Rose nodded. "One man. A nut from the look of him. Reminded me of Moses. He came around this afternoon and had a chat with Mr. Pennyman on the porch. I thought he was a friend of Mr. Pennyman, but it turned out he wanted a 'semi-permanent' room. Those were his words. I don't know exactly what he meant."

"Did you tell him two hundred a month?"

"No, never got around to it. And if I *had* gotten around to it, I wouldn't have told him any such thing. He had a beard. You should have seen it. He looked like Gabby Hayes and he was wearing a robe."

"A bathrobe?"

"No, a sort of Oriental robe, I guess. He said he was a member of a 'society.' I don't remember which. He was fascinated by the place, or so he said—particularly in your books. He said the house had 'a feel' to it. You should have seen his hat."

"My books? You let him handle my books? What hat?"

"It was a sort of what-do-you-call-it hat, like an old-fashioned clown's cap—a sort of cone with a round brim and coming to a rounded point on top."

Andrew nodded, still not liking the part about the books, but happy now that Rose hadn't rented him the room. That was just what they needed, a zealot of some weird stripe. Probably an Atlantean. Why were such people drawn to Southern California, to the coast, to the inn? "So you pitched him out?"

"No, *I* didn't. Mr. Pennyman rather discouraged him, I think."

"Pennyman again! And there goes two hundred a month. What filthy business does Pennyman . . ."

"His business isn't filthy at all. *You* wouldn't have rented a room to this man. Oh, wait. Yes you would have. Out of politeness, I suppose."

Andrew fumed. "What *I* would have done isn't . . . Pennyman can keep out of our business. We don't need his filthy money and we don't need the stench of rosewater and fish oil all over the place."

Rose stood up and began clearing away the plates, saying nothing. After a long minute of silence, she asked, "Why are you so against Mr. Pennyman? Is it that he keeps his hair cut and combed?"

Andrew's own hair was a mess. He'd admit that. It needed cutting badly and had taken on the appearance of a sort of wind-blown bush. He was above it, though. He had calculated once how many hours he'd spent in front of the mirror, arranging his hair, thinking, perhaps, that if he got it just so he'd be able to see someone else in there, the *real* Andrew Vanbergen, self-assured, rock-steady, able to walk on avenues of cobwebs without leaving an imprint. But his hair hadn't ever cooperated. Little curls of it would spring out on the end of a straight shock while the rest of it would stay put, giving his head the appearance of a broken cartoon clock with a ruined spring nodding from the top. The hours he'd wasted dabbling at it added up to about a year and a quarter. Well, no more.

Rose clinked dishes in the sink. "You don't have to be afraid of people just because they're different," she said, "just because you don't understand them. Sometimes you seem to despise everything you don't understand."

"*Me?*" said Andrew. "It was *you* who wouldn't rent the room to this poor bearded man just because he wore a hat. Who cares about his hat? *I* wouldn't have given a damn about his hat. I'd have envied the man his hat. God bless a hat."

Mrs. Gummidge wandered through just then, small and gray and bent and humming to herself as she stopped to root in the junk drawer. "I'll just be a sec," she said apologetically. "Don't pay a bit of attention to me."

"Fine," Andrew said agreeably. "What was I saying . . . ?"

"Don't we have a little plastic case of tiny screwdrivers?" said Mrs. Gummidge, fluttering her eyelids at Andrew.

"We?" Andrew widened his eyes, as if the phrasing of the question had thrown him for a loop.

"In the back," said Rose.

"Ah." Mrs. Gummidge inclined her head at Andrew, almost sympathetically, seeming to say that she knew just how tough things were for him, and didn't take offense. "I'm just repairing that lock on the bathroom door that you haven't got around to yet, Mr. Vanbergen. I *like* a little job like that."

He let it pass, smashing down the urge to hurl a chicken bone at her. When she left, insisting that she was sorry for the "intrusion," he said to Rose, *"We? Our* screwdrivers? What damned lock? What business does she have with locks on the bathroom doors?"

Rose looked at him blank-faced. "Settle down," she said. "Who cares? Don't be petty. She didn't mean anything by it."

They both fell silent. Andrew hated to be told to settle down. But you almost *had* to do it when you were told to, because if you didn't it was further evidence that you should have. You wanted to run wild, to scream and break things, but you couldn't. You had to see reason. He tried to force himself to see reason, realizing that because of Mrs. Gummidge he had utterly lost track of the conversation he'd been having with Rose. In the silence he could hear the toad chirruping on the back porch, talking, maybe, to one of the cats.

"And I'm *not* afraid of Pennyman," he said, lowering his voice. "But I can spot slime easy enough. I'm going to pitch him out; that's what. He's cost us two hundred a month, and that rather negates the two hundred he's paying us, doesn't it? We pitch him out and we're dead even."

Rose washed the dishes, hosing off bubbles and stacking the clean dishes on the sink. "Add it up again," she said simply.

"Add nothing. This isn't mathematics, it's—what?—morality.

That's what it is. Hanging about with something diabolic. Pretty soon all sorts of rottenness starts to seem normal to you. Let a man like Pennyman get a toehold and all of a sudden he's running the place. He acts like he does already. Chasing this bearded man off! Talk about offensive beards.''

"Done with your plate?"

"What?" asked Andrew. "Oh, yes. I guess so. What did this man want with my books?"

"He didn't want *anything* with your books. He simply peered at them for a moment. In the library. And anyway, it was Mr. Pennyman's books he liked, not yours at all. The foreign ones on the middle shelves. He pulled one out and started to thumb through it, and Mr. Pennyman rather discouraged it. I can't say just how. He simply made it clear that the man was taking liberties of a sort. The two of them didn't like each other a bit. I could see that right away. The man said that he'd decided he didn't need a room after all, but I think he was just mad about the books. He went out looking haughty anyway. But then he stopped for a moment on the front porch to chat some more with Mr. Pennyman, who was really quite nice about it all."

"Nice!" said Andrew. "How does he get off being nice? What does *nice* have to do with anything?"

"You wouldn't know, perhaps, but I rather like it. Cheap as dirt, niceness."

Andrew kept silent. She had him there.

"Anyway, the man hung around on the porch talking to Mr. Pennyman about coin tricks. It was easy as that. I don't believe he was ever serious. He just wanted to poke around, like people looking through houses for sale. Nosiness is what it was."

"Well," said Andrew "why in the world did Pennyman loan us the books in the first place if he didn't want the public meddling with them? They're nothing but trash anyway. And coin tricks, you say?"

"That's right. I wouldn't know about his books. I've got a few things to do yet. Can you find time to bring down Aunt Naomi's plate?"

"Yes, I can find time." Andrew shrugged out of the kitchen,

feeling like a wreck. Somehow the evening had gone to smash. The pain in his back was murdering him. It must be his sciatic nerve . . . That's how the day had gone: He had come home rich and jubilant and then, through no fault at all of his own, had run into no end of treachery from Pennyman and Mrs. Gummidge. Well, he'd do something about it. A man's home, after all, was supposed to be his castle. He'd throw the knaves into the moat. His conversation with Pfennig still bothered him. Half of him wanted to think that the whole thing was a case of mistaken identity; the other half of him muttered that he ought to know the name, that no mistake had been made.

He pushed into the bedroom, thinking to change into looser clothes and to idle away a few minutes before having to confront Aunt Naomi again. Heaven knew what she'd be up to—sitting in a trance again, probably, watching the foggy night through the open window.

His books—his good books—lined two walls. There was Burroughs and H. G. Wells. There was Wodehouse and Dickens. None of the volumes were worth much. He was a book-owner rather than a collector. He was a hoarder. That was the truth of the matter. He thought about it as he sat on the edge of the bed, leaning back against his elbows. His books added something to his existence—a sort of atmosphere. No, it was more than that. They were a barrier of sorts. They were like a concrete foundation on a house; they kept the structure of his life up out of the dirt. They kept the termites out of the sill and kept the whole place from shaking to bits when the earth quaked. Looking at them was satisfactory, even when he was in a foul mood. Pennyman! There was one insect that had crept in, disguised, to gnaw on the floor joists. He was a bug, and no mistaking it, even if Rose didn't see it.

Of course Andrew couldn't just throw him out. It was too much money, after all. Rose would hand him the hedge trimmers and the vaccuum and tell him to fix the place up himself. She'd quit, and then there'd be no inn, no nothing. He pictured himself happy, ten years older, maybe, a little bit stouter, sitting at a corner table in the restaurant, a cheery fire in the grate, a pint glass of Bass Ale in his hand, things upstairs being seen to, the chef going about his business in the kitchen, the money rolling in. It was a pleasant enough dream, all in all—a comfortable dream. And it was true that it wouldn't come to pass if he was all the time throwing the guests out.

He sighed, tugging on his slippers. Squinting at the book-shelves, he stood up and cocked his head sideways, reading titles. There was a book gone, missing. He was certain of it. He looked closer, studying the titles, remembering how the books had been arranged. There were two books gone . . . three. He'd been robbed.

FIVE

"Now, therefore, I think that, without the risk of
any further serious objection occurring to you, I
may state what I believe to be the truth,—that
beauty has been appointed by the Deity to be one
of the elements by which the human soul is
continually sustained . . ."

John Ruskin
Lectures on Architecture and Painting

"WHAT THE HELL?" he muttered, thinking at first that he must
recently have been looking at the missing books and then forgotten
to put them back. Or maybe he hadn't unboxed them yet. Maybe
they were in the garage. They weren't, though, and he knew it. It
was impossible; they were gone. That was the long and short of it.
Someone had taken them, and it was fairly clear who that someone
was. Angry, he plucked up a pen from the dresser and looked
about for a bit of paper. Finding nothing, he wrenched his
handkerchief out of his pocket, and, stretching it tight across the
top of the dresser, he wrote down titles on it: *I Go Pogo* was gone,
and it had been signed, too, to Morton Jonwolly from Walt Kelly.
There were two Don Blandings gone—*Hula Moons* and *Vaga-
bond's House*—both signed, although the signatures were almost
worthless. What else? Not much of value. An unsigned copy of
Witherspoon's *Liverpool Jarge* and a copy of Gerhardi's *Pending
Heaven*. That was it, at least from a hasty glance. It had been a

weirdly selective thief—either a lunatic or someone who had taken the time to study things out.

Andrew shoved the pen into his pocket. There was the spoon, still in there. He plucked it out, looked around for some place to put it, and when nothing better suggested itself he slid it onto a bookshelf, in behind Charles Dickens.

"Rose!" he shouted, striding toward the door. Thievery in the house—that was the last straw. "Rose!"

Rose stepped out of the den, a swatch of fabric in her hand. "What's wrong?" she asked. "What's happened?"

"Thievery, that's what. My books, stolen."

"*All* of them?"

"No, just selected volumes. He knew what he was after. It was your man in the hat. It had to be. I thought you said he only fingered the books in the library."

"Well he did," said Rose. "At least while I was there. He might have sneaked in, I guess, while I assumed he was on the porch with Mr. Pennyman."

"I dare say he did. Let *me* interview these people from now on, will you? We'll be robbed blind at this rate."

Rose turned back toward the den. "Gladly," she said. "Interview anyone you please."

"And I *will*, too," shouted Andrew, thinking immediately that the retort sounded weak and foolish. He wasn't sure *he* knew what he meant by it. By golly he wouldn't be robbed though, not in his own house. And by a fat man in an Oriental robe, too, and wearing a clown hat. What was the world coming to? Was it rotting away under his nose? He slammed upstairs and into Aunt Naomi's room, ready to give hell to the cats if they asked for it. But they'd gone out the window, apparently, and Aunt Naomi was asleep in the chair. He picked up her half-empty plate and went back out, muttering his way down the stairs.

He laid the plate on the kitchen counter and stepped outside into the backyard where he opened the lid to the trash can, thinking that he'd been hasty to throw out the bag of poison, though he had no clear idea why at that moment he wanted to keep it—who or what he wanted to poison. The thief, certainly, was long gone by now.

He realized suddenly that he was striding around aimlessly, as if frantic to keep the world from collapsing on his head but not knowing what to prop up first. He had to do *something,* though. He was apparently living in a world full of rats, and they were growing more bold by the day. The trash can was empty. The poison was gone. Surprised, he checked the other can. The 'possum was gone, too. Rat control must have come around for the 'possum, found the pitched-out poison and taken it, too. Well to hell with them.

He slumped back inside. It was just nine o'clock, and all in all the most hellish night he'd spent in months. Rose would be going up to bed within the half hour, and wouldn't speak to him first. She was miffed. But by golly, her inviting criminals in to have a go at his books—that was no damn good. He walked into the library and sat down, realizing at once that he couldn't sit. He needed a walk, that's what. A walk in the fog. He loved the smell of fog on concrete with the smell of the ocean just beyond. It was like an elixir.

He started for the front door, realizing as he reached for the doorknob that he couldn't just walk out. Rose would think he'd left in anger and there'd be no way later to insist that he'd just gone out to clear his head. He turned around and poked into the den, where she sat sewing up a slipcase for the cushion on the library window seat.

"Thought I'd step out for a bit," Andrew said, grinning at her.

"That would be nice."

"Just for a walk. I've got to think this out."

"What a good idea."

"That damned robed man . . ."

Rose shook her head and frowned. Then she held up the business she was sewing and turned it right-side-out, inspecting the seam at the corner. She didn't say anything more.

After a moment Andrew ducked away and out the front door, into the misty evening. He felt more doomful than ever. It seemed as if there were forces that conspired against him. He remembered suddenly Aunt Naomi's two thousand dollars, and it seemed that perhaps some few things had gone right that day after all.

But then, as if all the ghastly business this evening had seen its opportunity and leaped in to pollute things utterly, the money in his wallet was suddenly loathsome to him. What did it mean but that he was dependent on old Aunt Naomi? Here was Rose, sewing away in the den, *doing* something, for goodness sake. And what was he?—a man who lounged around and hoodwinked money out of an old cockeyed woman whom he pretended to despise but didn't. *He* was the despicable one. He was mean and base; there were no two ways about it. Rose had seen through him at last. He would be a lucky man if she ever spoke to him again. *She* hadn't stolen his books either. She put up with them, in fact. They cluttered up every room in the house. Rose didn't say a word about them. She dusted them. She shelved them happily when he left them lying around. It wasn't *her* fault if men from secret societies sneaked in and pinched them.

And what about this "society" business? What about the funny hat and the robe? There was a good deal too much of that sort of thing in the wind recently: Pickett with his talk about blowfish; Pennyman lounging about in the dark with the air of a man possessed of secret knowledge; Aunt Naomi with her spoon and her sudden fear of silver quarters; and now this Atlantean, or whatever he was, snatching books. He seemed to know what he was after, too, as if he'd been in the house before, perhaps, and had snooped things out.

The fog hovered heavy and wet. There wasn't a breath of a sea breeze. He walked down the alley, past the back of Señor Corky's, and then left on Main Street, past Walt's and the Potholder and a half-dozen darkened stores and out onto the old pier, scuffing along. What did it mean? Was Pickett right? Was something going on? Something secret and vast? Did a scattering of ancient men control the turnings of the world, and if so, what were they doing in Seal Beach? The idea struck him suddenly as being very funny. He nearly laughed out loud; only the night was so dark and foggy and silent that laughter wouldn't have worked. It would have made things horrible.

But the thought of it—a few old men like master puppeteers, working the rest of them, making them caper and dance and bow and scrape, as if humanity were a sort of enormous farce and in the sad position of never being able to see the joke because they *were* the joke. Somehow it seemed reasonable enough, especially on such a night as this.

Well, so be it. What did he care? *Someone* had to run the show. It might as well be these wandering Caretakers. Andrew couldn't begin to run an inn. It was a damned good thing that the business of running the world hadn't been left to *him*. Rose might make a go of it. All in all, though, it made little difference who was pulling the strings, as long as they left him alone, as long as they didn't yank the wrong string and bring the whole thing down in a heap. But they weren't entirely letting him alone, were they?

He found himself at the end of the pier, by Len's Bait House, staring off into the mist. He could just see the gray Pacific below, the ground swell humping through oily and smooth, almost the same color as the fog. The scarred iron railing, beaded with mist, lay cold beneath his hands and the air smelled of fish. Along the side of the bait house, water drip-dripped into a vast sink where fishermen, on more hospitable evenings, cleaned their catch.

All at once the shifting ocean seemed to him to symbolize all the mysteries in the universe. He recalled reading, as a boy, an account of the netting of a marine coelacanth by fishermen off the coast of eastern Africa. There had been a drawing of a black fish with an odd arrangement of fins and great scales the size of thumbnails and a mouthful of teeth. Science had been surprised. Such a fish was extinct. It had been relegated to the job of being a fossil. Now here was one in a net, which meant that there were more in the depths of the ocean, swimming through the dark waters among—what? Who could say?

The surprising thing was that anyone had been surprised. The fishermen, certainly, weren't surprised. They'd spent their lives on the ocean, bobbing along in small boats, peering over the side into seas of sargasso weed, tangled in the topmost branches of kelp forests, watching the sun sink and the night drift in and the green-tinged moon rising out of the water like a transmarine Venus and hearing the quiet splash of restless things disturbing the surface of the dark waters and then disappearing again into the depths.

They must have wondered a thousand times at the shadows that shifted beneath the evening swell, beneath their puny tacked-together boat. Nothing that came from the sea would really have surprised them. Something in them would have nodded and said, "At last. Here it is. It's come." That's how Andrew felt—as if nothing at all would surprise him: aliens landing in saucers, pigs bringing around a spoon early in the morning, the discovery that the Wandering Jew was at work tinkering with the earth as if it were a clockwork mechanism. He had read in a book of myths the story of a wizard who had gone out fishing on the Mediterranean Sea, trolling with a magical coin. The wizard had caught an enormous fish—the Leviathan itself—and just as the beast had swallowed the coin, a great, shadowy counterpoint fish had descended out of the shadows of the heavens and swallowed the moon. Coins, coins, coins. And now this telephone call from the man Pfennig. It was maddening, but it would put itself right in time. Everything put itself right in time. Either that or it didn't.

Andrew shivered. He'd forgotten to put on his jacket. He was wearing his bedroom slippers and it felt to him suddenly as if the loose, slip-on shoes were full of fog, as if he were tramping down the pier wearing a pair of ghostly fishbowls. Rose would have gone up to bed by now. She'd be asleep. He dreaded having to wake her up to set things straight. He wouldn't let the night slip by without it, though. There'd be no weighty silence at breakfast.

He turned around to set a course for home, nearly pitching over onto his face at the sight of Pennyman, holding his stick in one hand and with his reeking pipe in his mouth, not fifteen feet distant, all alone on the pier. He wore his white coat and he bent over the railing as if to catch a glimpse of the sea. It looked to Andrew as if he held a spool of fishing line and was dangling it over the side, thinking to hook a flounder, perhaps, and then pull it in with his hands. Lamplight shone off whatever it was that was tied onto the end of the line—a fishing lure, maybe a bass spoon;

it was too dim and foggy for Andrew to see it clearly. There sounded the plunk of it hitting the water and it seemed that at that instant the pier shook, as if a monumental wave had broken across the pilings. It was coincidence, of course, as if the universe were playing along with Pennyman, abetting him in his posing and pretense.

Andrew decided that he wouldn't even ask about Pennyman's fishing. He would ignore Pennyman and all of his affairs. He was one down every time he showed an interest in the man. Without looking up, Pennyman said, "Out for a stroll, are you?" and he tugged a couple of times on his line.

"That's right." Andrew's heart flailed like a machine stamping out nails. He set out at once toward Main Street. He could see the comfortable glow of streetlamps disappearing down toward the highway, and the headlights of a car that motored toward the mouth of the pier then swung off down the alley.

"Looking for something?" asked Pennyman as Andrew strode past.

"No, just walking. Getting a little air."

"Something *in* the air tonight, isn't there?"

"Fog," said Andrew, nodding and clumping away, wishing he weren't abroad in his bedroom slippers. He thought suddenly of what the fog must have done to his hair, but he chased the thought off, noticing that it hadn't, somehow, ruined *Pennyman's* hair, and wondering why that was. There *was* something in the air tonight; just as Pennyman had said. And it wasn't just fog and darkness, either. It had been drifting in for a week or more, and it would no doubt keep on drifting in until its features coalesced out of the gray and it made itself known.

The moon peeked through the parting mist just as Andrew stepped off the pier and out onto the sand, as if it were having a quick glance at what sort of man it was who was out fishing after mysteries. A wave broke softly along the shore, glowing with an eerie phosphorescence in the light of the moon, which looked uncommonly pale and distant and lonesome up there, winking and bobbing in the briefly starry heavens like the reflection of a dream. Then, in the slip of an instant, the fog billowed through again, swallowing the moon utterly. Andrew set out for home, scuffing along the deserted beach. He could just see the dim figure of Pennyman slouched over the railing at the end of the pier. In the now moonless night the waves no longer glowed, but out in the water, beneath the rolling swell, there gleamed a whitish light, as if a company of water goblins were gathering mussels from the pier pilings by the guttering light of an undersea candle, or as if some glowing, deep-water monster had drifted up out of a submarine grotto, attracted by Pennyman's lure.

The house was dark—everyone asleep. Pennyman, of course, was out fooling away the night on the pier, up to whatever it was he was up to. As Andrew stood outside, leaning against the curb tree looking at the house, he wondered exactly what it was he'd say to Rose. He decided to have a drink first—a glass of beer, maybe. He still was on the edge of feeling foul. The walk hadn't entirely done the trick. His books were gone; Pennyman had made a fool of him; and worst, he'd made a fool of himself, whining at Rose about nonsense.

He half-wished he smoked a pipe; it would be just the thing—outdoors on a night like this. It would be a comfort. But he numbered smoking among the vices he'd been spared, and he put the thought aside. There was a rustling off in the bushes—no doubt one of Naomi's cats, out fouling the flowerbeds. Damn them. He'd have to hit Farm Supply for some of those anti-cat stakes. If he couldn't bring himself to trap the creatures, then the least he could do was make it clear to them who ran the show—put them in their place.

But it wasn't a cat. It appeared just then, a 'possum, sniffing along behind its foolish pointy nose. It was a big one, out marauding. It wandered along to the crawlspace under the house, where it hooked its paw behind the wood-framed screen that covered the space and tore the screen loose, frame and all, ducking away into the darkness. Andrew went across and examined the frame and screen. It had never been fixed properly to the house, just tilted in, sort of holding itself up—as barriers went, it was apparently no match for a determined 'possum.

In the soft dirt around the space were a dozen of the creature's footprints, plain as day. Maybe Pickett was right; maybe he *would* show them to Rose. That would cement things. All suspicion would be swept away. He tilted the little door back into its hiatus and then stood up, debating with himself. He was a fan of 'possums. He liked the idea that there were wild creatures out and about in the neighborhood, living in the urban sprawl of Southern California as if the coastal chaparral and grasslands hadn't been swept away a hundred years earlier.

He remembered the first time he'd seen the flock of wild parrots fly past overhead. It had been in the autumn, some years back. There was something mystical about the green, raucous flock of tropical birds cutting across the gray skies above Long Beach, winging down to roost in the broken-out windows of an abandoned building. Parrots and 'possums—they were a sort of weird counterpoint to the deadening, soulless technology of the modern age.

He grinned. It *must* be late, for him to start dredging up shopworn philosophies over a 'possum living under the house. Having made up his mind, he bent down again and dusted away the thing's footprints. He wouldn't tell Rose after all. She might have taken him seriously about what sorts of monsters 'possums were, and demand that he trap them, get them out of there. And they were sort of an ace in the hole anyway. When push came to shove, and it was generally assumed that he was a madman, he could lead them all to the crawlspace and point. The nest of 'possums would be vindication.

Vindication, though, wasn't worth much to him at the moment. In fact, thinking about it made it all come flooding back in again, all of the day's lost battles. He went inside and into the kitchen to pour that drink. Drink, fortunately, was not one of the vices he'd foresworn. He jerked open the kitchen cupboard door and surveyed the glasses, wavering between the temptation of beer out of pilsner glasses and wine out of cut-glass stemware. Both had their advantages. The right glass was almost as important as the right drink.

It would be a glass of wine, he decided, instead of beer. Beer had a deadening effect on him; wine seemed to settle him down. It filled him almost at once with a sense of proportion. It was a balancing effect, a keel-evener. Except that if he drank too much of it he overbalanced and sank.

The wine glasses were wedged in behind non-descript, dimestore quality tumblers, and when he edged the tumblers out of the way with his hand, one toppled off into the sink, shattering into fragments. He stopped dead, not even breathing, waiting for the rustling to begin. Mrs. Gummidge would scurry in, chattering like a gibbon ape, lunging after the broom and dustpan, saying, "You just leave *that* little mess to me, Mr. Vanbergen. *I'll* see to it. Dropped a glass did you? Well, care killed the cat, as they say," and uttering this lunacy she'd shoulder him out of the way and turn the whole business into a production, further ruining the evening.

She didn't awaken, though. There was no rustling, no whispering, no sudden illumination. He'd have to clean the glass up himself.

He pulled out a paper sack and started fingering the larger pieces very daintily out of the sink, shoving the tip of his thumb almost immediately into a glass sliver. He blushed with heat, feeling the sliver half-buried there and not wanting to look at it. In a moment he held his thumb to the light. There it was. If he hadn't kept his fingernails chewed short, he might have plucked it out. As it was he had to go for the tweezers. Taking care not to brush his thumb against anything, he knocked the bathroom door open with his knee. Then, holding the tweezers in his left hand, he worried the piece of glass out, a drop of blood bubbling slowly out in its wake. He squeezed his thumb against the possibility of blood poisoning, and, cursing, dropped the glass sliver into the trash, put away the tweezers, and walked back into the kitchen. He wouldn't touch another piece of glass. There was nothing more treacherous than broken glass. He seemed to have gotten all the sizeable fragments anyway. He turned on the water, washing the last few chips down into the garbage disposer. Then he flipped it on. Immediately there was a terrible grinding and howling. He hadn't gotten all the big pieces after all. The disposer ground to a sudden stop, locked tight against a wedge of glass.

He stood in silence, listening to the laboring of the engine, thinking vaguely that he'd let it go until it overheated and burned itself out. That would show it. He'd catch hell for it, though, and it would mean having a man in to fix it, and the man would no doubt steal a half dozen of his books on the way out. So he reached up and flipped off the switch. He'd get a pipe wrench, is what he'd do, and beat the living daylights out of the garbage disposer. That was the only sane course. Except that it would awaken the house. That wouldn't do at all. Mrs. Gummidge would appear and, wiggling something, would have the disposer running again. Had he tried to grind up a glass? Had he this? Had he that? Didn't it seem as if the trash bag under the sink? . . .

Shaking, he opened the cupboard door to confront the glasses once again. There were the tumblers standing like so many smug little swaggering fools. There was nothing at all to recommend them, not even age. They were a sort of olive green, splashed with gold glitter—a half-wit's idea of elegance. He and Rose had gotten them as a wedding gift—from a blind man, it would seem. Andrew had always detested them. There'd been eight of them, and in the long years since only one of them had broken—the one he'd dumped into the sink. At that rate, losing one, say, every fifteen years, there would still be a set of them, four at least, when he was dead. The idea of it appalled him. And that was if he lived to be ninety. He'd die broken and gibbering, and in the cupboard, barely showing the use they'd had, these foul tumblers would wait, knowing that, barring major earthquakes, they'd see another sixty years out easily enough. He couldn't stand it.

He *wouldn't* stand it. He hauled two of them down—it would be madness to do for all seven of them at once—and he carried them out the back door. In the garage he found a gunnysack and an old paint-stained T-shirt. He wrapped the glasses in the rag, put the rag into the gunnysack, and, after laying it on the sidewalk just off the back porch, he wrestled a melon-sized chunk of smooth granite out of the flower bed, ascended the porch, and dropped the rock onto the glasses. There was the satisfying thunk of something smashing; not the tinkle of flying fragments, but the deadening smash of the glasses having gone flat. He felt as if he were striking a blow, literally, for—what?—art, maybe. Sensibility. General principles. He retrieved the rock and carried it up the stairs for another go, dropping it just as the porch light blinked on.

The rock thumped down again, rolling off onto the grass. Rose stood in the open door, looking puzzled. Andrew grinned at her, feeling like the prince of fools. He started to speak, but managed only to croak and shrug. He searched desperately for a plausible lie. Fish in the sack, perhaps. He'd gone fishing and caught two bonita and he wanted to kill them and clean them. No use letting that sort of job go until morning. Best get them into the freezer tonight. It wouldn't wash, though, him killing them with a rock as big as his head.

"What are you doing?" asked Rose, utterly humorless.

"Nothing," said Andrew. "That is to say, I'm messing with an idea I've had about glass—about building odds and ends out of shattered glass and melted lead. I got the idea down on the pier tonight. There was a burner for sale at the bait house, for melting lead into fishing weights. Why not cast it into shapes, I thought, mold it around scatterings of colored glass? Paperweights, bookends, doorstops—all that sort of thing." He smiled at her and stepped off the porch, fetching up the stone again, very purposefully, and setting it back into the flowerbed.

"Pickett called," said Rose. "He wanted to tell you about a pair of apes that escaped into San Francisco. A psychic, apparently, had a vision of them eating ravioli in a North Beach restaurant."

"He called to tell me that? What was the point of it?"

"I'm not sure. I thought at first it was a joke—apes and psychics and ravioli and all that—only there didn't seem to be any punch line. Maybe I've told it wrong. He seemed to be fascinated by it all and assumed you would be, too. Anyway, I'm going back to bed. I heard the noise and I didn't know what it was." She looked over the porch railing at the gunnysack. Then she yawned, shoved either hand up the opposite sleeve of her bathrobe, and walked away into the darkened house without saying anything else.

Andrew heard a cupboard door open in the kitchen, and then, a moment later, shut again. He looked down at the gunnysack. It was a sad, foolish object, lying there on the fog-damp sidewalk. Rose would know what he'd been up to, and her knowing would foil any future efforts at smashing up the glasses. If he broke one by accident now it would seem as if he'd gone mad and done it on purpose. He was as transparent as a sandwich bag. He'd have to use Aunt Naomi's money now to buy the sinker molder at Len's. Then he'd have to fake up some way to build something out of lead and broken glass, as he'd said. What it would be he hadn't any earthly idea, but he *had* to do it. If he didn't do it, he was doomed. He couldn't be caught in a lie. He had to turn the lie inside out, to meddle with reality until things were put right. Just like he'd done with the 'possum. He could do that again with the broken glass. If there was method to his madness, then it couldn't be madness after all, could it?

As he dumped the gunnysack onto the bench in the garage he wondered if that's how Pickett's Caretakers worked. If they effected vast upheavals of economies or governments or whatever they did by setting into motion, say, a trifling little calculated lie, or a wink tipped in just the right direction—some little bit of gravel, which, bouncing down a broadening hillside, would knock loose rocks and boulders, one of which, out of nowhere, would whack on the head some poor banker in a three-piece suit as he stood contemplating interest rates. Maybe he'd drop dead on the spot, and when alerted associates began to suspect that the stone out of nowhere signified something, there would begin a surreptitious movement of money in and out of vaults and through the electronic links of computer networks until the public got wind of it and undertook a fear-induced run on the bank. Just like that, an empire would sink in the dust, ruined entrepreneurs would leap out of windows, third-world governments would topple, and no one ever suspecting that the first jolly pebbles were kicked loose by a pottering old man in baggy trousers, pruning rose bushes with one hand and manipulating the lever-action works of the universe with the other.

Two weeks earlier, Uncle Arthur had bought twenty-two Exer-Genies from a door-to-door salesman. In the Leisure World retirement community door-to-door salesmen were frowned on. There was a wall around the place to keep them out. One had got in, though, past the guards, with a trunk full of these Exer-Genies, which a person would recline on in the interest of being folded up over and over again at the waist, fearfully fast, until he was healthy again. Uncle Arthur had bought the lot of them. He had become "the West Coast rep," as the salesman had said. And now the devices were stacked in the plywood cabinet screwed to the wall of the carport.

He'd done it on the afternoon of a full moon. Rose had pointed that out. Uncle Arthur was an old man. Rose couldn't remember a time when Uncle Arthur *hadn't* been an old man. It had always been common knowledge in the family that his age seemed to affect him most when the moon was full. When there was no moon, or just a sliver of it, he seemed chipper and spry and canny. It was a strange business. Andrew couldn't puzzle it out, except that it seemed to imply that the derivation of the word "lunatic" was a product of something more than mere superstition. That's how it went sometimes; there was often some little grain of truth behind the wildest folktales.

Uncle Arthur shouldn't live alone, Rose had said in reference to his moon-madness and to his buying the Exer-Genies. The family had shaken its head—the poor old man, swindled again. Last time it was a case of rechargeable batteries and a device to do the recharging, which had burst into flames after having been left plugged in all night and had nearly burned the house down.

Pickett knew better than the family. Senility, he said, didn't enter in. One didn't second-guess Uncle Arthur—not even Pickett, who suspected he knew who Uncle Arthur *really* was— *what* he was—although he said he couldn't tell anyone yet, not even Andrew. Why the twenty-two Exer-Genies had to have been bought, Pickett couldn't say. Where they were bound was an utter mystery. They might very well sit in their plywood cupboard until doomsday, what did it matter to you and me? They'd sit there because they *had* to sit there, because when it came to Uncle Arthur's dealings, said Pickett, *nothing* he did or said was random and without purpose. Everything was calculated. That's what Pickett had said about the Exer-Genies and about Uncle Arthur's late-night sojourns in his red, electronic car. Don't question the Exer-Genies, that had been Pickett's advice, at least that had been his advice until the arrival of Pennyman. Then Pickett had begun to question everything.

There were simpler answers, of course. There nearly always were, but Pickett didn't see any value in them. Uncle Arthur had been a prodigious traveling salesman in his day—going door to door, town to town, state to state, and, years past, continent to continent, wandering the earth like a tinker, peddling his wares. There was nothing he hadn't sold, to hear Aunt Naomi tell it, no front stoop he hadn't stood on, no bell he hadn't rung. He had accumulated the careers of ten standard-issue salesmen stacked one on top of the other, and there was scarcely a corner of the globe, no matter how far-flung, that he hadn't memories of.

Such instincts die hard, Andrew thought, wandering through the quiet house, carrying a glass of beer. The wine that had been in the refrigerator was gone—Mrs. Gummidge again, no doubt. It was after midnight, and he couldn't sleep. Squaring it with Rose had become impossible, what with their confrontation on the back porch. He sat down in the library, staring up at the books. He would read something to take his mind off things. It should be something substantial, nothing unsettling. Dickens would do— some funny Dickens. Or *The Wind in the Willows*. That was the ticket. It was clover-strewn meadows that he needed, running down into babbling rivers. It was talk of firesides and Christmas and glasses of ale, of picnics and boating and jolly companions. Things were out of balance, and if he didn't have a glass of wine to put them right, then a book would have to do.

He opened the book at random—he'd read it often enough so that beginnings and endings meant nothing any more—and found himself dabbling through "The Piper at the Gates of Dawn." Ratty and Mole were off to find the baby otter, lost down the river. Dawn was near. The world was turning toward the morning. There was faint music on the breeze, which stirred through the rushes. Something was pending—something . . . For a moment Andrew thought he knew what it was, that something. He *did* know, but he couldn't at all put it into words. It wasn't something you knew in your mind; you felt it with your spine, maybe, and with your stomach. And it wasn't the obscure machinations of men like

Pennyman that you felt, either; it was something else, something that such men were ignorant of, or that they hated—that they didn't have or want any part of, that they wanted to ruin. For that moment at least, Andrew knew that he himself wanted a part of it very badly, whatever it was. He closed the book and sat there. The late hour lent itself nicely to that sort of thing—to things of the spirit, so to speak. When the day dawned with its garages needing to be painted and its men in mystical hats coming around after rooms for rent, the feeling would be gone, dissipated, hovering just out of sight. But he would stumble upon it again when he wasn't at all expecting it—the promise of heaven on the soft wind, "the place of my song-dream," as Rat put it.

Andrew glanced up, surprised to see a light on in the kitchen. He'd turned it off an hour earlier. It must be late, one or two in the morning. There was the scraping of a chair being pushed back and of a spoon clanking against the side of a bowl. He stood up and tiptoed along. It might easily be Pennyman. Andrew had had enough of Pennyman for one day.

But it wasn't. It was Aunt Naomi in a bathrobe. Andrew stood gaping for a moment, startled by the idea of Aunt Naomi out and about. She so rarely left her room that he'd begun to think of her as another fixture there, and he'd have been no more surprised to see her nightstand or her coatrack dressed in night clothes and wandering through the kitchen. She was after a bowl of cereal. There were a half-dozen boxes on the table and she sat looking at them, unable, perhaps, to decide. The sight of them reminded Andrew that he was ravenous. It seemed to him that he hadn't eaten in months. Cereal would be just the thing.

"Hello," he said, smiling in at her.

She looked up sharply, surprised, it seemed, to be caught in the act of eating breakfast cereal at such an hour.

"Having a bowl of something?"

She nodded. "In fact I am."

"Mind if I join you then?"

"Not at all," she said, nodding toward the chair opposite. She seemed almost friendly, as if the act of eating breakfast cereal was naturally cheering.

"I'm a Cheerios man myself," said Andrew, digging a bowl out of the cupboard. "Most people pour the milk on first, then sprinkle on the sugar. I do it the other way around, to wash the sugar to the bottom. Then you can scrape it up later, when you're spooning out the milk. It's wonderful that way." It occurred to him as he said this that it was just the sort of thing that Rose had warned him against—the sort of nutty talk that a woman like Aunt Naomi wouldn't understand.

She nodded her head, though, as if she *did* understand, and she picked up the box of Wheat Chex and dumped out a third of a bowlful. "The trick," she said, "is not to fill the bowl. You want a taste of each of them. It's a matter of temperance, really. You don't want to give into the urge to stuff yourself with the first sort you pick up."

This advice sounded rock-solid to Andrew, who'd always felt more or less the same way. He was happily surprised to discover that Aunt Naomi possessed some cereal lore. "What about flakes? I've always said that the problem with bran flakes is that they didn't hold up. Immediately soggy."

She nodded again. "You put in too much milk," she said, "and drown them. Use less, then dig for the milk with your spoon. Leave half the flakes high and dry. They've gotten round that with Wheaties, I've noticed. They hold up longer. And with sugar-sweetened cereals, too. It's the sugar glaze that keeps the milk out. Until it melts off, of course. I've never had much faith in them, though. I've felt that it was gimmickry from the outset."

Andrew shrugged, not wanting to contradict her. In fact, he was partial to both Trix and Sugar Pops. But he was still half-afraid of setting her off, despite the growing evidence of her sanity. His coming in on the side of sugar-sweetened cereal might cause unlooked-for trouble. "Do you remember Ruskets?" he asked. "Those little biscuits of pressed-together flakes?"

"Indeed I do." She paused and squinted at him. "Were you a crusher or a non-crusher?"

"A non-crusher. Absolutely. The only way to do it was to lean them against the sides of the bowl, so that half of them were out of the milk, like you were saying before, then skive off sections with a spoon so that you got a little bit of the dry flakes with the rest. There was always a heap of soggy flakes in the bottom, of course, but that couldn't be helped. Have you, by any chance, come across Weetabix?''

''Not in years,'' she said, remembering. ''I ate them in London, when I was feeling better. I used to travel a good bit, alas. That's the problem with being bedridden. The world isn't your oyster any longer.''

''Well,'' said Andrew, ''it happens that I've got a line on some Weetabix. For the cafe. My friend Pickett is driving them down from Canada. I think I can keep you supplied, actually.''

''I'd like that. A person has so few surprises nowadays, so few little comforts.''

''It must be rotten,'' said Andrew. ''I don't at all mean to be nosey, Aunt, and you can tell me to mind my own business, but I've never entirely understood what it was that ailed you. It must be something fairly grim, to keep you holed up like that.''

She shook her head, staring out toward the kitchen door. ''It's merely a cross,'' she said euphemistically, ''that I've had to bear.''

''I see,'' said Andrew, who actually saw nothing at all. He decided not to press the issue, though, just in case there was nothing, really, to see, or in case it was some sort of vaguely indefinable female trouble that he didn't want to hear about anyway. ''How did the chocolates agree with you?''

''They were quite moderately nice, thank you. You say your new chef made them?''

Andrew blinked at her. Lies seemed to have a way of perpetuating themselves. He was stricken with the urge to haul out his wallet and give Aunt Naomi the leftover fourteen hundred dollars and to admit everything. He gasped instead and grinned and nodded, and just then Rose walked in, squinting in the light, and saved him. ''Well!'' he said, standing up. It was awfully good to see Rose all of a sudden, and not only because her arrival clipped off the French chef discussion. It was a chance to make amends. ''Bowl of cereal?''

She looked at the table, winked pleasantly at Aunt Naomi, and said, "Yes, I believe so. That looks awfully good."

Andrew scrambled around after another bowl and spoon. Anticipating her, he picked up the box of Grapenuts and inclined his head at it. She smiled and nodded, yawning and putting her hand over her mouth. "Aunt Naomi and I have just been discussing the mysteries of breakfast cereals," said Andrew. "She's something of an authority."

They ate in silence for a moment, and there was no sound but the scraping of bowls. A cat wandered in just then, looking around. Andrew bent down to pet it. He laid his cereal bowl on the linoleum floor. The cereal was gone, but it was still half full of sweetened milk. The cat sniffed it and then set in to lap it up, pausing now and then to look around, as if wondering why it was he hadn't made this a regular practice long ago.

"I'm finished," said Aunt Naomi, standing up and leaning on her cane. She looked dangerously thin, with sharp cheekbones and an aristocratic face that made it clear she was once frighteningly handsome. Andrew was struck with her resemblance to Rose. Both of them were tall and patrician, as if they'd come from some royal family in the mountains of Bohemia. But whereas Naomi was polished and prim, Rose was slightly disheveled and earthy. Taken together like this, they made Andrew feel just a little bit like a bumpkin.

"This has been delightful," Aunt Naomi continued. "Perhaps we'll meet again like this. I'm feeling very much better this evening. Better than I've felt in thirty years. It's as if I've had a fever for years and it's finally broken. Good night, Rosannah, Andrew." And with that she hobbled away, shaking her head at Rose's offer to help her up the stairs. Rose let her go.

"Time for bed, don't you think?" she asked, smiling at Andrew. "You've had a tiring day."

Andrew shrugged. That was the truth. "So have you," he said.

"That's why I've been sleeping. You've been wearing yourself out, wrestling with things. Quit thinking so much. Sleep more. Why don't you go fishing more often? Do you remember when we used to get up in the morning and be out on the pier at dawn? Why don't we do that any more?"

"Not tomorrow, you don't mean. Not at dawn?"

"No, not tomorrow. But sometime."

"Of course,"said Andrew. "I didn't think you liked that sort of thing anymore."

"Quit thinking, then, as I said. It's not doing you any good. You're full of anticipation—worrying about things that haven't happened yet and probably won't. You're half-wornout just getting ready to dodge phantoms. You don't have to dodge me. You know that, don't you?"

"Sure," Andrew mumbled, unable to say anything more. He *did* know it, too. What he didn't know was why he so often failed to remember it.

"You're probably right." He stood up and cleared away the dishes, running water into them and stacking them in the sink. "Look," he said, "paper towels. I'm being good." And he yanked two towels off the roll, dried his hands, and threw them into the trash. Rose shook her head, giving him a mock-serious look.

He was frightfully tired all of a sudden. It had been a long day. With Rose following, he wandered into the library to turn out the reading lamp. On an impulse, he read her a bit out of his book, and she took the book from him and read a little more to herself. Then she shelved the book and switched off the lamp, and the two of them went up to bed.

BOOK II

Reason Not The Need

"Oh, reason not the need! Our basest beggars
Are in the poorest thing superfluous."
William Shakespeare
The Tragedy of King Lear

SIX

"Let James rejoice with the Haddock, who brought
the piece of money to the Lord and Peter."
Christopher Smart
"Jubilate Agno"

ALL IN ALL, the changes in Vancouver appealed to him—the
ruination of Gastown especially. Every second shop was littered
with tourist goods, with ceramic dolls and souvenir plates, with
idiot wood carvings of non-existent totem poles and with pot
metal ferry boats—the china-hutch dreams of travelers who
preferred a homogenized, cleaned-up waterfront to what had
been the dark and gritty reality of the place. Jules Pennyman was
indifferent to the place itself, except that in general he preferred a
sterilized world with the wrinkles ironed out of it. The deadening, prefabricated emptiness of the new tourist-appealing waterfront was just the sort of thing he approved of. It had become a
place almost without spirit, a shallow place of surfaces and
mirrors. Although some of the old shops were left—a few
bookstores and bars—they'd be modernized and sanitized in
time, too, and the sooner the better.

His meeting with August Pfennig had been interesting.

Pennyman hadn't wasted words; he'd finished his dealings with Pfennig and slipped away, the whole business reminiscent of his meeting with Aureus in Jerusalem. He had driven south, boarded a ferry, and now had stopped at Vashon Island with about an hour to spare before the outward-bound ferry departed for Seattle. His flight left Seattle/Tacoma in four hours.

Fifty yards away, at the base of a hill, sat his rented limousine, its driver polishing the dust from the fenders with a rag. Pennyman sat on his unfolded handkerchief atop a step stool outside the rusty, white-painted metal shed that passed for a gas station. There were two pumps anchored in dirty asphalt, and beyond the asphalt was forest and more forest, with here and there a house hidden in the trees. It was too idyllic—all the greenery and outdoorsy atmosphere of the place, but its lonesome silence was attractive, empty and cold as it was and devoid of human illusion. Away behind him stretched Puget Sound, the gray and shifting home of pilot whales and porpoise and octopi. There was too much life beneath the surface of the sea to satisfy Pennyman. He could barely stand thinking about it.

The Cascades, snowcapped and stretching away south toward Oregon, were what the common man would call majestic and sublime. Pennyman didn't believe in such things; he despised the tendency of stupid people to want to turn dirt and rock into something more than it was. His shoes were murdering his feet, and he'd run out of Pepto-Bismol on the ferry. His throat was full of acid. This morning his hair seemed to have gotten back some of its life. It had begun to fall out in clumps, just before he'd paid his visit to Adams and then traded the carp for another bottle of the elixir. It hadn't seemed to have the same restorative effect on his feet, though. And of course it wouldn't have. He didn't dare remove his shoes, although it felt as if there were a rock in each, jammed in against his toes. It was as if his shoes were three sizes too small now and shoved onto the wrong feet. He thought he knew why.

He looked at his watch. It wouldn't do to miss his plane. There was no use exciting suspicions among the members of his new-found family in California—Rose especially. He rather liked the look of her, and there was a certain satisfaction in using her to torment her idiot husband. Alone, Andrew was too easy a mark; there was more sport in bringing the whole family down together.

Someone was coming from up the road. It was the gas station attendant and the boy. The boy had been the only witness to the sinking of a rowboat and the drowning of an old man, whom Pennyman knew to be a bearded Caretaker named Simon Denarius. Pfennig had told him that much before they'd parted company.

There had been a trifling little article in yesterday's *Tribune*. Pennyman would have missed it, except that Pfennig had circled it in red ink, and left the newspaper laid open on the countertop in his shop. There was damn-all Pennyman could do about it now, of course, except to make certain. A fish had been caught, according to the article, fouled in a drag net in Puget Sound. It had been enormous—the few eyewitnesses had agreed to that. It might have been a whale, they supposed, except that it was impossibly large and was coruscated with undersea life, as if it wore a thousand years of coral polyps and hydra and sea fans and blue-green algae—a deep-ocean coat of many colors.

They had towed it to Vashon Island and cut it open, only to find another fish in its vast stomach, and then another fish in *its* stomach and yet another and another, like a set of dwindling, Peruvian gourd dolls. Out of the stomach of that last fish—so the newspaper article read—they'd taken an old silver coin. Early the next morning the coin was bought for an unlikely sum by an old man with a vast beard like an Old Testament prophet, who'd come in out of the fog on the Seattle ferry. Directly afterward he'd rented a rowboat and gone fishing. That was the end of Simon Denarius.

The boy who finally stood goggling in front of Pennyman had a baseball cap cocked around sideways and pulled down over one ear. His jeans were torn out at the knees, and there were dirty, candy-stained smears around his leering mouth and down his chin. He chewed moodily on something—his tongue, maybe, or a half-dozen sticks of gum wadded together. Dull wasn't the word for his eyes; vacant was better. Probably inbred, Pennyman thought, repelled by the boy, who might have been eight. Pennyman shivered inadvertently and a wash of acid churned up into his throat. Children in general were intolerable, but a filthy, gum-chewing urchin like this was an argument for something. A hundred and fifty years ago he might have been crippled and set to begging, but in the modern world he was merely useless, a bit of filth. Pennyman smiled at him. ''So you saw the big fish, did you?''

''I ain't saying nothing.''

''You're not?''

''I ain't saying I ain't, but I ain't saying I am, neither.''

The gas station attendant grinned stupidly. ''That's it, Jimmy,'' he said, nodding and blinking his eyes. ''What'd I tell you?''

The boy looked up at Pennyman, screwing his eyes half-shut, and spit between his teeth at the ground, the result landing on his own foot. ''How much will you pay me? If you don't pay, I ain't telling you nothing.''

''Pay is it!'' laughed Pennyman, pretending to be vastly amused. ''This is a surprise.''

''It ain't no damn surprise,'' said the gas station man, running a greasy hand through his hair. ''This is business. The boy got a living to earn, ain't that right, Jimmy?''

''Yep,'' said Jimmy, and he chewed his gum and squinted. ''Maybe I see the old man go out, maybe I was asleep, maybe you can kiss my ass.''

''How much do you want?'' said Pennyman flatly. He'd had enough of both of them.

''Soak him, Jimmy!'' said the attendant, and he slapped Pennyman on the shoulder as he said it, as if Pennyman would especially appreciate it.

Pennyman recoiled in horror, in sudden revulsion, as if he were a slug curling away from a droplet of lye or as if he'd discovered a rat's nest in a clothes closet. He flailed at the sleeve of his white coat, which was smeared with dirty oil from the man's hand.

The attendant grinned at him. ''Sorry, pop,'' he said, wiping his hands on his pants as if to make amends. ''Jumpy bastard, ain't you?''

"Talk first," croaked Pennyman, pulling forty dollars out of his wallet.

Jimmy stared at it with faint loathing on his little-boy face. "That ain't shit," he said.

Pennyman started to speak, but stopped himself. His chauffeur lounged against the newly polished fender, talking to two men in overalls, one of whom waved happily back up toward the gas station and shouted something that sounded like, "Ream 'im, Gus!" The gas station man smiled wider. "That's me," he said, nodding. "Gus." He held a tire iron in his right hand and slapped it against his left.

"What do you got in your shoe?" asked Jimmy, blowing an enormous bubble that popped across his nose and chin. He plucked the gum out of his mouth, rolled it in his dirty hands, then, using it as stickum, tugged the glued-on gum off his face.

"In my shoe?" asked Pennyman, suddenly horrified.

Gus said, "He means give him all you got. And if you got any in your shoe, cough it up. We ain't a-going to talk to the whole world. First it was the newspaper, then yesterday a guy name of 'Fence post' or something who come all the way up from L.A. in a beat-up Chevy. Burnt oil like a fry pan. He give Jimmy fifty bucks, and here's a cheap-ass slick like you waving two twenties. This ain't the Salvation Army, Holmes. Empty it out."

"That's right," Jimmy said. "This ain't the Army."

Pennyman sighed, trying to contain himself. He couldn't afford to be beaten with a tire iron. He couldn't afford to miss his plane. He couldn't afford to think that the limousine driver would do a damn thing to help him. In fact, all he could be sure of was that the two men talking to the driver were doing something more than passing the time of day. He angled his open wallet at Gus and Jimmy and pulled out all the visible money inside—almost three hundred dollars altogether.

Gus yanked it out of his hand, then snatched up the wallet itself, pulling out bank cards and papers and dropping them onto the asphalt. Pennyman let them lie there. If it had been within his power, he would have killed both of them then and there. They found a folded hundred dollar bill hidden under a flap, and Gus said, "Look-a here," and nodded down at Jimmy, who in one swift movement kicked Pennyman in the knee, then dodged in around behind Gus, who cocked his head on the side and gave Pennyman a don't-you-try-nothing stare.

Pennyman shook with rage, biting his tongue until it bled, thinking that he'd be back for a visit. Soon. When he was immune, when all the coins were his and he could do as he pleased. He forced a grin, trying to look as if he'd come up against better men in his life and laughed at them, too. "You've got it all," he said. "Now what about the old man and the coin? What about the coin?"

"He was nuts," said Jimmy. "Sewed that coin up in the belly of one of them fish, rented a boat down at the dock from Bill Nayler, and rowed out onto the Sound, trolling with a big old marlin rig and using the fish for bait. Set out there for half an hour burnin' crap in a bowl. I heard him singin' to himself. Then this thing come up out o' the ocean and ate him up, boat too, like in Pinochio. I got that movie on video. Same fish, I suppose."

"You think the boy's *lyin'* to you," said Gus flatly, making it a statement rather than a question. "Goddamn rich bastard driving down here in a stinking limo. Ain't you a ungrateful . . ."

But Pennyman had turned to go, walking stiffly across the weedy asphalt toward the limousine. In fact, he didn't disbelieve it at all. It was just the sort of thing he expected—and half-feared. He wasn't sure what it meant. He anticipated a tap on the shoulder at any moment, Gus's hand spinning him around, a greasy shove on the back. He wouldn't travel again without carrying a gun. But there was nothing except wild laughter and the blubbering rip of a tremendous raspberry—probably the high-spirited work of Jimmy. Then a credit card zinged past his ear. There was the sound of small feet running. He stiffened up, ready for a blow, just as a hand shoved him on the back. It was the push of a small hand—Jimmy's hand, no doubt.

Pennyman stumbled forward, caught himself, and strode on. He wouldn't turn around. They wanted him to turn around. He bent into the limousine and ordered the driver to back out and go. He settled into the seat, and then, thinking for the first time about the man from L.A. with fifty dollars to spend, he bent forward to loosen his shoelaces. That was when he felt Jimmy's wad of gum stuck onto the back of his coat, stretching away from where it had glued itself to the upholstery.

The sunlit fog was white instead of gray—as if Andrew were sitting in a house among the clouds. It seemed to be thickening, though, as the morning wore on, and there wasn't a bit of a breeze. Everything was wet—sidewalks, tree trunks, roof shingles, the windshield of the Metropolitan. Andrew sat in his car, idly working the wipers and watching the street.

There had been dead sea gulls all over the lawn and sidewalk that morning. Andrew had kicked one, not seeing it in the fog. Then he'd kicked another, and when he had bent over to have a closer look, there was yet another, lying in the gutter. They were everywhere, fallen as if shot. Alone in the fog, he had collected sixteen of the creatures up and down the street, dropping them into a cardboard box and then lugging the box down the alley, pitching it into a dumpster. The whole business struck him as bizarre, and he wondered if there'd been a leak of some sort of poison gas in the night, maybe a screw-up at the Naval Weapons Station.

The news on the car radio had been odd too—reports of flooding back up the San Gabriel River, as if there'd been a monstrously high tide. Only there hadn't been. It was almost as if the river had flowed backward all of a sudden, and brackish tidal water had spilled out into backyards and overflowed storm drains. Andrew wondered at it all: the odd phosphorescence in the ocean last night, the storm surf, the rain of birds, the river. It all had a biblical ring to it, as if something were "coming to pass." The morning was peaceful now, though, and wearing on. He glanced at his watch.

It was past ten. He'd slept late—later than he'd slept in almost fifteen years. He sipped at a mug of coffee that had gone half-cold in the morning air. There was no sense in painting the garage, not in weather like this. It wasn't at all a day for work; it was a day for thinking and reading and generally recovering from the previous day, which had been arguably the longest he could remember.

He was happy and satisfied sitting in his car, though. He had run the heater for a few minutes, taking the chance of being discovered, and now he was warm and almost sleepy. There was something in the smell of the interior of the car, something familiar and enclosing, which, when combined with the fog and the coffee and the sea air drifting through the narrow window gap, seemed altogether to conjure up a sort of feeling; he couldn't quite describe it. It was as if he were aloft in a balloon, very comfortable and with a glass of something nice to drink and watching the crazy-quilt earth slip past below.

The fog seemed to weigh everything down gently, like a gray overcoat thrown across the shoulders of a huddled world. Water dripped from the curb tree onto the top of the car, slow enough so that until the next one came each drip seemed sure to be the last, and from somewhere, layered between the muffled noise of distant traffic and the occasional lonesome cries of wheeling gulls, came the slow rumble of waves collapsing along the shore not half a block away.

It would be a good morning for walking on the beach. The heavy surf of the past night would have tossed up seashells and polished stones, and what with the fog and cool weather, tourists wouldn't yet have picked them over. Andrew finished his coffee and set the cup on the floor of the car. He had intended to wait for Pennyman, if for no other reason than to have something to report to Pickett when he returned from Vancouver with the Weetabix. Pennyman hadn't come out, though, and it had begun to seem suspiciously like Andrew had missed him. Such were the risks of sleeping late.

He hunched out onto the street, shut the car door as silently as he could, and locked it. The fog was so thick that he wouldn't be seen from the house, either by Rose or by Pennyman, and although he would have liked to wear his hat, he couldn't risk going in after it. He thrust his hands into his pockets and walked southwest toward the beach, angling down a narrow alley past where he'd given the bonita to the cats and wondering all of a sudden if they hadn't been Aunt Naomi's cats. That would be just like fate, wouldn't it? Here he'd been working hard to rid the house of the fiends, unsuccessfully, and then very graciously feeding them whole fish in the alley. They'd think he was a lunatic. Everyone sooner or later would think he was a lunatic—the cats, Aunt Naomi, Rose, Pennyman—everyone except Beams Pickett, who wasn't the sort of pot who called the kettle black. It was funny, actually, his having given the cats a treat. Even death row prisoners were given a top-notch meal before they were led away, or so the stories had it.

And the cats seemed to like him for it. Over the past couple of days it seemed as if they'd been hanging about him. One had even wandered into his bedroom early in the morning. Andrew had drowsed awake to see the beast standing there, looking as if it wanted to tell him something or as if it were standing watch while he slept.

At the edge of the beach he took his shoes and socks off, stuffed the socks down into the shoes, tied the laces together, and hung the shoes around his neck. Then he rolled his pantslegs up to his knees. The sand was damp and cold and it scrunched under his feet. He couldn't see the ocean, but he could hear it. Momentarily he was entirely adrift on the open beach, with nothing in the gray morning but a little circular patch of sand surrounding him, and not a sound of human manufacture to be heard. He was utterly alone, and the idea of it suddenly terrified him. He was struck with the notion that *They* were out there: Pickett's bogeymen, contriving the fog itself, perhaps, with a machine bolted to the underside of the pier.

Just then a man loomed up out of the mists, extraordinarily fat and with a glittery sort of helmet on and a shirt with moons and stars on it. An alien, Andrew thought, and he very nearly leaped back to hide himself in the mist, but the man's thrift-store trousers and down-at-heel shoes made it clear that he hadn't flown in from the stars, and he seemed easily as surprised to see Andrew as Andrew was to see him. He was obviously a local eccentric—like the bearded man yesterday at the inn—some sort of mystic. He nodded and passed on mumbling, walking toward the pier. Immediately someone else appeared, and behind him another three or four, all of them dressed like maharajas and carrying little tambourines like you'd win at a penny carnival. Andrew hurried past, careful not to make eye contact with any of them.

In his haste he kicked an enormous seashell and it rolled away down the sloping sand toward where the edge of a wave licked the pebbly shore. He chased after it and picked it up—a black murex the size of his hand, which had been wrenched up out of deep water by storm surf. Near the water's edge the sand was littered with seashells and jellyfish and tangles of kelp and pickleweed and eelgrass. There were moonsnails and owl limpets and brittle stars and leathery, purple nudibranchs and sea lemons and pipe fish. It was as if half of the denizens of the sea had stolen ashore in the night and decided to stay. Enormous codfish with bulbous eyes lay tangled in the weeds. Half-buried in the sand, the cold tide swirling around its whip-like tail, was a bat ray bigger than the hood of Andrew's Metropolitan. Andrew wished he had a sack with him. There was enough wonderful flotsam on the beach to fill a sea chest with.

He could see, farther up, a man in a tweed coat and with an uncanny sort of Prince Valiant haircut poking at something with a bit of driftwood. Andrew pulled his collar up and headed that way. The beach, clearly, was as full of eccentrics as it was full of odd sea life. Maybe he'd find his Atlantean there, reading one of his stolen books. Maybe he'd find the remnants of Atlantis itself, tossed up onto the beach along with pop bottles and fishing line and cast-off shoes. It was impossible that it was all coincidence, all of these oddballs sifting through things and the rain of birds, all of the talk of backward-flowing rivers. The strange people on the beach were looking for something, perhaps, or else, just like Andrew, they suspected that there was something to look for but didn't entirely know what it was and had come out to browse around on the chance that it would make itself known.

All in all, despite his haircut this fellow seemed safer than the maharajas or the man in the glittery helmet—less likely to run mad or to strike up a conversation with a ghost. And the thing he poked at appeared to be a body. Andrew strolled up and nodded a greeting. It wasn't a body, not a human body anyway. It was an impossible squid, eighteen or twenty feet long, half-buried under the sand and with its doleful, sightless eyes staring at nothing. It smelled awful, too, and not as if it had rotted there on the beach. It smelled burnt, somehow, like a smouldering electrical outlet or like badly scorched meat in a hot steel pan.

"Big, eh?" said the man, smiling at Andrew and gesturing with his pipe at the squid.

Although he already knew what it was, Andrew said, "What is it, a squid?" in order to give the man a chance to show off. But as soon as the words were out, Andrew noticed the line drawn down the center of the man's face, and his heart jumped like a spooked rabbit. He forced his own face to relax and glanced quickly around just in case Pennyman was somewhere nearby, watching them through the fog.

"That's just what it is," the man said, and he looked up at Andrew and shifted his pipe. "Genus *Loligo*. The French call them *poulps*."

Andrew nodded, breathing through his mouth very slowly in an effort to calm down. There was no sign of Pennyman, who was probably farther up the beach now, playing the quarter trick on the rajas. "The French do?"

"That's a fact. The Spanish eat them in sandwiches. The Italians fry them in olive oil or stuff them with herbs and cheese. The Japanese eat them raw on little moulded rectangles of rice. And in the South Seas the natives make a sort of jelly out of the eyeballs, which they eat on toast."

"You don't happen to be a chef, do you?" asked Andrew, thinking for a moment to solve the current Aunt Naomi problem. The man could certainly pass for a Frenchman, with his hair and all. But he wasn't a chef. He shook his head. Andrew squinted at his face, which was honest enough, but was pale and almost transparent, as if the man got out into the sun about once a year, early in the morning. There was no mistaking it; down his face was drawn the same line that Johnson and Andrew had been afflicted with.

"Something wrong?"

"No," said Andrew. "That is, your face . . . Seems to be something smeared on it. Pipe ash, perhaps. Sorry to stare."

The man produced a handkerchief and scoured away, the line rubbing off easily in the foggy air. Andrew inadvertently touched his own forehead. "Haven't seen a man out and about this morning, have you? A man in a white suit, beard? Carries a cane?"

"Yes, indeed. I saw just such a man. Had a nice long talk with him, too. He was an amateur stage magician; showed me some of the most amazing coin tricks, and card tricks, too."

Andrew nodded. "Had you roll a quarter down your face, didn't he?"

"By golly," said the man, "how did you know?"

"He's always up to that sort of thing. Out walking, was he?"

"He was fascinated by the squid. Said he'd been an ichthyologist from Scripps, down south. Interested in the glandular functions of carp, he said. If you live long enough you'll meet people who specialize in any damn thing; do you know what I mean? Apparently squids were a sort of sideline with him, carp glands being his heart's desire. Look here."

Andrew looked. The squid had been sliced open lengthwise, the cut so clean and straight that Andrew had taken it simply for a natural flap of skin. What the slice meant, though, Andrew was at a loss to say. Had Pennyman been out on the beach dissecting sea creatures? Grimacing just a little, Andrew pulled the skin back to expose an enormous cuttlebone and organ cavity. The inside of the beast was burned black, as if someone had kindled a fire in it. Andrew stood up and stepped back, turning toward the ocean and gasping in a lungful of sea air.

"Damndest thing, isn't it? Stinks like anything," said the man, staring into the bowl of his pipe. "Your friend seemed to expect it though, the burned organs. Put his nose nearly in 'em, as if they were cut flowers. He had a pair of gloves to put on and a sort of apron. Didn't want his white trousers soiled, I guess. Do you know what he did?''

Andrew shook his head, half-expecting to hear that Pennyman had made a sandwich out of the squid's heart and eaten it.

"He rummaged around in there and came up with a silver coin tangled in a bit of fishing line. He nipped it free with a nail clippers, and then he washed it in ocean water, dried it on his apron, put it in his pocket, and walked away. Just like that. He had me going, too, for a moment. I didn't know what to think, until I remembered the magician business. It was a gag, is what it was, and I was taken right in. There was a stage magician in Las Vegas who did that—with a gold ring and a loaf of bread out of the oven. He'd get a ring from someone in the audience, you see, very valuable, and make it disappear, and then ten minutes later he'd holler at a random waiter to bring over a hot bun, and . . .''

But Andrew wasn't listening any longer. The story of the ring and the bun didn't signify. The story of the coin in the squid did—somehow. Had Pennyman been fishing for squid last night from the end of the pier? It certainly seemed so. He'd caught one, at least—and a big one, too. It must have broken his line, of course, and he'd come out that morning looking for it—which was odd, unless he was certain that the lure, whatever it was, would kill it and that the heavy surf would wash it ashore. That scenario worked, given what Andrew knew. What it *meant*, though, was hidden from him as he trudged back up the beach, idly rubbing sand off the murex shell.

He stood looking out over the ocean. The fog had thinned suddenly, and he could see the glassy green humps of smaller waves breaking inside on the sandy, suddenly shallow seabottom. Pennyman seemed to be fishing for more than just the idle squid. Andrew and Pickett and maybe Rose, too, were schooling around his lure. One day soon, if they didn't look sharp, he'd give it a bit of a jerk and they'd jump for it. He'd reel them in, just like that, and stuff them into an old gunnysack.

Well, Andrew would be ready for him. Pennyman foolishly underestimated him and Pickett. That was his error. It was high time that Andrew struck back—subtly, of course. It was enough at first merely to make Pennyman wonder, merely to make him peer over his shoulder a little more often and be a little less carefree and smug. Andrew nodded at the ocean and squinted into the fog, thinking that for Rose's own protection he'd keep this whole unsettling business away from her. Let Rose think anything about Pennyman that she'd like to think. When the time was right, Andrew would unmask him; he'd splash mud onto Pennyman's trousers; he'd muss up his hair; he'd clip the point off the bottom of his beard; he'd play the nailed nickel trick on him; he'd . . .

"Hey!" shouted Andrew, leaping and waving his hand in the air. "What!" He pitched the giant murex onto the wet sand and shook his right hand. A drop of blood oozed out from the soft skin between his fingers. He'd been pinched, and it hurt like hell. He rubbed it and bent over the shell. A hermit crab leaned out, enormous and hairy and menacing him with a single pincer. Its eyes stood on stalks, like the eyes of a moon creature, and it seemed to be looking at him from about sixty different directions at once. It hiked up its seashell and walked away into the ocean. For a moment Andrew could see it beneath the clear water—a dark shadow making for the open sea, going home to a pleasant, weedy grotto, where it had an easy chair, maybe, set up in the shade of a sea fan.

The sun broke through the mists just then, in shafts of piercing white light, and Andrew saw that he wasn't fifty yards from the pier. The beach was dotted with people now, sitting in folding chairs and setting up umbrellas. Suddenly there were children laughing and running. A trio of smart-aleck-looking surfers ran past, sliding their surfboards into the morning swell and leaping onto them in one smooth motion, letting a glassy little wavelet slap across the nose of their boards and full into their faces.

On an impulse, Andrew waded out into the shallows, thinking that the saltwater might brace him. It had been years since he'd swum in the ocean. He remembered how good it had been just to get wet. The water was stingingly cold, though, and when a wave washed through, splashing across his rolled-up pants, he turned around and fled, his feet already numb. Youth, thought Andrew, shaking his head. Go figure it. He waved two fingers back over his shoulder at the departing hermit crab to show it that there were no hard feelings. He understood well enough. A man's home . . . after all. He'd said as much himself, just last night. It was time to reach out of the shadows and give Pennyman a pinch. He grinned. There were a thousand ways to do it.

SEVEN

"... but when the truffle pigs were driven into the forests of Fontainbleau, a great fat sow escaped into a stand of birch, from which it emerged with a spoon in its teeth and a beggar at its heels, escaping withal from master and beggar both, and never seen again in the region."

Louis Vinteuil
Ahasuer: Le Juif-Errant
C. K. Dexter Haven, trans.

THE TRICK WAS to befuddle them. That's what would strike terror into their shabby hearts. You could send a man an anonymous letter that would paralyze him without his half-understanding it. Tom Sawyer had been a genius at it after all, but he hadn't known why. Andrew sat in the bar, doodling on a scrap of paper. It wasn't enough to write "You'll die at midnight" or "Beware the singing corpse" or something like that. Theatrical notes weren't worth a penny when it came to literate men like Pennyman. Nor was it worth anything to be straightforward, like "Quit meddling in our affairs" or "Cross me once more and you'll suffer for it." That sort of thing was childish. There could be no hint of the Marquis of Queensberry about it.

The message had to be cryptic, almost nonsensical. There could be no sane explanation for it on earth. "Give me back my sister's chewing gum" wouldn't be bad, but it might be misconceived to be humorous, which wouldn't at all do. Andrew scratched his head. It had to be something short, and it had to seem to be complete, although it couldn't *really* be, not in any recognizable sense. He had the envelope addressed and stamped. He'd purposely misspelled "Pennyman," making it "Pengleman" instead, just to frost the cake, to raise Pennyman's eyebrows before he'd even torn the letter open. And Andrew had perfumed the envelope, too, and picked out a stamp from the post office's fish collection—a Japanese koi, appropriately enough. Pennyman would be steamrollered by it.

He was struck suddenly with inspiration, and grinning, he bent over the paper, shifting the pencil to his left hand in order to make a general mess of the note. "MOKE DAT YIGARETTE," he wrote, in a laborious, back-slanted hand, all the letters cockeyed and barely resembling each other. It was perfect. It meant nothing at all, but it seemed to imply something—smoke, perhaps, maybe poison smoke, maybe what? Ziggurats, mystical pyramids— certainly nothing that Pennyman could be sure of.

Andrew had debated cutting letters out of a magazine and gluing them on, but that was cheap, certainly, and would deflate the whole thing accordingly. He traced over the letters, darkening them, and dotted the *i* with a happy face. That would kill him. Andrew nearly laughed out loud. What would Pennyman make of it? Nothing. There was nothing on earth that he *could* make of it, and therein lay the beauty of it.

It would purely and simply flatten him out, like drinking undiluted grain alcohol by mistake. He'd think it was written by a foreigner at first, but then it would seem less and less likely to him that a foreigner would choose to utter such a phrase at all, and less likely yet that he would so weirdly misspell it. After the first few moments of numbed confusion that would surely follow Pennyman's opening it up and reading it, then rereading it and turning it over, a fog of genuine bewilderment would rise in his mind. There would follow a moment of fear and wild alarm. Here, he would say to himself, is something I don't at all understand. And the idea of it would paralyze him.

Pickett would be proud of Andrew, although Pickett would be shy of sending it. In truth Pickett had a little too much fear of these Caretakers, whoever they were, and would balk at the idea of taking them on. He was the man to *study* them. It was up to Andrew to step out of the shadows and confront them. He misfolded the letter, crammed it into its tiny envelope, and sealed it with Scotch tape. All in all it was an impressive package. He decided to drive to the Naples post office to mail it, just to throw Pennyman off the scent. And on the way back he'd stop by the telephone company and order up a phone for Pennyman's room and an extension for the attic observatory. Andrew would graciously offer to pay the charges, except for long-distance calls, of course. Pennyman needn't know about the extension.

He considered for a moment whether he ought to push things just a little bit: not a bloody horse's head in Pennyman's bed or anything like that—but a lizard in his shoe, perhaps, or some fairly horrible substance like honey or cornstarch or sulphur dissolved in his hair oil, or maybe a gag from the joke shop—rubber excrement, say,—on the toe of his shoe. Andrew started to write out a list, a battle plan, but then he thought better of it and tore the list apart, stuffing it into his coat pocket. He'd keep no records. And for the moment at least he'd abandon the idea of those sorts of gags. They were the sort of thing that would give a man away, and they weren't half the ploy that the note was. The note was a corker.

It was just two in the afternoon. The fog had burned off entirely, but there was still just the hint of moisture in the air. He'd break out the paint and brushes in an hour, when it was drier. How long could it take to get a good section of wall painted? A couple of hours? He'd have a really solid go at it later, after he'd mailed the letter and hit the phone company.

Writing the note had cheered him considerably. He was finally *doing* something, for heaven's sake, and was no longer just the passive observer idling away his time in a chair and getting his toe trod on by people with destinations. He went out the door whistling, driving slowly past the house on his way toward the boulevard in order to assess this business of painting it, and calculating as he drove just how much a man like him might accomplish once he rolled up his sleeves and pitched in.

He hadn't driven for more than eight minutes—up the Coast Highway and across the bridge onto Second Street—when he saw Pennyman tapping along the sidewalk. He looked poorly, somehow, as if he were showing his age. In fact, with the afternoon sunlight shining on him he looked almost like a walking mummy, and his hair was slick with oil, as if it had taken half a gallon or so to make it cooperate. The sight of him in that state almost made Andrew whistle a tune.

He stepped on the brake and started to turn off onto one of the little streets leading up to the Marine Stadium, but then he swerved back onto Second Street again and angled in toward the curb. It wouldn't do to lose Pennyman. There were a thousand streets for him to disappear into. It was better to park the car and follow on foot. He locked the doors and jumped out, fed dimes and nickels to the parking meter, and loped along up the sidewalk in order to catch up. Pennyman was walking briskly and determinedly.

Andrew waited for a break in the traffic, keeping well away down the block and lingering now and then in the storefront shadows so as to appear leisurely. Pennyman rounded a corner and disappeared, heading toward the isthmus and Alamitos Beach, and Andrew jogged across the street in pursuit, slowing down as he came to the corner and half-expecting Pennyman to be waiting there for him, just out of sight. He found himself in front of Moneywort's Tropical Fish, run now by Moneywort's nephew, a man referred to only as ''Adams'' who'd worked there for years, making Moneywort's life miserable while Moneywort was still alive. He was a nasty sort altogether, and the place had declined and lost much of its magic since Moneywort's death.

Andrew put his hands in his pockets and slouched along. He'd have a quick look around the corner, and if Pennyman were there, anticipating him, he'd pretend that he was simply heading for Moneywort's, to buy feeder goldfish for the Surinam toad—which wouldn't, in fact, be a bad idea. The toad would be happy with some goldfish, and there was something cheerful and solid about the notion of a happy toad. He'd buy dried shrimps for Aunt Naomi's cats, too, just to cement the impression that he was a friend to cats. Well . . . He admitted it to himself. He seemed almost to *be* a friend to cats. It was a half dozen of them all at once in the attic that gave him the pip.

Here was the corner. He stepped past it, down off the curb and heading across toward the Texaco station, where he would conspicuously get a drink of water at the fountain. He'd wait until he was almost there to glance down the street, and make it look as if there was nothing anxious about him, as if the last thing in the world he was doing was following someone. But he couldn't wait. Halfway across the street he turned his head to the side and pretended to scratch his neck. The long block stretching away toward Naples Lane was empty; there wasn't a soul on it except for a woman in hair curlers who was watering her lawn.

Andrew continued straight on across, cutting over to the gas station drinking fountain, which was clogged with chewing gum. He turned away in disgust after having pretended to drink. Either Pennyman had slipped into one of the houses farther along the block or else he'd gone into Moneywort's, through the back door. Of course he had.

Andrew would have to make up his mind quickly. He couldn't appear to be hanging about. The die was cast. He pushed into the tropical fish shop, reaching up immediately to shush the bell that would jingle to announce his arrival, and prepared to be pleasantly surprised to see Pennyman there. But there was no sign of Pennyman. The outer room of the shop was empty.

Feeling like a private investigator out of a forties movie, he eased the door shut behind him and let go of the bell. There was silence except for the hum of aquaria. The shop was almost dim, lit only by a couple of incandescent lamps near the counter and by countless twenty-five-watt bulbs in aquarium reflectors, the light of which was darkened, somehow, by the shadowy water in the tanks, and cast a shifting, murky glow over the dank concrete floor. There was the sound of bubbling airstones and the pleasantly musty smell of waterweeds and wet sand and fish.

The shop comprised a half-dozen small rooms with corridors leading back and forth. Pennyman could be in any one of them, waiting for him. Andrew cocked his head and listened. There was the faint sound of murmuring in the back of the shop, and then the sound of low, unpleasant laughter.

He tiptoed past the counter and in among the aquaria, watched by a thousand hovering fish that blinked out of grottoes built of waterfall rock and weighted driftwood and kelp-like stands of elodea and foxtail and Amazon swordplant. The murmuring grew louder and then fell away. There sounded a brief clattering and splashing and then silence again. Andrew peered past a narrow doorway into another room of aquaria. Beyond that was a broad storeroom with a door that fronted the alley down which Pennyman must have come. *If* he were in the shop at all. He mightn't be, of course. Andrew slid into a shadow, peered back over his shoulder, and then crouched down onto his knees, peeking around the jamb. There was Pennyman all right, just as he'd guessed, but alone in the storeroom. He stood with his back to Andrew.

One wall of the storeroom was simply an enormous aquarium—easily a thousand gallons, probably more like two thousand. It stretched from halfway up the wall to the ceiling, encased in hammered steel along the perimeter and braced every four feet or so. It must have opened into the attic, so that it would seem from the floor of the attic to be a sort of rectangular pool. A dozen stupendous carp, scaly and golden in the glow of hidden, overhead bulbs, clustered in the corner of the tank. The water was agitated and water plants were torn loose and floating.

Suddenly a broad net plunged into the water of the aquarium, and directly after that a head appeared along with the hand and arm holding the net. It was the head of Adams, Moneywort's worthless nephew, who was trying to dip out a fish. He was shirtless and wore a skin-diving mask and snorkel, and his dark hair swirled in the moving water as he looked out through the thick glass at Pennyman, who gestured impatiently toward the tank. The man swung the net ponderously at a big carp that had strayed away from the crowd huddling on the bottom. The net crept along through the water, though, and the carp easily eluded it, but made the mistake of fleeing into a back corner. The net wavered in toward it, and the carp nosed frantically against either wall of the tank, befuddled by having too many options. It burst away in a wild rush, swirling up sediment from the bottom, straight into the net, which Adams hauled up and out of the water.

There were noises in the attic: drippings and splashings, a curse and the sound of compressed air being blown into a plastic bag. Then Adams appeared on the little tilted stair-ladder that angled into the attic crawlspace, struggling to carry a long, lidded Styrofoam box. Pennyman stepped across to grab the end of it, and Andrew pulled back out of sight. It wouldn't do to be seen crouching in the doorway. Then he stood up slowly and straightened his coat, expecting the two men to wander out toward the front of the shop now, and find him. Just then the bell over the front door began to jangle.

Andrew hunched over to peer into a tank full of marine tropicals. Reflected in the glass of the tank he could see two doors—the door to the storeroom and a kitty-corner door leading out to the corridor that connected to another room full of aquaria and also led out to the rest of the shop. He pretended to study the fish in the tank in front of him. Adams appeared and disappeared past the second doorway, going out to see who it was that had come in. He hadn't seen Andrew. Then there was the sound of the back door shutting; that would be Pennyman, going out the same way he'd come in.

Andrew thought hard and fast. Pennyman was gone—or so it seemed—and that was good. Should he follow? It would be easy enough to slip out the same door. Adams wouldn't see him that way—wouldn't wonder how Andrew had got in without dinging the front door bell. But somehow Andrew didn't want to leave, or rather, he didn't much want to follow Pennyman any longer. There was something mortally dangerous about the man and in the power he seemed to have over people. Today especially. In the watery light of the storeroom he had looked like Mr. Death, like the personification of evil and decay. Andrew would wait for Pickett. Pickett was due home soon enough. Why press it?

But where was Pennyman going with the carp? Certainly not back to the inn. Andrew wouldn't stand for that, for Pennyman setting up aquaria. Was he going to eat it? Bring it to Rose as a gift? It was probably a taste he'd acquired in the Orient. Heaven knew what kinds of tastes he *hadn't* acquired in the Orient. Adams slipped past the door again and into the storeroom.

The sudden appearance of Adams had been startling, but in a moment Andrew realized he was safe; he still hadn't been seen. There would be no chance of sliding out the back door, though. He waited. There was nothing to panic about. He was a customer now, and nothing else. He still wanted those feeder fish and the shrimps for the cats. In a bit, when he was sure it was a good idea, he'd step quietly back out to the front of the shop and tug on the bell a couple of times, pretending that he had just that moment come in.

He focused on the fish gliding around in the aquarium before him: fat clown fish lazying back and forth through the poisonous tentacles of blue anemones. Somehow it seemed to signify to Andrew; it seemed as if it ought to be a metaphor or something, and he thought idly about how the most disconnected things developed secret connections when you saw them in the right sort of light—moonlight, maybe, or the suffused light of an aquarium. He wondered what it might mean—the clown fish and the anemones—and he listened to the momentary silence and then to Adams in the back room whispering, "Mr. Pennyman?" Adams waited, as if he were listening, too, and then he said it again, like a conspirator, very low and urgently. Mr. Pennyman, of course, didn't answer.

There was a hand on Andrew's shoulder suddenly, and Andrew nearly shrieked. He couldn't, though: There was a hand over his mouth, too. He stiffened, wondering whether to slam his assailant in the rib cage with his elbow or to pretend to be a surprised customer—which he was, really. The hand on his shoulder had a ring on it that Andrew recognized—a round signet sort of ring that looked like an old doubloon, or some other vaguely familiar old coin.

He turned his head slowly, and the hand released his shoulder.

There was Uncle Arthur, standing behind him, the hand with the ring on it just touching his lips. The old man shook his head and took his other hand away from Andrew's mouth. Andrew relaxed. He'd been holding his breath, and he let it out now in a long whoosh. He started to speak, but Uncle Arthur cut him off with a gesture, then shook his head again and jerked his thumb back over his shoulder toward the front door. Andrew nodded and set out alone, muffling the bell again and squinting at the bright sunlight when he opened the door.

It wasn't until he was outside and walking back up Second Street toward his car that he began to wonder why in the world Uncle Arthur was messing around in Moneywort's shop. He and Moneywort had been friends, but now Moneywort was dead, and Arthur had little interest in tropical fish—no real reason for visiting the shop. Andrew would have plenty of mysteries to lay at Pickett's feet, although he wouldn't, alas, have any shrimps to lay at the feet of the cats.

So what was Uncle Arthur doing there? That's what Andrew wondered as he motored away up Second Street toward the post office. Coincidence wouldn't answer. Over the past week Andrew had come to disbelieve in coincidence. There were only two answers that were any good: Uncle Arthur had come 'round to Moneywort's shop for the same reason Pennyman had—to buy an enormous carp—or else Arthur himself had been *following* Pennyman, a development that wouldn't much surprise Pickett.

Pennyman had got home before him. He was going in through the front door when Andrew pulled in along the curb. And he wasn't carrying the Styrofoam box, either. Andrew sat in the Metropolitan again, thinking. It was nearly four o'clock, and once again Andrew had managed to do nothing at all that day but avoid Rose. He'd gone out after seashells that morning but had collected mysteries instead, each of which was pretty enough, in its way.

But one wanted the mysteries to add up somehow. What Andrew had was a jumble of them, like shells rattling in a bag, and he had the growing suspicion that one day soon he'd reach into the bag to draw one out and he'd be pinched by it. He had to get them sorted, to see which of them contained hidden crabs, which of them stank of dead things, which of them he could hear the distant murmur of the ocean in. He turned on the car radio and then turned it off again. There was no excuse on earth for wasting the rest of the day. He reminded himself of what had happened yesterday, a day that had started out so promising and then declined into despair. The two A.M. Cheerios powwow around the kitchen table had fetched it all back together just a bit, had saved him. Now here he was idling away his time, losing the little tract of ground he'd got back with Rose and Naomi.

It was time to haul out the paint. He had painter's coveralls in the garage. It wouldn't take him six minutes to pull them on and get started. He had the sudden urge to announce his intentions to Rose, but he squashed it. Let her stumble upon him at work. He'd be whistling away, paintbrush in hand, cap pulled down over his eyes. He'd hang his paint scraper in the loop in the coveralls and shove a rag into his back pocket, next to his putty knife. People would drive by on the street, and, mistaking him for a professional painter, they'd stop and ask him for an estimate, appreciating his work, happy that these old houses were being sparkled up. He was working late in the afternoon, wasn't he? Well, he'd say, nightfall was the only clock *he* paid any attention to—nightfall and sunrise, the two great motivators of mankind. He was a philosopher-painter. Which one of the Greeks had talked about that sort of thing? Plato, maybe.

He picked up his coffee cup, which had lain there on the floor of the car since that morning. There was a little dribble of coffee in it, dried on the inside in a sticky line. He wished suddenly that the cup were full, but he couldn't risk going in to brew up a fresh one. He couldn't risk going after a beer, either. He'd have to paint dry, which was a pity, really, painting being such a boring job. Having something to drink—whatever it might be—was an end in itself, a pastime. Hose water would have to do. He sat up abruptly, realizing that another ten minutes had passed. He'd been daydreaming again.

In a fit of determination he climbed out of the car, closed the door softly, and stepped around into the backyard, hurrying into the garage. There on the bench was the sack full of smashed glass. The sight of it depressed him hugely, and he picked it up and flung it into the trash can in the corner. To hell with melting lead. He hadn't the time to waste on it. There was no use trying to fiddle away old mistakes anyway; Rose wouldn't be fooled. Not for a moment. All he would accomplish would be to look like an utter moron, and he couldn't afford that sort of thing any more. He yanked on the coveralls, pried open his paint, and hurriedly stirred it with a piece of stick. In minutes he stood alongside the house, spreading out a canvas dropcloth. To hell with painting the garage, too. The house was bigger game.

He began to dust off the house with a horsehair brush, intending to clean a good-sized area before starting to paint. It was nothing, this painting business. He studied the edge of his paintbrush. It was a good one, a Purdy four inch—sharp and clean. He dipped it into the paint, slipped the back edge of it across the metal can rim, and cut in a two-foot section of one of the clapboards, catching a drip and smoothing it out nicely. He stepped back and looked at it happily. It seemed to him to be evidence of something—that he wasn't entirely a worthless crud, perhaps. He dipped the brush again and then stopped and listened. There were voices murmuring, one of them angry.

He laid the paintbrush across the mouth of the can and rubbed his hands on the rag. It sounded like Rose; the angry voice did. He wouldn't have that. He would put a quick stop to it. There was no one in the house who had the right to argue with her, except maybe himself. If it was Pennyman giving her trouble . . . A hot flush of anger surged through him and he stepped around toward the front door, nearly breaking into a run, his fists clenched. Then there came another voice; it *was* Pennyman, but he wasn't arguing with Rose. The woman's voice belonged to Mrs. Gummidge, and both voices were coming through the open window of Mrs. Gummidge's ground-floor bedroom. She was the only one of them who occupied a room down below—a sort of maid's quarters with its own bath and kitchenette. The window was open just a fraction.

Andrew braked and then skipped backward two steps, spinning around and lunging after the paintbrush and paint. He fetched them, then tiptoed back around until he stood just beside the open window, and then very quietly and haphazardly he began to paint the siding. He hadn't brought the horsehair brush, and there wasn't time to waste going back after it, so he splashed the paint on over ten years worth of grime. He barely breathed, listening to the rising and falling of voices.

"I should think I'd get more than that," said Mrs. Gummidge tearfully.

There was a pause, then Pennyman's voice: "I haven't got more. You can appreciate that. It's a tiresome, slow process, wringing it out like that and distilling it down and decanting it and aging it. It isn't done in a day. And the fish themselves are fearsomely rare. When Adams killed them all out of stupidity, with his cheap thermostats, it was six months before the damage could be put right. If it hadn't been for the quick trip up to San Francisco . . . Well . . . Thank heavens for Han Koi's man up in Chinatown. It's only in the last month that Adams has got it all going again, and that means a month or two more before there's a surplus."

"A surplus! I'm not asking for a surplus. I'm asking for a very little bit. A bit of yours is what I'm asking for. You can spare it. You'd think it was narcotics."

"And it works that very way," said Pennyman in a soft and fatherly voice. "You don't need any more than I've given you. I *do*, though. Certainly you can see that. Don't cut any capers now. We're days away from it. You know that. *I* can't sacrifice a drop. If my powers aren't honed and strong, then we're done for; we might as well not have bothered."

There was silence for a moment as Andrew continued to slap paint on the wooden siding, paying no attention to the finer points of his work. He idly painted upwards and sideways and crossways, his head cocked, waiting for the conversation to continue. He could hear Mrs. Gummidge crying almost silently—stifling it, as if she didn't want to be overheard by anyone chancing to pass by in the hallway. Andrew smiled. They had no earthly suspicion that the enemy stood right outside their window, got up in coveralls and a hat. He was killing two birds with one stone; that was the truth of it.

The conversation started up again. There was the sound of glass clinking against glass and of Pennyman muttering something about cups of tea. Andrew couldn't make it out.

"Just a little at a time," Mrs. Gummidge said.

"Why don't you give that up? This has nothing to do with personal vendettas. We're above that."

"I don't believe we are," she said after a moment. "What about the books? Aren't we above that, too?"

"Damn the books. What books?"

"Don't think I don't see anything. Don't think it's not me that does a bit of dusting and vacuuming around this house." Her voice rose. In a moment she'd be hysterical.

"Shh!" Pennyman hushed her up, cutting her off before she had revealed anything at all.

Andrew was baffled. The whole conversation was baffling. Now there was another baffling silence during which he heard the back door shut. That could only be Rose, coming outside. She'd see that the garage door was open and she'd go in to have a look. Then she'd find the lid to the paint can and his jacket hanging over the bench vise, and she'd come around to the front to see if her wondering eyes had deceived her.

There was a grunt of loathing, as if Mrs. Gummidge had swallowed a toad, and then an ungodly sort of fishy smell wafted out through the window, so putrid and overpowering that Andrew reeled back, turning his face away. There was Rose, standing on the sidewalk. He might have predicted it. He *had* predicted it. He smiled at her and waved his paintbrush. At least he hadn't been crushing water glasses or experimenting with cups full of cold coffee.

He moved away from the window before he said anything, hauling his paint can back around to where his dropcloth lay and setting it down. "Thought I'd take advantage of the sunlight and get in a bit of painting."

Rose nodded—not happily, it seemed to him. He stepped back

and looked at the house. There were two short strips of clapboard painted very neatly on the corner where he'd started in. Then there was a sort of mess of fresh paint near Mrs. Gummidge's window. It looked something like a psychological test. He waved his brush at it, as if in explanation, thinking hard for something to say. He'd been caught out again. But at least he'd been caught by Rose and not by Pennyman. It would have gone hard on him if Pennyman had discovered him listening at the window. And of course he *would* discover it, too, as soon as he saw the weirdly painted patch of siding. Pennyman wasn't an idiot.

"I'm amazed," said Rose, seeming suddenly to be happy with Andrew's antics, as if she'd taken the long view and come to the conclusion that *any* work was good work, any painting good painting. "What's the point of being so wild with it, though?"

"Bad grain in the wood. The redwood seems to be delaminating there. Probably a matter of too much afternoon sun. When that sort of thing happens you have to scrub it on, to get it in under the grain lines where the wood is coming apart. It acts as a sort of adhesive. Looks bizarre now, I'll admit, but once the whole thing is painted . . ."

Rose nodded. "Why don't you stick to one side at a time. That way if you don't get it all done, it won't look quite so peculiar."

"Absolutely," said Andrew. "I got carried away, I guess. I saw what the problem would be with the wood and all and decided to have a go at it. I couldn't resist. You know how I am when it comes to tackling little problems like that."

Rose nodded. "Shouldn't you clean it first? All that dirt . . ."

"Bonding agent," said Andrew, hating himself. "It'll look good freshened up, won't it?"

"*I'll* be pretty happy with it," said Rose. "But why don't you clean up? You don't have much of the afternoon left anyway."

Andrew picked up his paint can and moved across toward the open window again, talking loudly to alert Mrs. Gummidge and Pennyman, if they were still in the room, that he was out on the lawn. His spying was pretty much at an end. If he were smart, he'd haul out a floodlight and an extension cord and try to get the mess of paint smoothed out and cleaned up before he quit for the evening. Rose would admire his sticking to it, and Pennyman wouldn't wander out in the morning and find anything suspicious.

"Bring my dinner out on a plate, will you?"

"If you want," said Rose, heading back up the sidewalk toward the garage. "Don't wear yourself out, though."

That was just like Rose, worrying about him. He dipped his brush into the paint, straightened up, and looked square into the face of Pennyman, which was regarding him out the window, grinning slyly. "Good evening," rasped Andrew, startled.

Pennyman nodded, giggling just a little bit, then laughing harder, then bursting into such a paroxysm of laughter that for a moment Andrew thought he'd choke. And for as long as Pennyman laughed, Andrew couldn't step a foot nearer the house, and he began to hope very fervently that Pennyman *would* choke, that the laughter would simply explode him like an overfilled balloon.

EIGHT

"Our affections and beliefs are wiser than we; the best that is in us is better than we can understand . . ."

Robert Louis Stevenson
Virginibus Puerisque

IT WAS LATE—after midnight. Pennyman hadn't come in all day. Andrew was sure of it. He would give the old man another hour, maybe catch an hour of sleep himself, if he could. It was high time he had a look inside Pennyman's room, and this was as good a night as any. He punched buttons on his little battery-operated kitchen timer, setting it for sixty minutes. In order to muffle it, he shoved it under the pillow on the couch. Then he lay down and fell asleep almost at once.

He woke up from a dream involving pigs, wondering where he was, wondering at the ringing buzz in his ear, and he groped for the alarm clock. Then he remembered. He sat up groggily, rubbing his eyes. He could barely keep them wedged open. His back was nearly murdering him, and he was stiff in the joints. He suddenly wanted very much to go back to sleep, to lie on the couch forever. But he couldn't. He had a mission. When he stood up, though, he almost tumbled forward onto his face. An hour's worth of sleep had just made him more beat; his mind was a sandy pudding. Then he thought about the pending adventure, and the thought woke him up. He stretched, tucked in his shirt, and stepped out into the livingroom.

The tennis ball he'd set against the front door still sat there. Pennyman hadn't come in. He was gone for the night—something fairly common lately. Mrs. Gummidge had mentioned having spoken to him before dinner. She had said that Pennyman had spent most of the day in his room and then had gone out to a relative's house in Glendale, where he would doubtless spend the night. But neither Andrew nor Rose had seen Pennyman that morning, and Andrew suspected that he'd gone off early and hadn't returned, that Mrs. Gummidge had lied. Pennyman was using Mrs. Gummidge for an alibi, it seemed. From Andrew's point of view, a man who needed an alibi was usually guilty as a gibbon ape.

Andrew didn't much trust Mrs. Gummidge, not since he'd overheard them at the window. He was certain that they were up to something together, that they'd joined forces since coming to live at the inn. In one way it relieved him just a little. Mrs. Gummidge, after all . . . One would have thought that Pennyman could find more capable allies. Perhaps his liaison with Mrs. Gummidge was evidence that Pennyman was mostly show, mostly facade. He was the sort, certainly, who *seemed* to be. That was something Andrew could sniff out pretty accurately. Andrew had a good nose for falseness.

He looked around for something else—something that would make a clatter. The fireplace tools would do. He left them hanging precariously in their wrought iron holder and tilted the whole business against the door. If Pennyman came in now, the whole house would know it. Andrew would have some explaining to do, but it would be better than Pennyman sneaking in and catching Andrew rummaging in his room.

He creaked up the stairs, listening to the snores echoing down the stairwell from Aunt Naomi's room in the attic, listening for sounds of restlessness from the bedroom where Rose, by now, had been asleep for three hours. He couldn't help grinning.

There was excitement in skulking around a dark house after midnight, doing battle with the forces of evil—or the forces of something.

One of Aunt Naomi's cats strolled down from above and stood blinking at him on the stairs. Then it jumped past him and ran down the stairs to the ground-floor landing, where it sat on its haunches and stared out toward the front door. Another cat appeared above, coming along down to rub against Andrew's leg. It sat down outside Pennyman's door and meowed softly. The cat below meowed as if in response. Andrew had the uncanny feeling that the cats were up to something—that they were signaling each other. He was certain somehow that they were on his side, though—that once again they were watching over him.

He suddenly felt surefooted and keen. The thrill of it all had scoured the sleep from his head. He could picture the interior of Pennyman's bedroom—the chair, the bureau, the bookcases, the single bed tucked into an alcove in the wall and with a curtain hung across in front of it. He'd found and bought the furniture himself. Rose had sewed the bedchamber curtain, and Andrew had installed it on a wooden rod across the front of the bed alcove. There wasn't a square inch of the room that he wasn't familiar with. He really didn't need the penlight in his pocket; he could feel his way from stem to stern in the dark.

Suddenly and without a tickle of warning, he sneezed. He squelched it with his hand, sort of moomphing it into his palm. He pinched his nose to stop an inevitable second sneeze as he froze there on the darkened stairs, listening again, his heart slamming. No one stirred. The snores continued unabated from overhead, and in the still, enclosed air of the stairwell hung just a hint of the smell of cats. It was comforting, somehow, and hadn't the power anymore to disgust him or set him into a rage.

He still didn't like the idea of a house full of them, though. His resolve to deal with them had weakened a bit, but he still had a score to settle there. He had to be the master of his own house. One thing at a time, though; that was how it had to be. Pennyman first, the cats afterward. He wouldn't make the mistake of overreaching himself. He tiptoed past the cat, bending over to pet it and feeling guilty again for plotting against it. He paused outside Pennyman's door, listening for one last time. Then he steeled himself, shoved the door open slowly, and stepped into the dark interior of the room.

There was the smell of books and rosewater and bay rum. An octagonal, hinged mirror sitting atop the bureau caught a glint of moonlight through the window. Arranged atop the bureau were carefully laid out toiletries: tortoiseshell combs and brushes, a mustache scissors, bottles of hair tonic and skin lotion, an emery board and another mirror—for admiring the back of his head, apparently. It was an unimpressive lot of credentials, but it was all Pennyman had to recommend himself. Mess his hair up and he was a sorry-looking scarecrow.

Andrew abruptly considered tumbling the lot of it out the window. He could watch Pennyman's pride crack to bits on the stones of the pathway below. Walk with the proud, he thought, and you shall be scornful. That was true enough. If there was one thing that Pennyman surely was, it was scornful. Andrew was—what? —scornful of it. He grinned again. That's what tripped him up every time—his pride in being humble. It beat all. There was no way to lick it.

He found himself contemplating a hairbrush, idly thinking about philosophy. He shook his head, clearing it again. There was no time for that. At any moment the fireplace tools might clatter down on the hardwood floor and Andrew's mission would come to a bad end. What if Rose, waking up and stepping into the hallway, caught him sneaking out of Pennyman's room? What if she got downstairs before him and found the fireplace tools strewn across the floor? Who would appear to be the fool, the lunatic? He or Pennyman? He knew the answer to that. He also knew that Rose wasn't the sort to lie in bed and shake when there were strange noises in the house. She was every bit as likely to pull on her bathrobe and have a look. He wondered suddenly what he was doing there at all, meddling in Pennyman's room.

The business of the fish tonic—that was central. Come to think of it, that was the other odor, mingling with the hair tonic and the bay rum and the general old-house smell. And there was something more, too—the faint smell of something sweet and chemical. What was it?—perfume, perhaps. A woman's perfume.

His eyes were adjusted to the dark, but the faint moonlight wasn't quite enough illumination to do the trick. He pulled out the penlight and switched it on, shining it first at this, then at that. There was a plethora of drawers in the room—five in the bureau, two in the desk, six in the built-in cupboard below the bed. He wished he could look through them all, but it would be folly. What if Rose awakened and went downstairs out of kindness to him, to wake him up on the couch and urge him to come up to bed? He'd have to hurry.

There it was, as if it had been left for him. On the little mahogany table next to the head of the bed alcove sat a half-filled bottle, open and with a glass vial lying beside it. It was odd that Pennyman would leave it open, and even odder that he'd leave it out like that, unless he were so conceited and sure of himself that he couldn't imagine anyone slipping in like this. Andrew pulled his silver flask out of his coat pocket, twisted open the cap, tilted the fish elixir bottle over it, and drained off a quarter inch or so—no more than a half ounce, just enough to have a bit of laboratory work done on it.

He set the bottle down, recapped his flask, and put it away. He was torn between hauling open drawers and getting the hell out. What might he find there? Anything at all; that was the answer. It was odds-on that there was something incriminating in Pennyman's goods—some telling affidavit, some revealing letter, a photograph, a recipe for brewing up poisons out of blowfish. It was tempting, but far too dangerous. He'd be back—when it was safer and he had more time. He'd bring Pickett along and do the job right; one of them to rifle Pennyman's goods and the other to keep watch.

He shined the penlight once more around the room, but the tiny beam wasn't enough to reveal anything telling. One bit of real information; that's all he asked for. The elixir was well and good, but what could it reveal? That it had been extracted from a carp? He already knew that much, or at least suspected it.

He turned to the curtain across the bed, reached up and grabbed it below its wooden rings, and slid it open in a rush.

Mrs. Gummidge lay there, asleep.

Andrew shouted, hoarse and silent as if in a dream. He jammed his fist partly into his mouth and reeled back into the desk, paralyzed with heart-hammering fear and flinging his penlight away onto the floor. It blinked out when it hit, and he scrabbled after it, down onto his hands and knees. It had rolled under the chair. He flailed for it, looking back over his shoulder, certain now that Mrs. Gummidge was dead. He couldn't bear to have his back turned to her.

He twisted around and stood up, abandoning the flashlight and stepping toward the door in long, silent strides, squinting at Mrs. Gummidge and breathing through clenched teeth. He paused there for a moment. If she was dead he'd have to take action . . . Steeling himself, he squinted at her, lying there in the shadow of the alcove, stiff and awful like an old-woman doll. She was breathing, though. And she stirred just a little.

It struck him suddenly that it wasn't Mrs. Gummidge at all, but was Pennyman in a Mrs. Gummidge mask, and the thought propelled his hand toward the doorknob like a shot out of a sling. But that was madness, and he told himself so as he whipped the door back, stepped out into the hallway, and threw himself past the waiting cat and nearly head-first down the stairs. Straight into the kitchen he went and out into the bar. He poured a shaky drink out of the scotch bottle, and then for reasons he couldn't define he slipped out through the street door into the night air, striding around and into the backyard and then into the garage, where he set the scotch onto the bench and then held onto the bench himself, breathing like an engine.

He stood just so for minutes, not daring to turn on the light. All the old night fears of his childhood had rushed back in upon him. Mrs. Gummidge's curl-encircled face had been horrible. She'd nearly gorgonized him. He shuddered and drained his glass, listening in anticipation for the sounds of pursuit. He could picture Mrs. Gummidge coming out through the back door like a wraith, like Lady Macbeth, drifting toward him through the night air with bloody hands and a loathsome automaton grin on her face. He shuddered again, cursing himself for not having hidden a bottle of scotch somewhere in the garage. Minutes passed and his breathing leveled out. It was cold. The concrete floor felt frozen through his socks. There was no sound of pursuit—no lights blinking on or back doors whispering shut. What he wanted more than anything, suddenly, was to go to bed. Rose's company, even if she was asleep, was worth a fortune to him.

The next day, Andrew was sitting in the overstuffed chair in the library when Pennyman came home. Andrew was happy to see him. It was late in the afternoon, and the mail had dropped through the slot just a half hour earlier. The note was there.

Luckily, it had been beaten up in transit, no doubt having been routed through the downtown station, and seemingly used as a coffee cup coaster for a day or two and then trodden on before delivery. It had become a happy mess of wrinkles and dirty Scotch tape, of unidentifiable stains and childish, semi-literate lettering.

Andrew had avoided Mrs. Gummidge most of the day, but she'd gone about her business as if she'd no idea that Andrew had come across her sleeping in Pennyman's bed. In fact, she seemed weirdly high-spirited, winking at him once in an appallingly suggestive way. Andrew could hardly accuse her of being in the room, but in the cold light of day he'd begun to generate theories to explain things. It seemed fairly likely that, if nothing else, Pennyman and Mrs. Gummidge were tolerably familiar with each other, that they'd been carrying on in secret. There was nothing he could do about his suspicions except dwell on them, and he had been engaged in doing just that when in had come Pennyman, through the door, almost on the heels of the mailman.

Pennyman was carrying his coat, folded over his arm. He looked particularly proud of himself; he had almost a youthful, damn-all appearance to him, as if he'd just finished off a half-bottle of wine and the world was a rosy place. The sight of him in such a state would normally have made Andrew seethe, but given the circumstances, the arrival of the anonymous letter and all . . .

Andrew looked up and winked and said that Pennyman looked surprisingly well today, in such a tone as implied that on most days Pennyman looked uncommonly miserable and tired. Then Andrew began to whistle the tootling little melody from "Steamboat Willie," and pretended to read his book while actually watching Pennyman sort through the mail and willing him to open the note then and there and not carry it away to his room.

Pennyman picked it up and peered at it. Then he thrust it away at arm's length and cocked his head, wondering at it with what seemed like vague loathing, as if he'd supposed at first it were a twig and then discovered that actually it was a cleverly camouflaged insect. He looked up at Andrew, but Andrew was reading harmlessly, swept up in his book and with a pencil in his hand. Pennyman produced a pocketknife and slit the envelope open, holding it suspiciously now between his thumb and forefinger. He peered inside, removed the folded message, and flattened it out. Andrew looked out over the top of his book, watching Pennyman's eyes sweep back and forth across the note. He read it and then read it again, uncomprehending. He blinked at it, reading it once more, his lips moving this time as if he were concentrating furiously, thinking it to be in code, perhaps, and trying to unscramble it, to make sense out of nonsense.

"Something wrong?" Andrew asked innocently, sitting up straighter in his chair as if ready to come to Pennyman's assistance.

"What?" said Pennyman. "No."

"Not bad news, I hope?"

"Not at all. It's nothing at all."

Andrew shrugged, implying that it was none of his business unless Pennyman wanted to make it so. "You seemed to go pale there for a moment. Not feeling under the weather are you? Sit down for a moment."

Pennyman's face seemed to stiffen into something resembling the face of a skull, and he looked at Andrew with such a rictus of suppressed fury that a wave of cold fear washed down along Andrew's spine, and for a moment he wished to heaven he hadn't sent the note at all. Then the moment passed and Pennyman relaxed just a little, gaining control of himself. "I'm feeling very fit, thank you. I have no desire to sit down. The contents of this letter, I believe, are none of your concern." And with that he gave the missive one last glance and refolded it—neatly this time—and slid it back into the envelope. Then he looked up suddenly at Andrew again, his expression having changed once more. He seemed to be studying the episode, seeing it and Andrew both, perhaps, in a new light.

Andrew stretched his face into a look of indifferent resignation, shrugged, and said, "Sorry. None of my business. You're right. Didn't mean to butt in. You seemed almost helpless there for a moment, though, and . . . Well . . ." He waved the whole incident away, trying to give the impression that he would forget about it, that he had already forgotten about it, that *he,* certainly, wouldn't be the cause of Pennyman's further embarrassment. "By the way, the phone company came around today and installed a phone in your room. I thought it was high time. It's on the house—all but long-distance calls, of course."

Pennyman was forced to thank him, although the effort of it was apparently painful. Then he turned toward the stairs, whacking his stick a couple of times against the carpet as if to recall the spirit of determination that he'd first come in with. He strolled away, humming now, brushing at his sleeve.

He stopped at the first step, looking downward. Then he bent just a little, leaning on his stick. Andrew watched, biting his lip, suppressing laughter. Pennyman stooped to pick up the nickel that seemed to lie there on the bottom tread.

It wouldn't come up. It was stuck. He flicked at it with his finger, then whacked at it with his stick. Andrew leaned forward in his chair, ready with a comment. "Coin trouble?" he would say, raising one eyebrow as if mystified at Pennyman's antics. That would do the trick. It would imply things. The day belonged to Andrew, and no doubt about it—the nailed nickel trick coming on top of the anonymous letter. Pennyman was a living ruin: one moment a thing of clockwork dignity tricked up out of hair oil and an ostentatious cane, the next moment a slouched old humbugging fake, scrabbling after joke nickels on the stairs.

Pennyman stood up suddenly, not turning around. He gazed up the stairwell, straight ahead of him, thinking about something. Andrew couldn't force himself to talk to the man's back. He wouldn't be able to speak if Pennyman didn't look at him. Ah, well . . . Silence, perhaps, would say more under the circumstances. He watched Pennyman climb the stairs, humming again. Andrew didn't like the humming. There was something in the humming that wasn't good, as if Pennyman were humming him out of existence. Andrew popped up and stepped into the kitchen, pulling a little claw hammer out of the drawer and then heading out toward the stairs to pry out the nickel. It was a pity, really, to have driven the thing into the stair tread, although the runner would hide the hole easily enough. He worked out the nickel, shoved it into his pocket, and then pushed at the rug a little to press the hole shut. There it was, disappeared, and no one the wiser.

The cafe, finally, was almost put right. It seemed to Andrew as if there were merit in the mere bulk of kitchen apparatus—all the stuff that Aunt Naomi had sprung for six weeks back and was only now being delivered and installed. He sat at the bar polishing years of dust from old salt and pepper shakers and taking notes in his spiral binder as three men in blue jeans and shrunken T-shirts hooked up a Wolf stove. It was enormous—six broad burners, a griddle the size of a playing field, and two ovens, each of which could accommodate a Thanksgiving turkey. Alongside it was a vast warming oven, and next to that was a cupboard with a cutting board top. Andrew had designed the cutting board himself, and was moderately proud of it. It was as big as would fit comfortably into the relatively small cooking area, and it had stainless steel bowls mortised in, so that a chef could sweep chopped odds and ends off into the bowls, pluck the bowls out, and dump the odds and ends into pans on the stove.

He was itching to mess with it all, to make it work. It was impossible that the equipment could produce anything in the food line that wasn't first-rate. A friend of Pickett's had built the cabinetry and the bar—had done all the woodwork, in fact, under

Andrew's supervision, and it all looked just right. Andrew had bought the half-dozen draw-leaf tables for ninety dollars apiece from an importer of English antiques, and had searched out three dozen oak chairs at thrift shops in downtown Long Beach. He'd paid out ten or fifteen dollars for each of them, and so he had no *sets* of chairs to speak of, just a random lot of them that Pickett's friend had worked over, regluing joints and replacing missing spindles and shimming up short legs.

Andrew admired the general mess of old furniture and had decided to continue the theme. He'd bought up random silverware and cups and saucers and odd bits of china and porcelain and napkin rings. He'd found no end of old tablecloths of mid-fifties vintage, with deep pastel flowers and rectilinear designs. And he had collected pairs of salt and pepper shakers: comical ducks and head-bobbing dogs and painted clowns riding on happy-go-lucky pigs.

Every table would be a mish-mash of shapes and colors, would remind you of a carnival, of a kaleidoscope, of a wooden box full of marbles, of the kitchen and pantry in Mr. Badger's house. It would be a comfortable place, with a cheerful fire in the winter and the casement windows thrown open in the summer. There wouldn't be two forks the same, or two wine glasses either, and serious, frowning businessmen, talking about updating supplies and finalizing documents and impacting infrastructures, would suddenly find themselves salting their potatoes out of the end of an elephant's nose. He saw it as an experiment in the principles of Ruskin and Morris. It wouldn't just be the food that sent them out satisfied; it would be something else, too, something that they couldn't quite define. Satisfied and mystified at once, that's what they'd be—and better off for it, too.

He had sprung for the espresso maker just that morning. The old Andrew would have frittered away the bulk of Aunt Naomi's money on odds and ends, and then looked about frantically for a means to buy the espresso maker. But he'd turned over a leaf on the night of the Cheerios meeting. He was working hard now at developing a strain of practicality in himself, at becoming the-man-who-got-things-done. The house painting was evidence of it.

For the past couple of days, since the victory of the letter and the nailed nickel, he'd let Pennyman go pretty much about his business; he had acted as if what Pennyman was up to was no concern of his. He'd been tempted to listen in on one of Pennyman's phone calls, but he hadn't done it. Pennyman would suspect that very thing. Andrew would wait for Pickett's return, and then the two of them would hold a council of war. After that, who could say?

He'd been fiddling with a promotional notion, too—the idea of sewing up a couple of enormous chef's hats, one for himself and one for Pickett. There was no reason at all that they couldn't be inflated, say, with helium, like clouds hovering over their heads as they manipulated whisks and spatulas in the kitchen. A photo in the *Herald* would do nicely. It would advertise that here was no ordinary cafe, operated by ordinary chefs.

Ordinariness was cheap; everyone owned it by the bucketful. Here at the cafe was something you didn't quite expect, such a picture would reveal. What?—something pleasant, certainly, something compelling and utterly removed from the tedious humdrum of the workaday world. He'd get Rose to sew the hats up. She'd see the value in them. They were a practical matter, really, an advertisement. The tops, of course, might have to be cut out of thin, beach ball vinyl and the seams glued shut. It would be nothing for Rose—two hours' work. Andrew sketched a hat in his binder, then flipped the page and sketched another one, bigger. He drew a comical picture of Pickett with a caricature mustache and a fabulous inflated hat perched on his head, like a double-dip mound of vanilla ice cream balanced on the wrong end of a cone. There was no point simply in a *big* chef's hat. It had to be enormous— the sort of thing to make the public's eyes shoot open; a tall order in these odd latter days, when men in helmets and wizard shirts searched for mysteries on the foggy seashore.

Thank goodness the workmen were leaving. Andrew hated to have strangers mucking around in his cafe; they violated it, somehow, with their cussing and loud laughter and hooting out the doorway at women a block away on the highway. When their truck finally rumbled off, Andrew set in with a rag and a spray bottle of cleaner, swabbing down stainless steel and generally neatening things up. It was then that Ken-or-Ed walked in. Another man followed him, carrying a clipboard.

"Ken," said Andrew, standing up.

"Ed, actually. Look here. I'll get straight to the point . . ." At that juncture, though, the man with the clipboard snorted, and Ed looked at him, losing the point entirely. On the bar was a salt and pepper shaker set—two tiny ceramic tornadoes, interlocking and hanging on a ceramic fence rail. They each had winking eyes and flipper-like arms and hands, one arm of each entwined around the other one's shoulder. Of the two free arms and hands, one held a sheaf of wheat, the other a sign that read, "I been to Kansas." Andrew had been trying to wangle the jammed corks out of them.

The man with the clipboard winked broadly at Ed and fumbled at his shirtpocket, pulling a ball-point pen out of an inky pen holder. He jotted something down.

Andrew squinted at them both, wondering what in the devil they wanted. This didn't seem to be a social call. "What's the point, again?"

His neighbor crossed his arms, looking uncomfortable. "I was saying that some of us have just learned about the cafeteria you're starting up here, and . . ."

"Cafeteria?"

"That's right. You can hardly deny it, can you?" He swept his hand around in a broad gesture, taking in the newly installed equipment. "This inn idea wasn't quite as bad—was it? It wouldn't have ruined the neighborhood. But a cafeteria is . . ."

"Cafeteria?" said Andrew. "Do you mean like Clifton's or something—hot turkey sandwiches and meat loaf and roast beef with gravy? Mashed potatoes? People in a line serving themselves with enormous spoons?" Andrew looked at him incredulously, as if he couldn't quite imagine that the cafeteria subject had been broached. The second man wandered away, taking notes.

Ed gestured the whole business into oblivion. "I don't care about mashed potatoes. Will you listen to me? By God, we won't have it. That's what I'm saying. Mashed potatoes or no mashed potatoes. We don't want this neighborhood turned into a fast-food restaurant! It's illegal. This is Jack Dilton from the planning commission. He's a personal friend of mine.''

"I can easily imagine that he is," said Andrew. "Even the least of us needs a friend. I have a variance, actually. This was all settled long ago. You're a little late. And who set you off, anyway? Just the other night you were running around in the streets half-naked. It was an insult to my wife and to Mrs. Gummidge. Put on some clothes next time.'' Jack Dilton stepped back across, sensing trouble. Andrew nodded to him and smiled politely. "Glad to meet you, Mr. Dilman.''

"Dilton," the man said. "I'd like to see a copy of the variance if I might.''

"You can't," said Andrew. "You can't stay here another moment. Do you have a warrant of some sort? No, you don't. You can't have a warrant, because they don't entrust warrants to petty officials from the planning commission. What you've come around here for I can't imagine, but I have a tendency to think that it has something to do either with thievery or malicious mischief. Someone has been systematically stealing valuable books from my library and letting 'possums loose in the attic bedrooms at night. What *were* you doing on the street that night, Ken?''

"My name is Ed. Ed Fitzpatrick. *Mr*. Fitzpatrick. *You're* crazy. I'm going to have this place shut down. There isn't any parking and the neighborhood isn't zoned commercial.''

Andrew's face stretched with astonishment. He reached out suddenly and pumped his neighbor's hand, then let it drop just as suddenly. "You aren't *the* Eddie Fitzpatrick?—who played for the Dodgers one season? Old *Slider* Fitzpatrick?''

Just then the door to the house kitchen swung open and Rose peered in, holding a glass of lemonade. "Didn't mean to interrupt," she said.

Andrew stepped across to take the lemonade. He waved back at his neighbor. "Rose, this is Eddie Fitz*patrick,* of the Dodgers, remember him? Relieved Wally Moon that one night at the Coliseum. Walked eight batters in an inning. *You* remember. It was on the night that the hot dog vendor tumbled down the stairs and broke his leg. Who'd have thought? And right across the street, too . . ." He grinned at Jack Dilton. "Baseball fan, Mr. Dilman?"

Rose gave Andrew a hard look, a drop-this-nonsense look, and started to say something to the neighbor. Ken-or-Ed interrupted her though, his face having gone red. "Your husband is an idiot," he said, glaring past her at Andrew. "And what's more, he's a filthy Peeping Tom. That's what I think. That's why he was up in that damned tree the other night, peering into windows. By God, my wife heard a noise last night, too, and . . ."

Andrew had hauled off his jacket by then and tossed it onto the bar, accidentally knocking off one of the tornadoes, which cracked to bits on the hardwood floor. Doubly enraged by the broken saltshaker, Andrew pushed Ken-or-Ed's shoulder, spinning him half-around. "I don't care *who* you are," he shouted, waving a fist. "Call me an idiot! Call me a Peeping Tom! I'll . . ."

Ken-or-Ed hunkered over, both hands in front of his face in the style of a turn-of-the-century boxer. "Try me," he said. "C'mon!"

"Try nothing!" Rose shouted, stepping in between them. "Get out of my house, you and your friend both."

"That's right . . ." said Andrew, endeavoring to move Rose out of the way. This was a man's work. He'd bloody the fool's nose. One good blow . . .

"You shut up, too. You're both fools. Now get out. Andrew, sit down, for God's sake, before you turn yourself into the idiot he says you are. There's the door, Mr. Fitzpatrick."

Dilton had already retreated toward it, and was busily measuring it with a pocket tape measure. Suddenly Mr. Pennyman was standing behind him, having materialized, it seemed, out of the afternoon air. Dilton hopped back into the room, prodded by the tip of Pennyman's cane and turning around to protest. The idea of Pennyman showing up at all further infuriated Andrew, who was mad now in such a variety of directions that he couldn't speak.

"What seems to be the trouble?" asked Pennyman slowly, uttering the syllables in a voice that sounded as if it had come out of a machine. Instantly a quiet descended on the room, and Ken-or-Ed blinked at him, seeming to wonder why his simple presence was enough to strike them all silent.

Pennyman leaned on his stick and smiled. "You're from the planning commission," he said to Dilton.

"That's right. This entire business is illegal, if I'm not mistaken. The doorway isn't broad enough, there's no ceiling sprinklers—not even a smoke alarm. It's a shame."

"Save your catalogue, sir. I represent these fine people, and I can assure you that everything that goes on here is legal and aboveboard. I believe they attained a variance some months back and have a moderately good relationship with the Coastline Steering Committee and the Chamber of Commerce."

Andrew started to protest. Pennyman *represent* them! He wouldn't be represented by Pennyman on a bet. "We can . . ." he started, but Rose stepped meaningfully on his foot, and he shut up.

Dilton stared at Pennyman and Ken-or-Ed stared at Dilton. "Let's go," Dilton said, sliding his pen back into his pocket. "This is pointless."

"We'll be back!" shouted Ken-or-Ed over his shoulder, but the threat didn't amount to much, and Andrew yelled "Hah!" just to show him. It made him feel almost happy to see that the fat man's shirt had come untucked in the melee, and what was left of his hair had been jacked up into a sort of wonderful hedge.

"Tuck in your shirt!" Andrew shouted out the door, but Rose dragged him away. He was giddy with victory for a moment, but then there was Pennyman, smiling benevolently.

"I'll see what I can do," he said to Rose.

Andrew plucked up his coat and put it on. "Don't bother," he said. "There's nothing to be done."

Rose cast Andrew another look. "Thank you," she said to Pennyman.

Andrew started to speak again, but Pennyman had very gallantly kissed Rose's hand and was tapping toward the door, and the sight of the hand-kissing froze Andrew's words before they'd had a chance to be uttered. Speaking was no good at all here. The more he spoke, the worse it got. Andrew would have simply slammed

Pennyman in the back of the head then and there, except that there was something in him that wouldn't allow for the striking of an old man. Or else there was something in him that made him afraid to. He pushed this last thought out of his mind and bent over to sweep up the fragments of the broken tornado. And just before Pennyman disappeared, Andrew heard him mutter the words ''upset'' and then ''he'll calm down.'' Then he was gone, giving Andrew no chance at all to murder him.

Andrew stood staring at the backs of his hands on the bar. Then, calmly and deliberately, he picked up the unbroken tornado and threw it hard at the wall. It exploded in a spray of black pepper, the ''I been to Kansas'' sign snapping off entire and spinning away across the bar like a top. Rose gaped at him. Without looking up, he slammed his fist down sideways onto the little, hollow ceramic sign, crushing it. He could feel it slice into the side of his palm, and he was glad for it. It would show Rose something; that was for sure. *What* it would show her he couldn't say; not enough, maybe. To complete the picture, he smashed his closed fist into one of the wooden panels fronting the bar, with far more force than he'd intended. He winced in spite of himself, and blood from the cut sprayed back onto his pants. Rose walked silently through the door, back the way she'd come. Andrew watched her go, the wild energy emptying from him. He pressed his left hand over the bleeding cut and flexed his fingers, wondering if he'd broken one of them. He half-hoped he had. He deserved to. But then he'd have to live with the day-to-day reminder of it for the next six weeks, and that he didn't deserve. That would be too much.

He seemed to go limp all of a sudden. All his rage had leaked away like water out of a cracked jar. He wanted suddenly to chase after Rose, to explain himself. It was easy enough. It was Pennyman, is what it was—kissing her hand. He couldn't have that. It wasn't gallant, it was . . . a perversion. Pennyman was laughing at both of them. Andrew could stand the laughter; he was big enough to shoulder it; but he couldn't have the slimy old fake making up to Rose that way. He nearly punched his hand into the bar again, but he didn't have enough jazz. He was drained, empty. He slumped into a chair and stared out through the street door, thinking of nothing.

At dinner that night Rose didn't say a thing about the trouble in the afternoon. She was cheerful, in fact, and had opened a bottle of Spanish champagne, which Andrew was happy enough to see. He kept wanting to bring the subject up, conversationally, as if by chance, in order to get around to explaining himself. He knew, though, that he oughtn't to be *explaining* anything. He ought to be apologizing. There was a vast difference. It was easy enough for him to do the one; the other was tough.

And here was Rose, pouring him a third glass of champagne. Pennyman was out; Mrs. Gummidge was upstairs, eating with Aunt Naomi. It was just the two of them. That sort of rage—that cold sort of smashing and breaking—was something entirely foreign to Rose. She didn't engage in it. She couldn't be made to understand it, any more than a tropical native could be made to understand ice . . . But there he went again, thinking of explanations.

If she just weren't so damned pleasant, with the champagne and all. She very clearly had "forgotten all about it," so as to make it easier on him. And she *meant* it, too. There was nothing deceitful in it. She was simply good, in about a hundred ways, thank God, and her goodness made Andrew feel worse.

Then it occurred to him abruptly that she was taking Pennyman's advice, and letting him "calm down." That wasn't so good after all. Thinking of Pennyman made Andrew go cold. The champagne wasn't worth anything all of a sudden. The pleasant sense of proportion it had given him evaporated and he felt only a dull headache.

Things changed so fast. The days seemed to bolt past while he hurried blindly toward a destination that no one on earth could define for him. He never seemed to get there either. More than half his life was gone, and he seemed no closer to any of his nebulous goals than he'd ever been. He'd been closer, in fact, when he was eighteen and was full of dreams and spirit. What had Aunt Naomi said? The world wasn't your oyster any more. Well, that would take some getting used to.

He could remember when, not so very long ago, he'd been as even-tempered as the next man, more so even. Laugh-a-minute Andrew; that's what he'd been. Now the tiniest thing would set him off. The bad, out-of-temper mornings came around more often than the mornings full of cheerful whistling. Would it get worse? Would Rose tolerate him? Why in the hell *couldn't* he have just a little bit of Pennyman's gallantry and self-assuredness?

The champagne was gone. He couldn't suggest opening another; that would be going too far. It would be a disaster to end the day in a drunken stupor, desperately pretending that he wasn't. He smiled at Rose, marveling at how pretty she looked. She hadn't ever needed make-up, although she looked smashing when she had it on. When she was half-disheveled, at the end of a long, tiresome day like this one, she looked prettiest. *Capable* was what she looked, and just a little bit tough, as if there was nothing that she might do that would surprise you. How in the world had he ended up with a woman like her? Why didn't she just pitch him out? He felt the wild urge to ask her, but he stepped on it. There was no use pushing his luck.

Maybe things hadn't gone so badly for him after all. When you looked around, why there was a comfortable house full of books and the smell of the sea, and there was Rose being good to him, and a business to dabble in that let him do just what he wanted—even if doing it made him feel guilty. It occurred to him for the first time—as if the champagne, or something, had whispered it very clearly into his ear—that he'd be more satisfied, perhaps, if he thought less about his regrets and more about—what?—his many blessings, maybe.

He must be drunk. He was getting maudlin. In a moment he'd start singing, counting them one by one. He pushed himself away from the table in tolerably better spirits, though. There was nothing for it but to keep going, to put one foot in front of the other. Steady-on—that was what was demanded of him. And besides, Pennyman would get his one of these days soon. Andrew would have to bring it off in such a way that it was Pennyman, and not himself, who was made to seem mean and small, especially to Rose.

"I'm going out to work on the cafe," Andrew said, kissing Rose on the cheek. "It's pretty nearly ready."

Rose nodded. "I'll just clean up. Why *did* that man come around this afternoon? He turned out to be far more horrible than I'd have guessed."

Andrew shook his head, grateful that the subject, finally, had been brought up. "I don't know what set him off. He must have known all along what we were doing here. Now he's taken it into his head to start trouble. He's a lunatic. That's all I can think of. He can't touch us, though. Don't worry about it, for heaven's sake. I'll take care of it. I'll call Uncle Arthur tomorrow. He's connected; maybe he can help."

"I'd be relieved if you did. Don't go brawling with the neighbors, though. Promise me that. You know how you are. You'll hurt someone and then there'll be trouble. That seems to be what he wants, you know. To start something."

Andrew nodded. That certainly seemed so. "I wouldn't have hurt him much," he said. "Just a little poke in the nose." He was moderately proud of the idea. Once he got hold of a man, he didn't let him go until he'd wrung him out.

"And what was that nonsense about a baseball game? I don't believe I've ever been to one."

"That was good, wasn't it?" Andrew grinned, recalling how easy it had been to make Ken-or-Ed or whatever his name was both furious and mystified at the same time. That took a certain technique. "Sent him straight through the roof, didn't it?"

"But was it a *good* idea to send him straight through the roof?"

Andrew shrugged. "It did the trick. I'm glad you stopped me, though. I *might* have hurt the man after all. I'm a pretty dangerous character, aren't I?"

"That's why you need me around. Admit it."

"I admit it. Happily." He kissed her again and went out whistling. He'd have another go at the menu. It was due at the printer's day after tomorrow. Pickett would be home late tomor-

row night, and could give him a hand. Then, as a gesture, he'd run
it past Aunt Naomi the following morning. Who could tell?—she
might have something smart to say about it after all. He glanced
back at Rose as he shut the door behind him. She winked at him
very jolly and then gave him a mock-serious look, a no-nonsense
look, a behave-yourself look, as if she were keeping him in line.
And it made him feel almost whole again.

NINE

"Hey diddle diddle, the cat and the fiddle, the pig and the coin in the spoon . . ."

Archaic rhyme

ANDREW DECIDED TO risk a phone call or two. Pickett would be dead set against messing around like that. He would want to use the attic phone to listen in, simply in hopes of discovering something telling. Making prank calls on it would accomplish nothing, Pickett would say. But Andrew couldn't hang around halfway up the stairs all day, waiting for Pennyman's telephone to ring. He was a busy man, what with the painting and all.

He was getting the hang of it—this painting business. What sickened him was the idea of having to scrape all the old, flaked paint off the eaves. With the money left from Aunt Naomi, he could hire someone to clean the house up, to do the preparatory work; then he could wade in and paint it. But after his boasting and all to Rose, he would look like a fool hiring someone. It would be an admission of incompetence and laziness, among a number of other things—including the fact that he somehow had a large chunk of money in his pocket.

But that damned old paint seemed to chip off right under his nose. The slightest vagaries of weather set it off. He had been brushing away late that very afternoon when the most astonishing wind had blown up, seemingly from under the house. Hot and dry, it had come rushing out through the crawlspace, carrying almost chalk-fine dust on it and the dried exoskeletons and spindle legs of dead beetles. There had been a moaning, too, as if someone with an awful hangover were waking up beneath the house. The wind had come curling up around him, billowing out his shirt, dirtying his hair, and, weirdly, the old, dried paint on the clapboards had begun to alligator off in a little hailstorm of yellow chips, the loosened paint snapping, the clapboards groaning. A half-dozen nails had half-pried out with a single desperate skreek. Then the wind fell, the chipping paint lay still in the grass, and the moaning stopped.

Andrew had gotten a hammer out of the garage and beaten the nails back in, all the time wondering what on earth had gone on. The moaning, certainly, would simply have been wind blowing through the cracks around the crawlspace—either that, or it might have been the 'possum, yowling at the wind like a dog yowling at sirens. It was still under there, the 'possum was, coming and going at night. But where did the wind come from? Through the crawlspace on the far side of the house? It was sheltered over there. Andrew had gone back to scraping, half-expecting another blast of wind, which you *would* expect, if it were a natural wind. But there had been nothing.

If the phenomenon had occurred three weeks back, he'd have shrugged. He'd have forgotten it by dinnertime. But now, with things astir on the south coast . . . Maybe this wind was one of the "emanations" that Pickett's friend Georgia had carried on about. She was full of talk of positive ions. In fact she had said that the air around the house was saturated with them, and that Andrew ought to get some sort of machine, he couldn't remember quite what—an orgone box? An ionic bomb? She had said that the house was at the eye of a mystical *foehn* wind. As he understood it, the whole thing was a matter of electrical charges cast off by spirit forces—ghosts bumping into each other, like raindrops in clouds. It had struck him as funny. Ghosts lead the damndest lives.

But now this wind . . . And even if there were some sort of mystical business going on, what did it mean? Perhaps Pennyman was behind it. They were going at it blow for blow, he and Andrew were. Pennyman still reeled from the effects of the note and the nailed nickel. The old man had come back at Andrew there in the cafe, mumbling to Rose just loud enough to be overheard. And now, to leap ahead in the war, maybe he had manufactured this scaling paint business, although heaven knows how he'd done it. It seemed to argue that it was Andrew's turn. The telephone would do nicely.

Andrew decided not to go about it in any slipshod manner. It was just possible that he was involved in something more grand than he had suspected. If so, then subtlety was vital. What was called for was tomfoolery with a delicate touch.

He mixed up a pitcher of lemonade in the kitchen, then sneaked up the stairs to make sure Pennyman's door was shut. He would have to place the call from his bedroom phone, and his bedroom was just down the hall from Pennyman's room. He couldn't afford to be seen going past in the hall or hustling up and down the stairs. He couldn't call any attention at all to himself, not if he wanted to accomplish anything.

After the call, there was the chance that Pennyman would phone out, that he had accomplices, that he was part of a more nebulous conspiracy and that he would want to keep them informed. In that case, Andrew would have to listen in. He'd have to slip up the stairs into the attic to where the extension was. Clearly, if Pennyman spotted him going up, Andrew would have to pretend to be paying a visit to Aunt Naomi, and forget about listening in. Coming back down afterward, of course, would be riskiest. He could still claim to have been up visiting Naomi, but Pennyman would be certain he hadn't been. And if Pennyman tumbled to the gag phone call, or to the existence of the attic extension, then he'd be certain about the origins of the note, too, and would be on his guard. Andrew's entire battle plan would be exposed. He tiptoed along, holding his breath, listening hard. The coast was clear; the door was closed.

He got the best effect by talking through a Melitta coffee filter—a black plastic cone with a paper filter still lined with wet grounds. The effect was astonishing, like a voice out of an orbiting satellite. He slipped into his bedroom, and eased the door shut. Then, holding the coffee filter against the telephone mouthpiece like an upended bullhorn, he shoved his face into the cone and dialed Pennyman's number. He heard the phone ring across the hall an instant before he heard the manufactured ring inside the telephone. "Mr. Pennyman?" he asked, suppressing a giggle.

"Yes," Pennyman answered, immediately suspicious.

"Mr. Jules Pennyman?"

"Yes, what do you want?"

"I have a message for you. From a friend in the east." Andrew snickered, immediately sniffing and clearing his throat, as if it hadn't been a snicker at all. He pinched himself hard on the leg.

There was a silence, then Pennyman saying, "You do, do you?"

Very slowly and ponderously, enunciating as if he were talking to a half-wit or a foreigner, Andrew said, "He wants you to know that the key to the dilemma is a chew of tobacco. Tow-bak-ko. A chaw of . . . *terbackky*. His advice is Redman brand. This is generally unknown."

There was another silence, a long one, which Andrew had to break by hanging up. He buried his face in his jacket, laughing like a fool. Pennyman was right down the hall. If he heard Andrew laughing like that, heading up to the attic, it would be curtains for the whole campaign. Andrew pinched himself again, trying to make it hurt, then ditched the coffee filter under the bed and went out swiftly and silently, up the stairs, sliding past Pennyman's room. The door was still shut.

He waited in the attic for a full minute. Timing was the key here. He couldn't afford to pluck up the receiver while Pennyman was dialing. Pennyman would hear the empty silence of the off-the-hook extension. If he were talking, though, to a line already open . . . Andrew's hand hovered over the phone until, on the count of sixty, he eased the receiver out of the cradle. There was the sound of Pennyman's voice, already in conversation.

"Yes, that's correct."

"When?"

"On the agreed-upon night."

"Look, I'm not sure that the kind of money you're offering is worth the trouble that . . ."

The voice trailed off, interrupted, if that were possible, by an enormous silence—the silence of Pennyman listening, judging, and coming to conclusions. The owner of the voice on the other end had somehow understood the silence, had felt its weight pressing against his own words, his own whining.

Andrew listened hard. A moment of revelation was at hand. What did it mean, "the trouble"? The silence lengthened. Then Pennyman's voice again: "On the agreed-upon night."

"Yes. Of course. I just . . ."

Andrew wheezed into the phone just as the man paused.

"I just . . ."

Andrew made a noise like a bird, a sort of canary twitter involving his tongue and upper lip, only an instant of it.

"Pardon me?" asked the voice, half-apologetically.

"What?" said Pennyman. "I didn't . . ."

Andrew hung up—desperately carefully—and then slid out and down the stairs just as fast as he could manage. He heard Pennyman murmuring behind his door as he stepped past, and he was in the kitchen in seconds, lifting the receiver to the downstairs phone and dialing Pennyman's number again. It was busy, so he re-dialed—once, twice, three times, and then it rang. Pennyman picked up the receiver and listened for a moment before saying, "Hello?"

Andrew switched the faucet in the sink over to spray and turned both taps onto full, then, without saying a word, shoved the receiver down into the sink, aiming it at the cataract. He counted to ten slowly before pulling it out, biting his jacket sleeve, and mumbling through a mouthful of cloth, "Redman brand. Everyone agrees upon the night." Then he hung up, tense, wondering if he'd gone too far.

He started whistling very loud and stomping around in order to give the impression that he was hard at work. He poured a tall ice-filled glass of lemonade, then stamped away up the stairs, still whistling, but softer now, more subtly. He rapped on Pennyman's door, and the old man opened it almost at once, as if he'd been standing right there.

"Glass of lemonade?" asked Andrew. "Made in the shade by an old maid with a spade." He winked. "Just now brewed it up in the kitchen. I've been outside painting." He looked past Pennyman, into the room. Only a slip of it was visible through the crack between Pennyman and the jamb. On the floor, weirdly, was one of Aunt Naomi's cat boxes, or rather, one of her cats' cat boxes, well used, and with a little slotted metal scooper shoved into the sand.

Upon opening the door, Pennyman regarded him evenly, then glanced at the glass with a look of profound contempt. He started to speak, but Andrew's face betrayed his puzzlement over the cat box, and suddenly Pennyman's countenance changed. He pushed the door open a little wider, as if he had nothing to hide, and gestured back into the room with his free hand. "Looks odd, doesn't it?" he said. Andrew shook his head, trying to grin. "I thought I'd do my part. These little domestic chores . . . Rose is too busy for them, and heaven knows, what with the painting and all . . ."

"Of course," said Andrew. "And Naomi, certainly, still isn't up to it entirely. By golly. We appreciate it; I can assure you."

Pennyman took the lemonade now, smiling widely. Andrew was one up on him, and he knew it. Scowling wouldn't accomplish a thing for him. He stood for a moment, as if unsure what to do next, like a child who had been caught at something and had managed to lie his way out of it but was still edgy about the lie.

Andrew raised his eyebrows, thinking to follow up his little victory. "Something gone wrong?"

"No," said Pennyman, recovering. "Why?" His tone of voice seemed a challenge to Andrew to make something of the cat box.

"Nothing. This is really first-rate of you. Humbling sort of job, mucking out cat boxes—calls for something more than lemonade, really. And this is out of a can, I'm afraid, but not at all bad." The conversation had come to an impasse. Pennyman was clearly anxious to close the door.

"It will do just fine," he said. "I'm really rather busy."

"Yes," said Andrew. "I can see that. Well, there's more in the kitchen. I've mixed up a jumbo can. It's in the fridge."

Pennyman stared at him. He was gaining ground. "In the *fridge*," he said flatly. Then he smiled an ingratiating smile, started to close the door, but evidently thought better of it. "I'd like to recommend a book to you, by the way."

"Ah," said Andrew. "Which one."

"Anthropological text, actually. I know that's not your meat, as they say, but you'd find it . . . informative. Wonderful book, actually. All about a race of early men in South America who dismembered their dead, afraid that they'd walk again otherwise. Sawed them into pieces. Very nasty business, don't you think?"

Andrew gaped at him. "Yes. Now that you point it out. I mean to say—sawed them up?"

"Into fragments. Then generally mixed up the pieces of a half-dozen corpses and buried them like a salad. If the corpse still managed to rise from the dead it wouldn't have any idea who to haunt—wouldn't know whether to go after the cousin of its arm or the landlady of its right ear."

"Fascinating," said Andrew. "I'll look forward to it. But right now I've got to get on with the cafe, actually. Been at it steady. I just took a break to bring you up a glass. I mean to say that I've got to get back to the painting. Horrible job."

He turned around and fled back down the stairs, cursing himself. Why had he thought it necessary to face Pennyman down? His momentary advantage over the man had gone up in smoke, and he had quite likely given himself away, to boot. If he had just let it go after the phone in the sink gag! Maybe headed back upstairs in another half hour to make a third call—a breather call—and then another a half hour later. By dinnertime Pennyman would have been jumpy as a flea. Now Andrew had gone and spoiled the effect. And the old maid with a spade business had been far too hearty. He would have to train his face and his voice not to give him away. But the cat box . . . What in the world? Pennyman was going to lengths to ingratiate himself with Rose and Naomi, but for what reason? Just to be in a better position to do Andrew down? He picked up the lemonade pitcher, looked around guiltily, and drank off a third of its contents before wiping the rim and putting it into the refrigerator.

Andrew looked again at his pocket watch: almost one o'clock in the morning. Pickett was late. He had called from somewhere outside Bakersfield and had been driving for sixteen hours, all the way from Portland. He had sounded very mysterious, as if he'd learned something; he wouldn't say what—not over the phone. That was at ten. Anyone could have made it from Bakersfield to Seal Beach in three hours, even in Pickett's rattling old Chevy.

Andrew peered through the window at the deepening fog. Headlights loomed through the mists on the highway, appearing and disappearing like the glowing eyes of deep-water fish. It was eerily silent, as if the fog muffled all noise. He could just hear the drip, drip, drip of moisture plunking down into the saturated dirt of the windowbox from an overhanging branch.

The menus were finished. At first, until they got their sea legs under them, they'd offer a price-fixed menu—only two choices for the main course. There'd be a different theme, so to speak, every Friday and Saturday night, and breakfast served Saturday and Sunday mornings. But that wouldn't start for a week or two. Andrew had ordered handbills with the idea of giving them out to early-morning, weekend pier fishermen.

On Saturday, when they opened, Andrew would lead off with Cajun food, which was in vogue—something that was irritating, since Andrew had fancied it for years. He couldn't much stand the idea of liking things that were fashionable. People would assume that he liked them *because* they were fashionable, when in fact it was most often true that the opposite was the case. Cajun food though . . . He'd make a gumbo that would wake them up. With Rose and Mrs. Gummidge waiting tables, Andrew cooking, and Pickett generally maitre d'ing and helping out here and there, they'd do tolerably well. He'd have to give Mrs. Gummidge clear orders not to speak, though. He couldn't have her start yammering in front of the guests; that would be the end of their patronage.

Andrew's mind wandered, sorting through his list of current troubles. It seemed that there was always something leering in at the window, some ruinous little piper demanding to be paid. Rose still had no idea that he'd loaned Pickett the credit card merely to stock up on Weetabix. It would do her no good at all to know. She couldn't fathom it, and for very good reasons, too. Yesterday evening, after his making up with Rose, Andrew had popped down to the supermarket to search out sesame oil and oyster sauce in anticipation of Chinese night, and there in the import foods aisle he'd run into a shelf of Weetabix. His information had been wrong. They weren't contraband at all. They were a dollar and a half a box. With a dozen biscuits in a box, and two in a serving at ninety cents per serving, that was a profit margin of two or three hundred percent, not subtracting for overhead. Andrew sighed. He had sent Pickett after the Weetabix in good faith, anyway. He couldn't be expected to know *everything*.

Pickett wouldn't have charged more than sixty or eighty dollars in gas. Andrew would have to keep the thing silent and nab the credit card bill before Rose got to it. He couldn't afford to forget—as he'd forgotten about the coffee filter under the bed. She had found it later in the evening while searching for a bedroom slipper. After trying in vain to dream up a lie, Andrew had said simply, ''You wouldn't believe it if I told you,'' and she had nodded in agreement, not asking him to try. It depressed him, though, her having to protect him with her silence and her continually taking the long view. The house painting had made up for some of it. And when this whole thing was over, he would quit staying up late every night. That would help. She rarely said anything about it, but he was certain she felt his absence, so to speak, and he was happy she did.

Tonight, though, he had business to attend to. Rose was long ago in bed, and it would be a simple thing tonight to unload the cases of Weetabix like he'd done the whiskey, stow them away, and later on pretend that they'd come from some standard issue distributor in Los Angeles.

But where was Pickett? He'd been on edge when he'd called, had mumbled something about a newspaper clipping from the Vancouver *Tribune*, about a murder, about a curious book he'd bought in a Gastown bookstore. Andrew had pressed him for details but Pickett had clammed up.

Headlights swung round the corner and there sounded briefly the churning rumble of the Chevrolet. Then the lights blinked out and the motor coughed quietly and cut off. Andrew stepped out onto the side porch just as the pale bulk of Pickett's car coasted out of the mists and slanted in toward the curb. The door opened and Pickett hunched out from behind the wheel, carrying his leather briefcase. He grabbed Andrew's elbow and hurried him back in after shutting the car door softly behind them but leaving the window down. He stood inside the cafe, watching the street.

Andrew started to speak but Pickett shushed him, still holding onto his arm. His grip tightened as another pair of headlights appeared, and a taxi, navigating through the fog, stopped at the curb opposite. The door opened and out stepped Pennyman, smoking on his pipe. He handed the driver a bill, then counted change out of his open palm before tapping across the street with his stick, up onto the lawn. They heard the front door swing open and then shut, and then Pennyman's tread sounded for a moment on the stairs.

Andrew stepped across to the bar and with a shaking hand poured Pickett a glass of bourbon, neat. Pickett looked as if he needed it. His suit was rumpled and moist, and his hair had been blown silly by the wind on the open road. His shirttail was hauled out in back, and he made a gesture at tucking it back in, but accomplished nothing.

"He spotted me out near Leisure World," Pickett said, wrinkling up his face. "I saw him through a gap in the fog just as I was pulling off onto the boulevard. That beard of his is a dead giveaway." Pickett stared into his glass, then rapped against the bar with his fist. "What does he want? That's the trick. We don't know what he wants."

Andrew nodded as if giving Pickett's question serious thought. He determined to play the fool. It would be better all the way around to cool Pickett down. He was fatigued from the trip, and so all the more likely to make a mistake. There was no room for mistakes now. "Maybe he doesn't *want* anything. It's not much of a coincidence, is it? Nothing odd about Pennyman's being out and about this late. Night before last he didn't come home at all. Tonight he could have been anywhere. Mrs. Gummidge tells me he's got a relative of some sort in Glendale. That would be about right. If he came home down the Long Beach and the San Diego freeways, then he'd have every reason on earth to be passing Leisure World. You don't put enough faith in simple coincidence."

"He didn't come home at all night before last?"

"That's right. He's a grown-up. He can stay out all night."

"Mrs. Gummidge has been telling you this, about relatives in Glendale?"

"That's exactly what she's been telling me."

Pickett looked steadily at him, then brushed his hair back out of his face. "And you believe her?" He asked the question in a flat sort of tone, as if he'd been wondering whether it might have come down to this at last.

Andrew thought for a moment and then said, "No. I don't suppose I do. But it's possible just the same. We don't want to overreach ourselves, do we? We don't want to get jumpy now. Our big advantage is that he thinks we're largely ignorant."

"Maybe," said Pickett. "Look at this." He handed Andrew the newspaper clipping that he'd mentioned over the phone—the grisly account of a murder, of a man sawed in half lengthwise, so cleanly that the precision of it utterly baffled the authorities. He'd been frozen first. That was the consensus, although a coroner had speculated that a laser scalpel might have done the trick. He'd been found—both halves of him had—holding a silver quarter in either hand, for reasons no one could fathom. Had he been murdered in the midst of making change? It hardly seemed likely.

Andrew was almost giddy with dread as he skimmed through the article, wondering why on earth Pickett had brought it along and knowing why at the same time. It was ghastly, to be sure, and was the sort of utterly unlikely incident that would give the gears in

Pickett's head a good cranking. But beyond that, beyond all notion of reason and of reasons, was a muddle of instinct and gut fear—nothing but more unwoven threads from a tapestry they only suspected the existence of.

"The name," said Pickett. "Look at the man's name." Andrew staggered against the bar. It was August Pfennig who'd been sawed in half. August Pfennig—dead. That made it certain, didn't it? It made *something* certain anyway. But there was no way on earth that Pickett could know that Andrew knew the name. When had Andrew gotten the phone call, after all? Pickett was in Vancouver himself at the time. "This Pfennig—who do *you* think he is?" asked Andrew, giving his friend a sharp look.

"He was Moneywort's cousin," said Pickett flatly. "We met him that night in Belmont Shore, at Moneywort's shop. You remember. No, strike that. *I* met him. You weren't there that night, were you?" Andrew shook his head and said nothing. Pickett continued: "He had a tricolored koi that he'd paid a fortune for. I thought at the time that it was pretty weird, all of them fascinated with a big carp . . ." He stopped and looked edgewise at Andrew. "Who in the devil did *you* think he was, for goodness sake? You knew the name. How many August Pfennigs can there be?"

Andrew told him about the phone call, about the coin business. Pickett listened, his eyes narrowing. He slammed his fist into his open palm and waved Andrew to silence, then paced back and forth across the floor.

"It doesn't matter. All of this proves a theory of mine. I called the authorities in my official capacity as a member of the press. I asked them straight out whether the murder was connected with the recent death of Pfennig's cousin—Leyman Moneywort. The officer on the phone professed ignorance of any such cousin and insisted that I come around to talk. Then he covered up the mouthpiece and mumbled for a moment before another detective got on and said he knew all about Moneywort, and that the murders were unrelated. A string of bad luck for the Pfennig-Moneywort family, that's all. He accused me of sensationalizing the case—as if it needed such a thing."

Andrew nodded. "And this didn't satisfy you?"

"Satisfy me! Heavens yes it satisfied me. What could the denial be but confirmation of a *connection*. Pfennig isn't two days dead, and here's the police professing the certainty that the two murders are unrelated. That was a carefully calculated tale; you can take it from me."

Andrew shrugged. "Let's haul those Weetabix in before the fog through the open window turns the boxes to mush."

Pickett shook his head. "Wait a bit. Let your man upstairs fall asleep first." He put his finger to his lips to silence Andrew, then crept across toward the door that led to the kitchen. He snatched it open and stepped back, as if he were certain that Pennyman would be crouched there, perhaps with a glass tumbler pressed to his ear and a look of surprise on his bearded face. No one was there. Somewhere overhead a clock tolled—once, twice. "Two o'clock," said Pickett, and then pushed the door shut and turned once more to face his friend.

"Let me tell you about my little bit of detective work. I found a telephone book is what I did. And do you know what? There was a listing for August Pfennig Books and Arcana in Gastown. The man was dead—horribly murdered—but the shop was open for business as usual. That's where I bought this." Pickett snapped open his briefcase and produced an old book. The cover was ochre-colored morocco, brittle and torn with age. Pickett set it onto the top of the bar and then nodded at it, as if to say, "Look at *that*."

There was gilt writing on the cover, but it was so faded and dim that Andrew opened the book to the title page. *Le Cochon Seul* it said, translated by the Marquise de Cambremer. Andrew looked up at Pickett. "No author?"

"I think it's all old legends. Probably a pocketful of authors, like the Bible. I imagine that this marchioness had nothing at all to do with the writing of the thing."

"Sounds rather like a cheese, doesn't it?"

"A cheese?" asked Pickett, mystified.

"This woman's name."

"That's Camembert, the cheese is. This has nothing to do with cheeses. And it's not her name we care about anyway. It's the book itself, for heaven's sake.''

"It's Greek to me," said Andrew, grinning.

"Well hold onto your hat, then. The title means 'The One Pig,' or something very much like that. I can't quite figure it as a title, but look at the frontispiece. That's what struck me. The clerk was studying it when I came in.''

Andrew did. There, badly drawn in sepia-colored ink, were back and front drawings of a serrated-edged coin with the likeness of a man on one side and of a moon-enclosed fish on the other. It was a crenelated-looking fish, like a sea serpent, perhaps, like the Leviathan, and it was swallowing its own tail.

Pickett looked moderately pleased with himself and started to talk again. Andrew stared at the picture, disbelieving in its existence. His chest felt hollow all of a sudden, and he found that he was breathing in little gasping breaths. He started to speak, to interrupt, but then he didn't. He decided to let Pickett go on. Pickett had been driving for nineteen hours, waiting for the chance to confound Andrew with this book, with whatever bit of coin lore the French text revealed. Andrew wouldn't upstage him yet.

"Well, the fact that it was an illustration of a coin struck me straight off," said Pickett, warming to his story. "But what fetched me up short was that I'd seen such a thing before. You'll never guess where.''

Andrew shrugged. All he was sure of was that Pickett hadn't ever seen Aunt Naomi's spoon, or rather *his* spoon. He was suddenly short of breath again.

"On Moneywort's hat. Remember me telling you about his fishing lures? Well, this is the fish, swallowing its tail. It's a common enough symbol in mythology, of course, serpents swallowing their tails. But it struck me like a ball bat that the likeness of this very fish should have been hanging from Moneywort's hat. Think about it: Moneywort's dead, murdered. And so is Pfennig. And the book is in Pfennig's shop. And here's the clerk with a hell of an unhealthy interest in it. Look at the picture—the multiple dorsal fin and the too-big head and the way there's a crescent moon laid in behind it, half-hidden. There isn't a shadow of a doubt—a miniature copy of it had been hanging on Moneywort's hat. I saw it there. Ho, I said to myself. Here's an unlikely coincidence. And the more I thought about it the unliklier it seemed.

"So just for the dickens of it I asked for the proprietor, for Pfennig—you know, just to feel the clerk out. Pfennig was gone—out of the country, said the man. Which was a lie, of course. Pfennig was lying in a bag on a slab at the morgue. The clerk couldn't have been ignorant of it. I mentioned that I'd been a friend of Moneywort's, but the clerk shrugged. I asked to buy the book, which, like I said, the clerk had been messing with when I came in through the door. He was nervous about it—tried to put me off. He said he couldn't sell it at any price. It was just a 'curiosity,' he said. Nothing valuable. Nothing I'd want, really. I told him that in fact I wanted it very badly, and then he said that it was sold already. That he was holding it for a man who was a friend of Pfennig. I told him *I* was a friend of Pfennig and then told him to name his price. That's just what I said: 'Name your price, sir!' I said, and snapped your credit card down onto the counter when I said it. The long and the short of it is that he named it. These days a credit card is as good as cash." Pickett winked broadly, as if to underscore the story of his victory.

"I don't doubt it," said Andrew, sinking into a chair. Rose was going to kill him. He debated asking Pickett how much the clerk had soaked him for, but he didn't. It was too late at night. He'd never get to sleep if he knew. He'd have to watch for the bill to come in the mail, just as he'd planned, and pay it off entirely, then destroy the record. "So what about this clerk?"

"He knew about Pfennig; you bet he did. You could see it in his eyes—raw terror. I thought he'd bolt before he got the book into a bag; and he nearly did. He sold me the thing, stuffed all the cash from the register into his pocket, and was out the door and locking it before I'd walked halfway down the block to my car. I've thought it over all the way down from Vancouver, and what I think is that we have a book that we shouldn't have, and *that's* why I didn't at all like the idea of running into Pennyman out by Leisure

World. And now you tell me he was out of the house for nearly thirty-six hours on the day Pfennig was murdered. He was in Vancouver himself; that's what I think. And what's more, I think he was the 'friend' who wanted the book.''

Andrew was suddenly overwhelmingly tired. His head spun with the bits and pieces of the mystery. He thought about the squid on the beach, sliced lengthwise, and Pennyman rummaging in its guts to retrieve a silver coin. He thought about the spoon lodged behind the books in his room, about the face on the front of it and the moon and fish on the convex curve of the bottom. He thought about Aunt Naomi giving it to him, almost making a production out of it, a ritual. He thought of Pfennig, sawed in two. Then a new thought chilled him—the thought of the credit card. ''They've got my name,'' he said flatly.

Pickett shrugged. ''Forget about names,'' he said. ''They're living in your house, for God's sake. They don't need your name.'' He poured himself another glass of bourbon, and sat down, looking desperately fatigued.

Pickett was right, of course. Andrew opened the book again, to the frontispiece, just to make sure. ''There's something else living in the house,'' he said flatly. ''Wait half a minute.''

And with that he walked out tiredly, slumping through the kitchen and up the stairs to fetch the pig spoon.

He knew that the penlight belonged to Andrew Vanbergen, but he didn't know what it was doing under the bedroom chair. Someone had been in his room while he had been traveling. He smiled, regarding himself in the mirror. He tipped his head. There was a clinic in Paris that performed hair transplants in such a way that one didn't emerge with a head that looked like a palm grove. And there was a shaman, a Professor M'gulu, in Zambia who could restore hair outright. The African's process, though, involved the application of loathsome substances to one's scalp and the chanting of mystical phrases. Jules Pennyman rather preferred a more clinical approach. He didn't function at all well in earthy, ritualistic settings. That was the enemy's territory, for the most part. Pennyman preferred the antiseptic cleanliness of stainless steel and vinyl and Formica scrubbed down with chemical sterilizers.

While the coins worked well enough prolonging life, they weren't at all kind to hair. There was a subtle, gradual decay and debilitation that they generated, even after one had got around the initial wasting away, the aches and pains and brittle bones. Pennyman had been plagued with random baldness for the last fifty years. The elixir manufactured by Moneywort and his cronies had done its work, and as long as he had it, he felt tip-top. Not even a cold. But he was beginning to suspect that there was a limit even to the elixir's effects; it was as if slowly but surely he'd become immune to the elixir's effects—as if it were an opiate—and now even with increased doses . . . That would be the effect of the coins again. But there was nothing he could do about it. There was always a price.

He could see in the mirror that his hair was thinning, unnaturally, in patches. He brushed it back carefully, checking the effect in the hand mirror. He'd have to have something done to his ears, too. There were certain body parts that kept growing, regardless of age, and their growing was enhanced by Moneywort's potion. Ears were the worst of them, because you couldn't cover them up. He despised the idea of surgery. One was so vulnerable when lying on a surgeon's table. But he couldn't abide looking comical either, and oversize ears were nothing if not comical.

There were aspects of the problem that he wouldn't have minded when he was young—those bodily members which, unlike ears, *could* be covered up. It had got to the point at which he could command a ducal salary on the club circuit, but he'd lost his taste for that sort of thing long years ago. Debauchery had worn thin after a while, and he had abandoned it as he had abandoned everything else. Even when he was young, he'd never understood the nature of the urgings that the common man referred to as love. They were nothing but fear—a matter of clinging to each other, just as a blind man, finding himself on the edge of an unfamiliar street, might cling to a tree or a lamp-post simply to keep his bearings as he listened to the traffic whiz by. Pennyman had no such fears. The unknown held no secrets from him, and he was no stranger to darkness.

He liked to think of the human heart as a clockwork mechanism, a thing of gears and crystals. He'd seen one at a laboratory in Munich, during the war. It had been removed from its host and maintained artificially in a sterile glass box, a complication of rubber tubes and circulating fluids. There was nothing sentimental about it; it was merely a mechanical device, more ghastly, perhaps, than a man-made contrivance because of its awful fleshiness, because it was more authentically alive.

If his plans failed, he'd go to the Paris clinic and have his ears attended to. If his plans *didn't* fail, then it wouldn't much matter.

What he couldn't quite fathom was the faint smell of perfume on his blanket. He knew whose perfume it was, but what had she been doing lying atop his bed? They'd never had any such relationship. The idea of it appalled him. The idea of physical contact of any sort appalled him, and that sort doubly so. What in the world had she been up to? Some sort of odd fantasizing? If so, then she'd come unhinged, and he'd be better off if she disappeared off the end of the pier on the next foggy night. His mind wrangled with the mystery. Why on top of the bedclothes and not under them? Clearly it hadn't simply been a matter of her sleeping in his bed. And why Andrew Vanbergen's penlight? Had she taken it from him? Andrew carried it clipped into his shirt pocket on occasion; it would be a simple enough thing to steal. But why would she bother?

There was the possibility, of course, that she hadn't been in his room at all—that it had been Andrew all along, and that he'd soaked a tissue in her perfume and rubbed it onto the blankets. But again, why? Why not slip in and out again? Why leave telltale signs? Simply out of lunacy? That would almost seem the answer, especially when Andrew Vanbergen was involved. He was raving mad; that was the truth of it. There was no other explanation, certainly, for the note that had come in the mail. The idiot's face had been an open book. And the contents of the note, too—senseless, decayed jabber. There was no question about its being Andrew's work. The man was a case study in several of the more novel forms of insanity. And he was a pest. Sooner or later it would be necessary to reach out and crush him, too, now that Pennyman had ascertained that Andrew wasn't a Caretaker.

Why leave the penlight, though? And why the stolen elixir? Pennyman hadn't hidden that half well enough. He'd been sloppy. On an impulse he put away his brush and mirror and bent down by the bed, hauling open one of the drawers below it. Behind folded sweaters lay a package wrapped loosely in brown butcher paper. Next to it was a leather bag, a lidded Plexiglas cube, and a lead-lined silver and pewter box designed by Archibald Knox and made by Liberty and Company in 1904, during a time when Pennyman had fancied the trappings of wealth and pretended an interest in art. He had come to see through that, finally. It was as transparent as the rest, art was, and not worth his time. His energy had been focused over the years onto a tinier and tinier target, and he had shed his trivial, youthful enthusiasms for art and liquor and tobacco and the rest of the "productions of time." Let heaven be in love with them. He was in love with—nothing. Maybe love was the wrong word.

The boxes in the drawer hadn't been touched. He took the silver box out anyway. He'd have to find a safer place. *Someone* had been skulking in his room when he was out—at night, to judge from the penlight. Surely a nitwit like Andrew Vanbergen would have no interest in the coins. But Pennyman had traveled too many miles, dealt with too many powerful men, to take any chances now, especially with a man as irrational as Vanbergen.

And there was the matter of the last four coins. He'd see the emergence of two of them soon enough. And the third, he knew, he would have to fish for. The fish would come to him, though. He had discovered that accumulated coins drew the scattered coins; and the more he had accumulated, the stronger had been their attraction. He possessed twenty-six of them, and the few missing coins were even now tumbling and burrowing and swimming toward him through the earth and sea. And when they arrived, he wouldn't need to drink carp elixir in order to drag out a few more years of life. As had happened when Judas Iscariot had been tempted to suicide out of remorse; immortality had been thrust upon him as a curse. Well, it wouldn't be a curse to Pennyman.

Pfennig knew that too—what it was the coins granted. All his kind did. And they pretended not to be attracted to the idea of it. They hoarded their coin or two and assumed the role of Caretaker. But it was all affectation. Pennyman was certain of it. Old Aureus had accumulated more of the coins than had been good for him, and their attraction had begun to work on him, to debilitate him. He was tainted with them. The possession of any single one of them would have turned a common man into an invalid. Fourteen of them had brought Aureus enough power so that he'd been a formidable enemy, with his obedient beggars and his calling up of spirits. Pfennig and Moneywort had been nothing. Caretakers! If their business was to keep the coins dispersed, then they were a sorry lot, weren't they? And one by one they were a dead lot.

But the fourth coin—where was it? It clearly had been altered some time in the past, and then lost. Pfennig had been on the track of it. It was there somewhere. He was tolerably sure, though, that neither Andrew nor Rose *knew* it was there. He would have sensed it long ago if they had. The coin *had* been altered—that was the truth of it—and cleverly, too.

A vague doubt flickered across the back of his mind—just the ghost of one. What if Andrew Vanbergen and his idiot friend weren't the fools that he took them for? What if their tomfoolery was monumental cleverness? What if they knew *exactly* what they were doing, but were operating at depths that he couldn't fathom, on wavelengths that he couldn't detect? Andrew wasn't a Caretaker; their meeting on the front porch had told Pennyman that much. When Pennyman had confronted Pfennig for the first time on his way home from Jerusalem, his silver test quarter had been torn from his hand and had slammed Pfennig in the forehead. Pennyman hadn't had to bother with the pretense of coin tricks. If Pfennig had been smart, he would have left the country then and there. But he hadn't been smart. Was Andrew Vanbergen smart? Had he managed to hide the altered coin more cleverly?

Then there was the old lady—Aunt Naomi. Pennyman would look in on her that very afternoon. She'd be a tougher case. Interesting her in idiotic coin tricks would be more difficult than it had been with Andrew or with any of the rest of them. Naomi wouldn't be in the mood for light-hearted parlor tricks. He'd have to flatter her—bring her a bit of a present, perhaps. If she had one of the coins on her person, he'd . . . No he wouldn't. He couldn't; not with the alleged "treasure hunt" just a couple of days off. Anyway, he had promised to leave her to Mrs. Gummidge. He'd have to be patient.

Pennyman slid the drawer shut and carried the silver box back over to the dresser, where he examined himself in the mirror again. He stepped back, admiring the sharp thrust of his bearded chin. He would put the coins in a safe-deposit box. That would do nicely until the day of Andrew's treasure hunt. He'd better have them out by then or else there'd be an astonishing whirlwind of silver in the bank when the two earth-bound coins neared the surface. He didn't know whether there'd be enough attraction to yank out silver fillings or tear silver rings off fingers, but it was possible, especially if the last of the coins *was* in the vicinity. Then all thirty of them would be in close enough proximity so that their power might provoke anything at all. And he, possessing the coins, would wield that power.

Smiling, feeling better just thinking about it, he examined his teeth in the mirror, then opened the lid of the box. He heard a high-pitched keening, the sound of manufactured wind swirling the dust outside, and he heard the snapping of old paint buckling off the clapboards of the house and the strain of old nails yanking loose. Would the coins simply dismantle the house, turn it to rubble? Bring it down on the head of that idiot Vanbergen who painted stupidly below? He was half-tempted to see. But that, of course, would needlessly complicate things, just for a few moment's pleasure. And it might mean his own death, too. He shut the box lid, picked up his walking stick, and went out, startled despite his half expecting it when a dead sparrow plummeted out of the sky onto the lawn. He regarded it for a second with a smile and then went on.

Out on the pier, two days after Pickett's return, Andrew pushed a hook through a piece of frozen anchovy, then cut a chunk of shrimp with his slimy fishing knife and baited a second hook with it. On the third hook he hung an orange-brown remnant of mussel, then tipped the baited hooks over the iron railing and let them whiz down into the gray ocean. It was just sunrise, and he and Pickett had the pier pretty much to themselves. "Have another Mounds bar?" he asked, raising his eyebrows at his friend.

Pickett shook his head. "Another cup of coffee, actually. I slept till three in the afternoon yesterday. I must have been beat."

"And no wonder," said Andrew. "There's nothing easy about battling the forces of evil. It takes it out of you in spades. I slept late myself."

"We've got to go back in. Soon, I'd say."

Andrew nodded. He felt the same way about it. He hadn't learned half enough in Pennyman's room. There were answers there somewhere, but they wouldn't reveal themselves to timid men. He and Pickett would have to wade in. "What's wrong with today? Mrs. Gummidge said something about going out. Rose is driving Aunt Naomi over to Leisure World later on. Pennyman's bound to be out most of the day doing whatever it is he does. Let's slide in as soon as he leaves."

Pickett nodded, staring over the railing at the sea. Andrew reeled in his line. The anchovy was gone—nibbled off by perch. He broke off a piece of Mounds bar and pressed the sticky coconut and chocolate around the hook, dropping it back into the water and letting line reel out until the lead weight whumped onto the bottom. He gave Pickett a studied look and said, "But *why* was she in his room? Why was she sneaking around when they're in league together?"

"Maybe she *wasn't* sneaking around. If they're in league together then maybe she can come and go as she likes. Maybe he doesn't care if she's in his room."

"I don't buy that. They're not equal partners, that's for sure. He's the general. She's not even a lieutenant, if you ask me. She's a private with aspirations. There's no way he'd be happy to know she was in the room.''

"Then she was after the elixir," said Pickett. "Just like you were. She heard you sneeze on the stair and hid behind the curtain, just like in a movie. When you yanked the curtain back, she pretended to be asleep. And you're right about his not wanting her to be there. If she weren't worried about being discovered, then she'd confront you with *your* being there. She couldn't do that, though, because *neither* of you was supposed to be there, lucky for you.''

They fished in silence for a moment. Then Pickett tossed the dregs of his coffee onto the pier and said, "It's clear, of course, what happened to Pfennig.''

"Is it?" asked Andrew.

"As a bell. He was sawed in half because there was something in him that had to be fetched out.''

"Like the squid on the beach," said Andrew.

"Almost exactly like the squid on the beach. I don't suppose Pfennig had swallowed the coin, though. I think it had been surgically implanted.''

"Why on earth . . ." began Andrew, but Pickett interrupted him impatiently.

"To keep it out of someone's hands—out of Pennyman's hands, to be precise. All the evidence points to it. The newspaper clipping of Jack Ruby dead. The phone call from Pfennig. Pennyman slouching around town trying out the quarter trick on every eccentric he runs into. He sawed Pfennig in half is what he did, and retrieved a monumentally important coin.''

"Rose's cousin has a coin collection," said Andrew. "Some of them can be valuable as hell. He needs a curly quarter, apparently, but you can't get one for love nor money—or at least not for love. He'd need half a million to buy a good one, I understand.''

"This is not that kind of coin. You know that as well as I do. Nobody beats that sort of coin into a spoon. It wouldn't make sense. They'd beat a coin into a spoon to alter it, to disguise it.

Pennyman isn't a coin collector in *that* sense. Offer him a curly quarter and he won't react; take my word for it. How about all that nonsense in Puget Sound about the fish with the coin in its belly? That was no curly quarter either.'' Pickett shook his head, remembering his hurried trip down from Vancouver. "The man at the gas station there said I needed new rings. They'll always try to take you for something. He made fun of my name, too. Damned rustics.''

"What is it then?''

"What? The coin? I don't know. I think . . . I'm not sure. But I'd bet my bottom dollar that it's ancient as hell. Coins, originally, were magical totems. You know that, of course.''

"Of course,'' said Andrew. "Common knowledge, isn't it? Were they?''

"For a fact. Moon disks is what they were. Playing cards are the same sort of thing, distilled down from the tarot deck, which itself was a distillation of an even more ancient deck. I wouldn't at all wonder if the most commonplace coins were tainted with some little bit of magic which has strayed down out of antiquity. This spoon of yours, take my word for it, was fashioned out of a coin that's incredibly old. Older than either one of us would guess. The same with carp.''

"What?'' asked Andrew, puzzled. The mention of carp reminded him that he was fishing, and he reeled up his line to find a starfish eating the candy. He plucked it off and threw it back.

"Carp. You've seen pictures of two carp curled around each other like a yin and yang. That's part and parcel the same as the fish or the serpent swallowing its own tail. Like on top of Pennyman's stick and Moneywort's hat. And guess what—they were carved into a wooden sign over Pfennig's door in Gastown. Now you might think I'm nuts, but I'll tell you that all this magical talk isn't just symbolic: carp curled around into circles, like moon disks, like coins, like the buttons on your shirt, like bus tokens and the pattern of seeds in a flower and the cycle of the seasons and the planets going round and round in the sky. Read Jung. It's all the same thing. We're awash in magical totems. Surrounded by little portholes looking out into infinity, at glimpses of immortality, if you bring it down to earth. The most trivial flotsam and jetsam scattered on the beach and cluttering shelves of junk stores *means* something, if you look at it from the right angle, through the right sort of spectacles.''

''But *what* does it mean?'' asked Andrew, reeling in his line again. He had no real patience. That was his problem when it came to fishing. The Mounds bar hadn't accomplished anything. The mussel was gone and the shrimp was half-eaten. He hacked another anchovy into bits, baited all three hooks with it, and swept the head and tail off into the ocean as chum. ''I have these nagging doubts,'' he said as he released the catch on the reel. ''Let's say it's all true, all this business you've been talking about. Let's say my shirt buttons *mean* something besides just being buttons. So what? I mean, what about the man who's ignorant of it? What about the man who doesn't see—how does it go?—'infinity in a grain of sand'? He just buttons up his shirt and heads down to the cafe for a hamburger. *You* look at a hamburger and think about circles and then about moon disks and about curled serpents and about planets swinging through space. This other man looks at a hamburger and sees ground beef. Do you know what I mean? If you were both struck dead coming out of the cafe, you'd go to your grave with a head full of puzzles; he'd go to his with a full stomach. So what does it all *mean—really*?''

''I haven't any idea on earth,'' said Pickett. ''But I mean to find out.''

TEN

THE METROPOLITAN PUTTED along up Seal Beach Boulevard
toward Rossmoor Leisure World. Andrew and Pickett still
smelled of fish, because of cutting up anchovies, but Uncle
Arthur wouldn't much care. There was no way at all to anticipate
how he'd react to anything, given that he was ninety-two years
old, maybe older—probably older—and that he grinned and
winked and looked vastly surprised at what seemed to be
randomly chosen moments. So the fishy smell and the tarry,
scale-smeared jeans wouldn't matter a bit. Their wearing ape
masks or space helmets wouldn't have mattered. Uncle Arthur
would be every bit as likely to leap in startled surprise at the sight
of them in a coat and tie, fresh from the barber.

They turned in past the enormous, skeletal, revolving globe
that marked the Leisure World gate and were grilled by an
octogenarian guard, who rang up Uncle Arthur's townhouse on a
wall-hung telephone and then entered into a baffling conversa-

tion. He put his hand over the mouthpiece, turned to Andrew, and said, "He wants to know if you're the man with the sheep."

"Indeed we are," said Andrew.

The guard peered uncertainly into the back seat, suspicious, perhaps, that there weren't any sheep riding along.

"In the trunk," said Andrew. "Stuffed toys, for the grand-niece. Christmas." He winked at the guard, who nodded, as if he understood Christmas despite its being eight months away, and then he muttered into the phone again before hanging up. Suddenly cordial, he waved them through and watched as they headed west, toward the townhouses and apartments that skirted the oilfields. The air was heavy with the smell of oil-saturated earth mingling with the salt air in the onshore ocean breeze.

"Stinks, doesn't it?" said Pickett, rolling up his window.

"I love it," said Andrew. "It's a gift, is what it is—our ability to smell the world as well as see it and hear it."

"I say it stinks. What was that nonsense about sheep? We haven't got any sheep."

"Always agree with everyone. That's my motto. If they were expecting sheep, and we say we've got them in the trunk, then it's suddenly *us* they were expecting. *Ipso facto,* as the logician would say."

Pickett nodded. It made sense. "Isn't that Uncle Arthur over there in the rose bushes?"

Andrew angled in toward the curb, parked the Metropolitan in a visitor's space, and set the brake. "Ho!" he shouted, thinking to make themselves known. It wouldn't do to slip up on Uncle Arthur unawares. The old man turned and gave them a baffled look, as if he were expecting the men with the sheep, and this wasn't them. Then, squinting and shading his eyes with his hand, he seemed to recognize them, and he waved and motioned them over.

"Help me get this fellow out of here," he said.

Pickett peered past him, a look of intense interest on his face. "What fellow?"

"Turtle. Big one. There he is. See him there? His shell is almost the color of the stucco. Here, help me haul him out. Fellow wants to hibernate some more, I guess, and tried to disappear under the ivy."

There it was—the light brown shell of a desert tortoise. Its feet were drawn in and its little pointy tail bent sideways, as if the creature meant to weather a storm. Pickett bent in and pulled it out, grunting in surprise at the weight of it. It was as big around as a hubcap. "Where do you want him?" asked Pickett.

Uncle Arthur started away toward the garages. "In the car," he said. Pickett gave Andrew a look, and Andrew shrugged as both of them followed along.

The red electronic car sat in its stall like something landed from the stars. Andrew had always admired it, with its immense fins and tiny cab. It was what cars were meant to look like in an alternate universe. A cut-down cardboard box lay on the floor, wedged up against the steering bar. Pickett fitted the turtle into the too-small box, in among lettuce leaves, which it had to sit on.

"Won't steal your car, will he?" asked Andrew, grinning.

Uncle Arthur looked at him blankly. "Coffee?" he asked.

"Yes indeed," said Pickett. "I'll take a cup."

Uncle Arthur regarded Andrew again, seeming to see him for the first time. "Aren't you the nephew?" he asked.

"That's right. Rose's husband. Naomi's nephew-in-law."

"That's just what you are. Of course. And you must be Spigot."

"Pickett, sir. Beams Pickett. We met some months back, I think. On the pier."

"Ah." Uncle Arthur stared as if in disbelief at Pickett's face. "I remember the mustache." He grimaced. "You were bent over cleaning a halibut, I recall, almost upside down. It looked as if your mouth were in your forehead for a moment, and that you had an inconceivable head of hair underneath it. Then I saw my mistake. It was a mustache after all. Fancy a mustache. Grotesque notion. Do you know that in my day they patented a device for burning off beards and mustaches?"

Pickett blinked, his hand going inadvertently to his face. "Did they?"

"A mechanical device. Reduced them to ash. Touted as the end to razors. It was a miracle of the future."

"I don't doubt it," said Pickett.

Uncle Arthur gazed at him, as if he suddenly supposed that

Pickett *did* doubt it. "I sold them. Door to door. It wasn't like vacuum cleaners. There was no live demonstration. Just a patented dummy. Head was stuffed with hair. You'd pull out a beard's worth through holes poked in his chin, apply the machine to it, and immolate the beard. Made a terrible stink. That was what got in the way of sales. Set the dummy on fire once."

"Huh," said Pickett sympathetically, stepping into the living room of Uncle Arthur's townhouse. It smelled like a barn. Arthur turned to Andrew, winked broadly, and jerked his thumb in Pickett's direction. Andrew was mystified. He had no idea on earth whether the old man was playacting or was cockeyed with age. There was an atmosphere of shrewdness behind his eyes, of tired knowledge that gave the lie to the senility business. Andrew had faith in his own ability to read another man's eyes. And Uncle Arthur's talk wasn't so very odd, either. It often seemed so because of the old man's leaping from one bit of conversation to another; as if as soon as you broached a subject he would play the coming exchange through in his mind in an instant, and then leap ahead to some distant point, or some tangentially related subject. And there hadn't been anything the least bit off-key about Uncle Arthur when he'd appeared at Moneywort's shop. He hadn't been engaged then in loony pursuits; on the contrary. It was his baffling activities, more than anything else, that made people wonder about him.

"Excuse me for having forgotten," said Pickett, "but I'm confused about *your* name."

"Arthur," said Uncle Arthur, looking as if Pickett were insane.

"Arthur . . . ?"

"Eastman."

"Ah, of course. Eastman. Somehow I had it mixed up with another name. What was it Andrew? It was you who told me, wasn't it? When we were chatting about the old days, back in Iowa. I can't quite get it Lique-something. That can't have been it."

"Laquedem," said Uncle Arthur. "That was a good long time ago. I've anglicized it just a little."

There was a scuffling back toward the hallway. Both Andrew and Pickett turned around, and there was another tortoise, bigger than the first, wandering out of the bedroom. Someone had painted a landscape scene onto its shell. Behind it was yet another, nosing along the light green carpet, thinking, perhaps, that the carpet ought to be edible, and that if he nosed around long enough he would find a patch that was.

Uncle Arthur stepped away toward the kitchen, and so Pickett, as if seeing his chance, slipped off down the hall. Following along, Andrew found himself in Uncle Arthur's almost-empty bedroom. In it was an ancient pine table, tilted on wobbly legs, and an old straight-back chair that must have been almost inhumanly uncomfortable. In the center of the room lay a bed—an oversize cot. It might easily have been the room of a hermit. A third turtle peeked out at them from under the bed. There were two bits of ornament in the room: a short length of hempen rope hanging on the wall, so old and so fragile-seeming that it might have crumbled to bits at the slamming of a door. It was looped around and tied into a noose. And then over the bed, strung by more rope, were two old, earthy ploughshares, crossed and hanging from the ceiling.

Pickett glanced around nervously, seeming to Andrew to be looking for something telling. "This is a crime," he whispered to Andrew, who shrugged.

"He likes it this way," said Andrew. "He used to sleep on a gunnysack filled with coconut fiber, but Aunt Naomi made him switch to the cot. It was his only concession to comfort, as if he's trying to expiate some monstrous guilt or sin. Part of his nuttiness if you ask me."

"I don't buy that," Pickett said. "I don't hold with nuttiness. There's always something more behind it."

The turtle came creeping out just then, angling toward Pickett's shoe. Andrew leaned down to pet it, just as Uncle Arthur shuffled in bearing a coffee cup.

"They're everywhere," said the old man, gesturing tiredly. "Don't mind them. They won't hurt you. Did either of you know that squids, of all creatures except pigs, have the highest degree of innate intelligence?"

Pickett shook his head, accepting the cup of coffee—cold coffee, it turned out. The three of them went back out into the hallway.

"Ice?" asked Uncle Arthur.

"I don't think so," said Pickett. "Too early in the morning for ice. Pigs, you say?"

"No, squids. They've put them in lidded jars, science has, and the squids figure out within moments how to unscrew the lids. Give the jar to a child and watch him work at it."

"Maybe if the child had suckers on his fingers . . ." said Andrew, reaching down to pet the painted tortoise, which had lumbered out into the living room proper.

Pickett shook his head in quick little jerks at Andrew, meaning for him to keep his mouth shut, to leave off with his jokes. "What fascinates me are pigs," Pickett said, sipping the thin, chicory-flavored coffee. It tasted like ant poison.

Lying on an end table next to Andrew's chair was a Xeroxed catalogue. "Gators of Miami," it read across the top. On each page was a list of available, mail-order animals: hippos, giraffes, caiman, antelope, even elephants and wildebeests. You could pick them up COD at the air freight depot at Los Angeles airport. All you needed was a truck. Amused, Andrew thumbed through it idly until he came to a section on barnyard animals. Someone had filled in half a dozen of the blanks, as if to put in an order to outfit a farm.

"Nothing like a pig," said Arthur.

Pickett slapped his knee. "That's my feeling entirely," he said. "I understand you can house-train them, like dogs and cats. There was a fellow over in Buena Park who taught one to count. He had a sow that would stamp on the ground, counting out numbers, and then grunt when she'd calculated a sum. It was amazing."

"Makes you think about the glories of the universe, doesn't it?" asked Andrew, clicking his tongue at the painted tortoise, which had lodged under the coffee table and was attempting to paddle itself free.

Uncle Arthur nodded sagely. "I've always been a friend to pigs," he said.

Conversation waned. Pickett seemed to be grappling with some means of opening the old man up, but the talk kept going awry.

"Ordering animals, are you?" asked Andrew, waving the catalogue.

Arthur shrugged. "After a fashion. Years ago I set up for a time as a wildlife biologist. Took quite an interest in the migratory habits of certain animals, especially of swine—of feral pigs. Most people have no notion what happens to farm animals that escape the confines of the barnyard. They exercise certain—functions, perhaps. There's more of them out there than you'd guess, living their own lives, out from under the yoke.'' Uncle Arthur paused, gazing at Andrew shrewdly. Then he said, ''Quite a race, pigs. Let one of them out of a barnyard and there's no telling where he'll go. Rather like letting loose a balloon with a message inside, if you follow me. Liable to end up in the most puzzling lands, largely because of air currents, of course. Feral pigs are the same sort of phenomenon, except that they're indifferent to air currents. It's another sort of—what?—force, let's say, that drives a liberated pig. I've written a monograph on the subject, in fact. But that was fifty-odd years ago.''

Pickett nodded sagely and winked at Andrew. ''Quite a history in pigs, isn't there?''

''A deep one, sir.''

''By golly, Andrew,'' said Pickett abruptly, as if he had just then remembered something. ''Wasn't it a pig that brought the spoon around to Naomi's farm? Tall tale, I suppose?''

''No, the gospel truth or so I've been told. You haven't heard that story, have you, Uncle?''

The old man shrugged. ''It's true enough. Old silver spoon. Very curious. I wouldn't touch it with a dung fork. And neither should you boys. Don't, for God's sake, eat from it. Leave it alone. Pig didn't want it, did he?''

Pickett shook his head.

''Does anyone want it?'' asked Uncle Arthur.

''What?'' asked Andrew, thinking that the old man was speaking generally. ''*Want* it? I don't suppose so.''

''Only Jules Pennyman,'' said Pickett, and he looked at Andrew in such a way as to imply that he'd purposely ripped the lid off the conversation.

''Pennyman, is it? And has he got it?'' Uncle Arthur yawned suddenly, as if he were beginning to find the conversation trivial and tiring.

Andrew shook his head. ''Not at all. He . . .''

"Then keep it that way." The old man took out a pocketknife and began very slowly to pare his fingernails. He looked up suddenly at the open front door. "Damnation!" he cried, standing up. "Another one's got out."

Sure enough, there was the painted turtle, having heaved itself free of the coffee table, gone out through the door, and making away across the lawn. The third turtle teetered on the threshold, inches from freedom.

"I'll fetch him," cried Pickett, springing up.

"Put him in the car," Uncle Arthur said. "On top of the other one. I'm taking them out. For air."

In minutes three of the tortoises lay in a heap in the box, and the fourth sat on the passenger seat. Pickett sorted the boxed tortoises out so that the biggest was on the bottom. Together they made a little pyramid of turtles, like an icon to a pagan god.

"Quite a load," said Pickett. "Where are they going again?"

Uncle Arthur buttoned his tweed coat, then hauled out his pocket handkerchief and dusted off the car fender. "Out and about. Bit of a constitutional and all. Naomi tells me you boys are coming along to the treasure hunt." He climbed into the cab, putting on a pair of thin leather gloves with the fingertips cut out of them.

Pickett looked baffled. "Treasure hunt . . . ?" he started to say, but Andrew interrupted.

"That's a fact. I'd forgotten all about it." He wondered wildly how in the world Aunt Naomi knew about their going on the treasure hunt. It must have been the overheard conversation on the front porch again. But why had she thought it necessary to inform Uncle Arthur?

"Do an old man a moderate favor, will you, boys?"

"Absolutely," said Pickett.

"Carry your pig spoon along to the treasure hunt. I'd like to have a look at it. I haven't seen it in heaven knows how long. It would bring back memories, to tell you the truth."

"Sure. Of course. If you'd like to see it," said Andrew. "I can bring it around tomorrow—later today, if you want. There's no need to wait on something like that."

"No, no." He shook his hand at Andrew, almost wildly,

and his face seemed to pale. "I don't want it. Keep it tight between now and the treasure hunt. It's on the night of the hunt that I'll want you to fetch it along. We might have need of it. And not a word of this to Pennyman or anyone else. You two can't leave town for a couple of days, can you? Take it with you?"

"Impossible. The cafe is opening tomorrow night. And we've got to get the chef's hats ready. We're being filmed by KNEX—a little promotional gag I've cooked up. Why?"

"Nothing. Keep it tight, though. Don't trust Pennyman."

"Not very damned likely," Andrew said. "What do you know about him?"

"That he's no damned good. He and I have had our differences. But don't tell him I said that. Don't mention me at all. He doesn't know that we've had any differences. Don't mention turtles or pigs or anything at all. Mum's the word." Uncle Arthur winked in the manner of a secret conspirator and started up the humming little electric engine. There was a click, and the car navigated back out of the parking stall and weaved away down the drive. Halfway to the street, as if heeding an impulse to take a shortcut, the car shot off across the lawn, bumped over the corner of a brick flowerbed border, and banged down the curb. The car wobbled on its miniature tires, then hummed away out of sight, heading southeast.

"Let's go!" shouted Pickett, and immediately he was off and running toward the Metropolitan. Andrew followed, swept up by Pickett's urgency, and the two of them flung the car doors open and slid in, Andrew firing up the engine and the car leaping into the empty street in a cloud of black exhaust.

"Turn left at the corner, along the wall," Pickett said. "We've got to follow him. Out for a constitutional! Turtles, for God's sake!"

Andrew banked around the corner. There was Uncle Arthur, disappearing three hundred yards down, behind a bank of parking garages. "There's no exit gate down here," Andrew said, shifting down into second gear as he approached the little alley that ran along the garages. "He's not going out."

"Just follow him." Pickett gripped the metal dashboard, his

face hovering inches from the windshield. "Don't lose him. This is vital."

Andrew peered sidewise at his friend's livid face. "No problem," he said. "I won't lose him."

But just then they lost him. The alley behind the garages swung around in a slow arc, dead-ending against a fire hydrant which sat at the edge of a sward of grass and flowerbeds. Uncle Arthur didn't care about grass and flowerbeds; he'd shunted between the fire hydrant and a cinderblock wall and was tearing across the lawn, straight through a shower of lawn sprinklers, the tires of the electronic car leaving little curvy ruts.

"Back out, for the love of . . . Go around!" Pickett was wild with the chase.

Andrew threw the Metropolitan into reverse and slammed away backward down the alley, weaving with the speed of it, almost out of control. He rammed the palm of his hand down onto the horn, honking his way out onto the street again as a carful of gray-haired women jerked to a stop to let him in. The Metropolitan roared off, making a false turn into a cul-de-sac, squealing to a stop, and backing out of it, too. A horn honked in the street, but Andrew didn't bother to look back. He was fired with his driving, and he tore away, shouting with laughter, punching Pickett in the shoulder. "Relax!" he hollered. "We'll catch him!"

Lousy driver, was he? If only Rose could see him now, catapulting around the grounds of Leisure World, chasing a tiny automobile carrying God's own mob of turtles and driven by an impossibly strange old man. How many people could say they'd done that? He realized all of a sudden that Uncle Arthur had disappeared, and he throttled down as they approached a corner, swinging out toward the right gutter. What did the racing man say about turns? Go in slow; come out fast—something like that. He set his teeth and jammed down on the accelerator, sliding around, tires squealing. Maybe it was best that Rose *couldn't* see him.

"There he is again!" cried Pickett, grabbing his forehead.

"Hold on!" cried Andrew, and he bounced the left side of the car up over the curb, the right side rolling up a little concrete wheelchair ramp. They started off across the lawn as Andrew surveyed the rearview mirror for signs of pursuit. The idea of a carful of ancient Leisure World police tearing along behind appealed massively. Rose would have to bail him out of a makeshift prison on the grounds. Maybe she would bring him the clothes of a washerwoman as a disguise. She'd find him manacled to a shuffleboard pole. He laughed out loud. Stay out of the sprinklers, he told himself, angling away toward the street again. If the Metropolitan bogged down . . .

"Slow up, for God's sake!" shouted Pickett. A garage wall loomed ahead. Andrew hauled on the wheel, skidding past the edge of it, the tires skiving out a strip of wet sod. A woman carrying a golf club across the lawn ran for an open door, shouting. Andrew hooted and jammed his foot down onto the accelerator, spinning the wheels and then abruptly heading for the street again. They'd saved a hundred yards taking the lawn. He'd learned something from watching Uncle Arthur. The old man had guts; you had to give him that.

And there Uncle Arthur was, driving on the street again, down toward the shopping center. He was going out the south exit. They were traveling too quick now; in a moment they'd be upon him, and it would be evident that they were following. Andrew spun the steering wheel and they rocketed in behind a collection of dumpsters, where he braked to a stop. "Give him a second," Andrew said, breathing hard.

"Don't give him more than that," said Pickett. "We've got to get out of here. If anyone calls the gate and reports us, the guards will shoot us on sight. They carry weapons, damn it. These old men can't be expected to take the long view when it comes to ripping up lawns."

"Well it was you who were so hot to trail him. I was just . . ." Andrew suddenly put the car in reverse, backed around, and then headed out onto the street, looking back over his shoulder. He'd seen an official-looking car creeping along slow across the mouth of the alley some hundred yards distant. "They're after us!" he said, feeling a flush of excitement again.

"Out the gate!" cried Pickett, swiveling around to look out the rear window. "Quick, before they spot us and radio ahead."

Andrew hesitated. He was tempted to make a U-turn and confront the prowling search car—speed past it honking his horn, lean out of the window and gesture insanely with both hands, lead it on a wild chase through the twisting streets, clipping off fire hydrants, crunching down mailboxes, scattering pigeons on the lawns, straightaway through the fence and onto the oilfields, dragging fifty feet of chain-link with him. Motive? he'd say when they booked him. And then he'd laugh.

He grinned at Pickett as they set out—approaching the gate. There was a car in front of them, slowing down to cross the little, bent steel fingers that thrust out of the road. A single guard lounged in the gatehouse. Andrew could hear the phone ringing as the car in front of them sped off. On a wild impulse, he tromped on the clutch and shoved the Metropolitan into first gear, gunning the engine and rolling down his window.

"Don't," whispered Pickett.

Andrew nodded with an air of utter confidence. "I'll handle this."

The guard, holding the phone now, hunched down suddenly and peered out through the window at them, astonished. He hollered into the receiver. "Yes!" he shouted. "It's them!" and he let the phone drop and lunged toward the door.

"Go!" shouted Pickett desperately.

There was a click and a bang, and a long wooden gate began to sweep down across the road. Andrew regarded it coolly. Pickett slammed Andrew's shoulder and shouted. "For the love of God!" The guard fumbled in his coat—for what? A gun, a badge, a can of Mace? Andrew laughed out loud and started to speak, but then his foot was kicked off the clutch and Pickett's shoe was suddenly jammed atop his own on the accelerator. The Metropolitan shot forward, under the half-shut gate, careening toward a concrete planter, the steering wheel twisting to the left.

Andrew jerked around and grappled with the wheel, shouting incoherently and pulling it too far to the right, the car skewing around in a fishtailing slide. "Get your damned foot . . . !" Andrew shouted, pulling the wheel back again. All in an instant, Pickett sailed against the door. Off balance now, he pressed down

all the harder on the accelerator and on Andrew's shoe as Andrew
slammed his left foot down onto the clutch. The engine screamed,
a cloud of exhaust shot out, and Andrew let up on the clutch,
anticipating the sound of smashing engine steel. He heaved again
at Pickett's foot.

"Oh!" Pickett yelled. "Damn!" and they skidded past the tail
end of a parked car, spinning around into the parking lot of the
Leisure Market. A shopping cart flew. Andrew pulled his foot,
freed at last, off the accelerator, jammed on the brake, and then,
his hands shaking on the steering wheel, he drove slowly and
deliberately across the parking lot, out the exit onto Westminster
Boulevard and up the street until he turned into the parking lot of
the Haynes Steam Plant, pulling in among a clutch of cars and
cutting the engine.

He sat for a moment in silence and then said, "They won't find
us here." He breathed heavily to counteract the slamming of his
heart. Then he got out of the car and went around to the back to
examine the hubcap that had scraped the curb. It was mashed in all
the way around, as if someone had beaten it with a hammer. "Aw
hell," said Andrew. It wasn't just anywhere that you could get a
hubcap for a Metropolitan. The front bumper was dented too,
where he'd hit the shopping cart. The chase had taken its toll.

Pickett still sat in silence when Andrew climbed back in.
"Sorry about the foot on the accelerator," he said. "But what in
the world did you want to tell the guard? I told you they were
licensed to carry weapons."

"I had the wild urge to quote poetry to him," Andrew
admitted, grinning suddenly and recapturing some little bit of the
outlandish feeling that had surged through him when he had
confronted the guard.

"Poetry!"

"Vachel Lindsay, actually." Andrew let out a whoosh of
breath, calming down now. " 'Boomlay, Boomlay, Boomlay,
Boom!' " he quoted, slamming his fist against the dashboard.
" 'Banging on the table with the handle of a broom!' What do you
think? Would it have done the trick?"

"Of course," said Pickett. "Of course it would have. That's

just what it would have done.'' He twisted around and looked past the cars, back toward the street. ''He wasn't in the shopping center.''

''Who? The guard?''

''No. Your uncle. His car wasn't parked in the shopping center. He's gone on. Where in the world? We lost him because we were screwing around.''

Andrew frowned. ''Say it—*I* was screwing around. Let's go. They're not going to chase us. The guards don't have any jurisdiction off the grounds, and they aren't going to call the police over something like this. The city police don't send out squad cars over a chewed-up lawn. I didn't mean to do that—to cause any damage. I got carried away.''

Pickett kept silent.

''Let's head down to rat control and talk to Chateau—see what he's found out about the fish elixir.''

''Good enough,'' said Pickett, sighing. ''But where the devil was the old man taking those turtles, and why? How are we going to find out? This is vital. I'm sure of it.''

Andrew shrugged as they turned off into traffic, driving up Westminster Boulevard toward Studebaker Road, intending to make a U-turn, then head back again east, along the edge of the oilfields. *Vital*—Andrew couldn't fathom it. What was vital were about a dozen things: painting another swatch of house, getting the kitchen together, being *responsible* for a change. And here he was out hoodwinking around, as if he were eighteen. What he *wasn't* responsible for was the godamned fate of the world, for the machinations of Pickett's bogeymen. Damn all this business about coins and magic. What had come of it but a dented hubcap?

And damn the pig spoon, too. He hadn't wanted it anyway. Not really. He was half-ready to *give* it to Pennyman, just to have done with it. Except that Pennyman was a foul slug, and Andrew wouldn't give him a nickel, unless it was attached to a nail driven into the floor. He grinned despite himself. Well, he and Pickett could stop around to talk to Chateau, who would, of course, know nothing about the elixir, which was probably just fancy cod liver oil. Then they'd hotfoot it home. They could be there by eleven if they hurried. Andrew would make an issue of their returning, as if they were just then wrapping up a really solid morning of fishing. It wasn't *lying,* actually, to carry on like that; it was something like self-preservation. It would be the last time, too. For a couple of days he would be wrapped up utterly in the business of the cafe and the chef's hats, which Rose, in her infinite wisdom, had agreed to assemble. She was giving him a chance to prove himself in his own oddball way. He knew that. It was a matter of trust on her part. He couldn't betray her.

He banged his hand against the steering wheel. He'd very nearly disgraced himself that morning. For what? Well, he would turn over that leaf now; he'd be good, worthy of her . . .

"Speed up," said Pickett.

"What?"

"I said pick it up a little bit. This is a 45-mile-per-hour zone. What are you doing, about 20?"

"Yeah, sorry." He *had* been doing about 20, and drifting toward the shoulder on the right. He set his teeth and sped up, making the turn at the light and reversing direction in the suddenly gloomy morning.

A fog had hovered in, and the sunlight brightened and waned with each blowing drift. Dark oil derricks stood alien and lonesome in the mist, and the insect heads of oil pumps rose and fell like iron grasshoppers scattered randomly across two hundred acres of dirt wasteland. There was a tang of oil seeping into the trapped air of the Metropolitan even with the windows rolled up. The fields were deserted, empty of people and of structures, except for a couple of rusted shacks way off in the murk. Andrew slowed the car despite his determination. The rush of energy he'd gotten during the chase had entirely drained out of him.

"There! Wait!" shouted Pickett suddenly. "Pull over!"

Mechanically, Andrew twisted the wheel and bumped up a driveway into the dirt of the oilfield, the car behind them rushing past with a blaring horn.

"Around behind that shed," Pickett ordered, rolling his window down and shoving his head out.

The car slowed and stopped. Andrew cut the motor, listening to the foggy silence and to the creak, creak, creak of the pumps. "What?"

"Off to the north. That way," he said, pointing. "Isn't that his car? Of course it is."

Andrew squinted. The windshield was fogging up. Pickett was right. There was the rear end of Uncle Arthur's car, half-hidden behind a pile of wooden pallets. "Do you see him?"

"No," said Pickett. "Yes. There he is, off by the fence, by the oleander bushes. He's up to something. Let's go."

Before Andrew could protest, Pickett was out the door and running at a crouch toward a distant oil pump. Uncle Arthur was a hundred yards away, busy with something involving the turtles. Andrew could see the cardboard box lying on the ground ten feet beyond where the old man was bent over. Pulling the keys out of the ignition, Andrew followed Pickett, feeling like a fool. They'd be caught, is what they'd be, and arrested for trespassing. And when the police got a look at the Metropolitan, the two of them would be identified as the thugs that had terrorized Leisure World.

He hunched in behind Pickett, who was jammed up against a rusting chain-link fence and partly hidden by the machinery of the oil pump. "He's got the turtles," said Pickett. "What's on the other side of the fence?"

"Naval Weapons Station," said Andrew.

"What in the devil is he doing? Let's get closer. We can't mess up here." With that Pickett scuttled away toward the mountain of pallets, and Andrew followed again, looking back over his shoulder toward his car. There was still no one in sight. The traffic on the highway zoomed along, dim through the fog. He should have driven farther onto the fields, where the Metropolitan couldn't be seen from the road. That's what would give them away. Maybe they'd be lucky, though. Maybe the police, if they drove past, would suppose it belonged to workmen.

They peered around the edge of the pallet heap, deadly silent. They could just hear Uncle Arthur humming or singing to himself. Either that or he was talking to the turtles. He bent over and picked one up, then crouched into the oleanders, disappearing. There was a rustling of brush, and then he stooped back out and reached into the box, where the last of the turtles waited. He seemed to be setting them free, shoving them in among the bushes, maybe under the fence. It was obvious: He was directing his squadron of turtles, running them out into the fields of the weapons station. This was the last one.

There was something odd about the turtle; it seemed to be wearing a gaudy sort of belt. "What in the world . . .?" Andrew muttered. Then suddenly he saw what it was—a belt all right, made of Navajo silver in the form of great, strung-together squash blossoms. Uncle Arthur pushed his way into the oleanders again.

"It's the treasure hunt," Andrew whispered into Pickett's ear. Pickett turned to give him a look. Andrew put his finger to his lips and jerked his head back toward the car, tiptoeing along the pallets. They'd have to make a rush for the road, get out before they were seen. But it was too late. Uncle Arthur had got rid of the last turtle and was stepping along toward his machine, oblivious to their presence. If they ran for it now he'd see them for sure. Pickett, clearly realizing it, crouched as low as he could and jerked on Andrew's jacket, pulling him down, too. Both of them edged around clockwise, keeping just out of sight. They heard the tiny slam of the door and the click and whir of the engine. Quickly they hunched around counter-clockwise now, as Uncle Arthur drove away forward. They stayed hidden, watching the old man make a wide U-turn around an oil derrick and head back toward them, beeping his horn as he swept past on the far side of the pile, humming away east, bumping across ruts, bound, apparently, for home.

"Damn it," said Pickett out loud, standing up and thrusting his hands into his coat pockets. "He was honking at *us*. He knew we were here. We haven't fooled him for a moment."

"He couldn't have known. The Metropolitan is lost in the fog, and he sure as hell didn't *see* us. He was honking at the turtles, I think."

Pickett peered at him as the two of them set out toward the highway. "What do you know about this? It doesn't seem to surprise you?—him covering turtles with silver and scattering them in the fog? What about this treasure hunt? He's hunting treasure with turtles?''

They drove back toward Seal Beach Boulevard and the freeway as Andrew told Pickett about the mysterious treasure hunt. Pickett, true to form, didn't seem to find it half so innocent as Andrew had. Andrew told him about how such treasure hunts were carried out in the old days, implying that this wasn't any sort of precedent, any sort of real mystery. But Pickett swept his suggestions away with a belittling wave of his hand.

''It's the *key,* is what it is,'' said Pickett. ''And the old man wants the pig spoon there. Why? Why the turtles? Why in heaven is he trafficking in farm animals? That's what I want to know. What's all this pig business? *The One Pig*—strange title for a book, isn't it? It wouldn't signify much, though, except for the rest of this. I've got some work to do in the library. Care to run into L.A.?''

''Not me,'' said Andrew. ''I'm shot for the rest of the day. For the week. Are you still maitre d'ing?''

''Of course I am,'' said Pickett. ''I'll be there with bells on.''

''Well, look—don't take all this so damned seriously. It's probably a lot of silly nonsense and none of our business. It looks awfully wild and important at two o'clock in the morning, but in the light of day it's exposed as foolishness—a couple of old men cutting senile capers. Am I right?''

Pickett gave him a withering look. ''A man has been sawed in half in Vancouver. Another man has been swallowed by a fish in Puget Sound. There's a herd of decorated turtles scouring across the pumpkin fields of the Naval Weapons Station. There's . . . Wait a minute. Where did you put the spoon, anyway?''

''In behind my books,'' said Andrew.

''I'd do better than that if I were you. You rooted through Pennyman's bedroom; we better suppose that he's going to root through yours. Get it out of there. Bury it under the house.''

''I hate getting under the house. There's spiders under the house.''

"Put it out in the cafe then. He doesn't go out there much, does he?"

"No," said Andrew. "He's afraid to run into me, I guess. He's a coward when you get right down to it, and doesn't want a confrontation. I'll put it somewhere safe. Leave it to me."

Pickett nodded, gazing out the window, lost already in the idea of killing the day in the library, of stumbling onto The Answer. They drove off into Garden Grove, bumping up into the parking lot of Rodent Control, where two brown-shirted employees mashed cornmeal and rat poison in an enormous wooden tub. Andrew slipped into a parking space and cut the engine. Pickett twisted the mirror around and peered into it, smoothing away at his hair and mustache. "Damn it," he said, unable to subdue his fog-frizzled cowlick. Andrew grinned at him, and Pickett frowned and got out.

Pickett pretended to be very businesslike when they pushed in through the glass door, nodding at the receptionist, who at once smiled broadly and raised her eyebrows as if of all the people she hoped would walk in that day, it was Pickett she hoped to see most of all. He reddened and looked at Andrew, who grinned at him. Then he croaked just a bit, as if he had something in his throat. "Georgia busy?" he asked.

"She's in the euphemism."

"Ah," said Pickett.

Just then there were footfalls on the carpet behind them, and Pickett's girlfriend appeared. Andrew wondered whether, in her Oriental shirt and black, Chinatown slip-on shoes, she didn't look more like a mystic than a secretary.

"Andrew," Pickett said, gesturing too widely, "you've met Georgia?"

"About a half-dozen times, actually."

"Of course," said Pickett. "Of course."

"Hi, Beamsy," she said, winking at Andrew.

"Beamsy?" Andrew whispered, and Pickett grinned crookedly at him.

She was slight and pretty, with crinkly eyes and a nice mouth and half-unruly curly hair. All in all she radiated a sort of go-to-hell attitude—necessary, maybe, for a psychic in a world full of doubters. Andrew said to her, "Would you and Beamsy like to be left alone for a bit?"

She blushed, and Pickett stuttered for a moment, then bent down suddenly to peer at a display of stuffed rats in a case along with various examples of their enormities: a gnawed wire, a chewed bit of avocado encased in Lucite, the stuffing out of a chair. "Very informative," he said weakly. "Imagine what a rat could do in your attic."

"Almost inconceivable, isn't it?" said Andrew, smiling at Georgia, who stepped toward the counter as if to explain the curiosities in the case. Andrew motioned toward a nearby door that stood half-ajar. "Is Mr. Chateau in his office?"

"Yes," she said. "I don't think he's up to anything. There was a gentleman in there ten minutes ago, but he's gone out."

"I'll just pop in, then, and leave you two to hash over the rat display."

Pickett looked half-betrayed and half-relieved, and as Andrew pushed through the door and out of the room, the two launched into earnest conversation that Andrew made no effort to overhear.

"What ho?" said Andrew cheerfully to the man who sat holding his head at the cluttered desk.

"What!" he half-shouted, sweeping an illustrated book on insects off onto the floor in a gesture of startled bewilderment. His face had on it the look of someone who half-expected to see something ghastly coming in through the door. "Mr. Vanbergen! Why . . . It's you, is it?" He grinned oddly. He had a jolly round sort of a face, almost cherubic, but it was tainted now as if with the memory of a recent fright, and he peered past Andrew, toward the parking lot visible through a far window. He seemed to relax suddenly. The wall behind him was covered with tray upon tray of beetles—thousands of them, some enormous, some microscopic, and all, except for their size, identical to the untrained eye. Andrew had always thought that a man would be worn down by the perpetual stare of countless beetle eyes, and here, perhaps, was evidence to support it.

"Feeling well?" asked Andrew. "Sorry to have burst in."

"Yes. No. I'm . . . I dozed off for a moment. I . . . I think it's a matter of biorhythms. I'm in a downswing. Feeling poorly, to tell you the truth." He waved his hand in a little explanatory squiggle.

"Sorry about that. I won't waste your time. I'm in a hurry myself. What did you come up with on the fish elixir?"

The man grinned again weakly. "Oh, yes. The . . . what did you call it? Elixir? It's nothing for you to worry about, actually."

"Excuse me?" said Andrew, blinking at him. "I wasn't actually *worried* about it; I was wondering what on earth it was."

"Of course, of course. I'm terribly sorry about it."

"Sorry?"

"It broke. In the sink. Slippery stuff, I'm afraid. Cracked to bits on the porcelain and went down the drain. Nothing but cracked glass. All of it gone. And the water was running, too. That was the pity of it. Washed all the goop off the fragments even. There wasn't enough left over to have a look at. I was disappointed, of course. It appeared to be fascinating stuff, although not entirely in my line." He bent over to pick up the insect book, avoiding Andrew's gaze.

"It's *all* gone?"

"I'm afraid so." He coughed into his hand. "Swept the glass into the trash can. Jaycox hauled it away this morning at six."

Andrew opened his mouth to speak, then stopped and stared at the man. He took a step closer to the desk, bent over, and stared harder. He knew he was revealing too much curiosity, too much wonder. He was giving himself away entirely, but he didn't care. Down the center of Biff Chateau's forehead was drawn the telltale line, charcoal gray, wavering where the silver quarter had crossed onto the bridge of his nose, and smudged where he'd been leaning against his arm when Andrew had come in.

ELEVEN

"BOUGHT OFF!" SHOUTED Pickett as they bumped out of the
parking lot and turned toward the freeway.

"I don't think so," Andrew said. "He was terrified. I've
never seen the like. He thought I was Pennyman coming in
through the door like that—coming back to deal with him
further. You should have seen the look on his face. Stark terror. I
think he put up a fight before he gave in. He's an honest man,
Chateau is, and he wouldn't have given the elixir up easily.
Maybe Pennyman threatened him with the same sort of business
he'd pulled on Pfennig." Andrew shivered with a sudden chill,
thinking about it.

Pickett nodded. "Well, now we know what we're up against,
don't we? We've been pretty casual about all of this so far.
Pennyman's probably already found the spoon. He probably
hunted it out this morning while we were hightailing it around
Leisure World. *He* hasn't been lounging around. Clearly, he
followed you yesterday morning when you hauled the elixir down

here. He's a careful man. We know that. You say you heard him refusing Mrs. Gummidge—wouldn't give her a drop of it even though she begged. The whole business becomes plain: It was out in his room that night because Mrs. Gummidge had been setting in to steal it. You sneezed out in the hallway and she hid, just like I said. You only took half an ounce, but then, maybe, she took a bit more. And here comes Pennyman to find his store of it depleted while he's out of town sawing Pfennig in half. Maybe there's only an ounce gone—not much, we say. But who knows? What if it were drugs of some sort—an ounce of cocaine, an ounce of heroin? There'd be murder in his eyes, wouldn't there? So what does he do? He looks around a bit and finds your penlight; simple as that. One, two, three. And he follows you down the freeway next morning, and figures he's struck pay dirt when you stop in to talk to Chateau. He waits for you to leave, and then he goes in and has a little talk with Chateau himself. Do you know what Pennyman told Georgia?''

"No," groaned Andrew.

"He said that there were two very persistent rats that he wanted to exterminate. He finds their 'droppings,' he said. Shooting was too good for them—that's what he said. He was going to trap them, cut them up into a stew, and feed them to the cats in the house—one spoonful at a time. That was this morning. Not half an hour ago. He thinks it's funny.''

"I'm afraid he . . .''

"And what's more," interrupted Pickett, "there can't be any doubt at all that he was tailing me the other night when I got in from Vancouver. No doubt at all. Am I right? Admit it. No more talk about coincidences. I don't believe in them.''

"You're right, so help me. I've said this before and I'll say it again. We've got to act." Andrew stared out the window at the empty fields trailing past, fields across which trooped Uncle Arthur's league of silver-bearing turtles. "What I can't quite fathom," he continued, squinting at Pickett, "is what in the hell is going on.''

Pickett checked his watch. They banked down the off-ramp and turned up onto the boulevard, heading home. "I'll come around later," said Pickett. "I've *got* to spend a couple of hours in the library. Maybe I'll find out. Wait for me, though. If he catches you snooping through his room alone . . .''

"He won't," Andrew said. "He won't *catch* me at all. I'm too many for him. I know how to handle his sort. You should have seen his face when he got the note in the mail—utter bewilderment. He was a rudderless boat." Andrew was cheered for a moment by the memory, but it didn't last. He gritted his teeth with determination. Pennyman! The son of a bitch. Andrew would take steps, immediately.

"He's got to be kept that way then—off-balance. Especially until we've got a handle on this."

"Leave it to me," said Andrew.

Pickett slammed his fist into his open palm. "What we've got to know is *why* he's going around town threatening people. And don't lose that spoon, for God's sake. Get on it as soon as we're home. I'll go up with you."

"No, don't. Rose and all. We've got to make it look as if we've been out fishing all morning. We can't burst in full of mysteries and plans. Did you shove your tackle box into the gunnysack?"

Pickett nodded as Andrew pulled into the curb. "Haven't got much done on the painting end, eh? What's that mess of paint by the window there?"

Andrew cut the engine. "That's the result of espionage. How about the tackle box?"

"Yes. It's in the gunnysack, along with my fishing jacket and my thermos."

"Great," said Andrew, climbing out of the car and going around to the trunk. In a slightly too-loud voice, just for the sake of an open window, he said, "Not bad for a morning's work, eh?" And he held the weighted gunnysack up with both hands, winking at Pickett.

His friend took it from him. "Heavy!" he said. "Must be—what?—twenty pounds if it's an ounce."

"Whoppers," said Andrew. He felt guilty suddenly, but faintly proud of himself for not actually lying. And no one was listening anyway, probably. Or watching. He slammed the trunk and watched Pickett deposit the sack in his car, climb in, and finally drive away after an elaborate amount of warming up the engine and racing the motor. Then, steeling himself, he walked into the backyard whistling, as if he'd spent a satisfactory morning.

Rose was in the kitchen, washing dishes, and Aunt Naomi sat at the table sipping coffee, looking oddly well. "You smell like fish," Naomi said, wrinkling her nose.

Andrew smiled cheerfully. "One of the hazards of the sport. What's this? Trix? Aunt! Trix? You? You're after the prize! What is it?" He picked up the box and studied the back. "A glow-in-the-dark squid! Have you got it out of there yet?" He tilted the box, angling the little colored balls of cereal so as to see to the bottom, and nearly spilling them onto the table top. "Here it is!" He hauled out a little cream-colored, glitter-sprinkled squid, three-inches long and made out of rubbery plastic. Grinning at Naomi and then at Rose, he said, "You two should have been quicker. It's mine now. My advice is that you empty the whole box into a bowl next time. Then root out the prize, and pour the cereal back into the box. You don't really even have to wash the bowl afterward—just dust it out." He pocketed the squid.

Rose whacked him on the shoulder with the dish towel. "I'm glad you made a morning of it," she said, hanging the towel up and dusting the sink with scouring powder. "It's what you need. The prize in the Trix is your reward for getting up early. Catch any fish?"

Andrew nodded weakly. "You should have seen the starfish I caught on a Mounds bar." He clicked his tongue, as if to imply that the sea had been full of creatures that morning, that there was nothing he hadn't hauled in. "Pickett just tossed a full gunnysack into his trunk—must have weighed twenty pounds."

He was a pitiful case—sneaking around. It was shameful, and he knew it. If he'd been up to something important, really important, if he were sure of it, then why in the hell didn't he just up and *tell* her? Because he wanted to protect her? Partly. Because it all looked very much like nonsense? Yep. Because he wanted desperately to play the hero, to make it clear in the end that he'd had the entire business in hand all along, and that, like Uncle Arthur, his seeming madness had deadly serious method in it?

That was it. He'd like to be a hero, wouldn't he?—casting down the villain Pennyman. It was pride and vanity. He saw through himself too damned clearly, and sometimes, when he was in a mood, he half-hated himself for it. Why couldn't he let himself rest? Why was he possessed day to day with the knowledge that he just wasn't good enough? Sometimes it made him want to throw up. He kissed Rose on the cheek and hurried up the stairs and into the bedroom before he was forced into any more lies.

The spoon was still there behind the books. It was faintly warm when he picked it up, and his palm seemed to retract at its touch, to draw back into itself like the antenna of a snail, repulsed by the feel of it. And it seemed monstrously heavy. The weight of it made him sag. He was suddenly tired. He'd been up early. All this Pennyman business was draining him. It was Pennyman, God damn him, that possessed Andrew with all these doubts about himself. That was the man's nefarious strength. That was how he worked. Andrew's back ached awfully, and there was nothing in the world that he wanted to do more than lie down and sleep.

He fought it though. Sleep was too easy. There was a job to be done. There was the matter of his shredded self-respect. He pocketed the spoon and headed back downstairs slowly, hanging onto the rail, saying nothing to Rose or Naomi as he ducked out into the cafe. He looked around, wondering, then picked up a pint glass, chose a half-dozen random spoons from the silverware box, and dropped them in, sliding the pig spoon in among them. It was a perfect disguise. He put the glass up on the wooden shelf that ran around half the room, ending against the stones of the fireplace. Sitting among books and knickknacks, the glass full of spoons looked innocent—just another decoration—and well above eye level so as not to catch anyone's casual attention. Feeling considerably lighter, but still fighting the compulsion to sleep, he headed out for the garage to fetch the paintbrush pickling in thinner. It was time to roll up his sleeves.

Pennyman's room was almost exactly as it had been two nights earlier. The man was psychotically neat. The only change was that the room smelled differently—only the old-house smell now; the window was shut against the ocean breeze, and there was no telltale hint of fish elixir or perfume.

The rest of the house was quiet. Rose had gone out with Aunt Naomi—the old woman's first outing in nearly a year. Dr. Garibaldi had come around that morning and been sent away after exclaiming that Naomi's recovery had been almost miraculous. He'd never seen anything like it. But then he'd never seen anything like the disease, either, which he still referred to euphemistically as "general debilitation," and so his surprise, perhaps, didn't signify as heavily as it might have. He'd found just a hint of internal bleeding, and that bothered him, but until Naomi could come in for tests . . . Naomi, at the moment, wasn't interested in tests.

Pennyman was out, too. Mrs. Gummidge was out. Andrew and Pickett had fastened the chain locks on the doors. If someone tried the front, the two would hear the rattling and close things up, then head out through the back door and into the garage, leaving that door unlocked, and pretending—if the locked-door business were commented upon—that they had no notion that the front door had been locked at all. No one would guess that they'd been up rifling Pennyman's things—except Pennyman, of course. He was the type to glue hairs to drawer fronts with saliva, then check later to see if the bond had been broken.

Who cared though? Pennyman knew that they were on to him; and they knew he was on to them. So what were the odds? Andrew was tempted to make the break-in obvious. Maybe he should slip in two or three times a day all week long, just to confound Pennyman, who would have to begin to think that all the breaking in and subtle ransacking was without purpose—which it very likely was, since neither Andrew nor Pickett had the foggiest notion what it was they were after.

Andrew patted his pocket. In it was the rubber squid out of the cereal box. He pulled it out and regarded it, grinning at the look of morose wisdom on its face. It was bound for one of Pennyman's socks. Pickett wouldn't approve at all. He took this whole business deadly seriously. What he didn't grasp was that Pennyman apparently did, too, and therein lay the beauty of the squid-in-the-sock notion. Pennyman wouldn't be able to fathom it, any more than he'd fathomed the letter in the mail. And Andrew was fairly sure that the letter business had been over Pickett's head too. *"What* did you write?" Pickett had asked, puzzled. Then he repeated Andrew's phrase several times to himself, as if trying it out on his tongue. "I don't get it," he said finally. "Why cigarettes? Wasn't there a song like that—'Smoke, smoke, smoke that cigarette'? How did that go?" He had hummed a bit, remembering, convinced that there was a message hidden in the lyrics; there must have been. He'd never caught on. That sort of thing was entirely a matter of instinct, not brains; you couldn't think through it and come up with anything but nonsense. That's why it worked so wonderfully on men like Pennyman. Andrew knew it was best not to tell Pickett about the squid until later. He nearly laughed out loud, thinking of Pennyman slipping the sock on, unawares, and then starting in horror. Was it a tremendous insect? A severed toe? He'd shake the thing out onto the floor, standing back out of the way. His face would go blank, and he'd curse . . .

"You take the bureau," said Pickett suddenly from across the room. "Wake up. Let's get this done and leave, for heaven's sake."

Andrew blinked at his friend. "Of course."

Pickett bent down in front of the bed alcove and carefully slid open a drawer. "Easy does it, now. Let's not give him the slightest clue."

"Call me Slippery Sam," said Andrew, sliding open dresser drawers until he found the socks. There they were, all of them folded flat, arranged in neat little heaps from light to dark. Andrew slipped the squid into a cream-colored sock, halfway down the first pile, then very carefully felt around the edges of the drawer and between the socks. There was nothing. The drawer beneath it was filled with underwear—most of it silk. Andrew was disgusted with the idea of searching through it, but he did. Beneath the shorts and T-shirts was a monumental elastic supporter, strung with mesh plastic to better keep its shape and bringing to mind the exoskeleton of a cephalopod or a particularly loathsome amphibian. It was obviously custom-built. Andrew whistled under his breath and held it up.

"Put that back!" hissed Pickett.

"What on earth! . . ." Andrew began. "Certainly no human being . . . !" He was struck suddenly silent with the idea of retrieving the squid and of dropping it into the elastic garment like a bucket down a well. He could stretch the waistband across the frame of the casement and fire the squid through Ken-or-Ed's living room window. He eased the sock drawer open again in order to fetch out the squid, wondering if he was allowing things to go haywire. Shooting the squid out of the supporter would pretty clearly break the cardinal rule demanding artistic subtlety. Somehow. It was best not to determine exactly how. He would compromise, and merely leave the squid in the supporter. Pickett had agreed that Pennyman be kept off balance, hadn't he? Andrew glanced at Pickett, whose back was turned, and then shoved the doctored supporter back in among its neighbors, smoothing the whole mess out and sliding the drawer closed.

In the middle drawer he found nothing but shirts—a tiresome lot of them, starched, buttoned, and folded. It occurred to him that, in the interests of excess, he could with very little risk dredge up about a hundred rubber creatures and load up every blessed piece of Pennyman's clothing . . .

He found nothing in the fourth drawer but ties and handkerchiefs and a pair of suspenders in a plastic case. The top drawer was the inevitable junk drawer—very neat, though, and three-quarters empty. There was a can of spare change, a couple of pocketknives, and several road maps—one of downtown Vancouver. Andrew held it up for Pickett to see and then put it back. Next to the maps lay a vinyl checkbook—the broad sort of double book that a businessman would carry.

Here was pay dirt. Each of the checks had been torn off of an attached stub, and each stub had written onto it a neat record of whom the check had been paid to. It was Pennyman's fetish with neatness again—everything orderly and labeled. Andrew wondered how many times a day Pennyman washed his hands. The information on the stubs meant almost nothing to him—just random names and dates. He and Pickett could run the lot of them down, of course, but it would take weeks, and what good would it do them in the end? They'd discover, no doubt, who it was that cleaned Pennyman's shirts and where he had his hair cut, but they hadn't time for that sort of wasted effort.

On a sudden hunch, Andrew counted back on his fingers, calculating the date on which he'd tracked Pennyman to Moneywort's shop. Sure enough, there'd been a check paid out—to a man with an Asian name, on The Toledo. Andrew couldn't quite make out the spelling of the name, beyond the fact that it was short and started with a *K*. It was substantial, too—nearly a thousand dollars. That would be for the elixir. Pennyman had walked away in that direction carrying a live carp in a bag, and had appeared at home two hours later carrying a vial of the elixir. It stood to reason. Andrew pulled the pen off the checkbook and wrote the information on the palm of his hand, just as a precaution against forgetting it, then idly flipped to the next check stub. It had been written out to Edward Fitzpatrick.

Ken-or-Ed. Right across the street. Andrew was flabbergasted. What did it mean? Pennyman had paid the man off. All that business about the planning commission—that was all a charade, a hoax. Pennyman had set it up. It had cost him two hundred dollars. Jack Dilton! He was probably some drunk they'd found slumped on the counter down at Wimpy's.

For a moment Andrew was tempted to fly into a rage, to turn Pennyman's room upside down, the lying, stinking . . . Kissing Rose's hand! The whole incident rushed back in upon him, and it took an effort of will not to rip the checkbook in half. He counted to ten, very slowly. He heard Pickett whistle just as he was telling himself to put the checkbook back. He could *use* the information. If he tore it up, Pennyman would know all. Andrew would have played his hand, and a damned poor one at that.

"Look at this," Pickett said. Andrew slid the checkbook back into the drawer, closed it, and stepped across to help Pickett, who knelt in front of the lower, right-hand drawer beneath the bed.

In it, spread open, was a leather bag of silver dimes—thousands of them. "What in the world . . ."

"All silver?" asked Andrew.

Pickett slid his hand through them, letting them run through his fingers as if he were an adventurer in a pirate's cavern. He nodded. "Looks like."

"Do you think he just *keeps* them? I keep pennies, for heaven's sake. They're not evidence of anything."

"You're not going around town sawing people in half, either. Lord knows what they're for, though. They don't do us any good, do they?"

Andrew shook his head. "What's that wrapped in paper there? Looks like books, doesn't it?"

Pickett hauled it out—an almost-square parcel wrapped in butcher paper and with the ends folded and taped like the ends of a Christmas present. "Tape is pretty new," Pickett said, worrying up a corner of it. "It hasn't stuck tight yet. Should we chance it?"

"Of *course* we'll chance it. Let's steal them and replace them with *Reader's Digest* condensed."

"None of that," said Pickett. The tape pulled back without ripping a bit of the paper. It would stick down again well enough. Andrew bent in over Pickett's shoulder, watching his friend unfold the package carefully. The sight of the top volume staggered him: *Hula Moons,* by Don Blanding, the poet—one of the five books that had been stolen from Andrew's bedroom. It hadn't been the Atlantean after all. It had been Pennyman all along.

"The son of a bitch . . ." Andrew said. They were all there: the Walt Kelly, the Gerhardi, *Liverpool Jarge*—all five of them. Andrew plucked the pile out of Pickett's hands.

"Hey, watch it!" his friend said. "Don't mess them up."

"What do you mean 'mess them up'? They're my books. I'm taking them back, right now. Pennyman's a common thief! I had him pegged for a world-class criminal, and he stoops to stealing another man's books!"

"We've got to put them back."

"*Got* to? We've got to do nothing but expose him. I'll show these to Rose, wrapped up just like this. Evidence is what I call it, and so will she. She'll know they're my books. We'll give Pennyman the bum's rush. Him and his processed hair.''

Pickett shook his head meaningfully. ''I believe Pennyman to be one of the most powerful and dangerous men in the world. Don't even think about tackling him this way.''

''If he were such a man, then why *steal* books? These aren't *rare,* for God's sake. He could find copies just by driving around town. He could buy copies at Acres of Books. That's where I got most of these. Aside from the Pogo, there aren't ten bucks worth of books here. The most powerful man in the world doesn't *need* to steal books.''

''Don't try to reason it out,'' said Pickett. ''There's presidents and priests cutting the most amazing capers right now. Depend on it. They arrested that judge up in Bellflower just last week for going out naked except for a hat. He didn't *need* to go out naked, did he? God almighty, man, he sure as hell didn't need the *hat*. I drove a thousand miles to buy contraband breakfast cereal for you. What would Rose say if she knew it? Forget any of this business about what people need. Also, if you tell Rose that Pennyman stole these books from you, wrapped them in paper, and then hid them in his drawer, she's going to wonder, isn't she? She knows you've got it in for him.''

''I'll show her the checkbook.''

Pickett squinted. ''What checkbook?''

''Pennyman's checkbook,'' said Andrew, tossing his head toward the dresser. ''There's evidence that he paid off the fat man across the street. Sent him over to cause trouble. Rose witnessed the whole thing.''

''Maybe,'' said Pickett, looking doubtful. ''What will you tell her when she asks you what you were doing going through Pennyman's things?''

''I don't know.''

''In fact, what if she *does* believe it and wants to take action, to confront him? He's a dangerous man, like I said. We don't want to start him up over some damned petty thing like this.''

''Petty!''

"Yes," said Pickett. "Petty. Compared to what he did to Pfennig, this is petty as hell. A couple of books . . . Even you say they aren't *worth* anything much. Wait and watch, that's my advice. Don't involve Rose. Trust me. She doesn't want to be involved." He took the books away from Andrew again and folded them up laboriously, rubbing a finger across the tape to heat the glue and slipping the package back into the drawer. "One more box. Looks like opaque Plexiglas sealed with a neoprene gasket. Maybe some sort of waterproof . . . Let's have a look."

Andrew was silent, fuming about the books. He'd get them back; that was for sure. And he'd confront Pennyman with them, too. He'd make him sweat before he was through, he'd . . . "Damn it!" cried Andrew, reeling back. "What the . . . Close it up!"

A putrid, decaying stench filled the room. Andrew gagged and staggered toward the windows, throwing them open and leaning against the screens, sucking in air. He heard Pickett scrabbling around behind him. Gasping a lungful he turned and stepped back to where his friend wrestled with the box, trying desperately to shut the lid clean and tight enough so that the spring latch would compress the top of the box down into the neoprene. Pickett half-threw the box at Andrew, leaped up, and raced out, starting to retch, barely pausing at the door. Steeling himself, Andrew fitted the lid carefully, set the corner of the box against his knee and leaned into it, snapping the latch into place. Then he put it back into the drawer before jumping away toward the window again.

There was a heavy onshore breeze, thank heaven, angling in up the alley, straight through the window. In minutes it would have flushed out most of the reek. Andrew knew that he wasn't in any risk of being sick anymore. But that first whiff . . . Pickett had barely made it.

Again, why? Why a box full of decayed—what? Andrew had seen just a bit of it, and it made no sense at all. What he thought he'd seen was a scrap of the snout and eye of a dead 'possum—a severed head, probably. But that couldn't be, could it? It was too bizarre to believe. And there was more than that in the box— unbelievable filth. There leaped into his mind the memory of

Pennyman and the cat box. It was incredible, preposterous. There could be only one explanation—it was a joke. A sick joke. Pennyman had anticipated them, and he'd had a sealed box built *just so that they'd find it*. He had probably laughed himself sick over it. Rodent Control hadn't gotten the 'possum out of the trash can at all. Pennyman had. Andrew could imagine him cutting it up, just like the squid on the beach, just like Pfennig, and then going upstairs to strain the sand in the cat box. The man was a living horror.

Andrew shut the windows, took a look around to see that nothing was out of place, and went out. The idea of setting more traps of his own hardly appealed to him. He'd lost his appetite for that sort of gag.

"I can't imagine why," Mr. Pennyman said, sitting on the stool in the kitchen. Rose worked at the sink. It was evening. Andrew was out in the cafe chopping vegetables.

"Was anything gone? Stolen?" The information clearly bothered Rose. This wasn't good—someone sneaking into Mr. Pennyman's room. News of it would do nothing but ruin their chances of making a go of the inn.

"No, nothing stolen. Not that I could discover. I haven't much, really, that's worth anything. What is there to steal in an old man's room? Not even a pocket watch. It's the idea of it though—having one's sanctum sanctorum, as they say, invaded by garden-variety thieves. Thank God I was out. They probably came in through the window—rather like the crowd Andrew chased off the other night. I'm half-surprised that Andrew didn't hear them. He was probably busy with his cafe, clanking glasses and such. You wouldn't think a sleepy neighborhood like this was such a hotbed of garret thieves, would you?"

Rose shook her head, saying nothing for a moment, but looking as if she were collecting her thoughts. Finally she said, "Should we call the police?"

Now it was Pennyman's turn to pause. He shrugged and gave his head a little noncommittal jerk. "I suppose not. No need to drag the police in, is there? Nothing stolen after all. There's always the chance that suspicion is cast in the wrong direction when the police meddle in these sorts of affairs. They can be inventive. And then there's your troublesome neighbor across the street. If he came around yammering about Andrew's having been up in the tree . . .''

"Well," said Rose, "I'll take your advice here. I'd rather this got no further, actually. If Andrew could be spared . . .''

"Say no more." Pennyman held his hand up. "This is a stressful business, opening an inn. Andrew's eccentricities can be explained. Even justified. How is he feeling, better?"

Rose looked at him. "I don't know how you mean, but to finish my sentence, if Andrew could be spared knowing about the break-in, I'd appreciate it. It would only work him up."

"Of course, of course. I knew just what you meant. After the business with the planning commission the other day . . . I'm not a practicing psychologist, Rose, but Andrew seemed to me to be rather dangerously close to the edge there. Far be it from me to butt in, though. That's his affair—and yours, of course. I'm afraid he's already conceived a dislike for me. I rather wish he hadn't. I admire him, men like him . . .''

"I'm sure you exaggerate. He's determined, is what he is, and I wish sometimes that he weren't. I wish he'd put on his bedroom slippers and relax. But he can't. He's always got to be up to something, meddling around with half-finished projects, trying to make sense of things that maybe can't be made sense of. I'm pretty sure, though, knowing him like I do, that if he got rid of all his demons, what was left afterward wouldn't be worth as much as it should be. I rather like him the way he is, and I can tell you that you don't have to worry about him. I'll tell him half the truth. I'll tell him that you were afraid that someone had been in your room, but that nothing had been stolen and so it must have been Mrs. Gummidge straightening up. It might have been, I suppose?"

Pennyman nodded and widened his eyes. "We'll suppose so, won't we? She was out, though, wasn't she? I admire the hell out of your loyalty, do you know that? If I were a younger man, and you weren't attached . . . Well . . . You'd have to be curt with me.'' He smiled and winked. ''Hold onto that husband of yours. He can use a bit of your energy and strength.'' Pennyman strolled away, out of the kitchen, out the front door. Rose stood without moving, staring through the kitchen table.

Out in the cafe kitchen Andrew chopped vegetables on his cutting board. Every now and then he stopped and looked around him, satisfied. Tomorrow night would tell the tale. There were two reservations so far, but he expected more. The cable station was coming around to do a piece of filler on the chef-hat gimmick. He was damned lucky that they had called around to suggest it. It beat a simple photograph in the *Herald*.

Everything would have to roll out smooth and easy. Timing was the key in the cooking business—that and advance preparation. He hated cutting up onions. Somehow he always lost track of what he was doing and ended up with his face six inches away from the damned things, crying all over them. How many had he chopped? —eight? That ought to do it. There was no use making ten gallons of gumbo to feed a dozen people. He wouldn't be cheap with it, though.

He raked a heap of chopped bell peppers into one of the cutting board bowls, then dumped peppercorns into a mortise and ground them to dust. He'd already mashed garlic and cut up a picnic ham and three pounds of sausages. He'd peeled the shells off a mountain of shrimp, but had left the heads attached for style, and he had a flotilla of crab legs soaking in fresh water in order to leach out some of the salt.

When Pickett knocked on the street door at eleven, Andrew was three-fourths done. Aunt Naomi's cats had been in and out all night, looking around, winking at the shrimps, generally making themselves at home. At first Andrew had half a mind to throw them out, but he didn't. He had to admit that he'd developed a kind of regard for them, solitary creatures that they were. He wouldn't half-mind being a cat; they seemed so well informed. He was vaguely puzzled by his having come to like them. He could remember having been wild to pitch them out not two weeks past, and now here he was, feeding them the odd shrimp. It was what he'd felt on the stairs when he'd first gone into Pennyman's room—the strange notion that the cats were looking out for him, that they were players in the same game, on the same team. He wouldn't be surprised to find that Uncle Arthur fraternized with cats.

"Sit down," said Pickett, looking as if he were wild with discoveries. "They had to throw me out at ten. I would have spent the night there if I could have. This is monumental. I've been talking to Robb, the reference librarian. Do you remember him?"

Andrew drained the oil off the sausages and ham fat he'd been simmering, pouring the fat through a heap of cheesecloth into a measuring cup. "Slow up," he said. "You're about to explode. *I've* been taking it slow and easy—machine-like, that's my way tonight. Everything done just so. Measure twice, cut once; that's my motto. Rob who?"

"Randall Robb. At the literary society. He threatened Johnson that one night over Johnson's misquoting a phrase from Leviticus."

"Steely-eyed fellow with bushy eyebrows? Fierce?"

"That's the man! He's been running me all over the basement of the library. You wouldn't believe the stuff he's got stored down there: secret society stuff, apocryphal Masonic texts, suppressed Illuminatus tracts, hollow-Earth literature. It's astonishing. And just between the two of us, the authorities think that the recent library fire wasn't just a case of simple pyromania. There's stuff in that basement collection that someone wanted destroyed."

"Whoa," said Andrew. "I thought this man Robb worked up in one of the branch libraries. Up in Glendale."

"Eagle Rock. That was years ago. They transferred him uptown. A branch library wasn't big enough to hold him. He's one of the old-school librarians—wild hair, spectacles, arcane knowledge. They get that way. Nickel-and-dime information isn't worth anything to them. They run into an odd bit here, an unlikely coincidence there, and suddenly they're following a trail of hints and clues and allegations back into the murky depths of *real* history—the stuff that's glossed over and rearranged; the stuff they don't want us to know.''

"*They* again?''

"That's right. Depend on it. But listen. He knows Pennyman. Tell me this, where did Pennyman say he came from? Back east, wasn't it? Just blew into town like Billy Bones, right? Looking for a berth where he could watch the sea? Well it was lies. Robb knew him from the library. He'd been hanging around for six months, looking to find something but too sly to reveal what it was. He said he represented the British Museum in some sideline way. His research had to do with coins, though, and with biblical arcana. That much was sure. You and I know which coins he was after. But why? We ask ourselves that, don't we?''

Andrew nodded and turned the flame on under his cast iron kettle, arranging a big whisk and a long-handled spoon on the range top next to it. "Just this afternoon," he said. "But there's the 'what' element, too. I've seen a picture of this coin, and I seem to own one that's been beaten into a spoon and carried around Iowa in the mouth of a pig, but I don't have the earthliest idea what that means.''

"Well hang on to your hat. Robb's looked over my Vancouver book. The coin is definitely one of the thirty." Pickett uttered this last phrase slow and meaningfully.

"Ah," said Andrew, noting that the oil in his kettle was starting to smoke, and distracted by the process of gumbo-making.

"Thirty pieces of silver.''

"Ah. Thirty of them. Here goes nothing.'' He poured three cups of flour into the smoking oil and began flailing at it with the whisk, knocking out lumps. Flames shot around the blackened sides of the kettle, scorching the hairs on his arm. "Pot holder!" he shouted.

"*Thirty* pieces of silver," said Pickett again, looking at him fixedly.

"All right," Andrew shouted, grabbing the whisk with his left hand and waving his right hand out away from the pot to cool it. "I'll pay. Just give me the damned pot holder, will you, and then turn down the flame here. God almighty this is hot!''

Pickett blinked at him, then got up to fetch the pot holder, which Andrew had carelessly left lying out of reach on the counter.

Andrew transferred the whisk to his right hand and slipped his left into the pot holder. Pickett turned the flame down by half and peered hesitantly into the pot. ''What the hell?'' he said.

''Black roux. Or at least it will be. Touchy process. Watch, you can almost see it turn color. If you quit whisking for a moment, it's burnt like a cinder. Nothing to do then but pitch it out. Back away there.'' With that he picked up the bowl full of heaped vegetables and poured them into the bubbling oil and flour. A great reek of steam poured up out of the kettle, and Andrew dragged it off the flame, still whisking. The worst was past. The whole business was a success. He whisked away until the mixture quit bubbling.

''Looks like the devil, doesn't it?'' said Pickett. ''What do you do with it? You're not still thinking of trying to poison the cats, are you?''

''I was *never* going to poison the damned cats! You eat it,'' said Andrew. ''After you've mixed it into three or four gallons of broth and tossed in all this meat and shrimp and such and a little cayenne.''

''All that oil? What is this, oil soup?''

''It's God's reward for our meager virtues,'' said Andrew, rinsing off the whisk. He shut down the stove and closed the cookbook that had been lying on the counter.

Pickett, looking cross, picked the book up and took a look at the cover, on which was a picture of a startlingly fat man with a pudding face, grinning out across an appalling lot of sausages and crustaceans. ''You're cooking out of this man's book?''

''Look at him,'' Andrew said. ''The man knows how to eat. He's eaten more than the rest of us put together. What that man hasn't eaten you could put in your hat. What cookbook would you suggest, the *Hindu Diet Book*?''

Pickett shook his head. ''Oil soup with shrimp heads. *Burnt* oil soup with shrimp heads.'' He sat down pettishly, took out his pocketknife, and pretended to scrape his fingernails, saying nothing.

"Well, where were we?" asked Andrew, smiling pleasantly. Tomorrow's cooking would be a piece of cake. The yeoman's work was done, and at barely eleven o'clock, too. Rose would be proud of him. She was upstairs gluing up the chef's hats. She had protested mildly about the dimensions of the hats, about them being sewn up out of an expanse of rubberized nylon roughly the size of a bedsheet. Andrew had prevailed though, explaining to her his theory of the virtue of excess. In the morning Andrew would run down for a canister of helium. The camera crew from KNEX was due at four o'clock in the afternoon, an hour before the doors would open. It was a miracle, them calling and offering to do the story. They'd heard of the cafe, they said. They wanted to do a human interest story—local citizens make good, that sort of thing. The chef's hats were a natural, just the sort of comic slant the public would like. Things were certainly falling together.

Andrew became aware suddenly that Pickett was in a state. He'd been almost crazy with the idea of the coins, and Andrew had lost interest because of cooking up the roux. It was time to get back on track. "Oh, yes. That's right. That was it. Thirty pieces of silver. Just like out of the Testaments. Judas Iscariot and all."

"Not *just like*," said Pickett, folding up his knife. "The *same damned coins*! That's what I'm telling you. I've suspected it for days, but what I've found in L.A. cinches it."

Andrew whistled. "They must be worth a heap. How can anyone tell though? It would be just like any religious relic. Sell a man an old sea gull bone and tell him it's what's left of St. Peter's ring finger."

"Nope. Not this time. There were always only thirty of these coins."

"What do you mean, 'always'?"

"I mean as far back as anyone can discover. I mean thirty *magical* coins minted in antiquity."

"If you plant them, will they grow?" Andrew was giddy with the success of his gumbo, with the satisfaction of something going right. He grinned at Pickett, thinking to cheer him up.

"If you collect them all together," said Pickett evenly and

deadly serious, "you can . . . Lord knows what you can do. But the point is that Pennyman's been after these coins, and it looks as if he's got them."

"What do you mean, 'looks as if'? He certainly hasn't got them all, and won't, either."

"It's a damned long story, let me tell you. I haven't been sitting idle. But listen. All of a sudden ten million things fit. That's what struck me—even little things. Have you ever thought about the business of kicking over the money changers tables in the temple? I mean really *thought* about it?"

"Because He didn't go for money-changing in the temple."

"Half that story," said Pickett, "has never been told. The coins were being gathered. That's what I think. Right there, by the priests. A conspiracy so massive and far-reaching that it set the course of modern history. It was the collected coins that brought about the inevitable betrayal—the fall, if you want to put it that way, of heaven on earth. They're a physical incarnation of evil, and they've been purposefully scattered these two thousand years since, and . . ."

"And now Pennyman's got them together again. The two coins in the photo of him and the dead Jack Ruby . . ."

"Betrayal upon betrayal, evil stacked on top of evil."

"But he hasn't got *all* of them, because we've got . . ."

Pickett sprang at him, waving his hands and shaking his head. "Don't say it. Wink twice when you want to refer to it. Where is he, anyway?"

"Out, as usual. Or he was an hour ago."

"Is it hidden?"

Andrew nodded. "Brilliantly. But what is he going to do, anyway, when he gathers all the coins?"

"Save that," said Pickett. "I don't know. I don't want to find out, though. There's more to it. I haven't scratched the surface here. Look what Robb turned up. It's part of a dozen legends in the farthest-flung reaches of Europe and the Middle East. Latch on to something, though. It's going to throw you."

Pickett held up a Xerox and read: " 'When the moon is old, he is very, very old, but when the moon is young he turns young again.' And now this: '. . . and he can only rest beneath two crossed harrows or *ploughshares*.' '' Pickett put the Xerox down and sat silently.

"Who says?" asked Andrew.

"One Chrystostum Dudulaeus Westphalus. Seventeenth century."

"West*phalus*?"

"Assumed name. And the name doesn't matter anyway. The legend is everywhere, dating back to at least the second century. This man Westphalus just wrote it down. And here, listen to this from something called *Curious Myths of the Middle Ages:* 'We hear of the Wandering Jew again at the royal palace in Bohemia, in 1505, where he is assisting the prince to find certain coins which had been secreted by the great-grandfather of the prince, sixty years before. The coins were found in a leathern bag, beneath a boundary stone cut into the shape of a sow and her litter. On the advice of the Jew, the coins were dispersed, all but one, which the ill-fated prince hid beneath his tongue and later paid to a stranger for the murder and betrayal of the king, his own father. The prince's tongue clove then to the roof of his mouth, and during the course of his two-year reign, which ended when he hanged himself, he was known as Walter the Mute.' "

"Pigs again," said Andrew.

"Pigs is right. Here's another; this one translated from the French. It's an account—get this—of the legendary *Isaac Laquedem*. What do you think about that? The name is corrupted from the Hebrew and means Isaac the Old or Isaac of the East. He was believed to be the Wandering Jew, and had a sort of Francis of Assisi affinity to *farm animals,* for God's sake, especially pigs. Listen: 'When the truffle pigs were driven into the forests of Fontainebleau, a great fat sow escaped into a stand of birch, from which it emerged with a spoon in its teeth and a beggar at its heels, escaping withal from master and beggar both, and never seen again in the region. Six years later, its master identified it as one of a trio of swine driven along the roadway outside Chateau Landon by a man in monk's robes, who was identified by a passing peasant as

Isaac Laquedem, the Wandering Jew, who had been alive at the time of the Passion of Christ.' ''

"So who is he?"

"Wait, one more. Here's the *Britannica,* tenth edition: 'As Cain was a prototype of Judas, so was Judas of such doomed wanderers as Malchus in Italy and Ahasuerus in Germany, who along with a score of similar wanderers, were known variously as the Legion of the Coins or the Legion of Iscariot.' ''

"Iscariot? A sort of general then, of a band of wanderers? And you're telling me that they've been hightailing it across the western hemisphere keeping an eye on these thirty coins?"

"That's the long and the short of it. But they've failed, largely, in recent years, and what's gone around, as they say, is coming around."

Andrew sat for a moment, considering all this. Then he asked, "Who is Uncle Arthur?"

Pickett shrugged. "You know what I know, almost. It's all there, isn't it: the name, the murky past, the pigs, the farm animals, the phases of the moon, even the crossed ploughshares. For my money, every last dime of it, Uncle Arthur is Judas Iscariot."

Andrew stood for a moment in unbelieving silence, then said, "But living in Seal Beach? In Leisure World? Driving an electronic car?"

"Why not?"

Now it was Andrew's turn to shrug. Why not indeed? "And you think he's hustling to—what?—keep Pennyman from collecting the coins?"

"That's just what I think—to keep *anyone* from collecting the coins. Did you know that Pennyman was recently in the Middle East—at a time that corresponds exactly with all the mystical stuff, the rain of dead birds and the Jordan River flowing backward? What does that tell you about the impossible tide last week? About the sea gulls all over the street? Remember what Georgia said about the psychic disturbance in the area?"

"Are they still here, do you think? They weren't in his room. We'd have found them."

"Yeah, we would have. He wouldn't keep them here, not now that he thinks we're onto him. Where is it, by the way?" Pickett winked twice.

Andrew winked back. "That'll be my little secret, won't it? It's safe. So tell me, what about Pfennig? What about Moneywort?"

"Caretakers, just as I'd suspected. In league with Uncle Arthur. Aunt Naomi, too, the way I figure it. She inherited the you-know-what from her late husband. You know the story. She's lucky, though. She's still alive."

"Because she's given the damned thing to me!"

Pickett shrugged. Then he started, as if he'd had a chill, and he slapped his hand on his knee. "I just thought of something," he said. "Johnson was right—that morning down at the Potholder. It *was* pigs—back in Iowa, involved in the cow-pasture business. Of course it was pigs. And they took the man's coin! Wouldn't that cook you? I can't stand the creep anyway. It was a lucky guess on his part, an eyes-shut home run. Anyway, what I've pieced together is that Pennyman traced all the Caretakers down and stole the coins from them, ruthlessly. It was just like I said with Pfennig. Robb found mention of two of the coins in the Apocrypha. They were never recovered after Iscariot hung himself unsuccessfully; they were buried by a remorseful priest in the potter's field that's mentioned in the Testaments. Without any doubt, a third coin is in the belly of that fish up in the Sound. How it got there I can't begin to say. And do you know what? For my money that fish isn't in the Sound at all anymore. He's off the south coast, or on his way.

"The balance of the coins, we have to imagine, were scattered, and have been turning up far and wide and doing their mischief ever since. It was the coins that bestowed immortality on Judas Iscariot. That's their effect. When he tried to hang himself, he couldn't, and he set himself to a quite possibly endless lifetime of penance. He's had a mission for two thousand years."

"But he seems so happy, so cheerful, driving over lawns and all. You don't suppose that piece of rope on his wall . . ."

"Of course I do. And why shouldn't he be happy? He's turned back around, hasn't he? He wakes up every morning with a purpose. He's been a moderate success at orchestrating a vast and intricate plan—up until now. Then his officers start to die, to be murdered, and here comes Pennyman, pocketing a coin here, two coins there . . .''

"It must have taken him ages. How old can he be? How old can *any* of these Caretakers be? I get the immortality part as far as Uncle Arthur is concerned, but why the rest of them?''

"I'm not sure, but I suppose that possessing even a couple of the coins might have such an effect. And then there's the fish elixir, isn't there? I've got a few leads to run down there, including your Asian man on The Toledo.''

Andrew groaned. "I wish I could help. But with the cafe and all . . .'' He swept his hand in a wide arc, gesturing at the stove. "And if I slipped out again, Rose would kill me. She'd pack my bag and leave it on the porch. I'm going to have to leave the fate of the world to you.''

"On the contrary,'' said Pickett seriously. "As I see it, the world rests on the shoulders of the last of the Caretakers.''

"The last of the Caretakers?''

"Keep it well hid.''

"Oh,'' said Andrew. "Yes. No wonder I've felt worn out. Call me Atlas.'' But he said this last without much humor. It wasn't very funny to him.

Pickett stared at his friend's face. "Step over here by the window for half a mo. Let's check the street.''

Half-dazed, Andrew followed his friend. The two of them stood in the light of a gibbous moon, which had risen above the ocean. The fog had dispersed, and moonlight shone through the window glass, casting an ivory glow over the rubbed oak of the table tops. Pickett stared at his friend's forehead, but Andrew was lost in thought. "If we had a silver quarter and a bit of powdered ash . . . But it would mean your death if Pennyman saw the results.''

"He's already played that trick,'' said Andrew.

"When he did, he had the wrong man.''

"What was he looking for?''

"Stigmata, of a sort. There's mention of it in the *Britannica* and in the Vancouver book, both. Sympathetic markings that the silver and the ash would cause to materialize. The markings would fade eventually, but for a time they'd be indelible.'' Pickett produced another Xerox from his bundle, and read from it. '' 'Such a mark was indeed supposed to be on the Wandering Jew's forehead. Xemola says it was a red cross concealed by a black bandage, on which account the Inquisition vainly tried to find him.' That's the *Britannica*. Here's from *The One Pig*, Robb's translation of it. He's written it out for me. 'The mark of Iscariot can be drawn from the forehead of his followers by the use of silver and palm ash . . .' ''

''His followers,'' said Andrew, idly rubbing his forehead. ''I'd never have pegged myself as a follower of anybody, and certainly not of Judas Iscariot.''

''He's not the same man now as he was in the Testaments. And it's not *you* who does the pegging anyway. You're one of the chosen few. For the moment, you're the *last* of the chosen few. Many are called,'' Pickett said ponderously, ''but few are chosen.'' He shoved his Xeroxes and notes into his coat, reached for the doorknob, and said, ''There's a full moon on the night of the treasure hunt.''

''Is there?''

''That's right. It'll be a dangerous business. We can't depend on Uncle Arthur then, not if all this phase-of-the-moon stuff is accurate. He'll be feeble, doddering. Maybe outright loony. It'll be up to us.''

''Up to us;'' Andrew muttered as Pickett went out through the door, into the night. Andrew stood at the window, looking out at nothing, only vaguely seeing Pickett's car whoosh away toward the highway. He turned and looked in at the kitchen, which was a mess of splattered roux and the remnants of chopped vegetables. Somehow the mundane notion of cleaning a kitchen, when set against the mystical knowledge that Pickett had revealed, made Andrew dizzy. He decanted the roux into lidded plastic tubs and shoved them into the refrigerator, working in a sort of haze. His back ached. He was tired out, and tomorrow would be worse. He would clean the kitchen in the morning. It was sleep he needed now. His eyes were drawn to the pint glass full of spoons. It seemed to glow and jiggle in the gloomy twilight of the cafe.

"The last of the Caretakers," he breathed. "Maybe the single most important man in the world . . ."

The idea flitted around in his head like a sparrow, never really alighting anywhere long enough for him to grasp it, to study it, to draw some satisfaction from it. He went out and climbed wearily up the stairs, wishing he could tell Rose, but knowing he couldn't.

BOOK III

The One Pig

". . . One pig to rule them all, One pig to bind them
One pig to bring them all and on the pier-end find them
In Seal Beach, on the Coast."
                          William Ashbless
                          Myths of the Pacific Coast

TWELVE

"I am a man more sinned against than sinning."
William Shakespeare
The Tragedy of King Lear

THE TELEPHONE RANG at five in the morning. Andrew groped for it, nearly pushing it off the nightstand. It was Pickett, whispering. He sounded desperate. There was trouble. He was in the basement of a Chinese restaurant, the Bamboo Paradise, down on Broadway, near Cherry.

"What?" said Andrew, half-groggy. "Speak up. What time is it?"

It sounded as if the phone banged against something on the other end, as if it had been dropped maybe. Then it was hung up; there was a click and a dial tone. Andrew swung around and sat on the edge of the bed, trying to think. It was barely daylight.

"Who was that?" Rose asked.

"No one. Pickett."

She turned over and plumped up her pillow. "What for? More escaped zoo animals eating ravioli?"

Andrew forced a laugh in order to humor her. But this clearly wasn't any laughing matter. The ax had fallen. The enemy was finally moving against them. Andrew wondered if it was the squid in the supporter that had set them off, if that had been the last straw. He stood up, picked his pants up off the floor, and pulled them on, squinting around the room for yesterday's shirt.

"You're not thinking of going out," said Rose, waking up now. "Where?"

Andrew acted hearty, as if he'd had a little outing planned all along. "Fishing. There's a warm current in. Fish'll be biting like crazy. *You* were the one who advised it, after all, and now I'm just taking the advice. It's simple as that. I'll be back early."

"But we're opening today. *You're* opening today."

"No sweat," said Andrew, tying his shoelaces. "I got it all squared away last night. It's in the fridge. There's a couple of veggies to chop for the salad and the dressing to whip up, but that'll save for this afternoon. You might send Mrs. Gummidge in to tidy up the kitchen, though."

Rose pushed herself up onto her elbows. "Mrs. Gummidge isn't a maid. She's a paying guest. The kitchen is a mess and you're going out fishing?"

"Only for a bit. I'll be back in no time, like I said. I've got to meet Pickett down at the Potholder before word leaks out that I'm coming. There won't be a fish left this side of the Belmont Pier if I stop to scrub the kitchen down first. News travels fast in the ocean. Mr. Sardine tells Mr. Perch, Mr. Perch tells Mr. Flounder, Mr. Flounder tells Mr. Mackerel. Pretty soon it's a fish exodus. You know how it is. They live in fear of me and Pickett." He laughed, kissed her on the cheek, and went out before she had a chance to complain. He'd have to throw his fishing rod and tackle box into the Metropolitan, just to keep things straight. And this time he'd stop in at the fish market on the way home and buy a couple of cod or something to flesh out the gunnysack.

He was halfway down the stairs before he hesitated, turned, and crept back up, holding his breath. He tiptoed down the hallway to where the door of Pennyman's room stood slightly ajar. The door didn't creak; Andrew knew that. He pushed on the top panel, evenly and lightly. It swung open an inch, two inches. It was dark inside. Andrew was certain he could hear heavy breathing. A ghastly smell lingered in the air of the room, and Andrew wrinkled up his face at it, recognizing it. Could it still be the stink from Pickett's opening the box in the drawer? Surely by now it would have faded . . .

Pennyman himself must have been at the box. Strange, thought Andrew, his eyes adjusting. There was Pennyman, asleep on the bed, the curtain open enough to reveal his face. Satisfied, Andrew left the door where it was and backed away down the hall.

Just then the phone rang again. Andrew gasped and staggered, hurrying toward the bedroom, hoping to God it was Pickett, talking sense this time. There was another half-ring and then silence followed by someone murmuring. He stopped to listen outside the bedroom door. Rose wasn't talking to anyone; she was asleep again. It hadn't been their phone at all. He loped to the stairs and then down them three at a time, as noislessly as he could, out through the kitchen door, ducking through the garage, grabbing his rod and tackle box, and sliding into the Metropolitan, shoving his rod in through the open window. He threw the car into gear and cranked the ignition, leaning on the gas smoothly as the engine caught and the car leaped forward. It had been Pennyman's phone, and Pennyman had answered it.

In five minutes he was out on the Coast Highway, driving northwest, into Long Beach, wishing he'd brought—what? A gun? A ball bat? He had his pocketknife, a multi-bladed little toad-sticker. He could picture himself pulling the knife out, menacing thugs. How was that sort of thing done, exactly? Pickett was in trouble; there could be no doubt about that now. What was the restaurant called? The Bamboo something.

There was a fog bank out over the ocean. Andrew could see little trailing wisps of it stealing ashore as he sailed up Ocean Boulevard, the traffic lights still blinking yellow. Almost no one was out and about except him, which was moderately pleasing. He was a man with a mission. Maybe with a deadly mission. He recalled last night's conversation with Pickett. He *should* have told Rose, informed her, very placidly but squinting with secret knowledge, that he'd become the most important man in the world, that the mystical weight of the millennia had fallen on his meager shoulders. By God, he was bent, but not broken. She would have sighed and shaken her head. Who'd have thought? Then when the phone rang at five o'clock in the morning it wouldn't surprise her, although she'd react to the element of danger in it. "Do you have to go?" she'd say. "Stay with me another five minutes."

"It's duty," he'd tell her, his jaw set, his eyes focused on eternity. "They've called." And out he'd go, brushing back his hair, to face the bastards down.

There was an old green panel truck parked on Cherry, just around the corner, off Broadway. "Han Koi" it said on the side of it, and beneath the words was painted a stylized goldfish. Two Asian men, Chinese probably, stood beside it, eating doughnuts out of a Winchell's box. That had to be it, although what exactly *it* was Andrew didn't know. There was the restaurant, the Bamboo Paradise. Lights burned inside. Andrew drove on past, up Cherry, swinging around onto Appleton. He cut the motor and coasted to the curb.

The neighborhood was neat and fresh—old bungalows and Mediterranean-style flat-roofed houses sitting atop banked front yards with clipped lawns. The sycamores along the curbs were just starting to leaf out. A dog barked a few doors down and then abruptly shut up, as if he were sorry for it. Andrew sat and thought for a moment, realizing that he had no idea on earth what he was doing there. He hadn't been built for this kind of work, this saving-the-world business. Or had he? It seemed vaguely like fate to him, like destiny—his having ended up with the spoon—his being the last of the Caretakers. He wondered abruptly if that made him one of Them. It pretty clearly did. Maybe this *was* what he was built for. Maybe on this foggy morning the curtain had opened on the final act, and he was stepping out onto the stage to play out his destiny and the destiny of the world. He regarded himself momentarily in the rearview mirror in order to see whether he looked the part. His hair stuck up like flowerettes on a broccoli stalk. He worked for a moment winnowing them out with his fingers and smoothing them down but gave it up. They'd have to take him as he came.

He sat for a moment and thought. Pickett had been in danger—clear enough. But what sort of danger? How could Andrew go wading in? They'd both be up to their necks in it if he weren't careful. He had an edge, though. He'd been smart enough to check Pennyman's room. He'd heard the phone ring. If the old man had already been out, then Andrew could assume he was here, at the Bamboo Paradise. But Pennyman hadn't been out; he'd been home in bed, sleeping like a baby, at least until his phone had rung. Andrew had got the jump on him. What was Pennyman doing now? Styling his hair? Fetching out the blowfish? The laser scalpel? Until Pennyman arrived, Andrew could assume fairly safely that there was no one here who knew him, who would recognize him. But when Pennyman showed up . . .

Han Koi. That was the name on the check stub in Pennyman's book—the man on The Toledo! The carp truck fit. The way Andrew figured it, Pickett had gone meddling around down there late last night, trying to make sense of that corner of the puzzle. He'd run afoul of them, and now, for some unknown reason, they'd brought him around to this Chinese restaurant. There flashed through Andrew's mind the picture of Pickett lying on a Formica table, held down by hired men, and Pennyman setting in to saw him in half. And it wasn't a far-fetched notion at all.

He slid out of the car, feeling helpless. Then, in a fit of inspiration, he tugged one of his shoelaces out and tossed it back into the car. He yanked half his shirt out and went around to the trunk after his fishing jacket, which was coffee-stained and smeared with ten years worth of tar and fish scales. He mussed up his hair, although it didn't need it, and then kneeled in the muddy gutter, soiling his pants and smearing the wet dirt with his hands, wiping them off on his jacket. Three doors down, on a front lawn, was a thrown-away bag with an empty bottle in it—just the thing. Andrew retrieved it. He looked good—a custom-built hobo, the tongue protruding from his laceless shoe. No one would imagine who he really was, *what* he was—Andrew Vanbergen, restaurateur, Caretaker, last of the Legion of the Coin, a sort of twentieth-century Odin going out disguised into the foggy morning.

He made sure both sides of the car were unlocked, and he left the key in the ignition. It was risky, but it was a good neighborhood and there might easily be no time to be fumbling after keys. This might be a matter of running for it. He slumped away down the sidewalk, around onto Cherry, heading downhill toward Broadway. Overhead there sounded the raucous cackle of wild parrots, dozens of them, jerking along toward the south, toward wherever they went.

Andrew forced himself not to look up. He had to affect the indifference of a wino just having waked up on someone's stoop. But he was happy to hear the parrots anyway, strangely so, as if he suspected without knowing why that, like Aunt Naomi's cats and like Uncle Arthur's turtles, the parrots were allies, were looking out for him, were part of an ordered plan.

That was nonsense, though. He'd have to pay attention. This was no time for flights of fancy. The doughnut eaters were slouched against the side of the truck, sipping coffee now and talking. Andrew shuffled along silent as death in his crepe-soled shoes. If they looked up and saw him, he'd weave past and head south on Broadway, entirely unremarkable. If they didn't he'd . . .

Quick and quiet he angled across into the cramped parking lot behind the restaurant, forcing himself to walk slowly, straining to watch the two men out of the corner of his eye. They paid no attention to him. One of them laughed aloud and said something in Chinese. The other one laughed, too, and said something back. One more step, two . . . and they were gone, lost to sight behind the edge of the building. Andrew quickened his pace, ducking in past an open, foul-smelling dumpster, half full of garbage. He shoved the bag and bottle into the inside pocket of his coat.

There wasn't any time to wait. At any moment a taxi might pull up to the curb and spill Pennyman out; then he was lost, or at least the whole business would become frighteningly more complicated. A line of windows showed just above the pavement of the parking lot, dusty and covered with hardware cloth fixed with screws and strips of wood. They'd be basement windows. Pickett had claimed to be in a basement. The windows were large enough for a man the size of Pickett to squeeze through.

Andrew made up his mind. This was no time for debate. He pulled his knife out of his pocket, prying out the screwdriver and kneeling in front of one of the windows.

But he was in clear view of the street. Anyone cruising past would see him and suppose him a burglar. They'd sound the alarm and he'd be given away. He stood up and bent along toward a heap of cardboard cartons, pulling two big ones over to where he had been working, careful not to scrape them on the asphalt. Then he went back for two more, piling them up so as to hide him entirely when he crouched behind them. He went to work again.

There was no use trying to alert Pickett. Not yet anyway. What could Pickett do to help? Andrew would take it on faith that Pickett was inside. If he weren't, then Andrew would go in through the window anyway to have a look around. Either way, unscrewing the hardware cloth was a good idea. The screws turned easily in the weathered wood, but were too loose to back out. Andrew pried on them, shoving a big splinter of wood from a packing crate in under the blade to get some leverage. He peered around the boxes at the street. The seconds slipped by. The screws one by one popped out onto the pavement, and he brushed them away with his free hand. Finally two of the wood strips fell away and the corner of the hardware cloth was loose. He realized he was sweating in the cold, foggy air, but he was working silent and sure, surprising himself, thinking about Rose, thinking that if he tackled painting the house with this much attention and persistence . . .

He yanked on the corner of the steel screen, gouging his palm against one of the jagged edges. The still-attached wood strips cracked, popping loose past the screws. He tugged again and tore the screen away entirely, pitching the hardware cloth into the weeds beyond the parking lot and then leaping up and sweeping the litter of screws and wood fragments away with his foot before hustling in behind the dumpster again to lie low.

The smell was god-awful—old rotted fish and coffee grounds

and cigarette butts. He crouched there, catching his breath, half-waiting for the sound of the doughnut eaters coming to investigate the noise. There was nothing. He counted to ten, giving them time. Still nothing. He peered beneath the dumpster, past its little wheels. The parking lot was empty and silent. Back to the window he went, folding the screwdriver back into the pocketknife and drawing out the long blade.

Clearly, he was born to be a burglar. This was going as neatly as had the dead 'possum job. The transom window had a spring latch at the top. That was it. Over the years the building had slumped, the windows had worked their way out of square, and there was no end of gaps where gaps weren't intended to be. He slid his blade in, pressed the half-rounded point against the angled side of the spring-set metal triangle that formed the moveable half of the catch, and pushed it in, simultaneously pushing on the window.

He nearly tumbled against the wall as the window fell open, and at once there was the smell of garlic and fish and the sound of distant voices. The basement was almost dark. Clearly, Pickett wasn't in there. He'd have heard and seen Andrew breaking in. He'd be at the window, pulling himself through. There was nothing for it but to go in—head first, on his back.

It was easy. Inside, above the window, was a concrete ledge— the top of the foundation most likely. Andrew grabbed onto it, scrabbling for a hold on the rough wooden mudsill running along the top of it, and held on as he slid through and dropped to the floor, landing in a crouch and waiting again—this time for the talk to stop, for the hue and cry. There was nothing—just more hushed voices, a laugh, the sound of glasses clinking.

What if Pickett weren't there? What if, thought Andrew suddenly, he hadn't even been in trouble? What if he'd only been zealous, thinking that Andrew was equally so and wouldn't mind being awakened by a five o'clock phone call? What if he'd simply been cut off? Those were grim thoughts. It would mean that Andrew had broken into an innocent Chinese restaurant, that when frightened cooks took him apart with meat cleavers, there'd be nothing to do but grin and bear it.

That couldn't be the case though, not with the truck parked out at the curb. What had Pickett said about not believing in coincidence? Andrew crept forward. Despite the deepening fog, there was plenty of light outside, now that his eyes adjusted, to illuminate the basement. It was smaller than it appeared to be from the street, only a half basement, really, with almost a quarter of it taken up by a single restroom. Boxes of canned goods and crates of vegetables were stacked everywhere. A bare, unlit incandescent bulb hung from the ceiling by its cord. The scrape of table and chair legs sounded from above.

Andrew crept across the concrete floor and up the stairs, pausing with each step to listen. All he wanted was a peek. If Pickett weren't there, out in the restaurant itself, then Andrew would go back out through the window, weaving bum-like up the road, waving a groggy hello at everyone he saw. But if he were confronted now, on the stairs . . .

He'd act drunk, pretend to have broken into the basement in order to sleep. He wished to God that he had liquor on his breath instead of toothpaste, but he was glad he hadn't stopped to shave that morning. He paused long enough to pull the bag out of his coat pocket and unscrew the lid on the bottle. There were a few drops left inside. "Night Train," the label on the bottle read. He dribbled them onto his coat, surprising himself at the sudden, winy reek. He put the bottle away. It was a good prop.

Feet shuffled past above. There was clanking in the kitchen— off to the right he supposed, although he couldn't see the door. He crept up the last six treads on his hands and knees, ready to drop down and feign sleep. He was shaking wildly, as if he had a chill, and he knew if he were caught he'd never be able to convince anyone of anything. They'd have him. At best he'd find himself downtown, in a cell.

He could just see over the top tread, through the table legs. Three Chinese men in aprons, one of them a head taller than the other two and with oddly wavy hair, scurried around, setting tables, wheeling carts full of water glasses and plates. They were garden variety waiters, clearly, putting things right. An old man, very old, white-haired and thin and with a goldfish earring in one ear, sat a table sipping tea. There was no Beams Pickett. It looked suspiciously as if there was no Beams Pickett in the entire building. Pickett was probably sitting at the counter at the Potholder eating steak and eggs. By God if he was . . . What if Pickett *had* simply been cut off, and had called home again and talked to Rose, asking after Andrew . . . ?

Andrew would kill him—and to hell with saving the world. He backed away down the stairs, half-sliding. He had to get out of there. Suddenly he couldn't breathe. He was hyperventilating. He felt faint. If he tumbled back down the stairs . . . He sat down hard, fighting vertigo, shoving his head between his knees and forcing himself to breathe regularly. He would just take a second—it was better than passing out.

There was a shifting noise, like someone moving—below him. He listened sharp. It was impossible, unless someone had come in through the window after him, in which case he was trapped, fore and aft. He started down again, looking sharp, and there was the shifting and scraping, followed by a sigh. It was coming from the bathroom, which had, weirdly, a bolt on the outside of the door. The bolt was pushed in. Someone was locked in the bathroom. Andrew grinned. He knew who it was. This would be good—dangerous, but good.

He glanced backward up the stairs, turned the knob at the same time that he slipped the bolt, and swung the door open, dropping down into a sort of James Bond crouch, as if he were ready to tear to pieces whoever was on the other side. It was Pickett, wild-eyed, backed against the sink, expecting Lord knows what—Pennyman, no doubt, carrying some loathsome instrument of death and torture.

Pickett sagged like a stuffed doll, steadying himself against the sink. He opened his mouth to speak, but Andrew shook his head, gesturing, looking again up the stairs, and then nodded him out of the restroom, shutting the door and throwing the bolt. He pointed toward the rear of the basement and winked, then set out with Pickett at his heels. He helped his friend through first, and then Pickett half-dragged him out onto the asphalt of the parking lot. Andrew reached back in and pulled the window shut just as the basement light clicked on. Both of them sprang for the dumpster.

The seconds ticked by. They could just see someone moving around within, shifting crates, juggling vegetables. There was an airy little snatch of song, and then the light shut out again and all was silent. Andrew nudged Pickett in the ribs and grinned at him. His friend looked awful—rumpled and baggy-eyed—but he clearly hadn't been beaten. They were saving him for Pennyman, no doubt. There'd be time to discuss it in the car.

Andrew felt very satisfied with himself, and nearly laughed out loud. Quickly, he formulated a new plan, whispering it to Pickett, warning him about the thugs on the street, about the manifold dangers. Andrew would slouch out, bum-wise, toward the sidewalk, and if the doughnut eaters were gone, he'd give Pickett the high sign and Pickett would follow, the two of them beating it up to the Metropolitan and away. It was easy as that. He'd get Pickett out of there yet, and Pennyman could go hang.

Steeling himself, Andrew started out, peering past the edge of the dumpster and shoving his foot forward just as a yellow cab whipped around the corner onto Cherry and bumped to a stop at the curb. The rear door swung open and Pennyman himself hunched out, shoving his arm back in through the window to pay the driver.

Andrew ducked back, whispering "Pennyman!" and hauling Pickett down onto the asphalt, the two of them huddled and listening. A car door slammed and the taxi motored away. They'd wait for Pennyman to go in, and then they'd run for it. To hell with anyone at the curb. Once Pennyman unbolted the bathroom door and found that the prey had disappeared, there'd be half a dozen men at the curb.

But Pennyman didn't go inside. He walked straight in their direction, whistling "Zip-a-Dee-Doo-Dah," as if he were in tip-top shape and the morning was a good one.

Andrew and Pickett crouched amid the rubble of broken crates and cardboard boxes, watching beneath the dumpster as Pennyman's white bucks strode along toward them, the tip of his walking stick tapping along beside. There was no time to pull a carton over their heads; no time for elaborate plans. Andrew gave Pickett a look that he hoped suggested toughing it out. Between the two of them they could throttle Pennyman despite his canes and blowfish. If he carried a gun though . . .

Pennyman stopped when he got to the dumpster, close enough to it that he must have been gripping the edge, with his face nearly in the garbage. There was no way on earth that he could see Pickett and Andrew unless he walked around to the other side. What was he looking for? Some sort of vile fish guts to grind into poison? He stood just so. Andrew and Pickett held their breath. The morning was deadly silent.

No, not quite silent. There was a deep, almost hoarse irregular breathing and sniffing. Garbage shifted in the dumpster, as if Pennyman were stirring it with a stick, and the reek issuing from the rotted fish and vegetables and table leavings redoubled. Andrew nearly gagged, covering his mouth with his hand, still watching Pennyman's feet. The old man groaned, sliding the toe of one shoe up along the back of his calf, as if caressing it. He stood suddenly on tiptoe, bending farther over into the dumpster, and uttered a low, moaning wail, breathing like an engine, quicker and quicker, the toes of his shoes twitching on the asphalt.

Andrew was dumbstruck, and Pickett, given the look on his face, was nearly blind with disgust—not at the ghastly odor of decay and rot that had settled around them, but at Pennyman's insane passion, which, from the look of his twitching feet and the sound of his dwindling, throat-rasping wheeze, was almost spent.

Andrew suddenly stood up, slamming his open hand into the steel side of the dumpster, which thrummed like a bass drum. His vision had narrowed down into a tight little focus, as if he were looking down a tube. He couldn't speak. But playing through his head like a looped tape was the loathsome knowledge that this monster, ecstatic now with rot and filth and decay, had kissed Rose's hand, had been gallant, had been . . .

He lashed out with his right fist, pulling himself up and across the rim of the dumpster, taking Pennyman utterly by surprise. The old man reeled back, safe by inches, his mouth working. He raised his stick and swung it at nothing, as if he were half-blind. Andrew leaped around toward him, picking up an empty bottle and hurling it wildly, past Pennyman's shoulder. It smashed straight through the basement window where he'd torn off the screen. Glass shattered, crates toppled. Pennyman shouted, and there was the sound of running feet punctuated by a weird raucous chattering, coming, it seemed, from the sky.

Pickett slammed into Andrew's side, deflecting him away from Pennyman, who stood with his stick upraised, watching him rush in. "C'mon!" Pickett screamed, pulling at Andrew. "Leave him! Let's go!"

Andrew reeled after him, but turned back after half a step. Give up! Not now he wouldn't give up. He would finish Pennyman off and damn the consequences. he'd beat Pennyman with his own cane, by God! He'd . . .

The two doughnut eaters rounded the corner of the building just then, one of them carrying a little wooden baseball bat, and both of them springing straight toward Andrew. Pickett waded in behind them, smashing one of them with a packing crate, the spindly wood cracking to splinters against the man's head. He stumbled, mostly out of surprise, but he was up again in an instant.

The air was a tumult of sounds: Pennyman's cursing, Andrew's shouted threats, feet running on pavement, the airborne shriek of suddenly-appearing parrots. Andrew turned to meet the two new attackers just as Pickett threw himself onto the back of the one who had stumbled. But two more men—two of the white-aproned waiters from the restaurant—burst out through the back door just then, and although Andrew landed one good punch on his man's shoulder, half-spinning him around, the two reinforcements slammed Andrew against the stucco wall, pinioning his arms. Pickett lay on the parking lot, the man with the ball bat having shaken him off and standing over him now, the club poised in the air.

"Stop!" commanded Pennyman, and the man with the bat lowered it, snatching Pickett to his feet. Pennyman smiled, raising his left hand to his mouth and nibbling on his finger. *"I'll* attend to that," he said. "Hold them."

Andrew was aware that he was breathing hard, but he felt calm, considering what he faced. He vowed not to lose control over himself the way he had that afternoon with Ken-or-Ed. Pennyman fed off that sort of chaos. "Your hair is mussed," Andrew said matter-of-factly and squinting with disapproval. "I'd let you borrow my comb, but I don't . . ."

The tip of the cane whistled through the air, stopping a half inch from Andrew's nose. Pennyman grinned when Andrew flinched and gasped. He paused to take out a pocket comb, which he pulled through his hair with a trembling hand. Andrew wouldn't be put off. He was fired up and thinking. The morning was wearing on. Traffic had picked up. There was every reason in the world to waste time, to spend a few more minutes in the parking lot in order to attract the attention of neighbors or passing cars.

"Why those five books?" Andrew asked.

Pennyman looked sharp at him. "What?"

"The five books you stole. Why those five? They aren't worth anything, not really. I don't get it. Those are the five *I* might have stolen."

Pennyman made no effort to act surprised, to pretend. He shrugged. "It doesn't matter."

Pennyman liked to talk. He fancied himself a philosopher. Andrew knew that—all the wombing and tombing business had taught him as much. "I can't figure it out, especially the Pogo."

Pennyman widened his eyes, as if to tell him to go on, that he would hear him out.

"A month ago," said Andrew, "I'd have said that any friend of Pogo was a friend of mine. Anyone who reads Walt Kelly *has* to have the right inclinations. Nitwits and pretenders wouldn't understand it. I'd have taken you for the sort who nods over—who?—Sartre? Maybe Mann. Someone polished and full of . . . shit, I guess. But not Pogo. What does that mean, I ask myself. And it seems to mean that, well, you're something in the way of a lost soul. There's something in you yearning to be . . . might I say, good? Something that isn't at all fond of . . . of . . . collecting cat waste, let's say, or drooling over rotted garbage in a dumpster.'' Andrew beamed at him curiously, but with the moony-eyed, meaningful smile of a self-help psychologist, a benevolent, compassionate look, guaranteed to drive Pennyman insane. He tensed, readying himself to duck the inevitable blow of the walking stick. But there was none. Pennyman stared at him, breathing shallowly. A heavy pall of embarrassment had descended.

''Are you through?''

Andrew shrugged, glancing sideways across the parking lot. The street was empty. Talking was useless.

''Take them in.'' Pennyman's mouth was set, frozen in an expressionless line. ''Into the kitchen,'' he said, with such a ghastly intonation as to make it sound as if the kitchen weren't a kitchen at all, but were a medieval chamber of horrors.

Andrew screamed, simultaneously ducking away, carrying his captor with him. Taking Andrew's lead, Pickett screamed, too, and Pennyman, caught by surprise, stepped backward, thinking that Andrew was lunging at him, and swung the stick wildly, thudding it off the back of the man that held Andrew's arm. Andrew stamped his foot behind him, still shouting and screaming, trying to smash the man's toe and swinging around so as to keep the man between himself and the cane.

It was worthless. The man sprinted forward, driving Andrew into the wall of the restaurant. It was over, and all Andrew had managed was to drive Pennyman into a fury. He could hear the parrots circling above, and he stumbled as he was pushed toward the door.

Then, without warning, the parking lot was chaotic with parrots, flapping and reeling and shrieking. There was a cloud of them, a green, clamoring, raucous cloud of heavy parrots, dropping in like dog-fighters and slamming around and around them, tearing at faces with pronged beaks and claws, screeching and gouging. Pennyman threw his hands over his head after taking a wild cut at them with his cane. One of the waiters ran for the street, pursued by three or four parrots that tore at his ears like demons.

Pennyman hunkered lower, trying to keep the birds away from his neck, trying to curl up into a ball but terrified lest his white trousers touch the dirty asphalt of the parking lot. One of the parrots, a great, red-headed Amazon with an almost three-foot wingspan, clung to Pennyman's back and burrowed into the collar of his coat as the old man let go of his head with one hand and flailed away at the bird uselessly, trying first to bat it away, then to get a grip on it.

The parrots took no interest at all in Andrew and Pickett. It was as if the cavalry had arrived in the nick of time. For the long space of half a minute Andrew watched amazed, wafering himself against the wall of the restaurant, as he was jerked back and forth by the doughnut thug, who still gripped his left arm but was weaving and dancing and waving his free arm to keep off the parrots. Seeing his chance, Andrew hit his man in the stomach with his elbow, twisting away at the same time and kicking him in the knee.

Two parrots sailed in as if to help him, one of them clutching at the man's cheek with its talons and biting his nose, wrenching it back and forth as if to tear it off. Howling, he grabbed the bird but couldn't pull the parrot off without losing the end of his nose into the bargain, and so reeled away shrieking for help, blood spattering his shirtfront. Andrew ran for it, up Cherry, toward the Metropolitan, thanking heaven that the parrots were on his side, and that one hadn't latched onto *his* nose by mistake. Pickett pounded along after him as the men back in the parking lot were slowly backed up against the wall, fighting just to keep the birds away from their eyes.

None of the parrots followed Andrew and Pickett, and as they topped the hill and sprinted across a lawn, angling toward where the car was parked, they looked back to see Pennyman lurching through the door into the rear of the restaurant, his pants tattered, his hair wild. He tore at his coat, which still sagged under the weight of the determined parrot.

Andrew fired the engine and sped away, Pickett pulling himself into the weaving car and slamming the door on the run, the

Metropolitan barreling through two stop signs and sliding around the corner onto Wisconsin Street, bound for home. It was when they'd got to Ximeno that the flock of parrots passed squacking overhead again, heading out over the ocean. Mystified, Andrew and Pickett watched them through the windshield until they disappeared beyond the rooftops.

It was early yet, too early to go home. Heaven knows there was enough to do at home, but there was no way on earth that Andrew could claim to have done any serious fishing yet, and, at least for the moment, there was no way they could simply walk in and confess. Not yet anyway. They talked about it as they sat in a booth at the Potholder, eating breakfast.

What profit would there be in generally revealing things? Rose would become involved; that was bad. It would be expected that they'd call the police, now that kidnapping had entered the list of villainies. But what, the authorities would want to know, had Pickett been doing breaking into a house on The Toledo?

That's what he'd done, it turned out, just as Andrew had suspected. Pickett had driven off late last night with Andrew's Toledo address in his pocket, and just for sport he'd parked in Naples and walked to the right. It fronted the water and backed up onto an alley. There'd been an unlocked door, as if it were an invitation. Pickett had sneaked in, crept downstairs and into a basement, knowing he was an idiot for doing it, but fired up with his successes at the library. The basement was a laboratory, full of books and what seemed almost to be alchemical apparatus. A great carp lay flayed upon a table, laid open with a scalpel, but with its heart still beating, weirdly, as if Pickett had just that moment interrupted some half-finished experiment.

Which, of course, he had. They'd stepped out of the shadows and cut off his retreat, almost as if they'd been waiting for him. He'd sat tied to a chair for hours, waiting almost until dawn, unable to sleep. The man wielding the scalpel—an old Chinese who looked like Fu Manchu with goldfish earrings—had been friendly, although not out of compassion, but out of the certainty, it seemed, that Pickett was a dead man and so posed no threat and could be talked to with impunity.

Three hundred years old; that had been the man's age, or so he said. Pickett believed him. Why not? He looked it, certainly, in some vague and undefinable way—as if he'd seen at least three hundred years worth of tumult and mystery and wonder. He excised a little gland from the carp, a gland from which, he said, he generated the elixir that Pennyman guarded so jealously. It was a longevity serum, a way to circumvent the ruinous effects of possessing the coins. "Mr. Pennyman needs the elixir very badly," the old man had said, shaking his head as if it made him sad. "Very badly. He came to me in a sedan chair, a mummy, unable to walk, barely able to swallow. And now . . ." He shrugged, as if Pickett could see for himself. "He is a good customer. A very good customer."

Grinning, Han Koi had offered Pickett an ounce of the elixir, mixed in orange juice, thinking, maybe, that it was funny to offer a man something in the way of immortality one moment, knowing that the man's life would be snatched away the next.

One thing that Pickett became sure of before they hauled him away to the Bamboo Paradise was that Pennyman was merely a customer of Han Koi, an old and treasured customer, but not a partner. Pennyman paid well for the elixir—as the check stub testified—well enough so that Han Koi was happy to do Pennyman the favor of holding on to the snooping Pickett for a few hours, until dawn, until Pennyman had finished his sleep and would want to ask a few delicate questions.

Pickett sipped his coffee and shook his head, remembering. It had been a long night. They had driven him to the restaurant and led him inside, untied—very sure of themselves. They'd dead-bolted the street door and pocketed the key, going into the kitchen to brew tea. Pickett had lunged for the pay phone, dialing Andrew's number, barely able to get a sentence out before they were onto him. They locked him in the bathroom then, and there he'd sat, thinking that the first person he'd see when the door opened would be Pennyman. But there was Andrew . . .

"It was a pretty spectacular escape, wasn't it?"

Pickett nodded.

"And how about the parrots? If it hadn't been for the parrots . . ."

Pickett drew a finger across his throat, illustrating what would have become of them if it hadn't been for the parrots.

They ate in silence, both of them nervously watching the door. "What do we do about Pennyman?" asked Andrew.

"Nothing," said Pickett.

"Nothing? We let him get away with this? How about that garbage business. You don't think that he was . . ."

"I think that explains the filth in the drawer, doesn't it? Some men clip out pornographic pictures, some . . ."

"Good God," gasped Andrew. "He's twice the monster I had him pegged for. I can't allow him to stay in the house. He *won't*, I bet. For my money we won't see him again. He'll send for his things."

"Nope," said Pickett. "He'll be back looking sleek and happy and full of flattery. And you'll have to let him stay. The treasure hunt is two days away. The pot is on the burner, and we've got to let it boil. This isn't something that can be stopped; it's something that will *come to pass,* like it or not. And for your sake and Rose's sake and the sake of the inn, we better let it play itself out with as little mess as possible. If Pennyman tries to brass it out, we'll outbrass him, that's all."

Saying nothing, Andrew sopped up the last of his egg yolks with a piece of toast. Maybe what Pickett said was true. The sails were furled, the ship slanting through the growing swell. There was nothing to do but ride out the storm. Someone, Andrew was sure, was at the tiller—maybe it was Uncle Arthur, maybe an unseen hand. This was no time to start throwing over ballast, to try to shift course.

After breakfast they drove to the fish market on Ocean Boulevard, watching through the rear window for a tail. Then, with two rock cod and a sheepshead in the gunnysack, they drove to Naples, where Pickett's car was parked. Pickett drove off. He intended to be at the cafe later that afternoon, to do his part. It promised to be a curious evening.

When Andrew got home it was barely nine o'clock. He walked through the back door carrying his fish. He looked like hell, still wearing his jacket, although he'd tucked his shirt in and replaced his shoelace. Rose gave him a look.

"Catch anything much?"

"Didn't do too bad."

"Out on the pier?"

"Off the end." He held up the gunnysack.

"Cold out there?"

"Not bad," said Andrew, beginning to wonder. Rose was distant, clearly not chipper. He grinned to cheer her up.

"I wouldn't think that old jacket would be worth much. The wind must cut right through it."

Andrew nodded. "It *was* cold out there. But when you're fishing . . ."

"KNEX called early this morning and changed the time."

"What? To when?"

"This evening, while you're cooking."

Andrew grimaced. "That's no good. I can't actually *wear* one of these hats, not while I'm cooking. My idea was to get them in and out of here. Clear the decks, you know, before we opened up."

Rose shrugged.

"You should have told them I was out, that you couldn't change it. You should have told me first."

"In fact," said Rose, wiping the countertop with a rag, "I did more than that. I went out onto the pier looking for you, about seven."

"Damn," Andrew lied. "That's when we were down at the Potholder, eating breakfast."

"No you weren't," said Rose. "I looked for you there, too. The waitress said she knew the two of you and that you hadn't been in yet. When I couldn't find you anywhere I figured there was nothing to do but call them back and okay the time change. It seems to me that if this inn or the cafe made the least bit of difference to you . . .''

''Of course it does!'' It looked as if she were going to cry, just out of tired desperation, sick of his sneaking around, his weird behavior. Andrew stepped toward her, thinking to take her by the shoulders, to give her a bit of a hug. Maybe he *would* explain things to her. Maybe she should know. But she wrinkled her nose and stepped aside.

''What in the world . . .''

''What?'' said Andrew. ''Nothing. Alcohol from the kelp worms we use as bait. They pickle them.'' He spread his arms in a gesture of assurance, a gesture that revealed the bag and bottle in his inside pocket. The sight of it horrified him. Why hadn't he . . . ? He pulled it out, gesturing more wildly now, almost frantic at what this must look like. He was innocent. He was *more* than innocent. He . . .

The bottle slid out of the bag onto the linoleum floor, smashing to bits. Fragments of green glass slid away. The label, with a nebula of shards glued to it, spun 'round and 'round like a dervish until it slowed to a stop at the door to the living room, where Aunt Naomi stood in surprise, looking on. The old lady turned and hurried away, leaving the two of them alone.

THIRTEEN

"Let Tola bless with the Toad, which is the good
creature of God, tho' his virtue is in secret, and his
mention is not made."

Christopher Smart
"Jubilate Agno"

ANDREW WAS HORRIFIED. He was empty. This had knocked the
stuffing out of him. He couldn't bring himself to grope for
another lie; the kelp worm business had been bad enough. Rose
very deliberately opened the cupboard in the little pantry where
they kept the broom and dustpan.

"Let me do that," said Andrew.

"No."

"This isn't what it looks like."

"It looks like broken glass."

"What I mean is . . ."

Rose stopped dead still and gave him a level gaze, her jaw set.
"For God's sake *don't* start up about making paperweights out of
old bottles or something. Don't say anything at all about it. Don't
carry on. Let it alone. Go out and clean up the kitchen in the cafe.
I don't want to know what you've been up to this morning. I can't

imagine what it could be. I don't *want* to imagine what it could be. Get out of here and let me clean this up. I've got to take Aunt Naomi in to see Dr. Garibaldi in a half hour, so please stay out of my way; that would help me more than you could guess.''

Andrew nodded. ''Yes. Sorry,'' he said, stepping toward the door to the cafe. ''I'll be ready to go tonight. Don't worry. I've got it under control.'' Rose was silent, sweeping glass from under the kitchen chairs. ''I'd be happy to take Aunt Naomi over . . .''

Rose interrupted him with a meaningful look, and he scurried away, into the sanctuary of his cafe.

He managed to keep up a cheerful front all day, as if there were nothing wrong, as if he took what Rose had said to him at face value and that the morning's blunders had been scoured away. It was lousy for that to have happened right on top of his foiling Pennyman, though. Apparently he wasn't meant to revel in glory.

But he knew that the cheerful front was a lie. He couldn't get around that even for an instant. He was filled with the hollow fear that the bottle incident had caused damage that couldn't be repaired by winking and grinning and apologizing. It was a final sort of blow. And whose fault was it? His own. He'd master-minded Pickett's escape, but he couldn't, it seemed, keep himself out of trouble at home. He couldn't get through the most mundane chores around the house without everything going to bits and him looking like a jabbering clown.

Of course, part of it was Pennyman's fault. It was important to keep that in mind. It was Pennyman who was driving the wedge.

And it was Pennyman who rolled in at noon, dapper and smiling and without the look of a man who'd been torn to bits by parrots. Andrew was struggling with a rented helium canister. It would have been worlds cheaper to haul the chef's hats down to the gas and chemical company to have them filled, but that would require a truck with an enclosed bed to transport the full hats home in, and he didn't want to rent one. Also, if one of the hats leaked, then he'd have to run it home again for repairs and then back down for more helium, and the day wasn't long enough for that.

He was just levering the canister out of the trunk of the Metropolitan when Pennyman's cab pulled in. Andrew could feel his blood race. Would there be a confrontation? Pennyman wouldn't give him any slack at all next time. He'd strike first and talk afterward. Andrew would have to be ready for him.

But how, without starting Armageddon right there on the sidewalk? It would make a strange setting for the Last Battle.

Pennyman waved at him, very cheerfully. "Bringing in the sheaves, are you?" he called. "Give you a hand?"

"No thanks," Andrew croaked. He cleared his throat, determined once again to outgrin him. "Just one sheaf, actually, and I've got a dolly here. Nothing to it, really." The canister cooperated nicely, thunking down onto the little metal dolly and settling there. Andrew strapped it down. It wouldn't do to have it fall and the valve be knocked off. He heaved it up over the curb and across the parkway, making away toward the rear. He ignored Pennyman entirely, although he could see out of the corner of his eye that the old man stood there watching, as if Andrew might need him after all.

What he wanted, probably, was a chance to bandy words. Andrew had best not give him that chance, not with Rose home again. It was tempting, but dangerous. Andrew might easily lose control and reveal that he possessed the spoon, and that the spoon was the coin, and then he'd be a dead man. He couldn't take a chance on it. Uncle Arthur had advised getting out of town. Lying low was the best alternative—starting now.

Andrew would have liked to mention the parrots, though, just to see how Pennyman reacted. It would be nice to imply that Andrew hadn't at all been surprised to see them, that he half-expected them, or perhaps that he himself had timed their arrival for just that crucial moment, that his shouting and screaming had summoned them. Pennyman would respect him then; that much was certain. He would think that Andrew wasn't blundering along blind; he was part of an Organization, an officer in the War of the Coin, that each step he took was toward a fully anticipated destination.

But what did Andrew care for Pennyman's respect? That had been his problem all along—wanting to be liked or respected by people he loathed. What he ought to do was simply tweak Pennyman's nose, right there and then, on the sidewalk. But Rose was home now, along with Aunt Naomi, who was still bleeding internally. Dr. Garibaldi couldn't grasp the ailment. It was worsening, too. Her blood was thin. He'd prescribed megadoses of vitamin K and an avocado diet. That was a tough break.

Andrew found himself feeling bad for the old bird as he clunked up the steps into the cafe, hauling the canister. Just when she'd gotten the invalidism licked, this new ailment set in. On an impulse, he filled a bowl with Weetabix, sprinkled sugar on them, poured milk into a pitcher, and headed upstairs. He knocked on Aunt Naomi's door and went in. The sight of the Weetabix seemed to cheer her.

She'd been watching out the window again, staring at the lonesome ocean. She looked at him wistfully and said, "Don't worry, it'll be all right." At first he thought she was talking about her own troubles, but she wasn't. She was talking about Rose and him. "She'll see things straight soon," Naomi said, spooning up the Weetabix. "Just do what you have to do."

Andrew went back downstairs feeling a little bit cheered, and he stopped to pet the cats on the bottom landing. He chatted for a moment with the toad on the service porch on his way back to the cafe, asking after its health, but the thing just floated there with its fingers outspread, doing nothing. Andrew realized abruptly that he half-expected it to respond. This, he told himself, is insanity. But then he remembered the parrots, and he shrugged.

Turning toward the cafe door, he noticed that Rose had taken the brick off the top of the toad's aquarium and was using it to block the back door open. He stopped again and considered it. If *he* had done that, Rose would have pointed out his mistake. She still wasn't enthusiastic about the creature, and wasn't fond of the idea of it slipping out of the tank and making away through the house. And here she was, giving it just such a chance. Well, he'd be big about it, and not point out the contradiction in her behavior, not remind her of the lecture she'd given him. And if she neglected to put it back, and the toad got out . . . Andrew shrugged. It would give him a certain edge, wouldn't it? . . .

He felt suddenly like a jerk. He was working hard at feeling sorry for himself is what he was doing. If he could *invent* misdeeds for Rose, then it would seem to even things out. What he was thinking of doing was using this petty brick business against her, in order to gain back some lost ground. Only it wouldn't gain *anything* back, and he knew it; it would only make him contemptible.

He had caught himself—nipped his self-pity in the bud. He hadn't let himself make the stupid error of picking a fight over nothing, just to cast blame. His spirits lifted. He saw Rose heading across the backyard, toward the open door, carrying the library rug, which she'd been beating in the yard. He stood smiling at her. He would say something about the brick, is what he'd do, something lighthearted, that showed that he was aware of the possible trouble connected to removing it from the top of the toad's aquarium, but that he had too much faith in Rose to remind her to replace it.

But then just as abruptly as his spirits had lifted, they fell again. He was puffed up with pride, and he knew it. He marveled at the shifting of virtues and emotions. You couldn't keep them straight. One was always edging the other one aside or swamping it entirely. You had to juggle them continually, and when you thought you had them all balanced and spinning just so, down they came, in a tumble, and you were reminded all over again that you were the biggest fool of all when you put on airs. Well, sometimes that was a healthy reminder—because it was true, you were. And it was when you congratulated yourself most loudly that you were in the most trouble; that's when the fall was greatest.

Andrew laughed for the first time that day. There was a certain humor in the irony of it, in the up and down tangle of guilt and remorse and desire and joy that drove people along as if they were sitting in motor cars built by madmen, trying to steer but finding that the wheel kept coming loose in their hands and that the tires were out of round. And yet somehow, in the face of it all, he was sure that he would get to where he wanted to go—wherever that was—despite the fog and the joke car and the crooked and roundabout route.

He resolved again not to tell Rose the Pennyman business. He was big enough to shoulder it. He knew that he would have liked to abdicate some little bit of his responsibility to her in order to lighten the burden on himself, just like he'd left the mess in the cafe kitchen, half-hoping that Rose or Mrs. Gummidge or elves or cats or someone would clean it up for him. This was his chance to turn that around, his chance to come through.

When the battle was won or lost, when his tour of duty in the Legion of the Coins was through, Rose could be made to understand what had gone on. All would be revealed. He needed patience, that and a clear head, because he could feel it in his bones that there would be trouble tonight.

This had come down to a personal battle between him and Pennyman—an almost petty contest of wills that had begun that night on the front porch and had become a quite possibly deadly affair. Pennyman would act, and soon, too. That's why he had come home starched and pressed and cheerful today. Inside he was a festering mass of hatred; outside he wore the mask. But he would rip it off that evening. You could bet on it.

Trouble came early. It was six o'clock and KNEX hadn't shown up. Andrew's frantic calls to the station were useless. The crew was out in the field. They couldn't be called back. Canceling the piece was out of the question; if it was going to be done at all, then tonight was the night. There was static clicking and a dial tone. Subsequent calls turned up nothing but a busy signal, until finally, after a half-dozen tries, it seemed as if Andrew had got a connection again, except that on the other end there was nothing but silence and then a distant chattering voice sounding like a humanoid insect. Andrew was gripped with the suspicion that the phone trouble was manufactured, and he thought he heard muffled laughter just before the connection was cut.

Too many people were showing up at the cafe. It began to seem as if he wouldn't have enough gumbo, and if he were going to make more then he'd have to hustle. Even with help the process would kill a couple of hours. He felt like sitting in a chair. He wanted a pint of beer, but the keg wasn't working worth a damn. It was pouring out a steady stream of foam, leaving a quarter inch of beer in the bottom of the glass. Pickett had gone to work on it and failed, so now Rose was having a go. But Andrew would have to call her away to chop onions and bell peppers.

And just an hour earlier it had seemed as if everything was set. The fire was lit, and a pile of split eucalyptus logs sat on the side of the hearth, ready. Each table was arranged just so, with a tiny bouquet of blue sweetpeas arranged around a pink carnation; Rose had done that. There were ceramic salt and pepper shakers on each table along with a cut-glass sugar bowl and a pair of candlesticks and the flowers. The whole effect, with the print tablecloths and oak chairs and mismatched silver and china was so homey that he had suddenly wished *he* was eating there, carefree and waited upon. Then it had struck him that the idea of it meant that he had succeeded, that the cafe was going to work. Rose seemed to think so, too.

Pickett had come dressed in a black jacket and a bow tie and with his shoes polished. His very appearance made it clear that he was putting aside his demons and devils for the evening and was rallying 'round. He took Mrs. Gummidge in hand, the two of them agreeing on the folding and placement of napkins, on the topping off of water glasses. Mrs. Gummidge would pour conventional coffee; Pickett would brew more exotic coffees in the espresso maker and tend bar. Rose would bus tables and wash dishes, helped out generally by Mrs. Gummidge when Pickett could spare her. Aunt Naomi would tally and distribute the checks and would keep the cats out.

The cats insisted on coming in—hiding behind counters, under tables. Andrew had chased them out again and again, losing the patience he'd developed for them over the past few days. They wouldn't be persuaded, though. They *would* come in, like it or not, and Andrew finally threw in the towel, warning Aunt Naomi to keep them at bay, and to be ready in an instant to pitch them out if a customer complained. He had been certain, by four in the afternoon, that everything would work as smoothly and accurately as a seven-day clock. With only two tables reserved, they couldn't fail. They would come close to outnumbering their guests.

By five everything had been ready and there hovered in the air an atmosphere of anticipation. Pickett had polished glasses that were already clean, holding them up in the evening sunlight gleaming through the casements and buffing out traces of fingerprints and waterstains. Mrs. Gummidge had brewed Aunt Naomi a cup of tea out in the house kitchen. She insisted that tea was a natural curative, and that Aunt Naomi drink half a dozen sugared cups a day, which the old lady did, perhaps to humor her. There had been a generally cheerful bustle as the minutes ticked away toward six o'clock.

Andrew, finished for the moment in the kitchen, had stepped out to survey the bar—the pint glasses, the bottles, the little refrigerator case full of beer and white wine, the debris he'd picked up from Polsky and Sons. Their liquor couldn't be argued with. Most of it would be wasted in a mixed drink, though. They'd discourage mixed drinks. They weren't Pickett's forte anyway. Andrew had felt like a general, surveying the field before a battle, satisfied with the troops ranked just so about the hillsides, with the cannon and camouflage and with the satisfying smell of victory already in the air.

Then the first party arrived, dressed in suits and furs and looking very cheerful. Pickett had just seated them near the fireplace when the second party came in through the door, a very old couple and a very young couple—the young couple evidently the grandchildren. The old man was nearly deaf, and seemed to think he'd been mistreated. Pickett seated them three times, before, with a gesture of contempt, the old man was satisfied and asked immediately for dry toast. Pickett explained graciously about the set menu, about the unavailability of dry toast, and the old man had to be humored by the rest of the party. He picked up the saltshaker, a blue ceramic doggy with inflated cheeks. He stared at it as if in disbelief and then put it down, hiding it behind the flowers. That's where the cat trouble will come from, thought Andrew, looking out through the kitchen door.

Then there was another party, without reservations: four women from Leisure World. They revealed that they were on the staff of the *Leisure World Recliner,* and did the restaurant column. Behind them, to Andrew's indignant surprise, was Ken-or-Ed, looking very cheerful and accompanied by his wife. He caught sight of Andrew in the kitchen and swarmed in toward him, waving his hand and apologizing and leaving his wizened wife standing by the street door, wearing, of all things, a mumu intended for a woman six times her size.

Andrew gritted his teeth. This stank. Something was rotten in Seal Beach. Here was Ken-or-Ed, being big about it all. Andrew could hardly accuse him of being a hireling of Jules Pennyman, not with Rose and Aunt Naomi there, not without seeming to be a lunatic in front of the contingent from the Leisure World newspaper.

Andrew rousted himself. He would have to work like a fiend. He couldn't afford to drink beer. Rose had done something to the keg, and now it was flowing moderately well. There was a cat on the counter staring into the gumbo and another wandering out into the cafe, looking for a lap to leap into. Andrew hissed at the passing Mrs. Gummidge to see to the cats, but she hurried off to "lay tables" as she put it, and was looking for silverware.

KNEX finally strode in almost at seven o'clock—two of them altogether, with video equipment and looking tired and out of sorts, as if it had been a long day. God almighty, Andrew thought, watching the sudden turmoil in the cafe. Pickett ushered the crew into the back corner, then went around to the tables explaining things. The old man was skeptical. He squinted at the video camera and said, throwing down his napkin, that he didn't want a salad, that he couldn't stand "roughage." He wanted soup. Pickett grinned at him. The soup would be right up, he said, and explained again about the camera crew, who waved equipment around and talked too loud, joking between themselves. The old man asked where his toast was, and the young lady at the table patiently explained that there wasn't any toast.

Andrew hid in the kitchen. He hadn't even inflated the hats yet.

He had no idea whether they'd inflate at all. His brilliant notion of publicizing the restaurant by wearing floating chef's hats was turning out to be a nitwit idea, and he felt suddenly defensive about it. He heard the old man, talking too loud out of general deafness, say, "I've been told that there *isn't* any toast!"

Mrs. Gummidge came through the kitchen smiling just then, looking around. She had a vacant, bemused expression, as if she only half-remembered why she was there at all. She found a spoon on the counter, rinsed it off, dried it, and went back out, humming. Another batch of guests had arrived. The place was filling up. They needed salads, they needed silverware, they needed this and that and the other. Andrew was tired. His back ached and his elbow joints hurt. He had to have aspirin. He felt as if he'd aged ten years in the last two days.

Suddenly there was a shout from the cafe. Andrew knew the voice. He would have guessed it would come from the dry toast man, but it hadn't. It was Ken-or-Ed, cutting up rough. "You're God damned right!" he shouted, evidently at Pickett. "In my *salad*!"

A woman shrieked. Leaving his cast iron kettle on the fire, Andrew stepped across to the door and looked out. There was Mrs. Ken-or-Ed, standing up, her hands thrown across her chest, a look of surprised horror on her face. Her water glass was tipped over, her chair thrown back. The rest of the patrons were obviously restless, peering under their tables and lifting napkins. The cats! Andrew thought, suddenly seething.

But it wasn't the cats. "It was a beetle!" shouted Ken-or-Ed. "A big damned beetle! In my damned salad!"

"Must've been an olive," Pickett said.

"I saw it, too," said Mrs. Ken-or-Ed.

Pickett brassed it out. "Seems to have disappeared, doesn't it?" He turned around and looked at Andrew in the doorway. Pickett's face was white. Out of nowhere came a man from KNEX, waving a video camera, grinning. He was a tall Asian, Chinese probably. He looked familiar as hell.

"Come, come," said Andrew, strolling out among the tables.

"I put that salad together myself, piece by piece. I can assure you that there was nothing at all in it that shouldn't have been. I'd have seen anything out of the ordinary, wouldn't I? It's not one of your tossed-together salads. It's a bit of salad nouvelle. The arrangement, you see, is at least as important as the flavor. Texture is as important to the eye as it is to the palate. The byword in salad-building is . . . Ah, here's our man's toast!"

Rose had appeared, carrying two slices of quartered, dry toast. The old man was suddenly full of goodwill, as if at last he'd found someone in the restaurant who wasn't certifiable.

"And something's knocked over my water glass!" cried Mrs. Ken-or-Ed. "I don't know what it was. Something was on the table."

Andrew smiled at her and then, grinning almost wildly, he patted Ken-or-Ed on the back. The man jerked away, looking as if he would kick the table down. Andrew righted the water glass. "Did the bug kick it over?" he asked. Then to Pickett he said, "A fresh glass for Mrs. Fitzpatrick."

Meanwhile the camera whirred away, filming the whole thing. Andrew turned to confront the cameraman, grinning into the lens. "I'll sue you blind," he whispered, winking at the man. The Fitzpatricks snatched up their coats and stormed toward the door, slamming out, Mrs. Ken-or-Ed giving Andrew a look that resembled the face of someone who'd drunk turpentine. Suddenly Andrew knew who the cameraman was. He'd seen him just that morning, at work at the Bamboo Paradise.

So that was it. A beetle! "Sorry folks," Andrew said. "I'm afraid that the couple who left weren't feeling up to snuff. That was Eddie Fitzpatrick, who used to play for the Dodgers. He was hit by a line drive in his last season. In a coma for a year and a half. Maybe you've read about it. Never been the same. They live across the street, and we invited them 'round tonight to eat on the house. They haven't been out for nearly fifteen years, because he's developed a fear of insects. I thought we'd have a go at breaking him of it. But I guess . . ."

Rose angled in toward him, smiling very nicely. "The kitchen, perhaps . . ." Andrew waved at the troubled guests, hurrying back toward the kitchen where his kettle sat red hot on the stove. He collared Pickett on the way.

"Shit!" Andrew said, looking at the smoking kettle, "It's *hot* enough anyway," and with that he dumped in two cups of oil and two cups of flour, whisking away at the mixture. Rose went out carrying the first bowls of gumbo. "Pour everyone a drink on the house!" Andrew said to her. Then to Pickett he said, "Do you recognize the guy with the camera? The Chinese man?"

Pickett shook his head.

"He was one of your hosts this morning."

"Get the hell out of here!" said Pickett, incredulous.

"Honor bright. Hand me the damned pot holder."

"Well listen to this. There *was* a beetle in that idiot's salad."

"Couldn't have been."

"Big as a damned mouse. Must have been some sort of imported variety."

"Then the bastard put it there himself. It sure as hell wasn't in there when I put the salad together. Where would something like that come from?"

"My bet is . . ."

"Of course," said Andrew, anticipating him. "From Chateau, from Rodent Control. It was one of those prize bugs of his. Pennyman must have walked out with it, the dirty . . . It had to have been him. And KNEX, too. I should have known when they called out of the blue like that . . ."

"Wait," said Pickett. "That's not the half of it. Do you know what kicked over the water glass?"

"*She* did, I suppose. Or else her stinking husband . . ."

"Uh uh. Neither. It was your *toad*. That damned pancake toad from your back porch."

Andrew handed the whisk to Pickett and ran out to look in the aquarium. The toad was gone. The tank was empty. The thin reflector lid lay on the linoleum, and a trail of water led away toward the cafe door. Andrew hustled back into the cafe kitchen, where Pickett scoured away at the kettle with the whisk.

"Where the hell did he go?" asked Andrew, taking over.

"In among the logs by the fireplace. He's in there now, eating the beetle. He came out of nowhere—snatched the bug off the table and ran for it. Thank God she didn't see *him*. She'd have to be hospitalized.''

"We'll give him a medal," said Andrew. "It's the Toad Hall of Fame for him now." How convenient, he thought. Fancy Rose having left the brick off his lid today, of all days. And then the toad . . . Talk about timing.

Aunt Naomi stuck her head in through the door. "Mr. Pennyman's here," she said.

Andrew rolled his eyes. "Holy mother of . . .''

"Take my word for it, " said Pickett. "He's just here to watch. He'll be puzzled that your man across the street is gone."

The man with the camera loomed in the open door, filming Andrew just as a great splop of napalm-hot grease slid off the whisk and into the open flame, igniting in a wash of leaping fire. Andrew plucked up a dish towel and slapped away at it, dropping his whisk. Hunks of burning grease splattered across the back of the stove.

"Baking soda!" shouted Pickett, looking around wildly as the camera zoomed in.

Andrew flailed away with the towel. "What!" he shouted. "Out in the other kitchen. In the house!"

And right then Rose pushed in past the cameraman, shaking a can of beer, her thumb over the popped top. She slid her thumb aside and cascaded beer foam onto the islands of burning grease, then stoppered the can, shook it, and sprayed it on again. The fire smothered itself out under the foam.

"Turn the fire out first thing," she said to Andrew, who was just then twisting the knob under the burned-up gumbo. The kitchen was filled with smoke. Rose turned on the fan in the flared hood and a swoosh of smoke was sucked up and out. Then she closed the open door in the face of the man with the camera in order to keep the smoke out of the cafe itself. "I've got Mrs. Gummidge serving sorbets. That should kill some time. There's enough gumbo for almost everyone, although I had to tell the camera crew that there wasn't.''

Andrew waved his whisk, furious at the burned muck in the kettle. "I'll tell them more than that . . ."

"Where are the hats?" Rose asked, cutting him off.

"What? Out back. With the helium."

"Let's get that over with then. Get them out of here."

"That's a damned good idea," said Andrew. "See to it, will you?" He nodded at Pickett. "There's a flap in back with a clip to seal it off. Fill it there. The tank's simple. Just a valve. Don't overfill it though. We don't want a balloon; we want a sort of floating cloud effect. Tell them that I'm busy as hell in here, and that they'll have to get in and get out just as soon as you're ready."

"Right," said Pickett.

Andrew nodded cheerfully at Rose. "This will be good," he said. Secretly, though, he knew that it wouldn't be good. His chef's hat plan was spoiled. No matter how good the idea had been at the outset, this new Pennyman twist wrecked it. KNEX would find some way of making a hash of it. Pennyman would see to that.

But Andrew couldn't let on to Rose, could he? She had put hours into the hats, into his damned, cockeyed hats. He *had* to tough it out—to be entirely surprised when the whole hat plan went to bits. He couldn't reveal that there was a Pennyman plot afoot. He couldn't reveal anything. He had to pretend to be an entirely innocent victim. "So—what?" he said to Rose. "No more gumbo?" He was relieved about that. Making another pot of gumbo was the last thing he wanted to do. He put the kettle into the sink and turned the water on.

"Not now," said Rose as Pickett went out the door.

The other member of the KNEX crew, a man dressed like a lumberjack and with a beard, looked in just then and growled something about its getting late.

Rose shut the door in his face. "Mr. Pennyman is the last of the guests, I think, for the evening."

"Pennyman," said Andrew in a hollow voice. "Let's serve him dead rats just for the hell of it."

Rose ignored him. "He's sitting with the ladies from Leisure World. They're really very sweet. They loved the salad and place

286 / James P. Blaylock

settings and the fireplace. One of them apologized on behalf of Mr. Fitzpatrick. She said it was terrible about his being so long in a coma.''

Andrew smiled at her. Then the thought that Pennyman might actually fancy a plate of dead rats wiped the smile from his face. He pushed the door open and leaned out, to give things a look. The place had settled out now that the Fitzpatricks were gone. There was Pennyman, dressed all in white, sucking up to the four old ladies, gesturing expansively, talking about China. He tipped a non-existent hat at Andrew and smiled a jolly greeting. Andrew shut the door and took a deep breath.

"Are you all right?" asked Rose.

"Tip-top. Still recovering from the fire. The beer foam trick was neat."

Rose nodded. "Yes, well, portion out the gumbo then. We shouldn't need but five more."

"Piece of cake," said Andrew. He opened a cupboard, hauled out two cans of beef broth, opened them, and poured them into the finished gumbo. What else did he have—a big can of crab meat, a bottle of oysters . . . He'd flesh the pot out a little. To hell with making more. Rose went out into the cafe just as Pickett was coming in—or trying to.

He wore one of the hats, about three-fourths inflated. The whole cafe watched in disbelief. The old toast man had half stood up, gesturing with his spoon. The hat wanted desperately to float off, but Pickett had strapped it around his neck. He forced it through the doorway into the kitchen, plumping it sideways as if it were an enormous pillow.

"Put the apron on him," said the KNEX lumberjack. "This is good. This is theater, is what it is. Here, give him this big whisk. Dip it into the pot there, Mr. Pickett. That's it. What the *hell* is that thing there? A shrimp? That's a *shrimp*? Good God. That's right. Hang it from the whisk there. You getting this?"

The cameraman grunted, the camera whirring away.

"*Do* something with it," said the lumberjack.

"What?" asked Pickett.

"Bite its head off."

"Are you picking up voices, too?" asked Andrew. "Because if you are . . ."

"To hell with the voices. We'll dub this later. Who the hell are you?"

"I'm the owner . . ."

"Stand back, then. That's right, wave that thing around. Get a close up of that goddamn shrimp, Jack. Then back off and pan the whole kitchen. Get the hat. Hey! I got it. Let loose of the strap, Spickett. Let's float the hat out into the cafe. 'Runaway Hat,' we'll call it. That's it."

And before Andrew could intervene, the lumberjack leaned in and unsnapped Pickett's hat, which floated toward the ceiling. The man batted it toward the door, then tried to yank it through. It caught on the corner of a hinge, though, and hung itself up, at which the man jerked on it, pulling loose a seam. The hat deflated in a whoosh, sinking to the floor like a bottled genie that had granted its wishes and gone home.

"Shit," said the lumberjack. "Sorry. Someone fetch the other one."

Andrew gritted his teeth. *"Forget* the other one. That's plenty. You've got enough, I should think."

"Edited down, though . . ."

They were interrupted by the clatter of a plate hitting the floor out in the cafe. The cameraman flipped around, his eyes round with anticipation. What would it be, wondered Andrew: Cats? Ken-or-Ed having come back with an automatic rifle? The toad terrorizing the Leisure World women?

It was Mr. Pennyman, having a fit. He sat perfectly rigid in his chair. His bread plate lay broken on the tiles of the hearth. His face was all moony, and he was breathing quick and shallow, as if he were hyperventilating. Andrew had seen that look on his face before. Little gasping noises came out of his throat, throttling together second by second into a sort of high-pitched keening. His hair—perfectly neat when he'd sat down—seemed to dishevel itself in a little storm of dandruff flakes, and his shoes thumped against the floor, each thump causing a spasm of pain to lance across his face, only to reveal a mask of even more intense pleasure.

The street door opened and Ken-or-Ed surged in, followed by Jack Dilton.

"I'm the health inspector!" Dilton said aloud. Then he saw Pennyman carrying on and he lapsed into a grimace of startled surprise. He turned helplessly to Ken-or-Ed.

There was a sickening smell in the air—the odor of long-decayed fish, of bacteria, of sewer sludge. On the end of the bar, not two feet from Andrew's elbow, lay the pint glass of spoons that Andrew had put away on the shelf. Half the spoons were gone. It didn't take three seconds to figure things out. Mrs. Gummidge had found the pig spoon, and had given it, very innocently, to Mr. Pennyman, who had shoved it into his gumbo.

"For God's sake don't eat with it." That's what Uncle Arthur had said.

Mr. Pennyman was almost helpless, his strange urges uncontrollable. Pickett and Andrew launched themselves toward his table at the same time, Andrew arriving first, but when Andrew snatched up the fouled gumbo and tried to haul it away, Pennyman groped after it, mewling, and pitched out of his chair onto the floor, snatching out the spoon in one last heaving effort, just as Andrew shouted, "He's got it!" in order to warn Pickett to stand by.

Pretending to go to Pennyman's aid, Andrew tried to wrench the spoon away as the old man's face shuddered and shook inches from his own, livid and vibrating.

But Pennyman was recovering. His helpless grin was turning into a calculated smile. Andrew pinched him under the armpit, hard, leaning into it, twisting his hand as if to tear out a piece of flesh, pinching him for the sake of the whole human race. *"There* now, Mr. Pennyman!" he said through his teeth. "You'll be fine. Did you forget to take your medicine?"

"Poor man!" cried one of the Leisure World ladies, saddened at the very thought of Mr. Pennyman's having neglected his medicine.

"Brain lesion," said Andrew, just as Pennyman hooted in pain and released the spoon, half-throwing it toward the fire. Quick as a flash, one of Aunt Naomi's cats scooped it up and was gone—out the door, into the night.

"I'll just have a look at that soup!" Jack Dilton said to Pickett, who headed toward the door in the wake of the cat.

"Jesus! What . . .!" Ken-or-Ed began dancing and twisting, and Jack Dilton, giving him a wondering look, instantly did the same. The doorway was suddenly full of cats, an ambush of them, shredding pants legs, honing their claws on the legs of the two men who danced there, cursing and stomping. "Get 'em off! Hell!" Dilton yelled, and then pushed Ken-or-Ed so hard on the shoulder that he reeled, bending over to slam at the cats.

Pickett pushed through them with the soup, setting out to dump it in the alley. Aunt Naomi hobbled across, shouting "Shut the door! You're letting in every cat in the neighborhood. This is a restaurant, not a kennel!"

The man with the camera slouched in, filming the whole thing. Rose collared him, smearing a fingerful of peanut butter over the lens of the camera as if by accident.

"Hey!" he said, as she led him outside, pushing Ken-or-Ed and Jack Dilton in front of them both. Aunt Naomi shut the door. The cats had gone. The spoon was gone. The fouled gumbo was gone. Pennyman, his face clenched like a skeletal fist, apologized very graciously to the Leisure World ladies. He was beaten and was acting the gentleman.

"I'll just go lie down," he forced himself to say. Andrew could see in Pennyman's eyes the most obscene sort of pure hatred he'd ever witnessed. The sight of Pennyman's face struck him cold. He wanted to wink, to say something that would put the old man away, but he couldn't. He nodded and pulled off a weak sort of smile. Pennyman went out, followed by Mrs. Gummidge, whose head shook as if she were palsied. Rose came back in just then, followed by Pickett.

Andrew walked into the kitchen, rummaged in the cupboard until he came up with the kitchen bottle, and poured two inches of scotch into the bottom of a tumbler. He filled the tumbler with water and drank it down, steadying himself against the counter.

Then, breathing evenly, he went back out into the hushed cafe and announced that they'd all be able to use a round on the house. He pulled down bottles of sauterne and port and sherry, and nodded at Pickett. "Where's the spoon?" Andrew asked.

Pickett shrugged. "Trust the cats," he said, and set out to take orders.

"Where's Fitzpatrick?" Andrew asked Rose, as she pulled down glasses.

"I chased him off. Told him I'd call the police. He didn't want that. You were right. The man's stark. The other one, Dilton, wanted to fight him, right there on the street, and said something about his hundred dollars. They're out there right now, for all I know, beating each other up. I don't pretend to understand it." Andrew grinned, half-thinking to go out and watch. But things were too hot for that.

Aunt Naomi, appearing to be utterly unruffled, went over to talk to the four ladies. In a moment they were shaking their heads and clucking their tongues and exchanging reminiscences about medical troubles that they'd known. Aunt Naomi moved away, toward the old couple and the young couple.

"What was that *god-awful* smell?" the old man demanded. The couple at the adjacent table, the ones who had arrived first, nodded and leaned in.

Andrew heard Aunt Naomi say, "That's rather delicate, isn't it?" and he stepped up, clearing his throat, to save her the embarrassment.

"Sorry, folks," he said. "This has been a rough night. Poor Mr. Pennyman. When he's taken with this sort of fit, he suffers total muscle relaxation. I'm afraid he's . . ." And he bent over and whispered into the ears of the young man and the gentleman at the next table. Each of them whispered into the ears of their wives, and the young lady whispered to her grandmother, who said, "Oh, the *poor* man; *what* an embarrassment!" and then whispered the grim truth into the ear of the old man, who sat stock still and with a look of puzzled dissatisfaction on his face.

His mouth fell. "He *what*! Soiled his . . . The filthy . . ."

"He couldn't help it, for goodness sake. It was uncontrollable."

"A hanged man does that," the old man announced out loud.

"I dare say he does," muttered Andrew, moving off but happy enough that the old man had said it. The rest of the restaurant knew now. Or at least they thought they knew.

Rose collared him as he slipped toward the kitchen. "What on earth did you tell them about poor Mr. Pennyman?" she asked.

"Well," said Andrew. "I told them the only thing I could think of—that he'd had a fit and lost control of his bodily functions. What else would explain it? It's no crime. The man is old."

Rose looked at him steadily. "What was wrong with the gumbo? What did you do to doctor it up, to stretch it?"

"Not a thing!" said Andrew, looking hurt. "Take a look in the pot."

Rose did. In fact there wasn't anything wrong with it. It was fine. "Well," Rose admitted. "Don't get a swelled head, but the woman from the *Recliner* said she'd never eaten better than this or felt so at home in a restaurant."

"Did she?"

"Yes, and the couple across the way said the same. Your gumbo was a hit, apparently."

Andrew wiggled his eyebrows at her. Then the street door opened and into the cafe came the cameraman and the lumberjack, having put away their equipment. Andrew's face clouded and he headed out of the kitchen, but Rose grabbed his arm. "I've asked them to drink a beer. Let's not aggravate things. I told them that we were very anxious that their program, if they aired it, would reflect well on the restaurant and hinted that if it didn't we'd take action. But I don't want to put too fine a point on it. I don't want to make them mad."

"Ah," said Andrew, thinking hard. "Settle them down, is it? A beer, a friendly chat. Sure. You're right. They can take a stab at the gumbo, too. What the hell. There's some left. It's in their blood, I guess, waving cameras like that." He smiled at the two of them and gestured toward a table.

A half hour later the cafe was almost empty. Aside from Andrew and Rose and Pickett, only the two from KNEX were left. Aunt Naomi had gone up to her room, but had to have Rose's help climbing the stairs. Andrew considered every word he said to the two from the cable station. He was breezy, unconcerned, nonchalant. He supposed that they were mystified by the night's proceedings. They certainly couldn't have imagined that they'd be witness to such a wild display.

When they left, the cafe was six beers down, but the two seemed congenial enough. It was just possible that they'd changed sides, that they'd been good men who had been caught up in Pennyman's web without half-knowing how they'd gotten there, and had, over the course of the evening, been wooed away from the enemy by the cafe and the gumbo and the beer and the cheerful talk. Andrew almost felt friendly toward them.

Five seconds after they were out the door, the shouting began. Andrew, Pickett, and Rose headed for the street. "Trouble!" Andrew shouted, thinking that the two of them had—what?— been jumped? Maybe Ken-or-Ed had come back again, out of his head finally. But no, there the two were, arguing on the parkway. Yelling. The Chinese man was nearly out of his mind. Some damned thing had gotten at the camera, had torn all the tape out. Something with claws.

"It was the stinking cats!" shouted the lumberjack, suddenly sober and enraged.

But it hadn't been the cats; Andrew was sure of it. An almost electric thrill of joy and mystery shot through him, and he felt suddenly like a man with friends, like a shaman who could call up the wind and the birds and send them on missions, who could make oak trees dance in the forest. The frame over the crawlspace had been pushed aside. Andrew squinted at it surreptitiously, hardly believing that it could be true, but knowing it nonetheless. It was the 'possum that had dealt with the film, that had scuttled Pennyman's last ship. There it was, under the house. Andrew could just barely see it in the soft glow of the streetlight, looking out at him with goggly eyes. It ducked back into the shadows.

There was a monumental amount of tape on the street, ragged and dirty and trailed nearly to the beach and back. A car or two had run over it. Andrew wouldn't have guessed there'd be half so much tape in a video camera. Every last inch of it, apparently, had been hauled out and shredded, chewed and trampled on, heaped into the gutter, tangled in the bushes.

"Hell," said the cameraman, standing very still. And it seemed to Andrew as if he was worried, as if he had someone to answer to. Five minutes later they were gone, the wadded-up tape nearly filling one of the trash cans in the backyard.

Within a half hour, Pickett was gone, too, and Rose had shuffled wearily upstairs to bed. Thank God, thought Andrew, they wouldn't be open tomorrow night. Just cleaning up would kill half the day. So what? He whistled merrily despite his aching joints. Pennyman had come in smug and gone out a wreck. Ken-or-Ed was a broken man. The cafe would get a bang-up review in the *Recliner,* not to mention the *Herald,* Pickett's newspaper. Pickett had written his review three days ago; Andrew had helped him.

He went outside for the last time that night, wearing the second chef's hat, which he'd inflated dangerously full, and carrying with him a saucer of milk. Clicking his tongue outside the crawlspace to alert the 'possum, he lay the milk just within the shadow, and then strolled around to the front of the house.

A light burned in the Fitzpatricks' living room, but as Andrew drew up across the street, the light blinked out, as if they'd seen him, and wanted, perhaps, to hide behind the drapes and watch. He stood on the sidewalk, his hat billowing around his head, lit by the streetlamp and valleyed with shadowed folds, like a cumulus cloud blowing in the sea wind. After a moment he turned and headed back around, satisfied that they wouldn't know what to make of him, that the sight of him wearing the floating hat and standing dead still on the midnight sidewalk was a vision from outside their ken. They wouldn't be able to fathom it.

He slipped back into the house, tolerably satisfied, and climbed the stairs to bed.

FOURTEEN

"Since we have explored the maze so long without result, it follows, for poor human reason, that we cannot have to explore much longer; close by must be the centre, with a champagne luncheon and a piece of ornamental water."

Robert Louis Stevenson
"Crabbed Age and Youth"

THE SPOON WAS in his pants pocket next morning when he awakened early, well before dawn. It fell out and bounced on his foot when he picked the pants up. Who had put it there? The cats? Why not, Andrew thought, tiptoeing around the bedroom. The cats were probably downstairs right now, playing gin rummy with parrots and 'possums and toads, plotting against the Soviets.

Rose still slept, and the house was dark and quiet. Hustling downstairs, Andrew went out onto the service porch, took the brick and the lid off the toad tank, and buried the spoon in the gravel at the bottom, laying a lump of petrified wood over it.

The toad floated as ever, innocently, as if he hadn't just last night thwarted a lunatic and hid out among eucalyptus logs until Andrew had found him and put him back. Toads, thought Andrew, were an inscrutable lot. Andrew wished there was some sort of toad treat he could give it, but nothing came to mind. The toad drifted down to the bottom of the tank and sat on the petrified wood, giving Andrew the slack-faced, deadpan look of a serious martial arts assassin, as if anyone who dared retrieve the spoon would have to deal with him first, and would regret it.

Satisfied, Andrew went off to work, and an hour later was washing dishes moodily in the cafe kitchen. The casements were open, and he could smell the Santa Anas blowing again, the warm desert and sagebrush odor mingling with the smell of popping soap bubbles. The cafe itself was cleared and swept clean and the tables arranged despite their having to sit idle until next Friday night. On the counter next to him lay a cheap walkie-talkie, silent, but with the volume turned all the way up.

It might be today that the crisis would come. The treasure hunt was that night. The moon would be full, the tale told. The dawn light radiating now above the eastern rooftops was a bloody slash, dwindling into a gray and violet sky, and the air was heavy with the sighing wind. There had been a pair of jolting little earthquakes some time after two in the morning, and then a third two hours later, a deep, rolling quake that had brought him up sharp out of a dreamless sleep. Rose had got out of bed and wandered through the house when the first of the quakes struck, convinced that she'd heard something fall downstairs. She had slept through the third, though, and that's when Andrew had climbed wearily out of bed, thinking to get a jump on cleaning the cafe.

He had never before been so filled with premonition, with the absolute certainty that everything in the world was connected, that like Pickett's circles and serpents, everything whirled in a vast, complex pattern—the wind, the rhythmic crashing of ocean waves, the wheeling gulls and the distant cries of parrots, the earth-muted grumbling of subterranean cataclysms—all of it was linked, and all together it was the embodiment of something bigger, something unseen, something pending.

If Andrew were called, he would go. No trickery with fishing poles, no gunnysacks full of junk. Come tomorrow, Rose would understand. She might think he was crazy, but she'd understand. It was his destiny that was blowing on the Santa Anas, sailing along on the backs of newspapers and tumbleweeds and dust and dead leaves.

He'd been to the window a half dozen times, watching the sky pale and wondering at the cool, silent morning. There was fire in the foothills, out in the San Gabriels, and the northwest horizon was sooty-black despite the rising sun. He felt weirdly enervated, as if he were light and weak, built out of Styrofoam or woven out of the ashy smoke blowing up out of the hills. With luck, he'd have got through the dishes and drained the sink before the call came. That way, when Rose looked in and found him gone, at least she'd see that he hadn't been idle, that he hadn't left a mess again for Mrs. Gummidge.

He was just polishing the last glass when the walkie-talkie erupted into static. Andrew pushed the talk button and said, "Yo."

"He's come out." It was Pickett's voice.

Andrew threw down the dish towel. "Is there a cab?"

"Around on your side. You can see it through the window. Don't bother to look, though. Go out the back and around through the garden gate. I'm down on the seat. Don't make for the car until I honk. He'll have left. Then run like hell so we can catch him. He was carrying the bag of dimes."

"Dimes?"

"The bag of silver dimes that was in his drawer. He's got them."

Andrew switched off the machine, shoved it into his coat pocket, and rummaged in the pantry for a bite of something to take along. Then, leaving the light on so that Pennyman wouldn't see it blink off abruptly, he slipped out through the back door, leaped across Mrs. Gummidge's weedy garden, and pushed the gate open, peering past the corner of the house at the departing taxicab. Immediately a horn honked, and there was Pickett, sitting up and gunning the engine of the Chevrolet. Andrew was off at a dead run, climbing in through the thrown-open door as Pickett sped off.

They followed him down to the Pacific Coast Highway and around onto Seal Beach Boulevard. There was little traffic, so they stayed almost two hundred yards back. Andrew tore open the top of a variety pack box of Corn Pops, shaking out a handful and eating them one at a time, cracking them like nuts with his teeth.

"What else do you have?" asked Pickett.

Andrew patted his coat. "Let's see. Frosted Flakes and Honey Smacks."

They crossed Westminster, Pickett driving with his left hand and shaking Honey Smacks into his mouth with his right. "Bet you ten cents I know where he's going."

"Of course that's where he's going. But what's he up to? Is he going to dig?"

Pickett shrugged.

"Maybe we better head into Leisure World—roust Uncle Arthur. Maybe he ought to know that the game's afoot."

"Let's not," said Pickett. "Let's just follow along. If we sidetrack now we might miss the whole business. Besides, after the other day they might be watching for us at the gate. We can't afford trouble. Not now."

Andrew nodded, dropping his empty carton into the sea of trash and books and jackets on the floor. The cab pulled in just then at the Leisure Market. Pickett slid past, angling up a driveway farther on and cutting the engine in front of Mrs. Chapman's Doughnuts. "Duck," he said.

Both of them hunkered down, and Andrew watched above the seat as Pennyman tapped his way across the lot and onto the dirt shoulder of the street, down toward the oilfields. He disappeared from sight beyond the edge of a cinderblock wall. Andrew and Pickett were out, scrambling toward the wall and peering over. Pennyman picked his way along the road, dust blown up by the wind swirling around his feet.

"Half a sec," said Andrew, heading in after a doughnut.

"Two glazeys," Pickett said at his back. "And leave the coffee. This might take some running."

In minutes Andrew was back, trying to fit the edge of one of Mrs. Chapman's puffy, angel food doughnuts into his mouth. "I got a break on a half dozen," he said, holding out the open bag.

Pickett plucked one out. "He's heading for the oilfield across from the steam plant, where Arthur let the turtles loose. There's no use following him yet; he'd spot us in an instant. When he goes through the oleanders, though . . . ."

"Right," said Andrew, looking again over the fence. Pennyman was a good way down now, cutting across and into the field.

"There he goes," said Pickett. "Give him to the count of ten. Now!" The two loped across the road and down, ducking around into the field and behind an oil derrick fence, then across and behind the mountain of pallets from where they'd watched Uncle Arthur launch the turtles.

Pennyman peered through the foliage into the oleanders, then bent over, ducked in, and disappeared.

Pickett thumped Andrew on the shoulder. "There he goes. Give him a moment. Let's go!"

They were off and running again, as quietly as they could, certain that Pennyman couldn't see them but anxious not to be heard. The wind would cover most of the noise. The oleander was dense and deep, maybe fifteen feet broad, and from three yards away it looked impenetrable. Just inside the perimeter of leafy branches, though, someone had hacked out a tunnel, and you could shove in past the outer branches and get around to the back, in against the chain-link. The oleander grew right through the links, so that over the years the old barbwire-strung fence had disappeared into the bush.

"There it is," whispered Andrew. He could see where the fence had been cut and then hooked back together along one side with baling wire so that it was sort of hinged, the cut panel held up by oleander branches. The baling wire was clean and free of rust, very likely wound through the cut links within the last couple of months. On beyond the fence were the fields of the Naval Weapons Station, half of them up in tomatoes now, the other half fallow, waiting for autumn pumpkins. Bundled tomato stakes were the only cover in the open fields, so there was no question of their following; they'd be seen for sure. And besides, they could see Pennyman clearly, stepping through the clods of the harrowed pumpkin field. Some distance away to the west rose a cloud of dirt where a tractor cut the earth, and off to the east sat the green humps of sod-covered weapons bunkers.

Andrew could hear flies buzzing and the drone of a distant,

unseen airplane. "God, it's lonesome out here," he whispered, polishing off a second doughnut.

Pickett was silent.

"What's he doing, do you figure?" Andrew bit into his third Mrs. Chapman's and knew at once that he didn't want it. But he ate it anyway, wondering why he had such a passion for doughnuts, why he couldn't leave them alone.

"Watch," said Pickett.

Andrew watched, and it became clear at once what Pennyman was doing. He was sowing the field with silver dimes—handfuls of them, which he threw out in a glittering spray. Then he moved on, twenty feet farther, scattering dimes in a wide, purposeful circle that would lead him back around to the oleanders.

"What on earth? . . ." Andrew muttered.

"Same as the belted turtles," Pickett said. "To attract the two coins."

And it was just then that Pennyman found one of the turtles. They saw him bend over to pick it up, and then drop it abruptly when the thing urinated almost heroically on his pantslegs and shoes. They could hear the curse in the still air. Then he bent over again, and meddled with the creature, removing the silver belt before sowing another handful of dimes, peering closely at the ground now, alert for more turtles.

They were home by seven-thirty, after a half-dozen cups of coffee at the Potholder. The Santa Anas had kicked up, and the air was full of the rustling of tree limbs and the random banging and pounding and howling of the wind-blown seacoast. Andrew went up to visit Aunt Naomi, carrying another bowl of Weetabix and the fixings just in case. Predictably, she was sitting in front of the window again, watching the ocean over the several rooftops. Two of her cats sat with her.

Surf stormed through the pier, the wave crests licking the bottom of it and blown to foamy white by the offshore wind. The long, booming waves began to break some two hundred yards out, quartering hard in a tumble of churning ocean, re-forming quick and steep and slamming down in the shallows with a crack that must have been audible for miles. City lifeguards had cordoned off the entrance to the pier, which shuddered under the pounding surf, and every now and then a monstrous wave humped up along the horizon, drove in, and smashed straight through the pier railing, surging around the bait house and pouring off again in spindrift sheets of lacy white. The beach was almost inundated, and the tide was still rising.

Aunt Naomi's radio murmured. The early morning earthquakes had centered in the Hollywood Hills, and there'd been damage at the zoo. Griffith Park was alive with escaped beasts—apes and peccaries that had gone to ground, some few of them escaping over the hills and into the backstreets of Chinatown. Clouds of bats had swarmed out of the canyons from previously unknown caverns and rifts, and the dry bed of the Los Angeles River had cracked like the shell of a walnut, releasing torrents of subterranean water through a dozen fissures.

"Sounds almost like the first trumpet, doesn't it?" Andrew said, fixing up the bowl of Weetabix.

Aunt Naomi nodded. "I didn't think I'd live to see it." She petted one of the cats, who was looking hard at the cereal.

"Coming along to the treasure hunt tonight?"

She shook her head. "I'm too tired."

"Maybe Dr. Garibaldi . . ."

"Dr. Garibaldi is off the case," she said with a dismissing wave of her hand. "It's cancer, I suppose, all this bleeding, and he's too much the fool to see it."

Andrew didn't know what to say. Somehow he had come to like Aunt Naomi and her cats, once he'd understood what made her tick, or rather what had got in the way of her ticking. She'd become a sort of kindred spirit, what with her Weetabix enthusiasm and the joy she took in a cup of coffee. It had turned out, when he paid attention, that she wasn't a fool after all; she no doubt understood very well what he was doing with the money she advanced him—approved of it even.

Last night, before the cafe doors opened, she had talked

seriously about drinking glasses, about the differences in beer drunk out of pilsners and pint glasses and mugs, pointing out the easy to overlook virtues of paper cups. He had risked telling her about his war with the tumblers in the kitchen cupboard, and she had offered to do her part. She had been full of philosophy, and saw very clearly that all the cheerful little details of day-to-day existence, all the wonderful trifles, were, as she put it, knick-knacks of the human spirit. Andrew was almost teary-eyed now thinking about it.

"Well," he said, "Pickett and I are going to be there, at the treasure hunt. I expect it's going to be an adventure."

"Probably more of an adventure than you'll want," said Aunt Naomi.

There was a silence. Then the radio began to chatter about a collision at sea, about a fishing boat heading in toward San Pedro, trying to beat the rising swell and colliding off the tip of Catalina Island with a vast, barnacle-encrusted whale . . .

Andrew puzzled over it. "Something in the wind," he said.

"And in the ocean." She was silent for a moment. "Why don't you spend some time with Rose today? It's Sunday. Take a walk. Here." She hauled her purse out from under the night stand and fished around in it. "Have dinner somewhere nice." She handed him four twenties and squeezed his hand, not bothering to write anything down in her book.

Darkness came early. There was hardly any dusk. The full moon rocked above the troubled ocean, throwing a silver sheen across the plowed dirt of the pumpkin field, where two or three hundred people milled about, eating late-night picnic lunches and talking in hushed voices. The apocalyptic weather had somehow leached away the carnival atmosphere that Andrew would have expected. It was almost as if the mass of people, sitting on tailgates and at suitcase tables, felt the coiled tension in the air. The occasional ringing voice of a child sounded as out of place as it would have in church, and almost made the night vibrate.

Someone had brought along oil drums full of cut-up construction lumber, which had been doused with gasoline and lit, so that here and there around the parking area little imprisoned bonfires burned, throwing shadows onto the dirt. Somehow the effect was weird, almost cataclysmic, rather than warm or cheering.

When they pulled up in the Metropolitan, Andrew felt almost as if the people ought to applaud him, as if they ought to know who he was. But they wouldn't believe it even if they were told, and they were anxious only to dig, to find the hermetically sealed ring or the seafood dinner tickets. They'd brought spades and collapsible army shovels and clamming forks. Children carried trowels. Andrew had brought the spoon, and Pickett was empty-handed.

They spotted Pennyman straight off, walking alone fifty yards distant. And there, parked at the head of the line of cars, was his taxi, the driver waiting inside, reading a paper. Pennyman walked with a limp, as if he had something in his shoe. Andrew bet that it was some sort of detecting device, contrary to rules, but that even if Uncle Arthur's charity knew about it nothing would be done. For the principal players, the rules would be abdicated that night. Rules were perfunctory now.

Two tables with folding chairs had been set up between the bonfires, and a half-dozen ladies of Leisure World vintage sat around them, taking five-dollar bills, issuing tickets, handing out little maps, ready to keep track of unearthed treasures on lists drawn up on college-ruled paper. Andrew recognized the woman from the *Recliner,* but he was too nervous to make small talk. So after he and Pickett had paid their money, they hurried across toward the dirt trail that led into the field from the road, where a little rising cloud of dust swirled up from the wheels of the red electronic car, which bumped along toward them, swerving from side to side, carrying the oldest man on earth. It was Uncle Arthur finally, and Andrew was glad to see him.

His relief waned, though, when the old man pushed the door open and stumbled out. He was tousled and rumpled, and he looked so ancient that he might have passed for an unwrapped mummy in a glass case. Andrew and Pickett stopped short. The very sight of him cut off Andrew's hearty wave. Pickett stepped up and shook his hand delicately, unable to hide his fascination with

Uncle Arthur's forehead, which was marked quite clearly with a cross-shaped slash of pink. If Pickett and Andrew didn't know what they knew, they might have taken it for a scar.

The murmuring night was shattered suddenly by a voice behind them that said, "You!"

Andrew spun around, and there was Mr. Pennyman, looking past them at Uncle Arthur's forehead.

For a moment the old man's rheumy eyes cleared and he peered straight at Pennyman. "Me," said Arthur simply.

Pennyman laughed out loud, and Andrew wanted to hit him, to pop him one on the snoot. But they'd been through that, and there was no time for it tonight. Up close, Andrew could see that Pennyman wore an ostentatious belt of silver dollars in a triple row and linked with silver chain mail. He didn't have his stick, but rested instead against a silver-shod spade. He didn't in any way acknowledge Andrew's or Pickett's presence, but seemed satisfied simply with knowing at last who his real adversary was. He turned around and hobbled off toward the assembled crowd that pressed in anticipation against the ribboned starting rope.

"We've got the spoon in the car," Andrew whispered when Pennyman was out of earshot.

Uncle Arthur cupped a trembling hand to his ear and said, "Eh?"

"I say we've got the spoon!"

"God damn the moon!" the old man rasped, but the effort of it seemed to shake him. He stepped back, almost stumbled, and closed his eyes for a moment.

Then he blinked at them, as if he were just waking up, and gave Andrew a squint-eyed look. "I was up in Alberta once," he said, nodding.

Andrew swallowed hard, his mind racing to make sense of the Alberta business. It didn't compute, somehow. Maybe Uncle Arthur hadn't come to the point yet . . .

But it seemed he had. He stood blinking at them, swaying in the wind. "Little bit of railroad work," he said.

"Ah," said Andrew. "About the *spoon* . . ."

There was an explosion just then—a blast of yellow fire that lit up the whole western horizon, as if the entire city of Long Beach had detonated.

"Oil fire!" cried Pickett. "Looks like Signal Hill!"

Another explosion rocked the night, and a tongue of bright blue flame shot away and licked the sky. The air was suddenly full of the shriek of sirens and the hot wind blew out of the east.

The masses of people stood staring. If one had run, all would have followed. But in the full minute that they stood immobile, unbelieving, it became clear that there was nothing to do, no place to run. The fire didn't pose a threat; it was several miles away. They'd paid their five dollars . . . The woman from the *Recliner* rallied them, snatching down the rope, letting them out into the field, shouting about rolls of coins, diamond rings, toys. "Hurray!" someone shouted, and all of a sudden there was cheering and running, as if it had been fireworks igniting in the west, and not oil storage tanks.

Uncle Arthur squinted at Andrew suddenly and said, "Are you the son?"

"God help us," muttered Pickett.

"I'm the nephew," said Andrew. "Do you remember me?"

"Of course," said the old man. "Sure. The bearded man, with the sheep. Did you cut it off?"

"Cut what off? I don't wear a beard."

"We had a device," he said, thinking hard, "that would burn your beard straight off. Roast your head like a potato if you didn't look sharp. I sold them door to door. At least I think I did. Wish I had one now." He gave Pickett a particularly hard look. "Did I tell you I was in Alberta? Why don't you shave off that damned silly mustache?" he said. "Looks like a damned caterpiller."

"Get the spoon," said Pickett, smiling and nodding at Uncle Arthur. He jerked his hand at Andrew, as if to propel him toward the car. "Sit down, sir! Take a load off."

"Ach." Uncle Arthur waved him away in disgust, and then slumped back down onto the seat of his car. Lord knows how he'd driven that far, but his part in the War of the Coins was over, at least for the evening.

"The damned moon!" said Pickett as Andrew hurried back

toward him, the spoon in his pocket. "This *would* have to happen tonight."

"Maybe we better do something for him. Call someone." Andrew looked sadly at the old man, whose head slumped against his chest now. He appeared to be sound asleep, breathing laboriously.

"He's two thousand years old," said Pickett, heading out toward the fields. "He won't die until it's time, and if it's time, then heaven help all of us. All the doctors in the world wouldn't be worth the quarter it took to call them."

For an hour they had no luck. Andrew carried the spoon in his back pocket, and somehow he didn't like it at all. He'd always felt it was vaguely repellent, but now it felt as if his back pocket housed a throbbing, poisonous lizard. It was warm, too, and not simply because it was pressed against him. For ten minutes it had got hotter and hotter, and he had taken it out and wrapped it in his handkerchief. But then it cooled again, only to heat up and cool twice more during their stumbling search of the fields.

All around them people dug happily in the moonlit earth. There were shouts and cries. A boy ran past howling with joy, carrying a little plastic treasure chest filled with rhinestones. Another waved a tangled handful of chandelier crystals. A thin woman in a too-short dress unearthed a fist-sized hunk of amethyst, and then cursed under her breath and flung it down again, and then a little girl who couldn't have been above four picked it up and tilted it into the moonlight, oohing and ahing at the watery purple glow. A little over a half hour into the hunt there was a shriek from near the perimeter of the field. The diamond ring was found. Half the treasure hunters left grumbling.

There were silver dimes aplenty, scattered here and there. And they found a turtle, Andrew and Pickett did, beltless, and wandering purposefully toward the oilfield fence. They let it go. One o'clock came and went. Pennyman was still at it; they could see him methodically shoving the silver tip of his spade into the earth at calculated points.

Then the spoon started to heat up again. That's when Andrew figured it out. It was like a child's hot and cold game—literally. He would stake his fortune on it. They quit wandering then, and followed the spoon, pretending for Pennyman's benefit, though, that they weren't up to anything at all. When they passed the old man at a distance of some ten yards, the tip of his silver shovel jerked into the air and the shovel spun end over end, torn from his hands, skiving down into the dirt six feet away so that the whole blade was buried.

"Let's go!" whispered Pickett urgently, and Andrew pretended not to have seen the shovel's weird behavior. When they looked back, Pennyman spaded furiously in a cloud of rising dust, throwing big clods back out of the way.

"Did the *spoon* make it do that?" asked Andrew.

"We have to think so," said Pickett. "Either that, or he's found one of the coins. But even so we have to go on. We can't wrestle him for it. Not yet. Not with the spoon in your pocket. He'll end up with all of them that way. Is it still hot, or is it cooling off?"

"Heating up even more," Andrew said. "Whew!"

"There!" cried Pickett under his breath.

Down among the clods shown a glint of reflected silver moonlight. They bent over to look. The spoon began to vibrate in Andrew's pocket, and he was possessed with the intense desire to drag it out of there, to throw it as far and as hard as he could. It seemed to weigh a ton, as if it would push his feet right down into the dug-up earth and anchor him there forever.

It was a turtle that Pickett had seen. It was half-buried, as if he'd dug in to hibernate the rest of the spring away. On his back was the landscape painting, half-flaked off, and girding it around was the belt of Navajo silver.

"Watch it," Andrew said as Pickett bent over to pick it up. "Remember what happened to Pennyman this morning." The thought of Pennyman reminded Andrew that the old man might well be watching, and so he stepped in behind his friend in order to shield him. It wouldn't do to have Pennyman figure them out. Andrew could see that he still dug away, though less furiously now, as if he were tiring.

"Holy smoke," muttered Pickett. "Will you look at this."

On the turtle's underside, clinging as if magnetically to the silver belt, was a ball of fused dimes, big as an orange. Pickett jerked it off and turned it over in his hand, tilting it into the moonlight. "There's one," he said, tracing the outline of the edge of a larger coin that thrust up through the dimes. "No, both of them. They're sandwiched together, back to back. We've got them both."

Andrew slammed his hand against his pocket, where the spoon jerked and danced. He was certain that if he didn't hold it down it would tear the pocket right off. Both of them set out, pretending still to be searching. Pennyman was hard at it, poking randomly with his silver spade, having given up on the hole he'd been digging. Andrew was sure that at any moment he would figure out what had happened with the spade business and be onto them. He would certainly think it monumentally suspicious when they left the field and went home. Almost everyone had by now, but Pennyman would assume that Pickett and Andrew would stay until they were successful or else had been defeated. Their leaving now would point to their success.

The bonfires were out. Only a big propane lantern burned on the table where the woman from the *Recliner* sat reading a book. She waved cheerfully to Andrew, pointing toward her list and widening her eyes, as if wondering whether he hadn't found something nice. He waved back, trying hard to look calm and maybe just slightly disappointed, but nearly shaking with anxiety. If Pennyman hadn't seen them talking with Uncle Arthur, if he hadn't seen the cross on the old man's forehead, there would still be the chance that he thought they were simply there to dig for rhinestones and nickels, and were going home because they were tired, like the rest of the people.

He would know, though. Andrew was sure of it. "Put the ball of dimes in the trunk," he said to Pickett as the two of them hurried toward the Metropolitan. "I'll take the spoon up front with us."

"Right," said Pickett. "Keep them apart. Let's take it easy driving out of here. If Pennyman catches on and heads for the taxi, then step on it.'' They eased the trunk lid shut, then climbed in and backed out.

Andrew forced himself to drive slowly, bumping over ruts. "What the hell's he doing?"

"I think . . . Yeah. He's found it. The turtle. We should have taken the damned belt! Why the hell didn't we take the belt? He's onto us. He tossed his shovel away. Here he comes. Step on it.''

Andrew stepped on it, shifting back down into second and swerving toward the edge of the road where it was smoother going.

"Don't get stuck in the field!" warned Pickett, as they slewed into a rut.

"You know me," said Andrew, grinning at him and jerking the car back out, "The Terror of Leisure World."

The Metropolitan slammed along like a camel over the desert. The lights of the highway shone ahead, a couple of lonesome cars full of people thinking they had somewhere important to go. The moon was enormous and yellow, as if it reflected the fires that burned in the north and west. Signal Hill was almost entirely ablaze, a leaping ribbon of wind-driven flame. Dust swirled and flew as gusts buffeted the car.

"What a night," muttered Pickett.

"Just about what you'd expect," said Andrew. "Are they after us?"

"No. Yes. There's his headlights."

The Metropolitan banged down onto the highway, screeching left on Studebaker Road. "It's too open out here," said Andrew. "There's no place to hide, nowhere to lose him."

"Just go like hell. I'll watch for cops."

Andrew drove toward home. If it came to a fight, he wanted it to be on familiar ground, near allies—Rose and Aunt Naomi. And somehow the beach drew him, the pier, the crashing waves. He was jacked up with adrenaline. He felt sharp and canny. Things along the roadside seemed almost to glow. He could hear the ocean, too, as if in a giant seashell, rushing and sighing, the sound of the collapsing ages.

They rocketed down the highway, angling back onto the Pacific

Coast Highway toward the San Gabriel River. "Look!" Andrew shouted.

"What, what?" Pickett's head ratcheted around, staring, expecting Lord knew what.

It was a pig that Andrew saw. A monumental pig, big as a pygmy hippopotamus, coming up out of the bed of the river and bound for Orange County. It rollicked along on its too-tiny hooves, its eyes set on an unseen destination, glancing for an instant at the Metropolitan as they sailed past. Andrew slowed down, both of them craning their necks, and for no reason he could easily define, Andrew waved over the top of the car at it and then blinked his headlights. They banked around into town, past residential streets.

"He's going our way!" shouted Andrew, elated but not knowing why.

"Yeah," said Pickett. "That's a good sign. I can't see Pennyman. We lost him, I guess. We got out of there in time."

They slid around the corner onto Main Street, then down the alley and around beside the house. There was a light on in the kitchen. Aunt Naomi, no doubt, or Rose, waiting up for them, having a bite of something.

It was Mrs. Gummidge. Andrew was dumbstruck. On the kitchen counter lay a plastic bag full of white powder. On the stove was the tea kettle, singing away, and on the counter lay Aunt Naomi's mug and a box of Earl Grey tea.

"Oh!" she cried, throwing a towel over the plastic bag. But Andrew had recognized it. She hadn't been quick enough. It was the anti-coagulant rat poison that he'd stupidly thought to fool Rose with a week ago. Mrs. Gummidge had plucked it out of the trash can. The rest of the story was clear as well water— Pennyman's talk of "personal vendettas," Mrs. Gummidge's insistence that Aunt Naomi consume cup after cup of tea, the mysterious internal bleeding . . .

"Assassin!" cried Andrew, throwing aside the towel and

upending the bag into the sink. He turned on both faucets, flushing the powder down the drain, damning himself for ever having been fool enough to . . .

"Don't!" Pickett cried, waving the ball of dimes. "It's evidence! Don't pour it out!"

"Ow!" shouted Andrew, slapping at his back pocket. Smoke curled up from it, and there was the sharp smell of burning cloth.

"The spoon!" yelled Pickett, and Andrew flailed away at it with his hand, hauling out the smoking, handkerchief-wrapped spoon and dropping it immediately onto the floor, where it bounced free of the cloth and began to revolve, faster and faster, like a compass needle gone mad.

Mrs. Gummidge burst from her chair. She slammed past Andrew, who tried to push in front of her to cut her off, and she grabbed at the spinning spoon, understanding what it was now and hungry to possess it. Andrew kicked it away, toward the back door and the toad aquarium, then turned to chase it. "Get her out of here!" he yelled at Pickett.

Mrs. Gummidge backed away toward the living room, as if she were giving up, but then whirled around and jerked open the knife drawer, coming up with a carving knife. Without a word she slashed at Pickett, who yowled and tumbled backward out of the way. Astonished, Andrew abandoned his pursuit of the spoon and grabbed a ceramic pitcher off the counter, cocking his arm to throw it at her. She ducked out through the open door, cursing, with Andrew at her heels, carrying the pitcher, thinking to stop her and her murderous rage before she could do any damage with the knife.

The living room door flew open and there stood Pennyman, alone, with a pistol in his hand. His face was deadly white, and his hand shook dangerously. The corners of his mouth trembled, spasming downward in random jerks, and his head was twisted around stiffly, his chin thrust forward, as if he were being pressed on the back of the head by some unseen force. "I'll take that," he said to Pickett.

the stomach.'' The old man stank like a demon, his breath rasping out through darkened, mossy teeth. His eyes glowed with loathing and desire and corruption. There were footfalls on the stairs.

''It's on the kitchen floor,'' Mrs. Gummidge hissed. ''He dropped it.''

Pennyman waved them toward the kitchen with his pistol, then abruptly shoved it into his pocket, leaving his hand on it. Rose confronted them from across the room, tugging her bathrobe around herself.

''Well,'' she said, smiling sleepily. ''Back from the hunt?''

''That's right,'' said Andrew. ''Wonderful time. Plenty of treasures. I'll just be up in a moment.''

Rose nodded. ''I won't join you, if you don't mind,'' she said. ''I'm not dressed for socializing.''

''Of course,'' said Pennyman, controlling himself with a visible effort. Rose didn't seem to sense any trouble. She nodded and climbed back up the stairs. Andrew deflated. He didn't care what happened, not really, not if Rose could be kept out of it.

Waving the pistol again, Pennyman herded them into the kitchen. ''Where?'' he said.

Mrs. Gummidge hesitated, betrayal in her eyes. Quick as a lizard, Pennyman slapped her on the cheek with the back of his gun hand, knocking her into the kitchen cabinet. She mewled with pain, cowering there.

Andrew started forward, but Pennyman spun toward him, covering him with the pistol. ''Stinking coward,'' said Andrew, cursing himself for his helplessness. ''It's on the damn floor. Under the aquarium. Take it.''

All of them pushed toward the back door. The spoon wasn't there. Andrew glanced at the lid of the aquarium, thinking that maybe the toad . . . But no, the toad floated as ever, hovering, watching them, the brick securing the lid.

''Where?'' Pennyman grunted, threatening Mrs. Gummidge again.

''It was there!'' wailed Mrs. Gummidge, her eyes full of hatred. ''I swear it was. Five minutes ago. I tried to get it for you. I tried . . .''

FIFTEEN

"Patience, children, just a minute—
See the spreading circles die;
The stream and all in it
Will clear by-and-by."

Robert Louis Stevenson
"Looking Glass River"

BEFORE PICKETT COULD move, could drop the ball of dimes or throw it, or cosh Pennyman in the head with it, the old man stepped forward, pressed the gun to his forehead, and clicked back the hammer.

There was the sound of a slamming door, and feet on the hallway upstairs. It was Rose, without a doubt, getting up to see what was going on.

Stay upstairs, Andrew thought, half-closing his eyes. Stay the hell upstairs. Don't come down.

Cats peeked out from behind chairs, slinking around corners and blinking out of doorways. There was a scrabbling beneath them, under the house. What was it?—'possums? The wind buffeted the casements and moaned through the ma[il] slot.

"Now the other one," Pennyman said. He turned the pistol [on] Andrew, who shrank away in horror. "Quick, or I'll shoot you[.]

"Shut up!" shouted Pennyman. "Witch! You murdered your lover to get your hands on that coin. You'd betray me in a moment. I'll have it out of you though, before the dawn. See if I don't. Out the door."

They cut across the backyard in a herd, through the gate and around into the alley, heading up toward Main Street. Andrew strode along, keen and alert but having no idea in the world what to do with all his keenness. Run? What would that avail him? Should he jump on Pennyman and then be shot and left in the alley? Or worse, bring about Pickett's death? He wished he could communicate with his friend, make some sort of sign, but Pickett looked pale and tired and watched the ground as they stumbled along.

Pennyman walked on his heels, painfully. Halfway there, back behind Señor Corky's, he hobbled to a stop. With his free hand the old man rummaged in his pants pocket, hauling out a clasp knife. Watching them all the while and covering them with the pistol, he thumbed one of the blades out of the knife, shoved it through the leather on the side of his shoe, and slit the shoe open, his face sagging with relief. He sawed across the top of the shoe, excising the toe, tearing his sock out entirely when the knife blade caught in it.

Andrew nearly gagged. He hadn't expected what he saw inside Pennyman's cut-away shoes, in the dirt and trash of the alley. There were no toes visible, no real flesh. Instead there was the cleft, scaly black callous ridge of a cloven hoof, obscene in the moonlight. Pennyman worked the knife into his other shoe, cutting chunks away.

His face twitched and shuddered, and his hair stood out in patches from his head, his scalp flaky and mottled. He licked his lips with a tongue that was almost snake-like. Mrs. Gummidge watched him, fascinated, unbelieving, frightened. She had the look of someone both repulsed and attracted by evil, the eyes of a half-repentant torturer, whose special sickness was a groveling, hand-washing contrition.

Andrew backed away from her and the pistol swung toward him. He stopped dead. Pennyman stood up, smiling now. He threw the pocketknife into the weeds, reached into his coat, and hauled out his silver, jingling, lead-lined box. Steam seemed to seep from under the lid, smelling sulphurous and hellish. The bulge of the two dime-encased coins danced in his pants pocket, and he licked his lips again, wondering, maybe, if he could afford to pull the fused coins out, break off the covering of dimes, and add the two to his collection. He put his face into the reek and breathed deeply. His features stiffened and his gun hand jerked and spasmed as if he wanted to throw the gun away, to tear open the box right there and scoop out the tainted silver and let it run through his fingers.

The temptation tore at his features, but he put the box away again, unable, perhaps, to accomplish the juggling act without putting down the gun. He wanted two more coins. That's all. Two more coins before the sun rose again over the tired earth.

They were off once more, out onto the deserted asphalt of Main Street. He waved them toward the pier. The surf cracked and boomed, shaking the pilings. The pier lamps still burned, dim and watery in the light that shone from the now enormous moon hanging over the city like a gas lamp, threatening to blow out on the instant. Wind sheered across the face of the waves, blowing sand, scouring the beach where the tide had fallen. A wash of shooting stars fell into the sea.

Andrew watched for his chance as they ducked under the rope that the lifeguards had used to cordon off the pier. He didn't have any idea when it would come or what form it would take. He knew without doubt that he'd leap into the ocean gladly if, say, Rose were there and had fallen in and needed saving. He would step in front of a bullet to save Pickett. But would he do the same to save the faceless world? To stop Pennyman? Would the desperate time come when he would say damn the gun, and just wade in? Or would he leave it to Mrs. Gummidge? She certainly seemed posed for it. She half-hovered when she walked, watching Pennyman out of the corner of her eye, knowing that he carried with him a malignant treasure that it had taken a lifetime to amass, and that in one calculated move she could . . .

But no, Pennyman was no longer entirely human. He was a thing born of the coins, a thing of evil, and he understood the Mrs.

Gummidges of the world far too well. He knew how far to trust them. He prompted the three of them along, down the pier, past the concrete restrooms, the fish cleaning sinks, the lifeguard tower, the snack stands, toward Len's Bait House, which stood dark and wind-lashed on the pier's end.

The ocean was a vast, oily plain lined with the humps of waves driving in toward shore. An ivory ribbon of moonlight ran out across it like a dwindling highway, illuminating the depths with a weird, silver-green glow. In the west the oil fire burned on Signal Hill, low and intense now, casting an aura over north Long Beach. All of them stood in the wind finally, in front of the bait house, waiting for Pennyman to make his demands, to reveal his plan. Do what he might, Andrew couldn't help him with the spoon. He had no idea at all what had happened to it. The cats, perhaps, had made away with it, just as the pigs had done in Johnson's entertaining tale. The spoon was out of Andrew's hands now, and good riddance. Still, he would do his part . . .

Menacing them with the revolver, Pennyman took out the silver box of coins and laid it on the shuddering pier. Andrew hung on to the iron railing, watching the flying spindrift, anticipating the wave that would wash them all to their death in the sea. A vast black shadow passed across the ribbon of moonlight on the ocean just then, as if a single cloud had blown in on the night wind. But the sky was clear, and lit with a thousand stars. There was something in the water—*under* it—not in the sky at all.

Andrew watched the sea. There it was again. He could see the dark hump of it behind incoming swells, edging along over the sandy bottom—a whale, surely, summoned by the coins, and on hand, perhaps, to do the bidding of the man the coins possessed. The radiant sea was full of fishes despite the Leviathan, the waiting monster. Andrew could see them: schooling bonita and mackerel and jack smelt; plate-sized perch swarming around the pilings; hidey-hole fish, sculpin and rock cod, blennies and eels, nosing up toward the surface. The sandy bottom was alive with shellfish and creeping things, with sea slugs and hermit crabs and lobsters and moon snails. It was as if he were watching them in a dream. But it wasn't a dream. Pickett saw them, too. And Pennyman, surely he was aware of the thing in the sea. Of course he was; it was what he was there for. The creature contained within it the last of the thirty coins.

The pier shuddered just then, as if a wave had slammed through it. It rocked on its pilings, creaking and groaning, threatening to tear apart, to twist itself in half and pitch into the ocean. Andrew held on, flung sideways as it moved again. There was the sound of splitting wood and concrete, and one of the pilings shivered into bits, slamming down into the water.

Pennyman cracked the fused dimes like an egg on the old worn slats of the pier, cupping his hands over the two coins, trapping them as they fell out together, the dimes rolling away in a dozen directions. He tipped back the hinged lid of the box, and the two coins popped in among their brothers like tiddly winks and drew the silver lid down after them with a bang as the pier heaved again in counterpoint to the slamming of the box lid. Pennyman stumbled and caught himself. He smiled and looked out over the sea.

He was scarcely human. His white suit was ragged and soiled with dirt from the treasure hunt and from kneeling in the alley. His ripped-apart shoes only half-hid what his feet had become, and his face, as if in keeping with the rest of him, had warped into a goat-like parody of a human face. His tongue lolled above his pointed beard as if there wasn't room for it in his mouth. In the west the moon was setting over the sea, and its reflected light made Pennyman's eyes seem opaque yellow, like disks.

"I'll begin with you," he said suddenly to Pickett. "You seem to be the detective, the clever man. Let's see how smart you are when smart is at a premium. Tell me where the coin is, or I'll blow you to kingdom come." He aimed the pistol. Andrew tensed, ready to jump.

"It's here," said a voice behind Andrew, and he turned in disbelief to see Rose standing in the cast-open door of Len's Bait House.

Pennyman turned the gun on her, a flicker of surprise and the hint of a smile appearing and disappearing on his face, replaced in turn with a look of grimacing idiocy.

"Look!" Andrew shouted, pointing away down the pier, where a tiny car bumped up off Main Street humming along toward them. It stopped, and someone got out to take down the rope. It was Uncle Arthur.

The pistol cracked. Too late, Andrew threw himself wildly at Pennyman, caring nothing about saving the world, but wanting only to turn the pistol on him, to . . . His hand and arm smashed into something that felt like a wall of cold, wet clay, and then he slammed into it bodily, rolling down onto the deck of the pier and against the bottom railing. He was up in an instant, puzzled, but throwing himself without thinking at Pennyman again, who stood holding the smoking pistol. Pickett reeled away, grasping his shoulder, and when Andrew leaped the second time, Pennyman was leveling the pistol at Rose, who flung herself back against Aunt Naomi, the two of them disappearing into the bait house.

Again Andrew smashed into the clammy, rubbery, invisible wall and found himself on his back. He looked wildly behind him, only to see Uncle Arthur buzzing toward them at full throttle, agonizingly slowly. Pennyman turned and fired at the oncoming car, and the wind screen spiderwebbed with cracks as the car swerved, caromed off the railing, and came on again.

Mrs. Gummidge sprang out of the shadows just then, with a shriek that stood Andrew's hair on end. He'd almost forgotten her, so intent was he on foiling Pennyman. She flew at Pennyman's back when he shot at the car, and maybe because his guard was down, there was no barrier to stop her as Andrew had been stopped.

The shriek gave her away, though, and the old man turned as he fired, sweeping his arm around savagely, roaring through his wide-open mouth, his eyes lit with hatred and with the joy of knocking her down. She slammed back against the pier railing, which caught her in the small of her back, and in an instant Pennyman's hand was at her throat, smashing up into her chin with adrenaline-charged strength, cutting off her scream as her head snapped back with an audible breaking of bone, and she flew backward over the railing, falling headlong into the sea, all of it done in a moment.

Aunt Naomi pushed through the bait house door, swinging her cane at Pennyman's head as he turned back toward them, howling pointlessly, as if he knew that the killing of Mrs. Gummidge called for some expression of emotion—laughing or yipping or hooting—but was no longer human enough to puzzle out what sort. His eyes flew open and he snarled into Aunt Naomi's face.

Andrew saw her cane shudder to a slow stop a foot from the old man, as if Pennyman were walled-in again by magic, protected by the accumulated coins. He snatched the tip of the cane out of the air, and before Andrew could react, could clamber up and leap, Pennyman jerked Aunt Naomi toward him, grabbing her wrist and twisting her around, pointing the pistol at her head.

Everyone stood as if frozen. The electronic car stopped fifteen feet away. Andrew was stymied. Heroics would accomplish nothing at all. He couldn't get near Pennyman, not while Pennyman held the coins, not while he threatened Aunt Naomi. The pier shuddered, nearly throwing the lot of them onto their faces. The ocean had grown weirdly calm, and the shuddering now could have nothing to do with storm surf. There *was* no surf; it had fallen strangely flat, as if it were waiting. Pennyman laughed again hoarsely, like fingernails on a chalkboard.

''Take it,'' Rose said, holding out the spoon.

''Yes,'' said Pickett. Blood seeped through the fabric of his jacket in a growing patch. ''He still doesn't have them all. There's one in the fish. He can't get that one. The fish doesn't care about his gun.''

Pennyman nodded sagely, as if in response to the conclusions of an intelligent four-year-old. ''Put it in my pocket,'' he said to Rose.

''Don't go near him!'' Andrew shouted.

Pennyman shrugged, tipped the gun up, and shot through Aunt Naomi's hair. Rose screamed at the crack of the pistol, staggering against the doorway. Aunt Naomi flinched and bent forward, unhurt. Pennyman laughed. ''I want it now,'' he said.

Rose stepped forward to give it to him. He couldn't take it, though, not with one hand on Aunt Naomi and the other on the pistol. She would have to put it into his pocket, as he'd said.

Andrew waited, poised, ready to leap. If Rose wasn't repelled by invisible walls, then he wouldn't be either. He'd knock the old man down, kick him to bits. If he touched Rose . . .

But Pennyman jerked Aunt Naomi around, covering Andrew with the pistol, waving it back and forth between him and Rose. In an instant the spoon was in his pocket, and when Rose grabbed Aunt Naomi's shoulders and pulled the old lady away from him, Pennyman let her go.

His eyes were rolled half up into his head, so that crescents of bloodshot white shone under each iris. His teeth chattered and his breath came in gasps. He seemed to be twisted from within, as if he'd swallowed a handful of ten-penny nails, and his hand shook as he clutched at his silver box, laying it on the pier and pulling it open. Twenty-eight silver coins lay within, glowing an almost sickly green in the lamplight. There was a ghastly, rotten smell on the wind, as if Pennyman were a ripe cheese or was riddled with dead, gangrenous flesh. The pier shuddered again, the creature in the sea, perhaps, growing impatient.

The spoon wouldn't fit in the box. It was too long. The lid closed against the handle. The surface of Pennyman's face moved as if it were a swarm of insects, betraying a dozen emotions in a moment, and he sniffled and drooled over the box, kneeling on it finally to warp the lid down around the spoon handle. There was the snap of the lid catching, and Pennyman stood up, holding it, backing toward the very corner of the pier, staggering as the pilings shook, his mouth working, but nothing but babble croaking out of his throat.

He climbed onto the railing. The great fish lolled on the surface of the sea—an immensely long undulating whale, looking like something out of an illustration of a Paleozoic ocean.

It came to Andrew abruptly that the great fish was Pennyman's destiny. Pickett was wrong. Pennyman didn't need the pistol any longer. He was merely going to leap into the gaping mouth of the fish, into the belly of the fish where lay the last of the coins. Pennyman was a modern-day Jonah. But he was a corrupted Jonah. And when the fish spit him up finally onto a Southern

California beach, it wouldn't be the grace of God that brought him forth. Nor would Pennyman any longer be a man. He would be something else entirely.

There sounded the beeping of a tinny little electric horn, and Andrew threw himself out of the way as Uncle Arthur's red car surged past. It angled arrow-straight toward where Pennyman was perched on the corner of the pier railing, squatting like a wind-bedraggled sea bird, clutching the box, the pistol, and—in the crook of his elbow—the iron lamppost. He stood up boldly, flinging the pistol into the sea just as Uncle Arthur's car smashed feebly into the post. Andrew lunged forward, grabbing futilely for Pennyman's foot, over the tiny hood of the stalled car.

Pennyman swung around the iron pipe of the lamppost, waving the box of coins in his free hand, a wild, damn-all look in his eyes, intoxicated with coin-magic. He flailed at the railing, at the post, scrabbling to steady himself, waiting for the moment to deliver himself into the mouth of the fish.

The pier shuddered again, a vast, heaving, concrete-snapping quake that threw Andrew backward and into the railing. He grabbed for a hand hold, his legs slewing around and through, between the parallel rails. His head banged hard against an iron post as he latched onto the wooden curb along the very edge of the pier and hung on, nearly sobbing with the effort of stopping his fall and looking down at the roiling water, seeing Pickett out of the corner of his eye, hunkering along toward him as the pier tossed and groaned.

Andrew shook his head, and pain lanced across the back of his skull where he'd hit the post. He sagged with the weight of fatigue and defeat and pain. He hadn't slept for two days. What could anyone expect of him? He was powerless to help himself, let alone the world. He could do nothing but hang on, and steel himself for the sliding rush, the smash of cold ocean water.

Blood from his lacerated scalp dribbled down past his shirt collar, and somehow the wild rush of the world around him paled and he focused on that little tickling dribble. It would be simplest just to hold on and wait, to be acted upon instead of acting.

Pickett hadn't made it to him. He couldn't help. He hugged the railing ten feet farther down, his left arm bloody. Rose huddled with Aunt Naomi against the wall of the bait house, and Andrew could hear Rose shouting at him, hollering unnecessarily for them both to hang on.

Then Aunt Naomi lurched forward across the pier toward Andrew. She shouted something, but he couldn't make it out. She stopped, nearly pitching forward, then steadied herself for a moment and flung her cane. It bounced, clacked down, and skittered toward Andrew, and he let go of the precious rail to grab it, shaking his head hard, letting the shot of pain wake him up—call him back to the world.

Andrew twisted his face into the wind as the pier heaved again. He hauled himself to his feet, the cane in his right hand. He could see Uncle Arthur slumped behind the wheel of his car, the electric motor still humming. Pennyman balanced on the top railing for a long, gasping moment. A hundred sea birds swarmed around him, snatching at his clothing, pecking at his eyes. He batted at them, slamming away with the box. There was one last shuddering quake, and Pennyman was thrown backward, off balance, clutching the coins to his chest as the entire corner of the pier—deck, lamp post, sink, railing, and all—began to crack loose from the rest of the pier with a groaning of twisting metal and a snapping of wood and bolts.

Andrew lunged, shouting, and swung the cane like a baseball bat, with both hands, slamming the hooked end across Pennyman's knuckles. There was a shriek and a clang—the sound of Pennyman screaming and of his coin box banging against the cold iron of the lamppost that fell now as if in slow motion into the sea.

Andrew whipped the cane back to hit him again, just as the badly latched box sprang open and the coins sailed out in an arc, into the ocean, across the pier. For an instant Pennyman had a look of horrified, uncomprehending defeat in his eyes, and then he went down end over end, scrabbling after the flying coins like a man in a cartoon as the corner of the pier collapsed piecemeal into the sea. Andrew dived back toward the railing to save himself, throwing away Aunt Naomi's cane, tearing out the knees of his trousers on the rough deck of the pier and hugging the splintered wooden curb.

He held on and watched Pennyman fall, watched his cloven hooves shiver and metamorphose into the feet of an old, old man, his magic gone, the coins no longer his. Pennyman turned his face to the sky, betraying the yellow, sunken-eyed features of a mummy, of a man long dead but half-preserved by potions. And then he splashed into the sea like a something built of sticks and twine.

The red electronic car geysered in after him, carrying Uncle Arthur inside its little cab. And just as Andrew thought of letting loose, of sliding in after it all, of trying to drag poor Uncle Arthur out of there, the dark bulk of the whale gave one last heaving lash and it opened its mouth like the door of Aladdin's cave, swallowing them up, Pennyman and Arthur both, and the car into the bargain.

The great fish humped around and slipped away, into the shadowed depths, and was gone.

The surface of the sea boiled with fish, but almost immediately it was still, and the dawn light illuminated the depths enough for Andrew to see that the fish were diving toward the bottom, darting after the coins that shimmered and disappeared into deep water.

The sky, suddenly, was full of birds—sea gulls and pelicans, parrots and crows and curlews—dropping down and pecking at the scattered coins on the pier, flying off with the coins in their beaks. Andrew heaved himself through the twisted railing, rolling over onto his back on the deck of the ruined pier. Something gouged him in the shoulder blade. He sat up and looked. It was the spoon.

He picked it up, and on an impulse, cocked his arm to throw it into the sea, into the newly rolling swell and the ribbon of sunlight that had just then blazed up across the blue-green water. Let the fish have it, he thought. Let them swim it away to some other continent, out of his life entirely. But then he stopped himself.

The light of the rising sun shone on the back of something running toward them down the center of the pier, running with an odd, short-legged, rolling gait. It was The One Pig, and no mistaking it, its hour come 'round at last. It trotted indifferently past a company of sleepy fishermen just arriving with the dawn, and followed the course of the Uncle Arthur's lost car, straight through the hovering birds, past Aunt Naomi and Rose, past the open-mouthed Pickett, trotting to within a foot of where Andrew sat holding the spoon in his outstretched hand.

Neat as clockwork the pig plucked it up, turned immediately around, and trotted off again. Andrew watched it grow smaller and smaller and smaller, disappearing up Main Street, bound for heaven alone knew where.

Epilogue

BEAMS PICKETT FELT a little like Tom Sawyer, as if his wound were a badge, a trophy. He'd only been winged. He liked the sound of the word—"winged." It seemed to conjure up the notion of it having been very close, his ducking away and foiling the concentrated efforts of a world-class murderer.

Georgia had announced that the inn was almost clean of mystical emanations. There was a residue, maybe in the dust under the house, like the lingering smell of aromatic cedar in a sweater just out of the chest. Ocean winds would sweep it away.

The little car he rode in jolted as it went off the curb, straight out into traffic, weaving crazily around a stalled truck and under the nose of a startled pedestrian. Pickett held on, one hand on the dashboard and another on the edge of the cardboard carton wedged behind his seat—an Exer-Genie. Apparently they were marvelous things for toning stomach muscles. Heaven knew he could use some of that. The thirty-five bucks had been well spent. Georgia had him on a new regime—diets, stylish clothes, twenty-dollar haircuts. She was going to civilize him, bring him up to date. Rose had been threatening the same ever since Andrew had made a clean sweep of things and admitted to the credit card outrage. She seemed to be softening, though. Georgia, on the other hand, had taken Pickett on as a sort of challenge.

"New battery, then?"

Uncle Arthur nodded, looping the car around an insanely wide turn and onto Main. "Corroded all to hell. Bumper all strung with kelp. They patented a machine for processing kelp. Did you know that? I sold them off the coast of Maine."

"No, did they? Where were you these three days, anyway?"

"Out. Constitutional and all. Holiday. Ever been to Scottsdale?"

Pickett shook his head. "No, is that where you've been? Arizona? We thought you were drowned."

"Not me."

"You weren't in Scottsdale?"

"I wasn't drowned. What happened to your mustache?"

"My girlfriend made me shave it off."

"She's a good woman. Keen eye."

"So you were in Scottsdale?"

"Once. Hell of a place. I sold rain gutters. Losing proposition in Scottsdale, you'd think. A man would go broke." Uncle Arthur grinned at Pickett and widened his eyes, possibly to imply that he hadn't gone broke.

Pickett was satisfied. *He* knew where Uncle Arthur had been. You could smell it in the upholstery. That the car still ran after being dumped in the ocean and swallowed by a fish was a testament to something—although whether to something mechanical or something spiritual he couldn't quite figure. Maybe both.

Pickett had tried to make it clear to Rose and Andrew. He himself had anticipated Arthur's return. Pickett had driven out to Leisure World on a hunch that morning. He had knocked on Arthur's door, and when it opened, there the old man had stood, in reading glasses and a suitcoat. He had got Pickett's name wrong and then taken him out to the garage and sold him the Exer-Genie.

Just like that. Now they were on their way to the Potholder,
together.

Pickett grinned and slapped his knee. The real corker was that
Andrew and Rose still thought the old man was dead. In almost
exactly a minute and a half—less, even, if Uncle Arthur ran
another red light—Pickett and he would lurch up to the door of the
Potholder, maybe take out a parking meter or slam into the curb,
maybe park on the sidewalk. Andrew and Rose, sitting at the
window table, would doubletake, spill their coffee. Andrew would
choke and stagger out of his chair, toppling it over. They would
rush outside, wild with wonder and joy, appearing to be lunatics,
and Uncle Arthur, very calmly and deliberately, as if there were
nothing else in the world to interest them, would talk about selling
rain gutters in the desert, the red electronic car smelling of whales
and kelp and the sea, like a tiny, deep-water submarine, a tangle of
waterweeds still trailing from the smashed front bumper.

They couldn't fish off the pier because of what the storm
supposedly had done to it. It was cordoned off again, and from
where they sat they could see the sparks of a cutting torch where
three men worked on a scaffold above the ocean. Rose and
Andrew, of course, knew that it hadn't been the storm at all, that it
had been a giant fish that had knocked the end of the pier to bits,
but there was no profit in saying so. The less said the better.

So they fished off the rock jetty just to the south, Andrew and
Rose did, drinking coffee out of a thermos. The fish weren't biting
so far, but it didn't matter to either one of them. The sunrise had
been worth getting up for. And fishing there together like that,
with all the turmoil and villainy behind them, was like a holiday.
In a little under an hour they were meeting Pickett at the Potholder
for bacon and eggs. There was summer in the air, and the morning
was warm and fine.

"So it was you," said Andrew. "You were onto the whole
business all along."

Rose shrugged, flipping her plastic lure twenty yards out into the
water. She reeled it in slowly. "It belonged to me, too, just as it

belonged to Aunt Naomi when her husband died, or when Mrs. Gummidge murdered him, I guess. *That's* something I didn't know. I should have though." She sat silently, thinking. "Poor Uncle Arthur," she said at last.

"I wish, well . . ." He let the thought go and pressed on to more cheerful subjects. "So you were feeding the 'possum under the house, weren't you? Admit it. And the brick on the toad tank—you left that off on purpose. I'm astonished. I wouldn't have thought it. Not for a minute. I bet you're a closet Weetabix eater, too. Sometimes . . . Sometimes I don't figure you very well. Sometimes I wish . . ." His cheerful train of thought had sidetracked again.

"Sometimes you should quit figuring. The house looks great, by the way—the paint that is. Did I tell you that?"

"Yeah," said Andrew. "You did. But you can tell me a couple more times if you want. God I hate painting."

"Want some help?"

Andrew started to say no. Then he caught himself. Actually he wanted help very badly. "Sure," he said. "Mounds bar?" He held one out to her.

Rose looked skeptical. "A Mounds bar? This early in the morning? Where did you get that?"

"I keep a few in the tackle box, actually. There's nothing like them when you're fishing."

She slid one of the pair of candy bars out of the wrapper and ate it. A crab sidled out from under the rocks and looked at her. She tossed it a hunk of coconut and chocolate and called him Mr. Crab.

Andrew grinned at her. The crab scuttled out of sight, carrying the treat. Rose folded up the fishing knife and dropped it into the tackle box. There was only a half hour to go before they were due at the Potholder. She reeled in her line and began to dismantle her pole. "We'd better get," she said.

Andrew nodded. "One more cast." He was using an old spinning reel with fourteen-pound line and a one-ounce pyramid sinker. "Watch this," he said, and he baited the bottom hook with a hunk of Mounds bar and cast it way out into the water in a long, low arc. He waited for the telltale thunk when it settled on the bottom. Rose, cheerfully skeptical, watched Andrew take the slack out of the line.

Then, almost at once, as if the universe were playing along, the line jerked, then jerked again, and Andrew set the drag down just a bit, winked at Rose, and leaning back against the heavily bent pole, began to reel in his fish.